PALLISER PARK

Historical Suspense

ANNE MERINO

Printed by Village Care Corp.
Village Care Publishing
99 King Street #1822
Saint Augustine, FL, 32085

Editor's Note

This is a work of fiction. Names, characters, places, and incidents are either products of the author's imagination or are used fictitiously. Any resemblance to actual persons, living or dead, events, or locales is purely coincidental.

Anne Merino

Anne Merino was raised between the United Kingdom and Arizona, surrounded by horses, hounds, and a deep love of books. Her childhood – steeped in the rhythms of British country life and spine – tingling ghost stories whispered along haunted byways – naturally inspired a lifelong passion for storytelling and the theatre.

A former professional ballerina, Anne eventually turned her creative energy to writing, drawing on her vivid imagination and deep love of history. She is the author of the critically acclaimed *Hawkesmoor: A Novel of Vampire and Faerie*. Now retired from the stage, Anne lives with her filmmaker husband and their two remarkable sons, continuing to craft stories that enchant and intrigue.

For my husband,
Tom – a filmmaker who loves a good action story.

And to Colonel Sir Henry Darlington.

My sons' great – grandfather,
Sir Henry served gallantly at Gallipoli.

Acknowledgements

Often the hardest part of producing a novel is thanking everyone who contributed to it in one way or another. There are so many and I would hate to think I'd forgotten anyone.

Family. They are the ones who suffer through what airy – fairy types might call *the process*. All of those hours tucked away at the laptop, unavailable for coffees, walks, dinners, movies and the odd session of *Baldur's Gate*(Go, Team Astarion!).

My husband, Tom – a filmmaker and a fine writer himself – is always good for a great conversation about plot and dialogue. He's direct and honest. If Tom likes something, it's pretty solid stuff. I had started *Palliser Park* just before getting a cancer diagnosis. It would have been easy to fold up the writing tent and shove creative projects on a shelf. Tom was adamant that shouldn't happen, stressing that the act of creating something, *anything* was a kind of medicine.

Son, David – a screenwriter with an almost uncanny sense of how to capture action on the screen and on the page, made a very difficult year so much easier. Some of *Palliser Park* was written on a little cruise he took me on, once I had recovered sufficiently from cancer surgery. Those days and nights at sea, walking with decks with this wonderfully funny, kind and talented young person will stay with me forever.

Son, Emlyn – a working journalist in Manhattan – is witty and wise. His wry observations about American society, pop culture and the world make life worth living. Also, I am frequently envious that I didn't come up with his *bon mots* first.

I am so grateful to Dr. Ardain Isma, that most elegant of authors (*Bittersweet Memoriesof Last Spring, Midnight at Noon*) and editors for wanting to put *Palliser Park*out there.

Most authors have beta readers – those intrepid, noble friends who will actually read a first draft and let a writer know if it all holds together. These are a rare breed. *I* have Suzanne Elusorr. Her astute and elegant takes on *Palliser Park* kept me pounding the keys. Whenever I send Suzanne a new section, I chew my fingernails until she gets back to me. Her invaluable contributions to *Palliser Park* are forever appreciated.

Someone who can bring up any day is my dear friend, Sanjay R. Singhal. He is a complex and lyrical writer (*Stories I Never Told You, Tales of the Nightwatchman*).One of the most sophisticated human beings knocking about the planet, gifted with a wicked sense of humour. An hour on the phone with Sanjay is a tonic for the weary soul.

My partner – in – ballet crime, Mark Nash. Gentleman, sportsman and a ballet professional of extraordinary ability, he makes life in the ballet a joy and a genuine hoot. We laugh a lot.

Anya Wong has not only been my ballet muse for so many years, her work as a massage and movement therapist has kept me at the barre as a teacher and choreographer.

Thanks to Joann Goodell for being everything a friend should be.

War (Rhyfel)

Bitter to live in times like these.
While God declines beyond the seas;
Instead, man, king or peasantry,
Raises his gross authority.

When he thinks God has gone away
Man takes up his sword to slay
His brother; we can hear death's roar.
It shadows the hovels of the poor.

Like the old songs they left behind,
We hung our harps in the willows again.
Ballads of boys blow on the wind,
Their blood is mingled with the rain.

Hedd Wyn (Ellis Evans)

Table of Contents

CHAPTER

1

June, 1919

Death held no surprise for Major Simon Fairlight, even a death that had sent a baronet plummeting from a Belgravia rooftop. He gazed down at Sir John Redgrave, now impaled on iron finials of the garden fence. An errant breeze pulled at Sir John's bloody tweed jacket, flapping the lapel up and down. It was a gentle movement, almost playful, reminding him that nature took no particular notice of murdered men and their fondest plans. Poppies still grew in the fields at Ypres.

"Sharpish wind," remarked Sir Vernon George Waldegrave Kell, founder and still head of the British Secret Service. He pointed to the Georgian stonework that enclosed Sir John's roof. "But not enough to knock poor old Pidgy off his roof. Anything, Major?"

"He went over at this point, I suspect," murmured Simon, dropping down to examine a section of the wall. "The angle's right and there's a little blood."

"Don't suppose it could, possibly, be a tragic accident? Gentleman of advanced years and all that."

"I think Sir John was taken by surprise – defensive wounds in the struggle – and then shoved over the edge."

Sir Vernon's fierce blue eyes glinted with regret. He walked away from the rampart, heading for a series of beautifully constructed cages holding a number of querulous grey and copper banded birds.

"The world's leading authority on the Egyptian Swift Pidgeon," said the spymaster, reaching out to touch the elaborate casing. Some of the Egyptians Swifts skittered away from Sir Vernon's powerful presence. "Keen on birds since our days at Eton. Poor Pidgy."

Simon returned to his full height and watched as Scotland Yard entered the rear garden to retrieve Sir John Redgrave's harpooned body. In a way, luck was with the Service. The Redgraves kept very few servants – not an uncommon practice for many genteel households after the war – and Lady Redgrave was out of town. Sir John could be cleared away without much drama.

"You'll have a word with the Yard?" asked Sir Vernon, still gazing at the milling Egyptian Swifts. It wasn't an actual question, merely a reminder.

"That's two for Britain," said Simon. "Five for France and Belgium including two of our own field operatives."

"Yes." The spymaster looked grim. "You might be right, after all. This German – this *Grabrauber* – we're sure he's not just a legend from the trenches, a Will O'the Wisp?"

"Sir, I …"

Sir Vernon waved a hand, acquiescing. "You've convinced me. *The Gravedigger* is in England. Your summer holiday must have been planned by the Almighty himself."

2

To an American girl, the title – Major, the Lord Simon Fairlight – was ornate and formal in the suffocating style of a Victorian sarcophagus. A perfect irony, Alice thought, not for the first time and not without deep sadness, since her husband was a ghost. The sunny, quick – to – laugh university student she had seen off to war in 1914 had been killed on a French battlefield and in his place was a shadow, a shade.

Alice gazed at her husband. He sat, lost in thought, as the car rumbled along a country road on the Essex coast. Always tall and slender, Simon was gaunt when he returned home from France and despite the best efforts of several Fairlight cooks, had failed to regain his optimum weight. The beautiful, highly planed face that she thought so poetic as if he were an elven king from a child's fairy story was now marred by a bayonet scar that ran from his right temple to his cheekbone. Yet – even more striking was the wound to his personality. Whatever had happened on the battlefields, whatever Simon had seen in the trenches had torn away all frivolity – random joy, a bit of a laugh.

Her first sighting of Simon Fairlight, by contrast, had been *all* frivolity and dizzy laughter. An American new to Oxford, she had been invited to view an utterly baffling October ritual by a fellow classmate. She stood at the entrance to Christ Church, surrounded by a cheering crowd of town and gowners, enchanted by the student spectacle. In Christ Church's storied Tom Quad, house members gathered for a giddy celebration – ancient, silly, and indisputably British – to lampoon the college's founder, Henry VIII. Carrying burning torches but dressed in flawless white tie, festooned with bejeweled Tudor hats and fanciful chains of office, they called out nonsensical questions in iambic pentameter to their elected sovereign. That glamourous young man – Henry's proxy – was carried around the quad in an open Jacobean palanquin, tossing out improvised couplets in reply and showering his litter bearers with champagne. He was wildly handsome with thick, unruly black hair – and an askew metal crown – falling about crystalline features animated by good humor and a keen intelligence.

Alice stifled a sigh, remembering the laughter and the champagne fizzing in that cold October air. She loved her husband *and* his shade – profoundly grateful he survived the war when so many young Britons had not. Perhaps, one day, a little of Simon's daffy student charm would return.

"It's going to come down in a minute," announced their driver, Reggie Spinner, shifting down to slowly pass a farmer who was securing a paddock gate. "Saw some lightning off to the east."

"How far are we out?" asked Simon with a small frown.

"Not bad, Major," shouted Spinner as competing rumbles from thunder and car threatened to drown him out. "Half five if the roads hold up."

"These sea storms can be nasty. Pull off if it gets dicey."

13

"Righto, Major!" The retainer patted the car's dashboard proudly. He had been Simon's batman for the entire duration of the war and had been glad to retain his valet duties in peace time. "Not much the Crossley can't handle, though. She's a proper gem."

A clap of thunder broke overhead. It was grey and dreary beyond the confines of the touring car. In the distance, the silvery sky was shifting to ominous black.

"Not quite the seaside summer I had in mind," said Alice, shivering. The Crossley's Burbank cloth top was very stylish but couldn't keep English weather at bay. "So much for treasured visions of lying about in the sun, knocking back cold drinks with abandon."

"Cold?" Simon held up an arm.

Alice nodded and slid across the oxblood leather seat. He draped the arm about her shoulders, drawing her in against his slender frame. She let out a long breath, enjoying the affectionate gesture from her haunted husband.

"Bit better?" he asked, using his free hand to pull the car rug over her lap.

"Yes, thank you." Alice laid her head against his chest and sighed. "Oh, I hope this was a good idea."

"How can it not?" Simon gave her an encouraging squeeze. "Lawn tennis, croquet, bathing in the sea, big engagement party for your friend ..."

"I know but ..." Alice paused, trying to find the best words. Since Simon's return from the war, he evinced a distinct distaste for frivolous things and ostentatious displays. Her friend, Lady Constance, was a frothy, dizzy girl – prone to fits of giggles and spending huge sums of her doting father's money.

"What if I promise to be on my best behavior?" said Simon quietly. "I realize I've become something of a bore."

Alice lifted her head. "Darling," she breathed in dismay. "I didn't mean to suggest you were …"

"Alice," he brushed her cheek with his long fingers, "you deserve to have a holiday. Lord FitzRobert can feed us peacocks stuffed with Baroque pearls for all I care."

Alice felt a sob rise in her throat. He had lost so much in the war but never his disarming kindness. She awkwardly pretended to laugh instead and threw her arms up around his neck. Simon seemed a little taken aback at her effusiveness, patting her back as if she was a skittish horse.

Outside the motor car, the weather moved from a steady drizzle to hard rain. It hammered the Crossley's cloth top, obliterating the engine's roar and any real conversation. While the intrepid Reggie Spinner battled visibility and the Essex country roads, Simon and Alice were content to just sit together, wordlessly. Simon had returned to his thoughts, idly toying with a lock of her blonde hair. She closed her eyes, happy to be under a warm rug and tucked away in the small of his arm. Long minutes passed, the dull patter of rain and intermittent jostling of the Crossley over the rough country road nearly lulled her into genuine sleep.

"Major," she heard Spinner say when the rain relented a little, "have you seen it?"

"Yes," Simon replied, enigmatic. "The last fork in the road. I'm told the gates to Palliser Park are impressive – hard to miss. Any glimpse?"

"Not as yet, Major, but we must be close."

"Steady on then."

Alice opened her eyes and sat up. "Is something wrong?"

"No – nothing," Simon replied with a shake of his head. "Just another motor having trouble in the rain. Not everyone is as adept as our Mr. Spinner."

She looked behind her, over the top of the car seat. Through a small rear window built into the Crossley's heavy Burbank cloth, the glowing headlamps of a vehicle could be seen behind a curtain of pelting rain. Rather close considering the wretched weather.

Then, as if the following driver had wearied of the Crossley's pace, the headlamps suddenly jerked to the right and ploughed forward. Alice could hear the other motor car's engine roar with effort.

"What's he on about?" growled Spinner, steering the Crossley as far as he dared to the left.

Alice gasped as what now appeared to be a lorry barreled towards them. "My stars – he's going to try to pass! What a palooka!"

Simon leaned forward, peering at Spinner's driving mirrors. "Did you really just say *palooka?*"

"American for a very stupid man," cried Alice, still watching out the rear window. The surging lorry was nearly to their rear right fender. "Here he comes!"

The rumbling lorry's engine was screaming with strain. Older than the state – of – the – art Crossley – it was large and ungainly, painted a cheery blue color but heavily stained with soot and oil. On its heaving wooden sides, *Meredith and Sons – Wanstead* was just visible under all the grit.

Meredith and Sons hampered by the wet conditions, remained on the Crossley's right rear. Unfortunately, despite superb all – weather systems , the touring car hit a rut made invisibleby rainwater. It jack – knifed – losing speed and the front end sliding to the right. The lorry driver saw its best chance and gunned forward with a tortured grinding of the gears.

Reggie Spinner corrected sharply to the left, avoiding a direct collision with the larger vehicle as it howled past like a freight train.

"Hang on, Alice!" Simon pulled her against him as the Crossley slid in the mud, drifting into a lurching spin. It seemed possible that the touring car would actually flip. The centrifugal force sent them tumbling into the rear passenger door and then forward into the footwell behind the front seat.

Alice let out a cry of pain as she slammed against a hard bracket of the seat. She felt the Crossley struggling to stay upright as it swung around wildly. Then the car began to roll backwards, its rear wheels dropping down off into a ditch.

"Are you in one piece?" asked Simon, his mellifluous voice urgent and unusually harsh. The Crossley had come to a full stop in the ditch. In the front seat, she heard Spinner uttering a string of sprightly epitaphs probably understandable only to natives of his parish in London.

"Alice!" her husband repeated.

"Hunky dory," she murmured as her wits tried to return. "Banged my shoulder, but it's fine."

"Define *fine*," he demanded, helping her up out of the footwell.

She began to feel distinctly woozy as if the sharp hit against the seat bracket had rattled her brain. "Poetry," Alice said with a giddy laugh. "Pure poetry. *Define fine.*"

Simon kicked open the rear passenger door and pulled her free. "Damn the motor, Mr. Spinner! Lady Fairlight is bleeding!"

"How exciting," said Alice with a strange brightness. She wondered why Simon sounded so effusive, so confounded. They were all fine despite Meredith and Sons' best efforts.

"Define fine," she laughed. Everything was fine – even poetry was returning. Alice took a giddy step closer to her husband. "Shower us with champagne, King Hen …"

Then Alice wobbled and fell against Simon. Drizzle and the Essex countryside began to weave into grey ribbons that seemed to wind around and through her. Then she was sick.

CHAPTER

3

"God's humor reveals itself yet again," Simon murmured, gazing across the road at a set of lofty, imperious Georgian gateposts that had revealed themselves as the heavy rain abated. Constructed from costly oolitic limestone, Palliser Park's honey – colored towers existed to announce that an exclusive residence existed somewhere at the end of a very long drive.

He refocused on Alice, who was sitting on the disabled Crossley's running board. "More the old self?"

"Yes, thank you." She smiled over the rim of a thermos cup from their travel hamper. "Funny – I don't usually keel over from nosebleeds. Sorry about your clothes."

Simon glanced down at the ruinous yellowish smear that now dappled his vicuna topcoat. He had been stained by worst things.

"If it's any conciliation," Alice added, examining her splattered silk chiffon blouse, "I don't think my Doucet original will ever be the same again."

"Don't imagine you're going to elude a doctor's visit – summer hols or not. As soon as we ..."

Reggie Spinner scrambled down from the road, interrupting him. "Wretched lorry's long gone, Major. Can't help but think a right – minded lad would have stopped to help."

"There's nothing right about Meredith and Sons, I feel," said Simon. "Time for you to leg it for Palliser Park, Mr. Spinner, and secure reinforcements."

Simon's former bat man nodded. "On my way, Major."

Once Reggie Spinner had hopped it for the Palliser Park gates, Simon walked around the Crossley. The lovely touring car, painted a deep lustrous red, seemed in reasonable order. The strike to its right rear panel from the road – hogging lorry had left a strip of dirty blue but no real damage. Not a serious blow. Not a kill shot. A warning, perhaps? He wondered. But who and why?

Ostensibly, he was Major Simon Fairlight of the Royal Horse Guards, 7th Cavalry Division – a career officer doing post – war mop up in London. His actual attachment to Waldegrave's relatively new secret service was known only to the department itself and the Prime Minister's immediate circle. Even Alice was unaware of his reassignment.

Simon reached out to touch the blue paint. It was running in the rain. One more good downpour and Meredith and Sons' particular blue would be gone. Just a driver with a more than a couple of pints under his belt and behind schedule to boot? Just an accident – just their bad luck? Or was *Der Grabrauber's* reach wider than they had anticipated – not a lone wolf at all. And more ᠁ disturbing still, was Sir Vernon's intricately assembled MI6 compromised? Was he about to take Alice up and over into a covert No Man's Land?

"Simon," called out Alice from the other side of the Crossley. She sometimes seemed to possess an eerie prescience.

"Do you think the truck driver was absolutely blotto? I mean, to knock us off the road."

He forced a pleasant expression on his face and came round the front of the car. "What's that American phrase? Spiffed?"

"Spiffed will do. Can't we just follow Mr. Spinner on foot?"

"Not while you're *hors de combat*, Lady Fairlight."

"Oh, piffle." Alice made a sour face. "I could be halfway to one of Palliser Park's fancy new bathtubs by now."

Simon bit his bottom lip. Lord FitzRobert, the current owner of Palliser, was one generation away from new money – *mountains of new money* – and the War – To – End – All – Wars had only added substantial sums to his fortune. His family made their initial mark in weapons manufacturing and had been happy to supply the British military with all that was needed from Crimea to conflicts in India, Egypt, Burma and Africa. They had seen their star rise spectacularly under Queen Victoria with royal warrants and splashy titles from a grateful nation. An almost complete renovation of Palliser Park, a vast Georgian property on the Essex coastline, had started before the war and had finally been completed in the months after Armistice. FitzRobert treasure had been poured into every aspect of the house and its extensive grounds until the only words gobsmacked locals could gasp were *palace, grandiose, opulent.* He had a word for Palliser Park too – meretricious.

"You look vexed," said Alice disapprovingly. "Remember it's Constance's big moment."

"Jack is a good egg," murmured Simon, scanning across the country road for any sign of rescue. "Survived the war just to end up with Constance's little heel on his neck."

21

Before Alice could respond, a shout of "Almost to you!" cut through the renewed patter of rain. A pair of heavy horses pulling what appeared to be a farm wagon rumbled down the driveway, the tack jingling cheerfully.

Simon smiled. FitzRobert had not deployed his undoubtedly flashy motor to fetch them. He hadn't the slightest doubt that if it had been his father, the Marquess of Tash, or his older brother, Viscount Blayloch stranded on the literal side of the road, a gleaming Rolls Royce would have swept down to the rescue. But a mere second son with a military commission and an American wife? The farm dray would do – *so much more room for the luggage and all that.* Meant to be a subtle social cue signaling the mighty ascension of a former family in trade from an unsubtle bore. Lord FitzRobert, however, had failed to realize that Fairlights from father to sons vastly preferred horses to motorized vehicles. They would be far happier climbing up into a dray behind a pair of working farm horses.

Simon waved at Reggie Spinner and the stable lad who drove the pair of bay Shires. He almost laughed out loud – it was going to be a jolly summer holiday all right.

CHAPTER

4

Rain pelleted down as they neared the palatial main house. Lady Alice was sitting up next to the driver while Simon and Reggie Spinner sat on Goyard trunks in the rear of the jostling wagon.

Simon blew out a stream of cigarette smoke. It vanished immediately into the hard rain.

"Despite our combined military experience, we both failed to secure umbrellas," he observed.

Reggie Spinner jumped slightly at a clap of thunder – an anxiety directly traceable to trench nerves. "Clear dereliction of duty, Major," the valet admitted, wiping water away from his face.

"I blame last week's recce by the aunts," said Simon, referring to a recent visit to the Fairlight family's London house by a frothy collection of his relations determined to see Anna Pavlova dance *La Fille Mal Gardee* at the Victoria Palace Theatre. Cheerful, dithery guerilla raiders, they had blown through the Upper Grosvenor Street townhouse and its stores in an exhausting three – day sortie.

"There was a run on brollies, sir," agreed Reggie Spinner.

"We can hardly be blamed for cracking under assault from superior forces."

"No, sir."

Simon crushed the last of his cigarette out on the dray's floor and pocketed the ends – a habit he retained from battlefield reconnaissance. "Well, Mr. Spinner, dismount and fight on foot."

"Yes, sir." The valet rose as the farm wagon jiggled to a stop by Palliser Park's front steps where a retinue of the house staff waited to be of service.

"Settle in and then find me. Let's discuss Meredith and Sons in more detail," Simon murmured as he, too, pushed to his feet.

"Righto, Major. I'll see that the Crossley's tended to first, though."

Simon jumped down, his feet stinging as he hit the wet gravel in the drive. He nipped around to assist Alice's descent from the driver's bench seat. She was dripping wet. The once immaculate fawn colored walking suit hung in water – logged layers, seeming to weigh more than Alice herself.

"Thanks, darling," she said, wincing slightly as her feet touched down on the drive. "*Yowzers!* – as we say in New York."

"Your Lordship," huffed a voice behind Simon, "I am Crumpling. May I suggest ..."

"Vastly prefer Major," interrupted Simon, turning to see Palliser Park's perfectly appointed butler gliding towards them with a large black umbrella aloft.

"Of course, Major Fairlight." Crumpling continued to advance with the umbrella with the steely purpose of a shark. "May I suggest a restorative in your rooms? Drinks will be served in the library at 7:00, sir." He turned slightly to acknowledge Alice. "Lady Fairlight."

"And the rest of the household?" Simon almost flinched when Crumpling reached them and held the umbrella high over their heads. He realized how much he had come to loathe the fuss of such domestic scenes and that a respectable middle – aged man was expected to stand in the rain shielding them from inclement weather.

"The majority of the FitzRobert household have yet to return from a trip to view Viking artifacts at Dankworth Hall, sir. I fear Lord FitzRobert is indisposed in his study."

"Heading to our rooms sounds positively tiptop!" piped up Alice, taking Simon's elbow. She was clearly eager to be inside by a fire somewhere.

"Very good, Your Ladyship." Crumpling said, his eyes brightening with the knowledge that Lady Fairlight, despite being an American, was a team player. She understood that English country houses ran to the servants' requirements rather than their betters. Lady Fairlight was not going to be a *nouveau riche* irritant. "If you would so kind as to follow me."

One of the largest houses in Southern England, Palliser Park reared over a bucolic eighty – five acres of coastal landscape like a Palladian dragon. Crumpling led them up its wide stone steps, past a collection of chilled staff members wearing practiced smiles of welcome and into the beast itself.

Often his breezy American wife, when confronted with an example of Britain's stately architecture liked to let out a low whistle and murmur in a stagey voice stolen from Vaudeville – *Well, ain't this the Taj Mahal?* But her first glimpse of what Lord FitzRobert had dubbed The Marble Salon silenced the usual bonhomie. Simon saw her suck in a breath as she absorbed the grandiosity of FitzRobert treasure – and she was the daughter of an industrialist, who had grown up on Manhattan's Park Ave and a Hudson River Valley country estate modeled after Fontainebleau.

The Marble Salon was the size of a massive rectangular riding school but instead of soft footing for the horses, there was an ocean of Calacatta marble veined in gold. Walls painted a Robin's Egg blue soared up three stories and were segmented with ornamental Italianate columns and marble statuary. The room featured not one but *two* formal staircases facing each other at the top and bottom of the rectangle. These led up to leviathan landings that presumably led to other glamorous rooms. Simon could well imagine Lord FitzRobert swaggering down one of the staircases, making his all – important entrance to a tenant ball or hunt breakfast. He did not, however, deign to appear for the mere second son of a marquess and his Yankee wife.

He looked up at a barrel ceiling heavily plastered in the Rococo style and gilded with gold. Indeed, it seemed any surface that couldn't get up and run away was gilded with gold from the Roman columns to the ornate iron – worked staircase balustrades. The Marble Salon glimmered in the grey afternoon light like gold doubloons half buried in sea silt. Fully lit for a party, Simon expected occupants might feel as if they were standing on the sun.

"We shall be ascending this stair," said Crumpling, indicating the one nearest. He turned and headed for it with a crisp economy of movement that spoke of years of dedicated service in the best houses.

Simon felt a momentary pang of pity for Crumpling. He suspected that Lord FitzRobert made it a requirement that all visitors should be led through the Marble Salon upon first entering the house. Surely there were more convenient ways to ascend to the guest rooms. Such gaucheness would offend a dedicated butler.

Onwards they marched, up the grand staircase and down labyrinthian hallways that were only slightly less grandiose than the Marble Salon until Crumpling opened a white beveled door and announced "The Green Room" without fanfare.

"Lady Constance has arranged for one of the servants – Polly – to act as ladies' maid," the butler said. Simon and Alice, well – trained troops, filed past him into the Green Room. "Polly's usual duties are that of an upstairs maid."

"How kind," said Alice automatically. She was shivering in her wet walking suit.

"Drinks at 7:00 in the library," Crumpling reminded them with a small bow of his head. "Major Fairlight, Lady Fairlight."

The moment Crumpling returned to stalk the highways and byways of Palliser Park, Alice ran to the fireplace and began shedding her wet clothes by the brightly burning fire.

"I'm so cold!" she cried, tossing her jacket down and fumbling for the buttons on her skirt. "Where's that wretched restorative he was so happy to dangle in front of us?"

Simon scanned the room and spotted a silver tray on a side table. Tea cozies embroidered with the FitzRobert crest announced that there were hot pots underneath the fine needlepoint.

"Tea or coffee?" he asked.

"Oh, a coffee sounds lovely." She stepped out of her skirt. "Hey – no gold gilding in here!"

"Such is the fate of those consigned to the second – tier guest rooms," said Simon as he began to arrange cups and saucers, although he was forced to admit that the Green Room was a very comfortable place to garrison. Taking its name from walls which were painted a deep shade of bluish green, the room was well appointed with an exceptionally large and handsome fireplace as its centerpiece. A bathroom had been installed in what once had been the sitting room – a definite bonus not always available in country houses. From where he stood pouring coffee, he could see gleaming white tile and thick towels that promised a glorious hot bath was well within reach.

"You know," Simon carried a cup of coffee across to where his wife was sitting in her slip by the warming flames. He pointed at a large, impressively framed portrait of an Elizabethan lady that hung over the chimneypiece. "The FitzRoberts don't have any old family pictures so they've just put other people's ancestors to use."

Alice took the coffee cup and laughed. "You *do* remember my family's house? My mother bought most of Europe's art and had it shipped home."

"I remember Manets, Cezannes and the occasional Degas," Simon said, sipping his own coffee, grateful for a hot drink. "Rather different."

She smiled. "We're here for Constance and Jack. We can just ignore her father, surely? You promised to eat roasted peacock stuffed with Baroque pearls without complaint."

"I did, didn't I?" He almost smiled.

"Mr. Spinner is my witness!"

A quiet knock came at the door before Simon could ask her if she thought swan livers shot with eatable gold flake might be on offer during the blessed distribution of alcoholic beverages.

"Yikes! The luggage bearers." Alice jumped to her feet and retreated towards the bathroom, unwilling to be viewed in her silk slip. "As Chicago gangsters say, give me da high sign!"

CHAPTER

5

Alice was grateful for a bath. Even with Simon popping in and out while changing into his dinner suit, it was a balm to drift in a deep well of hot water scented with Gardenia soap powder. She was surprisingly stiff after the Crossley's run – in with the predatory blue truck.

"I'm off to recce with Mr. Spinner," said Simon as he cracked open the door a sliver. "Crumpling has sent up your maid. Polly – Polly Piety. She's putting away your things."

"Oh, gosh – thank her for me! And tell Polly Piety I'll be wearing the *soie verte* with the lemon ice satin bits."

"Green with yellow – got it." Simon pulled the bathroom door shut and departed to confer with Reggie Spinner.

Alice gave herself permission to float in the massive ball and claw bathtub for a few more minutes. As was the way with Constance's father, no expense spared. She hadn't seen such an ornate adjoining bath since a luxurious stay at San Francisco's Palace Hotel.

The green dress would make a splash on their first day at Palliser Park. A delicious confection of apple green silk piped in yellow satin. It had been designed by House of Worth especially for her. The strong lines – high waisted and full skirt with two wide ruffles of frothy silk – suited her tall, athletic frame perfectly and its luminous green lit up her blonde American complexion. But the Worth gown was not only a sophisticated work of art, it was also a breathtakingly expensive bespoke creation. Something Lord FitzRobert with his constantly assessing eye would not fail to note. Hopefully he would reckon that there were a few Americans he could condescend to suffer under his expansive gilded roof.

Although she had been educated at an excellent American school and received a first in history at St. Hilda's, Oxford, there were still Englishmen such as Constance's father who would patronize her as an American thicko. It was important to her that Simon should not have any more excuses to put Lord FitzRobert firmly in his place. Exquisitely turned out in her *soie verte* and matching satin shoes with the whimsical curved heels, she ought to be able deflect any anti – American commentary for one evening at least.

Constance – Fizzy to her close friends – would help manage her supercilious father. Despite Simon's opinion that Fizzy was silly, reckless and had a laugh resembling a hyena with a chest infection, she liked Lord FitzRobert's devil – may – care daughter. They had met at a party in London before the war, bonding over a shared love of sports such as tennis and golf. Fizzy had been excited to invite them to visit to Palliser Park with the massive renovation finally complete. It had been years in the making – – almost as long as she had known Fizzy – and Lord FitzRobert resolutely refused to entertain in his new property until all the work had been completed. It was something of a coup to have been invited to Palliser Park for a summer holiday *and* Fizzy's engagement ball which would have the honor of being the first social event at the newly renovated Georgian house.

Alice sat up with reluctance. It was time to leave the lovely deep well of warm water and face her temporary servant. She was positive that Polly Piety would be more bother than she was worth. As an upstairs maid pressed into service, Polly would require much direction for not much in actual assistanceand she imagined that Polly's limited skills would be shared with other ladies who needed a dresser.

Her own, Elsie, had just retired to marry Simon's head groom and take up residence in one of Castle Fairlight's staff cottages. A new lady's maid had yet to be hired. Alice despaired at ever finding anyone as thoroughly excellent and pleasant to take Elsie's place.

She emerged to find the maid had finished unpacking. The first thing that struck Alice about Polly Piety was the girl's striking beauty. Polly, in her crisply starched white apron and grey uniform, could have stepped right out of an overly sentimental Victorian portrait of a dairy maid. Gifted with a perfect, creamy complexion, vibrant chestnut hair and an hour – glass figure, she also possessed a face that rightly belonged to a matinee idol. For a moment as Polly stood waiting for instructions, Alive had the thought that the stunning young girl really ought to be directed towards a career on the stage – she was the very vision of Midsummer's Titania or George Bernard Shaw's Saint Joan. And then, Polly Piety spoke.

"Owamya, miss," she said in a pronounced Birmingham dialect. "What needs doing?"

"Oh, a Black Country girl?" asked Alice with a kind smile.

Polly brightened. "Yay, miss. Me mam took terrible sick so me da found work by the sea."

"That was very good of your father. Is your mother better now?"

The maid nodded, pleased to be asked about her family. "Yay, bostin, miss … um, mean *fine*, miss. The sea suits her, it does."

"I'm glad," said Alice sincerely. She decided that asking Polly to refer to her as Your Ladyship was just fussy and unnecessary. "Shall we have a go at sorting my hair first?"

"Oh, yay, miss!" Polly darted towards the dressing table where silver backed brushes and combs had been laid out. She seemed genuinely excited at the prospect of tending to a lady's locks.

Once Alice sat by the mahogany table – a Jacobean piece with a large oval mirror sensitively added to the original design – her maid – on – loan unpinned her long blonde hair and began vigorously brushing it out. Unlike Elsie, who could sense when Alice might want or need a little time to ponder the evening's events, Polly was a chatterbox. The girl cheerfully burbled along in her heavy Brummie dialect about what seemed to be a reasonably pleasant albeit busy life at Palliser Park, her visits home to see her parents and a dog named Fan, her favorite foods – kippers and summer pudding – and her interest in learning how to knit a proper vest.

Polly also intimated that she had fallen in love and that her choice of mate would come as something as a surprise to both her family and fellow servants, especially Crumpling whom she described as keenly aware of the servant hierarchy. Alice didn't doubt the spectacular Polly might have caught the eye of Palliser Park's gamekeeper or a local farmer. Either would be a very nice hop up the social ladder for a young girl from the Black Country.

By the time Polly had described the fastest walk to Palliser Park's beach, then the prettiest walk around Lord FitzRobert's ornamental lake, her nasty run – in with one of the lake's swans *and* a funny story about Crumpling slipping on a wet floor, Alice was ready for a necklace and stiff drink.

"Let's do this one," said Alice, opening a blue leather case that had been stacked neatly on the dressing table. Inside was a pearl choker centered with a large oval peridot. "You know, they say this stone brings good cheer to those who gaze at it."

"Ooh, miss," cooed Polly Piety as she gingerly took the necklace from Alice and held it up to better admire the luminous green gem. "Maybe me own man'll give me own!"

"It would be a lovely gift," agreed Alice politely.

Polly went on to describe the wedding dress that she'd been thinking her mother could help her sew. It sounded rather old fashioned and stodgy – almost late–Victorian with a big, complicated skirt, puffy sleeves and lots of ribbons – to Alice who realized, with a guilty pang, that she had always had the very good fortune to be able to wear what was modish.

"Thank you, Polly," said Alice as the girl shut the clasp on her choker. "You have been most helpful."

Alice watched in the mirror as Polly bobbed a curtsey behind her chair. The maid had done a very respectable job of dressing her hair. It was a simple, sleek style that coiled her blonde hair at the nape of her neck – perfect for the *Soie Verte* and its three flounces.

She reached into another little leather case where some pin money was often tucked away and retrieved a sturdy handful of five – pound notes.

"I know this is not the usual time," said Alice. She pushed away from the dressing table and stood, handing the notes to the astonished girl, "but, please, I hope you and your mother will be able to acquire just the right materials for your dress."

"Oh, miss!" Polly Piety breathed; her astonishingly blue eyes were as large as saucers as she gazed at the money in her shaking hand. "This be too much by half, miss."

"Nonsense," Alice replied, reaching out to pat the incredulous maid's shoulder. "Your dress has to be absolutely perfect. Now, I won't need you after dinner. I'm quite capable of getting ready for bed on my own."

Mindful that it might seem suspicious if the chatterbox Polly tripped down to the servants dining room with a pocket of fivers, she added in a kind voice, "And I will let Crumpling know that I've given you something for your dress."

"Thank ye, miss," Polly breathed, still staring at the money. "Thank ye."

Alice threw the flabbergasted girl a last look and left the Green Room. With some luck, she would be able to navigate the vast hallways to one of the main staircases. With even more luck, Lord FitzRobert would be offering substantial alcoholic rewards to his guests. She was an American – land of jazz and speakeasies. After a long day, an American appreciated a strong shot of hospitality.

CHAPTER

6

Simon met Reggie Spinner outside the main house in the new garage that Lord FitzRobert commissioned in one of the two stable blocks. As with everything at Palliser Park, it was massive and completely *au courant* for modern motoring. The Crossley had been rescued from indignity on the side of the road. It now sat inside the garage awaiting a minor repair from Lord FitzRobert's personal mechanic who lived in a flat above the motorcars.

"He's a good man," said Reggie, patting the Crossley's wing. "Survived Gallipoli. 5th Manchesters. He'll have her ready to go in the morning."

"It'll be a long couple of days, Mr. Spinner."

"Piece of cake, Major," Reggie said. "It's not Gallipoli, is it?"

"It's not Gallipoli," Simon repeated in a soft voice. He had a flash of days spent digging out trenches in the mud and in the blazing sun, ending the lives of terribly injured horses with a bullet – good horses that had given their all.

"Wanstead first, Major?" Reggie Spinner asked, coughing.

Simon shook off the memories. "Yes – find out what you can about Meredith and Sons. Lorry was probably stolen but maybe there's something to be discovered. Then London and Sir Vernon. See him alone."

"Will he see me alone, sir?"

"Tell his aide de camp that Major Fairlight has sent you to finalize transport arrangements for the horse. Sir Vernon will understand. When you see him explain what happened on the road and that we may have a breach."

"Righto, Major!" Reggie Spinner tapped the wing again. "I'll leave as soon as the Crossley's repaired."

"You might send me a wire. I'll walk down to the village and pick it up. Be happy for any interlude away from Castle Perilous." Simon reached for his cigarette case. He automatically offered the contents to Reggie Spinner – an instinctive gesture from the trenches. Working class, middle class, landed gentry and titled officers were all one in the trenches. They shared everything – the work, the fighting, the death, the wretched rations, tea swirling with dust and cigarettes which could be difficult to obtain especially in the second half of the war.

Reggie accepted one. "Better get back, Major. I need to finish unpacking your kit."

"Your quarters acceptable?" Simon struck a match. He lit Reggie's cigarette and then his own.

His former bat man grinned. "Clean, well appointed. No gold though."

"Crumpling an all – right jack? He seems to run a tight ship."

"Served in the Second Boer War under Buller. No fuss or silly business. No deviations from duty. The servants certainly march to his drumbeat. Reckon he's earned that, Major."

Simon thought of the disaster at the Tugela River in which Buller's men stepped into a deadly ambush set by the Boers. Yet another collection of brave British soldiers who lost their lives in a land far from the green byways of Britain.

He abruptly blew out a stream of smoke. "Almost seven, Mr. Spinner. I can't leave Lady Fairlight to meet Lord FitzRobert's forces alone."

"Right, Major. I'll wire from London as soon as I can."

"Good man – and thank you," Simon said with sincerity. He moved quickly, leaving the newly minted garage and heading through a light drizzle across the gravel drive to the main house. Having ferreted out a side door conveniently located near a second staircase, he now had a way to quietly enter and leave Palliser Park. Trench warfare brought out the fox – he liked having a back door to the burrow.

The library was located on the ground floor, along with all the other really important rooms with which Lord FitzRobert enjoyed dazzling his guests. In the east wing – seemingly miles from the central Marble Salon – the library was situated in such a way that views over the manicured lawn and gardens would always be visible through several sets of French doors.

Terrible for the spines of leather books as sunlight was always the enemy, Simon noted upon entering and getting the lay of the land. The French doors were obviously a design choice of Lord FitzRobert, who had probably had period correct Georgian windows knocked out to accommodate them. He had a moment before he was seen to have a gander at the guests who were congregating by the new doors, admiring the view. The rain had stopped. Clouds had momentarily drifted away, allowing the late sun to reveal a perfect English summer evening.

Simon made rapid assessments in his head about what was obviously the core group visiting Palliser Park: Lord FitzRobert – still cutting a good figure for a man in his fifties – was pontificating by one of the glass doors, remarking on the excellence of his grass tennis court. Listening with various levels of interest were five houseguests. Two he recognized instantly as Lady Constance and her brother Perry. While Constance was sporty and outgoing to the point of coarseness, Perry was kind and more introverted. The only FitzRobert he actually liked, Perry – burdened with the aftermath of childhood pleurisy – had been rejected for active duty and had spent the war filing information for the War Department in London. Perry had also long disappointed his father by being bookish and deeply interested in classical music, especially the opera.

The others were an odd gaggle. One was a great beauty – almost unnervingly sophisticated in the theatrical manner. Dressed in an eye – catching scarlet dress and diamonds, she leaned into Lord FitzRobert as if he were the most fascinating creature she ever dared hope to meet in her journey through life. Simon had a shrewd idea as to why she might be included in the summer holiday at Palliser Park.

The final two were clearly a married couple and in the same age group as Lord FitzRobert but lacking his vigor and good looks. A quick reassessment and Simon recognized the husband as Alastair Rothermore, a highly connected member of the House of Commons. He could guess why the MP had been invited. Trust Lord FitzRobert to use his own daughter's engagement as an excuse to apply genial pressure for a political outcome he desired.

He was startled out of his social diagnostic when someone slipped an arm under his.

"Sorry I'm late," murmured Alice. "I got turned around. Two footmen and a maid had to leave their appointed tasks to provide directions. They practically had to wave flags."

Simon squeezed her hand. "Glad you're here, darling. I was too frightened to move forward by myself."

She laughed under her breath. "You, frightened? That's a good one."

"You might be surprised at what I'm terrified of," he said truthfully and pulled her forward. "Into the breach we go!"

They approached with Alice's green satin heels clattering cheerfully on the polished wood floor. The group by the French doors turned to acknowledge their arrival, perhaps grateful to miss more tales of the tennis court.

"My god – *at last!*" cried Lady Constance as if she were at a rugby match. "Alice! Simon! So glad you could get away."

She surged forward to take Alice's outstretched hands – pretty, modern in a pale blue frock and a bobbed head full of auburn pin curls. "I just couldn't wait for you two to arrive!"

Simon didn't see how that could possibly be true since she had shied off to Dankworth Hall to goggle at Viking swords and pickaxes. He just smiled politely. Constance wasn't really interested in him anyway.

"Fizz!" replied Alice, kissing Constance on the cheek. "We couldn't miss your big event! Where is Jack anyway?"

"Coming in very late. They keep him so busy at the War Department. It's a scandal! Simon – can't you do anything about that?" She threw him a dimpled look of mock entreaty.

"Sadly, I fear not."

"Everybody," Constance turned back towards the others, "may I introduce Major the Lord Simon Fairlight and one of my best friends, Alice – Lady Fairlight?"

Amid the murmurings of welcome, Lord FitzRobert looked mildly irritated at the casual introduction and sailed out to shake Simon's hand. He kissed Alice on both cheeks in the continental fashion.

"So good of you to join us! Allow me to introduce you to Mr. and Mrs. Alastair Rothermore."

The fifty – ish couple stepped forward for the obligatory social exchange of niceties. While Mrs. Rothermore engaged Alice in polite chat, her husband held out a hand to Simon. "You're a genuine war hero, Lord Fairlight," said Rothermore with real admiration. "I've been told how you led The Blues at Sambre – Olse. An honor to shake your hand, sir."

Simon saw Lord FitzRobert's jaw tighten. The host wasn't best pleased at any attention drifting from the family. The FitzRoberts before him had worked hard to catapult the next generation into a house such as Palliser Park. No second son of a marquess ought to be able to take center stage.

He shook Rothermore proffered hand. "Simon, please. Everyone did their bit at Sambre – Olse. All brave lads."

"Well said, Simon!" The MP looked delighted. "Perhaps you could tell me more about it over our stay here?"

"If you would like – but not the happiest of holiday talk, I fear."

"But it is so *important!*" Rothermore said soundly. "We must never forget what you chaps did over there."

Lord FitzRobert seemed to have had enough of the Sambre – Olse Canal and the British blood shed there in buckets. He gestured irritably to the lady in the red frock who immediately drifted in his direction. Possessed of an arresting and highly polished beauty, she was an urbane creature more usually found at London or New York watering holes. She was accustomed to being gazed at in admiration and expected nothing less when on the game. To that end, a theatrical edge was deployed to ensure center stage. Dark glossy hair had been ingeniously cut into sleek, utterly modern bob that brushed her high cheekbones and brought her striking violet – colored eyes into focus. Her figure was slim, perfectly suited to the chic dress and the circlet of diamonds she wore about a swan – like neck.

FitzRobert held up her slender arm as if she was a prize dairy cow he was showing off to a buyer. "I'm persuaded that even a soldier will have heard of *Miss Dorothy Brier*?"

Simon caught a brief flash of Constance rolling her eyes before ignoring Dorothy Brier entirely by concentrating on catching up with Alice. He extended his hand to the well – known actress who took it with a touch so light it barely registered in his palm. Her violet eyes flickered over his face and lingered for a moment at his bayonet scar. For one thrilling moment, he thought she might actually recoil from it. Disappointingly, she steeled her spine and did not.

"So pleased to meet you," Dorothy said without much enthusiasm. Married second sons were clearly not prey in her private hunting ground. He rather thought a widowed weapons manufacturer might well be though.

"Delighted, Miss Brier." He dropped her limp hand as quickly as it was polite to do so. "I saw your Lady MacBeth in New York."

The actress perked up at the magical words. "That production was showered in critical praise. President Wilson came to see it several times. He told me my portrayal of Lady

MacBeth revived his interest in Shakespeare. Those evenings at the theatre helped drive his mind from weighty matters. Such a powerful thing, great art."

Simon wondered how Woodrow Wilson managed to get his sentiments communicated fully before Mrs. Wilson stamped on his instep and drove him back to weighty matters.

"And, of course, you've known Perry for a long time," jumped in Lord FitzRobert, eager to send him off to the ranks of his children. "He's somewhere abouts. If you will excuse me, I must have a word with Crumpling."

FitzRobert strode off, leaving a somewhat discomforted Dorothy Brie behind. She shifted from one foot to the other – bored by conversation with a second – tier guest. Now that her reflections on the acclaimed run of MacBeth were depleted, the actress appeared to be searching for a suitable escape. Simon decided to throw her a reprieve.

"This has been … nice. If you don't mind, I ought to steer my wife to one of those drinks."

Dorothy Brier lit up as if her horse had just won a pile at Goodwood. "Oh, you must! She's very pretty. American?"

"You should see her on the 4th of July," Simon lowered his voice confidentially. "No one plays a fife with more feeling."

"How charming," Dorothy's voice flattened as she registered that he was taking the mick. She swiveled on her fashionable heels, heading in the direction of the nearest liveried footman. There were two who had been instructed to sweep the room with silver trays of martinis and champagne.

A rather ostentatious maneuver for a small summer gathering, Simon reflected, watching her zero in on shimmering gin like a cobra tracking a rodent. It screamed Lord FitzRobert's personal style.

"Darling," said Alice, interrupting his thoughts. He felt her slip an arm under his. "Fizz tells me that a *Russian prince* is languishing upstairs."

Simon turned to his wife. He had an instant to think that Alice looked lovely and refreshingly free of harsh artifice before Constance and Perry encircled them.

"Prince Andrei Volkonsky!" Perry piped up cheerfully. "He's frightfully poetic."

Constance laughed – a harsh hoot. "Swans about composing symphonies, waxing nostalgic about the tsar and drinking Dad's best firewater."

"But why is he languishing upstairs?" Simon asked. "Rivers of blue ruin are freely flowing."

"A nasty summer cold has stuffed up the imperial flame." Constance hooted again. "The village doctor ordered him to bed for a few days. Dad's hoping he'll be back to rights for the engagement party. Wants to show Prince Andrei off – doomed royalty in a Hussar's uniform on the dance floor."

"Well, he's more laughs than *Miss Dorothy Brier*," Perry volunteered, snagging a couple of champagnes from a passing footman's tray. He handed one to Alice at his left with an instinctual politeness. "The only thing she expounds upon is herself."

"Of limited appeal?" Simon accepted a champagne from the same passed tray, noting that the footman was an anxious teenager, perspiring in his too – hot velvet livery and gold braid. Britain had just lost a generation of young men and that loss was apparent in almost every aspect of everyday life. He also doubted that fussing about as a footman had much draw for battle hardened survivors.

Constance shook her mass of auburn curls. "She doesn't understand Dad, that's for certain."

"You step out with them, you never marry them!" said Perry, imitating his father's humorless voice. "Them includes the professional theatre, trade – oh, the irony – and Americans. No offense, Alice!"

Alice grinned. "None taken. Your father's not my cup of tea either. No offense."

"Ha!" Constance screeched like a hyena.

"None taken," said Perry with a short bow.

Simon held up his champagne glass, saluting his wife. Alice winked back. Her wonderful, clear – eyed American beauty again caught at his thoughts. He drank in the delicate lines of the peerless Worth dress that spoke to Alice's exquisite taste.

So many had met brutal deaths – mustard gassed, broken apart by explosives and weapon fire. He had survived, returning home to unquestioned privilege and the glorious Alice. Guilt stabbed at his heart and mind with the fury of a German bayonet. Lord FitzRobert's ornate library with its auction house pictures, predatory actresses and overdressed footmen seemed stifling. His stomach lurched.

"The sun is still out," he murmured to Alice with more urgency than he had wanted to reveal. "Fresh air?"

7

Alice saw her husband relax once he'd stepped free of the FitzRobert library. Simon walked to the edge of the newly installed terrace, gazing out at a countryside dappled with a summer evening's sun. It seemed as if a crushing weight had fallen from his shoulders.

Despite years fighting in trenches ravaged by rain, mud, snow and the sun, she knew Simon still preferred being out in the countryside. When not required to be in London, Simon fled to Wiltshire and Castle Fairlight where he had started a special project with the enthusiasticassistance of his father and brother.

After Armistice had been declared, Simon bought at auction large numbers of former cavalry horses and mules that had been abandoned on the continent. He had them transported to Castle Fairlight where they were fed and cared for properly. Once returned to healthy condition, the sound ones were put back to work and thoughtfully reschooled. Permanently injured war horses were given a dignified retirement in lush Castle Fairlight pastures along with the mules and heavy horses that would never again pull cannon. Riding horses were matched with vetted equestrians, leaving the castle to become field hunters, show jumpers and pleasure horses.

Simon's project had proven to be a striking success. British horse lovers, deeply critical of the War Department's harsh decision to abandon animals that had done so much honorable and brave duty, rallied to support the effort. Such popularity brought additional benefits beyond those granted to the horses. Just the Fairlight family and their small number of stable lads looked after all of the former military animals at the inception of Simon's idea. Every spare moment was spent in the stables, exercising, doctoring and grooming. It became clear that a substantial augmentation to staff was desperately required. Simon's father, the Marquess of Tash, had been delighted to hire former cavalry grooms and stablemen to live and work at Castle Fairlight – men who might have had difficulty finding suitable work after the war.

A riding school had also been established to teach children and interested adults. This had the effect of both promoting the joys of equestrian activities and creating prospective owners of a former cavalry horse. Success meant that agents for the Fairlights returned to Europe several more times to locate more abandoned war horses and bring them to safety.

Alice was profoundly grateful to the rescued war horses. They came to Castle Fairlight thin, rough and dejected, traumatized by what they had endured. Helping them gave her husband a few moments of genuine happiness. She knew Simon felt he was repaying a debt both sides of the conflict owed to the noble and generous horse.

"You know," she murmured, "there's no reason we have to stay after Fizzy and Jack's party. We could light out for Wiltshire first thing."

Simon turned towards her. His face brightened. "You really wouldn't mind?"

"Not a bit. I miss my Orson!" A keen horsewoman and proud winner ofnumerous silver cups for equitation over fences, she had fallen in love with a buff – colored old mule who had pulled an ambulance wagon. Orson was chatty, cheerful and occasionally naughty. He pulled a lightweight pony cart for her and she loved to take him on jaunts to the village and surrounds. Orson would do almost anything for a butterscotch candy.

Simon swallowed roughly. Alice thought for just the barest moment, his grey eyes glittered with something like tears. He coughed a little to clear his throat. "Darling, I …"

A full – throated scream abruptly cut Simon off. Harsh and terrified, it came from above and obliterated everything – auditory, visual or sensory – in an electric instant. Alice looked up. In the golden light of a summer evening, she registered the elaborate Palliser Park roofline with its decorative statuary representing Roman deities. It seemed possible one of the imperious Roman gods was moving …

There came a second cry – shattered, shrill – and what had appeared to be one of Palliser Park's statues started to fall.

Alice felt Simon throw an arm around her waist, dragging her backwards. In the next breath, a body slammed into Lord FitzRobert's fashionable new terrace. Blood, bone and brains sprayed up and outwards. House of Worth's *Soie Verte* – along with her green satin shoes with the charming underslung heel – was instantly splattered. The damp weight of gore on delicate silk seemed to burn her skin with horror and revulsion.

She gulped for air, staring at the distorted body, arms and legs grotesquely broken. They twisted unnaturally against the stone floor – one forearm ripped open by a snapped radius bone. The victim's head had been destroyed by the terrible fall. Jagged shards of skull jutted out from pulped flesh and chunks of bloody scalp. Scalp attached to long hanks of vibrant chestnut hair …

"Poll … Polly." Alice's voice broke. She had taken a real liking to the cheerful, thoroughly pleasant young woman. "Polly Piety."

Simon pulled her tightly against him as the rest of Lord FitzRobert's house party and various servants crowded through the open French doors. Voices rose in shock. Someone was sick. A dramatic swooning announced that Dorothy Brier was intent on collapsing. Alice buried her face into Simon's dinner suit, shuddering.

She heard Lord FitzRobert's incredulous tone. "God – one of our uniforms."

"Yes," said Simon. "I believe it's Polly – the upstairs maid. Crumpling will have to confirm."

"God," Lord FitzRobert repeated. "I have never …"

"You will have to call for the local police immediately." Alice heard Simon interrupt coolly. "Cover her with a sheet and post a guard so nothing is disturbed. You there – what is your name?"

"Hawkins, sir," came an unsteady reply.

"Go fetch my man, Mr. Spinner, and have him come at once." Alice felt Simon squeeze her waist. "Let's go in – you could use a cup of tea."

Alice nodded and took in a steadying breath. She lifted her head from his chest, turning to step gingerly around what was left of poor Polly Piety. Lord FitzRobert had returned to full strength, barking at his footmen to secure the scene.

Black clouds were beginning to drift across the horizon. Another sea storm was approaching.

8

Simon left the ashen – faced Alice with Lady Constance and Perry. They both seemed genuinely grateful to have a job fussing over his shaken wife that allowed them to ignore Dorothy Brier. The actress had flung herself onto one of the reproduction William and Mary chairs to knock back a manly portion of scotch. After the heavy crystal glass had been drained, she slammed it down on a side table.

"Another," she said flatly into the ethers as if the entire household was waiting to facilitate her next demand. As the footmen were preoccupied with assisting Lord FitzRobert to protect Polly Piety's broken corpse from the elements and everyone else was doing their best to pretend that she didn't exist, Dorothy sat, unheard and unattended.

Simon sensed an oncoming wobble in which the actress would, metaphorically, throw all her toys out of the pram. He darted out of the library, uninterested in intervening. Dorothy Brier could go to bloody blazes for all he cared.

Reggie Spinner was waiting just beyond the library. FitzRobert servants were beginning to gather in the hallway. They all looked as grey and shaken as his Alice. Some were crying. There was a palpable grief. Polly had been liked by her fellow *uniforms* as Lord FitzRobert condescendingly called his staff. If he wasn't there to ensure Lord FitzRobert's survival for Sir Vernon, Simon thought he might enjoy killing the owner of Palliser Park himself.

"Major," said Spinner quietly, "how can I be of service?"

"Come with me." Simon headed for nearest servant staircase. "We're going walkabout."

"Righto, Major. The roof?"

Simon nodded. "Before the next storm comes in."

They nipped up the lesser staircase, clipping past maids who were rushing to join the other servants in their shared upset over Polly Piety. The less flamboyant steps led them quickly to the third floor. Primarily the servants' domain, it lacked the elaborate plasterwork, classical statuary and gilded hallway furniture of Palliser Park's main floors but was bright, clean and comfortable.

The war had devastated servant classes as well as the more genteel. Even selfish bastards such as Lord FitzRobert had to make an effort to entice staff into his service, Simon thought as he and Reggie Spinner ran down the central hallway. He noted a couple of nicely appointed common rooms and even a little library as they jogged past in search of roof access.

"Guest staff are housed in the wing to the right," said Reggie as they approached a fork from the main thoroughfare. "There's a little twist up some steps near my room, Major. I'm guessing it must be one of the attic entrances."

"Lead away, Mr. Spinner!" Simon's voice echoed a bit. The third floor was abandoned as the excitement below had drawn the domestic household away.

Reggie Spinner's "little twist" in the tidy Georgian architectural design was a small alcove off the secondary hallway. It existed to contain curving steps up to another level of the house. Simon suspected there were several just like it dotting massive Palliser Park's third floor.

They darted up the narrow staircase and through an unlocked door into one of Palliser Park's interconnected attics. Cold and dimly lit by handsome Georgian windows that existed to provide a balanced design to the exterior facade, it contained carpentry tools and substantial amounts of materials used in FitzRobert's renovation. The attics – a much smaller rectangular cap to the building – allowed direct access to the rooftop that appeared as a deck to a great ocean – going ship.

"I don't see a convenient exit, Major," said Reggie Spinner. "Shall we try one of the other rooms?"

Simon gestured to one of the large windows. "Let's see if we can throw open the sash and get out that way."

He found the nearest, grasped its latching mechanism and gave the glass a good shove with his shoulder. The window obediently swung out, allowing them to step over the ledge and out onto the roof.

Despite the golden light of an English summer evening, there was a chill in the breeze that foretold the arrival of another storm. In the distance over Lord FitzRobert's verdant lawns, the North Sea glittered black and brutal – nature's glower that threatened the land and all who stood upon it.

"Time is the enemy," Simon said, scanning the low wall that edged the roofline and provided a base for pedestals displaying Palliser Park's Roman gods and goddesses. "You head to west and run the roofline. I'll go east towards the library. See if you can find how she got onto the roof – a door, another open window."

"Righto, Major," his valet murmured and took off at a jog.

Simon began walking the roof, scanning the surfaces for any sign of disturbance. He was reminded of his recent investigation on Sir John Redgrave's roof and wondered at the statistical chances of two fatal falls occurring within days in the average life of a cavalry officer. Extraordinary, he assumed.

"Major!" shouted Reggie Spinner, his voice faint in the distance.

Simon broke into a run, sprinting ahead until he had reached the library's quadrant of the house in record time. He found his valet around the corner of the most easterly aspect of the attic system, holding a door open for his inspection. A heavy, neatly painted door suitable for withstanding the elements and further proof that Lord FitzRobert's renovation of Palliser Park had left nothing untouched.

"Guessing this might be Miss Piety's way out to the roof, sir?"

Simon paused to catch his breath. He had been gassed on the battlefield and his lungs still hadn't fully recovered. "Most likely," he got out once the pain had passed.

He turned away from the attic entrance to scan the area from which Polly had probably launched herself. The tarred surface was damp from the recent rain and despite Lord FitzRobert's scrupulous care, a few cobwebs clung to imperious Roman statues and shimmered in the waning sunlight. There was nothing. Nothing at all to mark that a young, healthy girl had passed by on her way to a crushing death on the stone terrace below. Simon found it a very melancholy notion.

"Well," Simon said, returning to the attic door, "no obvious notes to suggest why she might have taken a flyer."

"Unhappy with her lot in life, Major?"

"Actually, seemed quite a jolly girl." Simon sighed, remembering how Polly Piety had cheerfully attended to unpacking Alice's cases, even humming off – tune as she did so. "Let's go down and make sure Lady Fairlight is holding up. You could probably use a stiff drink too."

"It has been quite a day if I might say so, sir," Reggie agreed. "I will endeavor to ask around a bit and see if any of the staff noticed anything amiss with the young lady."

"Thank you, Mr. Spinner." Simon stepped across the threshold and down three stone steps to the attic floor. There was slightly sharp smell of dust and damp in a room much more crowded with wooden crates, trunks, unwanted furniture and mundane oddities such as ugly Victorian oil lamps.

"We'll lose the light soon, Major," came Reggie Spinner's voice as he closed the door to the roof with a solid thud.

"Right you are," murmured Simon gazing at a cloyingly sentimental porcelain shepherdess from the late Victorian era that sat on a squat walnut chiffonier. Probably to Lord FitzRobert's mother's taste, it was the *objet d'art* equivalent of teeth rotted from candy. Reminded him of something his great – aunt Adelphia would have given as a wedding present to a departing governess who had been fortunate enough to snare a husband.

It was then he noticed something shoved behind the mincing agrarian. A green wine bottle – an uncorked green wine bottle. He pushed aside the porcelain figure and leaned in for a better look. A 1919 Ayala Champagne – a good, traditional choice and only half consumed.

"Now this *is* interesting," he said, retrieving the bottle for better inspection. "Recently opened – still has some fizz."

"Look, Major!" Reggie Spinner pointed at an unfortunate green chesterfield sagging next to the chiffonier. At the back of its lumpy seat cushion, rested two crystal champagne glasses. They lay on their rounded sides as if tossed there by an impatient hand.

Simon dropped down next to the musty sofa and gently picked up one of the glasses. He could see a hint of golden fluid stripling the bottom of the bowl. The fading green velvet under the jettisoned glasses was still damp.

"Is it possible that Miss Piety had a friend?" he asked aloud. "Someone she met up here, perhaps on the regular?"

"Servant romances are not unknown, sir," said Reggie Spinner. "A footman or a kitchen lad could nick a bottle of His Lordship's standard issue – wouldn't be missed especially with Lady Constance's engagement party so close – and arrange to meet with the girl."

"These were tossed aside in a hurry." Simon handed the bottle of Ayala to his valet. "This footman or kitchen lad hid the bottle behind the hideous figurine and threw the glasses on the chesterfield as he made good his escape."

"So, Miss Piety …"

"Might have had some help taking the plunge."

Reggie shook hishead, genuinely dismayed by the grim prospect. "Oh, I hope not, Major."

"Secure the evidence, Mr. Spinner." Simon rose to his full height. "Let's see if we can duplicate our kitchen lad's dubious success and get out of here without attracting any notice. Rather Lord FitzRobert not be appraised of our efforts."

"Very good, sir, but I don't much like leaving you and Lady Fairlight tomorrow under such circumstances." The former batman was now not only dismayed but clearly uneasy.

Simon reached out and patted his valet's shoulder. "A panicked footman will nay get the jump on me. "It's not Ypres."

"It's not Ypres." Reggie Spinner swallowed hard and nodded.

"Next we must have a look at Polly Piety's room before anyone else has the same notion." Simon suspected there would be other maids, friends of Polly's, who would shortly appear to divide some of her belongings before the housekeeper collected what was left to return to a grieving family. "Do you think you can ferret out the location?"

"Cook *has* taken a bit of a fancy to me, Major."

CHAPTER

9

"Everything that can be done has been done, for the moment at least," said Lord FitzRobert to his guests and by extension, his regiment of anxious servants who clustered in the library doorway and the hall beyond. "I suggest we adjourn to dinner as planned. The local police are on their way. They will see that everything is cleared up."

"Father," said Fizz, clearly unhappy at the idea of resuming social niceties. " I don't see how we can ..."

"A girl has killed herself!" cried her brother Perry before she could finish.

Lord FitzRobert threw them both a warning look. "We are all desperately sorry that this young woman chose to end her life in this dramatic ... um, tragic fashion, but we owe it to the household to keep to the schedule. They have worked very ..." he searched for a positive word that would suit, "*hard* to put on a good dinner."

Dorothy Brier rose from her chair, the severe red dress giving her the momentary impression of an Angel of Death launching into orbit. "It's the very least we can do," she said in her best lady of the manor voice. "I, for one, have been looking forward to one of Palliser Park's excellent dinners."

Alice watched Fizz and Perry roll their eyes in exasperation. The Rothermores, who had been politely trying to stay out of the way, glanced at each other uneasily. She had the shrewd notion that if they could find a way to extricate themselves from the house party and run like the wind to their car, they'd do it in a flash. But they would all be needed to make a statement to the local constabulary so there was no immediate escape from FitzRobert hospitality.

"Well said, Dorothy." Lord FitzRobert turned to the hovering Crumpling. "Dinner can be served, I assume?"

The butler swallowed and gave a nod. "Please allow me a few minutes to ensure staff is ready, my lord."

"A few minutes, yes."

Alice watched Crumpling retreat to where the servants were gathered in the library doorway. He made a pushing gesture towards them that left little doubt about returning to service despite Polly's tragedy. Obediently, they backed out to general murmuring in the hallway.

She sipped her sherry. It was not going to be possible for her to sit at a dinner table with Polly's dried blood on her clothes. Replacing the glass on what was once a map table, she stood up.

"If you will all excuse me, I *must* change into different clothes."

Fizz immediately came to her side. "Of course, you must, darling. I'll come help you. My maid, Dilys, is a genius with refreshing clothes."

"Yet here's a spot," intoned Dorothy as Lady MacBeth. Her four or five drinks were on display as a cautionary tale. "Out damned spot, out I say! Tis' time to do't."

It was in such execrable taste that an appalled silence fell across the room. Even Lord FitzRobert had the grace to look abashed. Dorothy, oblivious to her impact, sauntered to one of the tables where the footmen had left a tray of decanters and glasses.

FitzRobert coughed slightly. "Perhaps we should all retire to regroup before dinner. I shall inform Crumpling to hold things for an hour."

Alastair Rothermore and his wife murmured their appreciation of the idea, escaping the library with almost unseemly speed. Lord FitzRobert wasn't far behind as he went to instruct the servants on his new dinner plan.

"Come on, Alice, " said Fizz, her handsome face wreathed in concern. "You must be desperate to get out of those things."

There was a clattering sound as Dorothy uncorked a decanter and splashed some whisky into a glass. "Where's that husband of yours – the beautiful monster?" she asked, swerving around with her drink. "His dueling scar has a strange allure."

"He was bayonetted," Perry's voice managed to be both utterly incredulous and disgusted, "in the bloody *war.*"

Alice spun on her apple green shoes splattered with Polly's blood. She had no patience left for Miss Dorothy Brier, West End actress. She headed for the library door, not completely sure about the way back to the guest quarters.

"The bloody war!" Alice heard Dorothy drawl as she strode over the library threshold. "I'm sick of the bloody war."

"Hang on, Alice!" cried Lady Constance, catching up on her right. "You can't escape without me."

"Or me," added Perry, on her left. "Thanks for an exit. If we're really lucky, she'll be sleeping it off under a table soon."

"I don't think you give Miss Brier enough respect." Alice gratefully accepted their company. "It would take a lot more than your father's hooch to lay her out."

"How deliciously blunt and American! Is that how gangsters speak?" Lady Constance led the way, taking them efficiently through down the gilded hall and towards the central region of the vast house. "Father has had a lift installed. Much faster than tromping up the old – fashioned way."

Alice was genuinely surprised. Installing – what she was happy to call an elevator back home – in an 18th century country house was a monumental choice both in terms of cost and alteration to the original architectural design. It was a bold decision. Still, an elevator in an enormous pile such as Palliser Park did make some practical sense. She wondered if the servants who really could use it to best effect were allowed to step aboard. She rather thought not.

Lord FitzRobert's lift had been constructed in the center of one of Palliser Park's secondary staircases. The stair – once an open, airy spiral featuring pretty iron – worked railings – now wrapped its Georgian curves around a golden cage. Alice thought it looked exactly like a fussy Victorian birdcage with gilded rails and multiple finials in an Arabic pastiche.

"Isn't it something?" asked Constance upon reaching the golden cage first. "I don't think the original owners ..."

"The Tudaburghs – frightfully fusty and dusty," interjected Perry. "So particular about proper bloodlines that the family is reduced to two dithery antiques – a brother and sister!"

"Imagine how delighted they were to sell up to father." Constance unlatched the cage door and opened it so that they could come aboard. She sighed. "You'll note the FitzRobert cypher painted on the floor. It's as if we live in a hotel."

Perry offered a hand to Alice in case she might trip over the minute gap between the main floor and the cage. "The Tudaburghs were pretty desperate to offload. They had more house than money. Dad had them over the proverbial barrel."

"Does this go all the way?" Alice peered up as she stepped onto the elevator's platform. The elaborate metal bars and heavy chains seemed to go on forever. There was something eerie about it all in the dimming light of evening, reminding her of a clanging maw of some industrial monster. A perfect metaphor for Lord FitzRobert in its way – the emperor of mechanized warfare.

"Pretty much," said Perry as he shifted the operating lever. "Not the servant floor, of course."

Lord FitzRobert's gilded cage rattled and lifted from the main floor. It made slow but steady progress up to the next floor and bumped gently to a halt with remarkable precision. Only the very best for their host, Alice thought as she hopped off.

"Can I send you, my maid?" asked Constance. "She's very adept."

"For God's sake, Fizz," Perry groaned. He pushed the metal door shut and hit the latch. "You have all the sensitivity of a dockworker."

Constance winced. "Sorry."

"Yes. I'm off ladies' maids for a bit." Alice cocked her head as the rumble of distant piano chords caught her attention. It was meant to be dramatic music – sweeping and epic. Rachmaninoff or more likely, Rachmaninoff copyist, she guessed. But the composition was wildly uneven. One moment a flashy run down the keyboard and next, maudlin tinkles and trills.

Perry laughed at Alice's puzzled expression. "Dad's pet Russian, Prince Andrei Volkonsky. He insisted on a piano in his rooms. Actually, he's not *terrible* … completely."

"At least he's feeling better."

"Drunk, probably," said Constance as they continued along Palliser Park's wide, gilded hallway with Rococo cabinets, heavy satin upholstered chairs and settees strategically grouped every few yards. "Prince Andrei is almost always plastered."

"Where is the prince garrisoned? So, I can avoid him." Alice was not relishing running into an inebriated Russian as she attempted to negotiate Palliser Park's complex system of hallways and rooms.

"His Imperial Highness – by the way, Dad insists we call him *His ImperialHighness* – is situated in the Chinese Room: main hallway, east wing. You are in the Green Room, hallway north." Lady Constance winced again. "Just like a hotel."

"And all that gobblety gook means?" Alice threw her hands in mock frustration.

Perry pointed to a set of double beveled doors looming just before the hallway took a sharp bend to the left. "Prince Andrei's lair is there and your Green Room is around the corner. You can always tell his digs by that huge picture of Sir Edwin Darnaway, high court judge, hanging by his door."

Sir Edwin was a tall, elegant figure in late 18th century robes of office. His aquiline face was hawkish, highly intelligent and he gazed out at his viewers with calm interest. Alice quite liked him.

"An ancestor?" she asked politely.

"As if!" said Constance, her red curls bobbing as she laughed. "I wish he was though."

"Dad's agents bought him at auction – along with several others – A younger head of chambers decided landscapes were more modern than portraits of legal worthies apparently." Perry sighed. "However, Dad would like you to imagine that Sir Edwin is one of us."

A moment after Alice realized that the faux Rachmaninoff had ceased, one of the double doors fell open and an extraordinary character appeared, leaning on the doorjamb. He was of average height but it was his only ordinary aspect. Somehow, he managed to be both florid and frail simultaneously. An exquisite heart – shaped face worthy of representing Cupid in a sculpture was surrounded by thick, burnished gold curls worn quite long. He was wrapped in an ornate dressing gown of Oriental design edged in mink. The very definition of *precious*, there was an exotic, almost lascivious manner to how he rubbed up against the door frame. His fantastical robe had slipped a little, revealing an alabaster bare shoulder.

"It is good to see friends," Prince Andrei Volkonsky said in a slightly slurred but very pronounced Russian accent. His glacier blue eyes took each of them in turn. "How are you, my friends? I have been very ill as you know."

"You must return to bed, Your Highness," said Constance coolly. "A tray will be brought up to you soon."

"How kind you are, Lady Constance," murmured Prince Andrei, still gazing at Alice. He licked his full, perfectly formed cupid bow lips. "I see a new friend has been added to the house. Prince Volkonsky of Imperial Russia at your service, dear lady." He made an airy, spiraling gesture with one of his hands and attempted a little bow but staggered forward, off – balance instead.

Alice recoiled as he seemed to be flailing in her direction. Not only did she find his overripe beauty repelling, His Imperial Highness also smelled of sour sweat and cigarettes.

"No – this will never do. Perry, help His Imperial Highness to his bed." Lady Constance took Alice's elbow and pulled her out of the way. "Come on, Alice. Just enough time to dust off before dinner."

Alice saw Perry's face wrinkle in disgust as he moved in to assist the unsteady royal.She felt for him but not enough to turn back and offer aid.

"What an embarrassment. I'm sorry," Lady Constance said as they hurried around the bend and into the hallway where the slightly less grand guest rooms were located – Green Room, *hallway north*.

"Oh, have seen blotto men before. It's all right." Alice threw an arm around Fizz's shoulders and gave her an affectionate squeeze. "Listen, I'll see you downstairs for dinner."

"Just enough time to pour myself a substantial scotch. Dad's showing off with a flash extravaganza. If you're wise, you'll tank up too." Lady Constance raised her eyebrows to emphasize that she was almost completely serious and pushed off to return to her rooms in *Main Hallway – East Wing* where the favored of Lord FitzRobert's purview resided.

Heavy Victorian cream sauces, blood and brain splatter, a drunk Russian who smelled of the sick room all pooled together in her mind's eye. Alice felt her stomach lurch, bile rising in her throat. She broke into a run – there might just enough time to find the Green Room before she was thoroughly ill.

CHAPTER

10

Simon glanced up and down the staff hallway. Lord FitzRobert needed all hands to the tiller so the floor was conveniently abandoned. But it wouldn't stay that way forever.

"Well done, Mr. Spinner," he said, opening the door to Room 4 and stepping into Polly Piety's little space.

Lord FitzRobert, needing high – quality staff in a post – war Britain no longer able to provide unlimited supplies of domestics, was forced to offer amenities unheard of in an earlier era. One benefit of Palliser Park's vast size was that it allowed him to lure servants with private accommodation.

Polly's room was small but it had been her own. No dreary garret, the walls were painted a cheery sky blue with the window and ceiling moldings a crisp white. A brightly polished brass bed draped in pretty bed linens with pink roses sat in one corner and an oak washstand in the other. A plain but solid oak wardrobe offered her a place for her belongings and a comfortable chair upholstered in the same pattern as the bed linen had given Polly a place to ponder life's mysteries. All in all, not a bad place for a young girl from the Black Country.

Then again, it *had* proved to be a bad place for Polly Piety. A very bad place indeed. Simon wondered what could have transpired on the rooftop to snatch such a young life away – her own despair or someone who needed to destroy a connection with the maid? Had Polly gotten herself in a bad way? Unmarried and pregnant would be devastating to a servant. He found it hard to imagine Lord FitzRobert as a sensitive employer who would forgive such trespasses against his household. Polly would be promptly exiled without references. If she possessed any remnant of luck, her family might take her back. If not, Polly Piety was completely and utterly ruined. Good enough reason to take a plunge off Palliser Park's roof and end it all quickly.

"Look for anything that might tell us more about Miss Piety," he said, heading to the wardrobe. "Hopefully, a diary of some kind. Might be hidden if it held any real secrets."

"Righto, Major." Reggie went for the bed and searched the mattress for any secreted material. With no success, he dropped down to peer under the bed.

The oak wardrobe was divided into two sections. One half had the clothes rod on which Polly's meager collection of uniforms and off – duty clothes were hung, a second pair of sensible brown shoes laid out at the bottom. The other half had four drawers and a shelf for personal effects. The shelf supported a few books – penny romances titled *Country Nurse*, *Miss Jane Goes to Rome* and *Spring Holiday* – – and a magazine called *Sunday Parade* that featured articles of cheerful interest to schoolgirls along – side lots of banal poetry about flowers and seashells.Items she probably bought at the village tuck shop or borrowed from another servant.

Simon rifled through them but found no hidden letters or notes. Beyond those, there was a bottle of scent and a framed photograph of two people he assumed were her parents. It was an artificial and stiff portrait of young people in late Victorian dress, posing by a plaster Doric column. The kind of picture taken in an inexpensive photographer's studio to mark something important – an engagement or a wedding day. It might well be the only photograph ever taken of those who came from the working classes. He'd seen a lot of them over the course of the war, spilling out of the pockets of dead soldiers or stashed in their kit. Sacred items rendered meaningless by death.

Polly's wardrobe was tidy and devoted mostly to clothing items. A small jewelry box made of tin and featuring a romanticized picture of Princess Mary on the lid sat in a top drawer. It revealed a small bottle of cheap scented water – *Bouquet of Violets* – and just one handkerchief with the letter P embroidered in gold silk as well as an imitation pearl necklace probably given to her at a first communion.

Simon almost smiled. He and Polly both had Princess Mary boxes. Hers was a little trinket from a department store or a costermonger's cart. His – a brass box embossed with the image of the princess – had been a 1914 Christmas gift to him and every serving member of the British armed forces. It had come filled with cigarettes, chocolate and Christmas cards from the royal family. A real boon at the time and presently, it resided on his dressing table at Castle Fairlight – a reminder of genuine kindness.

Polly's bottom drawer was considerably more intriguing. Simon was both surprised and touched to discover how she had wiled away some of her free time. Colored pencils, children's watercolor palettes, a collection of cheap brushes and a sketchbook with heavy cardboard covers – all showing considerable use – sat neatly stacked in the drawer. He pulled out the sketchbook and retreated to her floral chair to examine it.

"Nothing, sir," announced Reggie Spinner, pushing a wicker traveling case back under the bed. "No convenient angst filled diaries."

Simon gave a nod. "We may be on a fool's errand. If the poor girl did, in fact, have a suitor, she didn't flaunt it even in private."

"I bet Crumpling put the fear in all the girls about the dangers of in – house romance. Mrs. Kent, the housekeeper is a right sharpie too, runs a tight ship."

"Wonder what she thinks of *Miss Dorothy Brier*, actress and professional confidante to wealthy men?" Simon murmured as he studied Polly's sketchbook. The pages held pencil drawings of a few local birds, the kitchen cat and flowers from the formal garden. She wasn't terrible. She wasn't good either. The overall effect was schoolgirlish and ordinary but not without some charm. He admired her interest in exploring something more ephemeral than her daily household assignments.

"Don't need to wonder," said Mr. Spinner. "I can verify the description; *A black widowspider* was employed while I was getting my tea earlier. Mrs. Kent has a keen eye for social distinctions, sir."

"The Mrs. Kents of this country kept the home fires burning while we were away ..." Simon's voice trailed off as he turned another page in the sketchbook. Polly, completely shifting gears from vapid flowers, had drawn a Mediaeval knight. Not particularly accurate in a historical sense but very much a fantasy figure from some child's book about King Arthur.

The knight stood noble, stalwart; his overly large eyes gazing out to an undefined horizon and overly luxuriant hair waving in the wind of olde England. A sort of blond, dream – like Every Prince in a flowing scarlet surcoat and holding out a chevron shield – possibly because Polly didn't want to attempt drawing human hands. On the shield was an unusual coat of arms – two merged black griffins holding an older heraldic shield in their talons.

"Something of interest, sir?"

Simon flipped around the sketchbook so Reggie Spinner could also study it. "What strikes you about this?"

The former batman frowned as he scanned the drawing. "Looks like something my thirteen – year niece, Elspeth, might knock out on a rainy day. Not very memorable... well, no ... the shield is different – very ... I don't know ... very ..."

"Specific?" suggested Simon.

"Yes," Reggie Spinner brightened. "It's a very specific design."

"As if Polly was drawing something she had seen somewhere. Something that meant something to her." Simon tore the page from the sketchbook and stood up. "Probably nothing but let's hang on to it anyway. Time to erase our steps and back out of here before anyone takes note of our intercession."

"Righto, Major."

"Besides," Simon sighed, "there's Lord FitzRobert's opening dinner to report to. Bound to be gruesome gobs of fancy French cooking. My stomach can't take it anymore."

"Hard biscuits and coffee," said his valet, referring to the spare rations they ate in the trenches.

"Brutality ruins all, Mr. Spinner," replied Simon as he pocketed Polly's drawing.

CHAPTER

11

The ethereal, frothy apple green dress and its matching satin dancing pumps had been consigned to the bin. She would never be able to wear them again. Even if Polly's blood and brain matter could be sponged away by a clever ladies maid, it would always be there like Dorothy Brier's *damned spot*.

Alice replaced the *Soie Verte* with the most somber dinner dress she had brought along on a short summer holiday – a Wedgewood blue trimmed in cream – and slipped into a pair of plain kid leather shoes. She had returned the peridot and pearl choker to its traveling case. No need for splashy jewelry now. Reassuring Lord FitzRobert about the social worthiness of an American no longer interested her.

Feeling a little more confident about the Palliser Park geography, she had made her way back to the revolutionary elevator and down to FitzRobert central for entertaining guests.

"Lady Fairlight," said one of Lord FitzRobert's overdressed footmen, "dinner is in the second dining room. May I show you the way?"

"Yes, please! I might end up in the kitchens."

"This way, Your Ladyship." The footman bowed slightly and held out an arm to indicate the way.

"Has Major Fairlight turned up?" She was actually feeling quite annoyed with her husband. It might have been nice to have his full attention after Polly Piety's death.

"Not as yet, Your Ladyship. But the rest of the FitzRobert household is present."

The second dining room appeared sooner than she would have liked. Given her druthers, she'd ask Mr. Spinner to ready the Crossley for a break out from FitzRobert Jail. What had seemed like such a good idea – whisking Simon away for an old – fashioned summer holiday – now felt like a real misfire. What had she been imagining? That Simon would actually delight in both Lord FitzRobert's company and his gilded Palliser Park? Alice remembered how she had swirled together daydreams of walking on the Essex coastline with her husband while enjoying deep, meaningful conversations or soaking in the English summer sun together by the sea, perhaps even with a packed lunch and white wine.

Alice groaned. *She was a complete moron.*

"Your Ladyship?" asked the young footman in concern.

"Please, not to worry," she said, shaking her head. "It's just been a very long day."

"Yes, Your Ladyship." He gave her a sympathetic look. "I understand."

Alice took in his obvious exhaustion. The FitzRobert servants worked for difficult taskmasters – relatively new money who expected far more from their staff than old line aristocrats such as her husband's family – and had just lost one of their own in a tragic event. In addition to being a moron, she was oblivious to others.

"Thank you," she replied sincerely. "You have been very kind."

He flashed a tired smile and lifted a hand towards a set of double doors. "The second dining room, Your Ladyship. They've just gone in."

"Thank you *again*." Alice returned his smile and stepped forward as he grasped the doorknob to allow her entrance.

She stepped through the door to find Lord FitzRobert, the Rothermores and Perry gathering at one end of the large dining room for one more drink before dinner. A momentary frisson of annoyance rippled through her that Simon was nowhere to be seen. What was he getting up to? – wherever he was in vast Palliser Park.

"*Sorry!*" cried Constance's voice behind her. She stretched the word out in such an entitled *I'm the daughter of the manor so I'm never actually sorry about anything I do* fashion that it managed to make Alice even more irritable. Maybe she could talk Simon into clearing out in the morning. Surely an excuse could be found.

"Constance – good!" said her father with rather more cheer than a dead servant on the terrace might suggest. "Will you have one more glass of champagne before dinner? Lady Fairlight – champagne?"

"No, thank you," she replied although drowned out by Lady Constance's cry of *Oh, pour away, Dad, pour away!*

Alice took a moment while Constance sailed into the group to secure her champagne, to take in the glories of the second dining room. With the denomination of Second Dining Room, the inference was clear – *not* as large or formal as *the* dining room. Unsurprisingly, Lord FitzRobert's second dining room was the size of the average cricket pitch and featured a massive round table worthy of a particularly prosperous Camelot. Its crisp white linen laden with a massive bowl of summer roses, gold – rimmed dishes and crystal.

"Why, where's our Dorothy?" asked Constance as she took two champagne glasses and handed one automatically to Alice. "Completely sozzled? Sleeping it off?"

Lord FitzRobert's handsome, hawkish face betrayed nothing beyond the mask of a genial host. "She wasn't feeling well and thought to make an early night of it."

"Won't the local police want to interview her?" Alice had a sip of the wine anyway. It did actually hit the proverbial spot.

Constance's father gazed at her for a moment as if momentarily nonplussed that an American would question his arrangements. Then he shook his head, seemingly in part to drive away the offending notion, "I can't imagine they'd need to speak to Dorothy. There's really nothing to be done about it – the girl fell. Straight forward."

"Dad," murmured Perry reproachfully.

"Well, it *happens*." His father bristled. "Flighty girls in service away from home. Sad but in big houses such as ours … Lady Fairlight, just where has your husband got to?"

Alice swallowed her champagne roughly. FitzRobert's sharpish tone taking her by surprise. "He … umm, He …" she coughed.

"Evening, all," came Simon's voice from the doorway. "Apologize for being slow."

Alice spun to see her husband amble into the second dining room. He looked relaxed and even genial. She didn't know quite what to make of it.

"Dad was just asking after you," said Perry quickly, possibly as a helpful forewarning.

74

"Yes – sorry. I was checking on the Crossley." Simon actually smiled. "Is that champagne? Thank God for small miracles."

Constance handed off one as he joined their knot. "Here you are, my darling."

"Thank you, Constance," Simon said and turned towards the Rothermores who were standing next to Lord FitzRobert. "How lovely you look, Mrs. Rothermore."

Alice actually thought both the genteel MP and his wife looked tired and on the edge of exasperation. She bet Mrs. Rothermore wanted to leap into the family car and head home as well.

The lady beamed at Simon. "You are very kind, Lord Fairlight."

"Simon, please," he said. Alice noted that he didn't wince as he sometimes did at the mention of his title of birth.

"Edith," Mrs. Rothermore replied, more cheer entering her aspect.

Lord FitzRobert cleared his throat. "Since we all seem to be here, shall we go to table? The servants are more than ready to serve dinner."

Alice was seated between Lord FitzRobert and Alastair Rothermore on his lordship's right. On his left were Edith Rothermore and Perry. Simon had been marooned at bottom rim of the table next to Fizz. Without the actress and obnoxious Prince Andrei, it was an uneven seating made a bit better by the circular table. She immediately loathed the French formal setting of the silverware with the forks and spoons reversed with tines and bowls down. It was old – fashioned, pompous and announced that the meal would be complicated and heavy.

She glanced at her husband as exhausted FitzRobert footmen moved in with the first course. The menu card described it as something called *Amuse – bouche* and appeared to be individual plates of heavy hors d'oeuvres set in little crystal cups. Simon winced slightly as the footman placed the plate in front of him. It was just the sort of frivolous excess he had come to dislike so much. She watched him mask his momentary dismay and then pretend to be interested in whatever Fizz was bubbling on about.

While Lord FitzRobert spoke to Edith Rothermore about a recent fishing trip to Scotland, Alice had a quick look at the menu card to confirm her suspicions about formal French table settings. *Amuse – bouche* would be followed by a Mulligatawny soup, curried lobster with rice, lemon ice, larded guinea fowl and creamed onions, raspberry sorbet, beef with pan – fried foie gras in a truffle sauce, green asparagus with raspberry vinaigrette, chocolate mango tart and finished off with assorted cheeses and fruit. Finished off indeed, thought Alice, almost sighing out loud.

"Your husband's scheme for rescuing our military horses on the Continent," said Alastair Rothermore with genuine interest. "Such a good, decent idea. My niece, Emily, acquired two a few months ago and dotes on them."

Alice took a moment to retrieve a memory of a cheerful, ginger – haired teenager who was utterly mad about horses. The girl stood out for having convinced her patient parents into collecting two geldings and whisking them off to their farm in North Wales.

"Emily Parry – Jones?"

The MP looked delighted. "Yes, indeed! My sister's girl. She loves those gee – gees. Got to see her ride the bay at the Flint and Denbigh show. They won the junior silver cup!"

"That would be Baker," cried Alice, remembering the big bay gelding who had seen a lot of action but had taken to reschooling as a hunter with generosity of spirit and common sense. "He's just such a good boy. How is Fleet doing?"

Fleet was an exceptionally pretty 16 – hand chestnut, rescued from the butcher's pen by Simon, who remembered him as having belonged to a fellow officer in the Blues who had been killed in action. A sensitive and sweet – natured fellow, Fleet had a little more difficulty with loud noises. He'd be as sober – sided as a judge with some time and thoughtful handling.

"Emily told me she's paying a lot of attention to him – sugar cubes and all that. Lots of grooming and long walks on a loose rein. Advice from your gallant husband apparently."

Simon had an unfailing sense about what horse would suit a rider best. Emily Parry – Jones rode beautifully with a strong, independent seat and soft, kind hands. He wouldn't have allowed Fleet to go off with most teenagers.

"I am so pleased," said Alice. "Thank you for the news."

"Happy to oblige! I wish all post – war schemes were as humane and successful."

"Speaking of post – war schemes," interrupted Lord FitzRobert who had shifted his attention from the MP's wife, "have you studied my recommendations in regards to the committee?"

Alice saw a flash of irritation cross Rothermore's face. It was gone in an instant as he picked up one of the hors d'oeuvres – a salmon and caviar concoction – and ate it. After chewing thoughtfully for a moment, he turned slightly to FitzRobert.

"I have."

"Well, your view?" Lord FitzRobert was gazing at him as if the MP was the single most enticing *Amuse – bouche* offering. "Once Constance's wretched engagement fete is over, we must make progress."

"Hardly the moment, Elleston, don't you think?"

"Understood but an inkling, perhaps? There is so much preparation to be done. It weighs on me." FitzRobert lifted his wine glass and had a sip, shrugging as if this was actually of little consequence.

"An inkling?" Rothermore threw Alice an apologetic look. "In short, too punitive. No one wants to punish the Huns more than I. They deserve to be crushed under our collective bootheels but if we cripple Germany as the French are planning to do, then we will reap the whirlwind."

Before Lord FitzRobert could respond, a very somber Crumpling appeared.

"Your Lordship, the local constabulary have arrived. They were delayed by a fatal accident near the village – a motoring accident."

His Lordship let out a short, impatient breath. "Thank you, Crumpling. I ..."

Alice was surprised to see Simon push away from the table. "Perhaps I could be of service?" he said. "Allow you to attend to your guests."

Lord FitzRobert nodded as if the idea was very appealing. "Thank you, Major. Very good of you. If they need to speak to any of us, we will make ourselves available, of course."

"I'm sure they will," said Simon as Alice tried to catch his eye. She wondered why he was taking such an interest. Maybe he saw Polly Piety in the same light as one of the abandoned war horses. A faithful servant who deserved a better end.

Simon didn't immediately head for Crumpling and the door. Alice was grateful when he came round to where she sat and bent over to murmur in her ear, "Do your best. Talk soon." Then he was off, leaving his *Amuse – bouche* behind, untouched.

CHAPTER
12

"DI Saxby, Brightsea Constabulary," said a young man – fair – haired and immaculately dressed in a grey wool suit. He held out a firm hand. "I take it you are representing His Lordship?"

"Major Simon Fairlight," replied Simon, shaking Saxby's hand. "And I take it that you've met Lord FitzRobert?"

A smile ghosted DI Saxby's serious countenance. "I have. His Lordship has a keen sense of his place in the world."

Simon held back a smile of his own. He liked Detective Inspector Saxby. He recognized another soldier although that was no real surprise as they were close in age and every reasonably fit young Brit had been sent out.

"Been mustered out long?"

"1918. Essex Regiment. Came back to my work here. You – still in then?"

"The Blues."

They were standing outside on the library terrace. A light, steady rain was coming down, low rumbles of thunder rolling in with the sea. Polly Piety still lay on the expensively laid stone tiles, underneath a black gardening tarp.

"What can you tell me about this poor soul?" asked DI Saxby nodding towards the wet tarp.

"Polly Piety – upstairs maid. Black country girl. She fell from the roof," Simon moved to point up at the corner, "about there. I was out here at the time, having a drink with my wife."

"I have spoken with Mr. Crumpling," said DI Saxby, gesturing towards the butler who stood under an umbrella, awaiting instructions. "He informs me that Miss Piety has been in service here about a year, was well liked and seemed quite content."

"That seems the general consensus, yes." Simon came to a decision – one he'd hoped to avoid but given his sense that DI Saxby was immensely clever and wasted in Brightsea, he had no choice. It was time *to liaise* as Sir Vernon had decided to term such situations.

Simon glanced at Crumpling who, as a superior example of his species, never missed anything that might affect his employer. "Can we release Crumpling? I'm sure Lord FitzRobert's dinner will go more smoothly with his presence."

"Yes, of course," Saxby turned towards the waiting butler. "We will take care of Miss Piety for now. If you would be good enough to retrieve her family's particulars, I will see to it that they can collect her body."

Crumpling nodded, grim. "Thank you, sir."

"I will be needing to examine her things and room. Please don't allow anyone to disturb the same."

"Very good, sir." The butler turned under his umbrella and retreated through the French doors into the library.

Detective Inspector Saxby gestured at Polly's form under the garden tarp. "Cliveden and Brown – fetch the stretcher. Need to get her out of the elements and back to the infirmary as soon as possible." He looked over at Simon, clear but unapologetic. "We don't have our own morgue … yet."

"Could we talk?" Simon asked as Saxby's constables hopped it, following Crumpling into the library. "On the quiet?"

Saxby frowned. "Do you know something more *illuminating* about this sad event?"

"I'm not sure," said Simon, also clear and unapologetic.

The DI threw another look towards Polly's tarp. It was glistening in the gentle rain. Then he returned his full attention to Simon, who saw that he was both intrigued and potentially, on the verge of becoming highly annoyed. He attributed that to Lord FitzRobert. There could be little doubt that FitzRobert had swanned about Brightsea, making sure everyone in the village understood as master of Palliser Park, he was above the petty world of mere shopkeepers,farmers, local council or coppers.

"Go on," Saxby stretched out the words to emphasize his concerns.

"Lord FitzRobert …"

DI Saxby's face shifted into full irritation. "If this girl's death isn't what it appears, Brightsea Constabulary will not be looking the other way for His Lordship's comfort."

"Polly Purity's death – in my opinion – was not an accident and I have doubts about suicide as well," said Simon before proceeding to tell the detective inspector what he'd found in the attic. When he finished, the detective inspector's intelligent face had returned to cautious interest.

"Major Fairlight, are you *investigating* this misadventure?"

Simon knew the moment had come. "I have a remit to look into a certain matter that may or may not extend itself to Palliser Park."

"Very vague and Home Office – y," said DI Saxby, crossing his arms.

"Yes – which is why I have to ask you to drag your feet on Polly's death. Just a few days until I can better assess the situation,"

Saxby actually laughed – without any humor. "Brightsea Constabulary should just stand down and go home while you fix something for the Home Office?"

"Quite the contrary, Detective Inspector," said Simon. "I would like you to make a right nuisance of yourself at Palliser Park for a few days – just don't act on anything significant until I've got my end in hand."

"A license to annoy Lord FitzRobert?" Simon could see genuine amusement shimmer through Saxby's nervous system. "And you'd freely share information along the way?'

"Happily."

The Detective Inspector gave a small nod. "Brightsea will muck in – just for a few days."

A clattering sound announced the arrival of Saxby's constables with the stretcher to carry Polly off to the Brightsea infirmary. As they stepped free of the library with wooden rails wrapped in canvas panels, Simon was immediately reminded of the times he'd seen the dead and gravely injured carried from one nightmare to the next. He shivered.

"Sir,' said one of the constables as he knelt by Polly's form under the tarp, "it's going to be really tight in the motor with three of 'em."

"You have three corpses?" asked Simon in surprise. Three bodies in Brightsea had to be a bumper crop not seen since the plague pits.

"Yes," replied DI Saxby as he moved off to oversee Polly's removal. "Try to keep the tarp in place, Cliveden, to preserve her from the rain. Yes – we had a nasty accident. A lorry spun off the main road and hit a tree. Two dead inside. Delayed our arrival here."

The constable named Brown dropped down to assist in lifting the maid onto the stretcher. "Strange business," he said. "Bless me, never seen the like."

"Strange indeed. They were dead before it hit the tree," explained Saxby with a warning look to Constable Brown. "Both shot in the head."

Another shiver ran across Simon's body. "Blue lorry – Meredith and Sons?"

DI Saxby and both constables stared at him.

"Blue lorry – Meredith and Sons," affirmed the Detective Inspector quietly. "Are you a fortuneteller as well, Major Fairlight?"

CHAPTER

13

Alice let out a breath as the footman placed a massive chocolate tart with candied oranges in front of her. She'd managed the *Amuse – bouche* all right but had run out of epicurean steam after an excellent Mulligatawny. Other courses had been pushed about in a polite pastiche of dining although the taste cleansing sorbets had been refreshing and settling to a system still struggling with the events of the day. Alice had a guilty flash about her husband's ruined vicuna topcoat. Mr. Spinner had promised to see what could be done but even he seemed awed by the breadth and width of the stains.

She snatched up her water goblet and drained it, hoping no one would notice her slip from genteel standards. But then Fizz laughed loudly at her own story about a clumsy hotel steward in Brighton and Alice realized there was really no need to have any pangs about not measuring up on the gentility scale. The Old Dutch worthies of New York were a much tougher crowd. They had no pity – no quarter given for water goblet mismanagement. Social death meted out for gesturing with silverware and crimes against napkin use.

Alice wondered if she had too much of the freely poured FitzRobert wine stores. She feltlight – headed and a bit silly, on the verge of either giggling like Fizz or being sick.

A footman appeared quietly at her side. "May I refresh your water glass, Your Ladyship?"

"Yes, please. Thank you." Alice thought she might roar through two or three more glasses in hopes of clearing her head and settling her stomach.

"I fear tomorrow will be a complicated day," said Lord FitzRobert as he attacked his chocolate tart. "With Constance and Jack's party on Saturday, some guests will be arriving tomorrow. I'm reliably informed that the stormy weather will clear out tonight so, at least, we shall have decent weather."

Alice heard the young footman let out a small breath as he replenished her water. She understood his quiet reaction to Lord FitzRobert's news. The servants would be hard pressed over the next few days. Not only did they have to welcome a number of guests on Friday into immaculate rooms, serving them properly imposing FitzRobert meals and tending to every wish, Palliser Park had to be made ready for Fizzy's engagement party – one of the major private social events of a post – war summer. After the party, staying guests would still have to be looked after with extreme care amid a general clean – up. She couldn't imagine how exhausting it all would be for the well – meaning servants. Alice felt a familiar guilty pang at how serendipity of birth had allowed her to know nothing but comfort.

"Jack will be in late tonight," added Fizz before she knocked back the dessert wine – a lovely pre – war Semillon.

"Remember to have Crumpling send the car to meet the train," her father said, offering his daughter an affectionate smile. "Jack is an essential element."

Edith Rothermore laughed. "I should say so!"

"I *did* tell you days ago Jack is motoring. Borrowing his father's new automobile."

Lord FitzRobert looked unimpressed. "The train is faster from London."

"Alice – you motored," Perry said in genuine interest. "Train or the motor?"

Alice put down her water goblet. "Well, I …"

"Why, this is wonderful," came a singsong – y Russian dialect. "Chocolate on a rainy night! May I join you?"

Prince Andrei Volkonsky drifted across the threshold, as frail and florid as before. Alice saw that the decadent velvet dressing gown had been exchanged for an aristocratic version of a traditional Russian *rubaha*. The high – collared tunic was made of heavy scarlet satin and embroidered in gold thread. It was the perfect foil for Prince Andrei's sybaritic beauty, producing a fascinating kind of exotic romanticism. Edith Rothermore stared at him, slightly dazed.

"Of course, Your Imperial Highness," said Lord FitzRobert, making a show of standing up. He was followed by polite Perry and far more slowly by Alastair Rothermore, who looked distinctly put upon. Alice was grateful that the ladies remained seated. She was an American and had no intention of snapping to attention over a precious prat like Prince Andrei Volkonsky.

One of the footmen rushed to pull out a chair for the Russian while another poured a glass of the Semillon. The prince slid into the proffered chair, taking no notice of the respectful gestures around him. Lord FitzRobert and the other gentlemen retook their chairs. Alice saw Alastair Rothermore throw his wife an exasperated look. She had the grace to return her gaze to her unfinished dessert.

"I hope you are feeling better, Your Highness," said FitzRobert as one of the chocolate desserts was dutifully placed in front of his guest by an attentive footman.

"Oh, yes," replied Volkonsky in his overly rich drawl, "much better. I look forward to celebrating Lady Constance and her dear man although I think he has … how do you say so amusingly in English? – – *done a runner, has cold feet!*"

Alice saw Fizz clench her jaw. "Jack is arriving late tonight. He will be on hand for Saturday without fail." She added pointedly. "Jack has a *job*."

A slow smile crossed the prince's indolent face and he speared a section of chocolate. "I have written a special piano sonata for the occasion, Lady Constance. I hope you will allow me to play it for you."

"How very kind of Your Highness," purred Lord FitzRobert, raising an eyebrow at his daughter before returning his attention to the louche Russian aristocrat.

Alice thought Lord FitzRobert gazed at *His Imperial Highness* with a kind of unsettling avarice as if the Russian aristocrat was also a massive chocolate tart adorned with candied oranges. She wondered if FitzRobert saw Volkonsky as a doorway to Eastern Europe – a region that would need armaments. As soon as the thought occurred, she dismissed it as silly. Surely someone as shrewd as Lord FitzRobert could see that Prince Andrei Volkonsky was a parasitic nothing whose only powerful connections had all been cheerfully murdered by the Bolsheviks.

Alice drank some more water, relieved to find that her system seemed to have settled down a bit. She didn't feel as if she would have to flee the dining room in search of a convenient bathroom at any moment.

Pretending to eat her dessert by pushing around bits of it on the plate, she wondered where Simon had disappeared to and whether being in fellowship with the local authorities was a lot more enjoyable than being in fellowship with Lord FitzRobert.

CHAPTER

14

Simon gazed down at the two bodies in the back of the Brightsea Constabulary's slat – sided Garford truck. One young, one middle – aged, both wore Meredith and Sons embossed uniforms and both had been shot in the head. He no longer had the capacity to be shocked by such sights or the human cruelty that produced them.

"Small arms," he said to Reggie Spinner as he jumped down from the bed of the Garford.

"I'll take Wanstead off my docket then, shall I, Major?" His valet looked grim.

Simon nodded, then turned his attention to DI Saxby. "We didn't get much of a look at the driver. I'm guessing it was neither of them."

"Careening up the road with a stolen motor, dead bodies in the back rolling around with the furniture – why risk charging ahead of you?"

"Excellent point," said Simon, hoping to avoid any notion that the Crossley had been deliberately targeted. "Did you say furniture?"

"Meredith and Sons is a removal service. These lads were taking household goods somewhere when they were waylaid.

I'll know more tomorrow about that aspect." Saxby gestured at Cliveden and Brown who were standing with Polly Piety's broken body between them. "Get the poor girl in. Then prepare to come with me into the house."

"You'll be interviewing the FitzRoberts?" Simon retrieved his cigarette case and opened it, offering the Detective Inspector one.

DI Saxby shook his head. "Thank you, no. Smoked enough special blends over there to last a lifetime." He was referring to the makeshift fags that the lads used to cobble together from scraps and whatever vegetation was left near the trenches. "Yes – the FitzRoberts, guests and staff. Any observations you'd share?"

"FitzRobert's a pill but you know that," Simon paused to light his cigarette. "His son, Perry, is a good lad – worked for the war department in London in a minor capacity."

Saxby squinted in the drizzle. "File clerk?"

"Weak lungs. The daughter, Lady Constance, is exactly what you might imagine – pleasant enough but spoiled, clueless but not a snob like her father. Of the guests, I know very little. Alastair Rothermore is a rather important MP and his wife, Edith – genteel but unremarkable. I suspect Rothermore was invited early to the big engagement do because he intends to push for lighter sanctions on Germany in Reparations Committee. FitzRobert wants to ..."

"Crush the Germans and their weapons manufacturers so he can corner the market?"

Simon was again impressed with DI Saxby's intelligence. This was no country copper to fob off and underestimate. He actually felt better that the Detective Inspector would be about the place. Alice would be safer if things went south.

"*Jawohl*," Simon said and blew out a stream of smoke. "One in the regiments of Russian aristocrat refugees is floating about. A Prince Andrei Volkonsky. Haven't seen or met him. From what I've been told Volkonsky's young, vaguely artistic and drunk most of the time."

"Lovely," said DI Saxby.

"My wife, Alice, is American and highly intelligent. Good observational skills. She probably had the last real conversation with Polly Piety on our side of the green door. Alice does *not* know I am on the job."

Saxby raised an eyebrow then nodded. He didn't look especially happy with all the surreptitious baggage that had come to Palliser Park.

"I will be highly irritated if your *certain matter* puts my lads at a disadvantage."

"Promise to fully brief, should it prove necessary," Simon said in a quiet voice, "and it might."

"Yes, very Home Office – y," DI Saxby replied, patently unimpressed.

He pivoted on his heel. "Cliveden – keep an eye on things. Brown, come with me."

Simon watched the detective inspector stride away followed by his constable. The rain came down harder, almost as if it was a stage curtain closing at the end of a scene. He turned to acknowledge Saxby's other constable who had stood up and was trying to find a place next to the Garford to huddle against the weather.

"Thank you, Constable Cliveden," he said. "I know it's been a difficult night."

"Isn't that the truth, sir? The last time we had this much trouble was the apple pickers' dispute of '18 and well, 11's flood – that was a bad one."

"Brightsea floods?"

Constable Cliveden nodded, the rain bouncing off his policeman's helmet. "The whole area's a trencher between River Wivenhoe and the sea. We expect a bit of mild flooding in the fields every year but 1911 was one for the history books, sir."

"I'm sure you lads did a fine job for Brightsea." Simon lifted a hand to let Reggie Spinner know they ought to head in after the DI.

Cliveden had a moment to sigh. It was clearly remained a painful memory. "Thank you, sir."

"Mr. Spinner, I am soaking. Shall we get under roof?"

"Righto, Major," Reggie turned to offer a wave to Cliveden. "Good night, Constable."

Constable Cliveden echoed his thought and retreated back to the Garford to find some modest reprieve from the rain. Another in the vast army of quiet, competent, largely anonymous men who made life safer and sounder for the many. Simon was profoundly grateful that there were still solid constables doing their bit for Britain. Almost a complete generation of Clivedens and Browns had been left, moldering, on the battlefields of Europe – holding a line there for the rest of time.

Once inside a side entrance of Palliser Park, Simon shed his raincoat and handed it to Reggie Spinner. He felt for Polly Piety's drawing in his pocket, confirming that it was there and still dry. The very specific drawing of a shield framed by two black griffins with outstretched wings.

"I've decided that you should take Polly's artwork to London," he said, wishing – not for the first time – it was possible to heat piles such as Palliser Park or his own Castle Fairlight properly.

"Oh, yes?" Spinner was expertly shaking out the raincoat and folding it over his arm.

"Hand it over to Sir Vernon," Simon threw his valet a pointed expression. " You know, I'm beginning to wonder if it just might be *Russian*."

15

Alice took in the young police officer as he came across the threshold and into the second dining room. He was something of a surprise. The popular view of policemen was of stolid, bland fellows in either a proper uniform or a second – rate suit. A diametric contradiction, she thought, to the gentleman now approaching a displeased Lord FitzRobert. Slender with elegant proportions, the young man was attired in a beautifully tailored grey suit and if she remembered rightly from her St. Hilda's days, a Magdalen College tie. He possessed a strikingly handsome face and burnished coppery blond hair worn a little long but in an immaculate managed blunt style. The piercingly blue eyes belied the innately aristocratic exterior with something wary and harsh. Alice knew it well. He was haunted – another ghost from the fields of Europe.

"DI Saxby," he said, producing a badge from his breast pocket, "Brightsea Constabulary. Would it be possible to take basic statements from witnesses to Miss Piety's fall?"

Lord FitzRobert did not rise to acknowledge the DI as a genuine old line aristocrat might have done. He leaned back in his chair and picked up a wine glass for a long sip. All to keep DI Saxby waiting like a servant.

Alice saw both Fizz and Perry wince at their father's spoiled behavior. Fizz, to her credit, stood up and took the reins away from her desultory parent. Immediately the rest of the table followed her example.

"I'm Constance," she said, moving towards the young policeman. "Lady Constance. You'll be needing a room to conduct the interviews?"

Alice watched DI Saxby turn towards Fizz. Admiration for the pretty and confident daughter of the household flashed momentarily across the blue eyes like an errant streak of lightning. He shook her outstretched hand.

"Yes." DI Saxby even smiled briefly – another flash of lightning. "Thank you, Lady Constance."

"You must call me Fizz – everybody does." It was tacitly clear that *everybody* was a reasonably exclusive group.

Lord FitzRobert – still stunned that he'd lost control of his dining table – scrambled to his feet. He cleared his throat, sounding as if he was snarling like an irritated lap dog over a biscuit.

"Crumpling, show the detective inspector to the breakfast room," he sputtered, deeply annoyed. "Will you require the servants as well?"

"Possibly. If I do decide it's needed, tomorrow will suit."

Lord FitzRobert's face reddened at the idea. "I have guests arriving from every corner of Britain over the next two days. That will not be, at all, convenient for the household."

DI Saxby acknowledged FitzRobert's words with a polite tilt of his head. "A woman has died at Palliser Park, Your Lordship. You will be seeing a lot of me over the next day or two. I will endeavor to stay out of the way of your social engagements – for the most part."

"Dad," said Perry in a cajoling tone, "we must do our bit to help Brightsea officers."

Both Rothermores, Alice noted, looked alternately aghast at Lord FitzRobert's arrogance and absolutely fed up. If FitzRobert had hoped to put an important MP in his pocket for various business concerns, Alice was pretty sure the dream was dead.

His Imperial Highness, to the contrary, showed no superficial reaction to the policeman at all. He seemed to have gone into a kind of blankness – devoid of any emotion, positive or negative. All of his gauche indolence packed away, leaving behind a mannequin wearing a Russian costume. Alice found it most interesting. She wondered if the prince had run afoul of the police before in his colorful existence.

"Yes, well ..." FitzRobert cleared his throat again. "Crumpling, give DI Saxby whatever it is he requires."

"Very good, Your Lordship,' said the butler. "This way, please."

DI Saxby nodded and turned to exit the second dining room. "Constable Brown will collect you. Thank you all for your assistance in this matter. Perhaps Lady Fairlight will come now? I already have Major Fairlight's statement."

Alice took in a surprised breath and stood up after the footman darted in to assist with her chair. "Thank you so much," she murmured, not quite sure if she really meant the attentive footman or DI Saxby for throwing her a rope and yanking her out of Lord FitzRobert's vicinity.

CHAPTER

16

"Darling!" said Simon, as Alice, DI Saxby and the noble Crumpling exited the second dining room. He thought Alice looked very tired and not at her vibrant American best. Not difficult to understand – in the parlance of her American cowboy brethren, it had been *onehelluva day*.

She notably brightened at the sight of him. Both tenderness and guilt pulled at his heart. Alice did so love him. Wholeheartedly and without reserve. The kind of love everyone trapped in filthy battlefield trenches hoped to return home to find or keep. So many did not.

"There you are, at last." Alice ran a couple of steps to grasp his hands. "I was marooned on FitzRobert Island!"

Simon pretended to shudder. "Sorry, darling. Couldn't be helped. You up first with the good inspector here?"

"I shan't keep her long," said DI Saxby as he caught up with Alice. "Very interested, though, in hearing about Miss Piety's state of mind."

"Well, I can say Polly was not at all morose or melancholy." Alice turned to the young policeman. "She was very excited about getting married soon. Apparently, it would be quite a happy surprise to both friends and family. Marrying *up*. I was glad for her."

"Really?" Simon cocked his head to the side in interest. "Did she say who the fortunate chap might be?"

Alice sighed. "No, unfortunately. I expect you might want to talk to the gamekeeper or a local farmer, Detective Inspector. She was beautiful enough to catch the eye of any man."

Crumpling, who had been politely hovering at the periphery, coughed with excruciating politeness. "If I might respond to that, sir."

"You have intelligence regarding Miss Piety's paramour?" Saxby asked.

The butler looked unhappy. "Mrs. Kent and I endeavor to provide a safe home here with appropriate structure for staff ..."

"Yes, yes," said Saxby. "Understood."

"Miss Polly was, as Her Ladyship notes, extremely beautiful and a kind little soul. I do not wish to infringe on my employer's ..."

"Understood. Go on."

Crumpling swallowed hard. Simon was intrigued. It would take something fairly universe tilting to cause a retainer of Crumpling's years and experience to swallow tightly.

"Over the past year, it has been clear to us that St. Michael's – our village church – young curate, Mr. Hayter, had taken a real interest in Miss Polly. *Besotted* might be the word a writer of romances would use, sir."

Simon almost gasped and he heard Alice do just that. Miss Polly Piety, as the wife of a curate, would be stepping up to upper edges of the middle class. A breathtaking rise for a poor girl from the Black Country. Could it possibly be true?

"Do you happen to recall the last time Mr. Hayter was about the place, hoping to catch sight of Polly Piety?" asked Simon, thinking of glasses that had been thrown aside in an attic and the bottle of champagne with its still fizzy cargo.

Crumpling's intelligent brow furrowed for a moment as he considered the question. "Mr. Hayter," he said finally, "came to dinner early last week. His Lordship likes to play Bridge."

Hayter's last assignment as a table balancer left him off the list of potential champagne tipplers. Simon wondered if Polly Piety had two admirers. His initial impression, garnered from her belongings and other people including Alice, was not a Dorothy Brier type.

"Did Miss Piety return his fervor to your knowledge?" asked DI Saxby, beating him to the question.

Crumpling looked downcast. "I am afraid I do not. Miss Piety was not required for His Lordship's Bridge parties. Beyond that, neither Miss Piety nor Mr. Hayter took me into their confidences."

Simon had a pretty shrewd idea what Crumpling might have advised Polly Piety if she had intimated that she planned to marry the village curate. It wouldn't have included time tested tips on packing a honeymoon trousseau. More to the order of packing her one wretched suitcase without a reference.

"Well, Polly did say everyone would be very surprised," Alice reminded them. "She was a very sweet girl. Mr. Hayter would have been fortunate if she'd accepted his offer."

Simon threw his wife an affectionate glance. As an American, she had a natural affinity for the underdog. She was less impressed by bloodlines and social boundaries. Her paternal grandfather had inherited the family business – a small bank in Tarrytown, New York – and built it into an enormous financial concern with lines into every aspect of American life. Her maternal grandparents were cattle ranchers in Arizona who vastly preferred campfire dinners to cocktail parties. Alice thought people should listen to their hearts without a care for what society might make of it. An admirable idea if completely wrong – headed for Mr. Hayter and any dreams he might harbor for his career.

"Darling," he said, "why don't you go along and talk to DI Saxby? I'll take your place at table."

She laid a hand on his forearm. "Any hope of escaping soon? I'm really tired."

"That is entirely up to the detective inspector." Simon murmured. He had to concede that Alice looked exhausted – something that would be a little unusual for his vibrant, outdoorsy wife – had she not survived an automobile wreck, witnessed a violent death followed by a long, overly complicated dinner next to Lord FitzRobert.

"I promise to keep Lady Fairlight only a few minutes," said DI Saxby. "But we should be getting on."

"Go straight up." Simon covered her hand with his own for a moment. "I'll join you as soon as I can."

She gave him a small smile and then turned to follow Crumpling who was, once again, leading the way to the prospective interview room. Simon watched until Alice turned left and disappeared into yet another one of Palliser Park's rooms. He let out a long breath. Lord FitzRobert and his table awaited.

17

Crumpling had conducted them to a much smaller dining room. In a less fraught frame of mind, Alice would have admired its simpler elegance – a cherry wood Regency table set near a pretty fireplace with plasterwork painted with bluebells and other English wildflowers. She imagined it might be where breakfast could be served on quieter days when the house lacked visitors.

"Would you be requiring anything else?" asked the butler, preparing to return to Lord FitzRobert.

"Yes," said DI Saxby as he waited for Alice to be seated. "You can rouse the actress from her rooms and have her join the others."

Crumpling nodded. "And shall I have the servants ready themselves as well, sir?"

"We'll be back tomorrow," replied the detective inspector, yanking out his own chair. "Just the FitzRoberts and their guests tonight but thank you for your readiness to assist."

"I will have a coffee service brought in," Crumpling murmured and politely evaporated from the room.

Alice leaned back in her chair, feeling as if she'd been at a dining table since Shakespeare scribbled *The End* on his manuscript of Hamlet. She was utterly knackered.

"Perhaps you could tell me about Miss Piety's fall," said DI Saxby. "Your husband has given me his recollection."

"Of course. She was a *very* nice girl, detective inspector."

"That seems to be the general consensus." He opened his small leather bound notebook and flattened it against the cherrywood surface of the table in preparation for taking notes. "But Miss Piety also had a secret, did she not?"

Alice conceded that he had a point and then carefully related all that she could remember about the moment when Polly Piety fell from Palliser Park's ornate roof. She saw that, at one point, DI Saxby wrote something down with particular emphasis.

"You're absolutely sure that you heard Miss Piety scream twice?" He gazed at her in marked interest.

"Yes – once before she fell and then again, *as* she fell." Alice almost gasped. It was a most intriguing aspect. Why would Polly cry out twice? Had she been frightened *before* losing her balance?

Before she could pursue her thought, DI Saxby threw her a sympathetic look and closed his notebook. "Your husband's report matches up with yours, making it the definitive version. I appreciate you going through it all again for me. If you return to the dinner table, please don't share your account with anyone."

Alice pushed back from the table. "No need to worry on that account. I plan to run and hide, detective inspector."

"Very wise. Perhaps, I shall see you tomorrow, Your Ladyship." He stood up quickly – a reflexive politeness. "Good night."

"Good night," she echoed, studying the young policeman for a moment. He was a very appealing figure – another gloriously handsome young Englishman. Britain had lost so many during the course of the war. Almost an entire generation lay under foreign soil, everything that they were and could have been falling into dust. Alice wondered if the great sadness that flared up, often unexpectedly, about the tragic effects of the War to End All Wars would ever really fade.

Alice left the small dining room and returned to the highways and byways of Palliser Park. Anxious to avoid spending any more time at Lord FitzRobert's table, she pointedly headed in the opposite direction. With some luck, the way back to their guest hidey hole would become apparent.

She walked along at a reasonable clip, finding some pleasure in being alone and under her own steam. It had taken her a few minutes to wind her way from the southerly region of Palliser Park that housed dining rooms and secondary sitting rooms to the Marble Salon with its twin formal staircases. It was the long way round but she knew she could manage to retrace her steps to their rooms from the main staircase.

Rain was coming down heavily beyond the gilded walls as Alice stepped into the vast Marble Salon. Empty of human frailty with the exception of herself, the space was an intimidating vacuum. Rain struck the windows with a drumbeat staccato. She felt as if she were marooned deep inside an Egyptian pyramid or another sort of ancient pagan burial mound from which the appropriate deity had long fled. Buried alive in the tomb like Juliet.

Unsettled, she actually shivered and focused on the rain instead. So much for treasured dreams of lawn tennis and lemonades down on Palliser Park's massive private beach. Alice turned to look at the formidable staircase with its gold gilded banister. She wondered just how fast a girl could careen up such stairs in a pair of dainty heels. It wouldn't be very aristocratic but, then, Lord FitzRobert wasn't loitering around the Marble Salon to look down his long nose at her. Maybe just dispense with shoes at all – hop it in stocking feet …

"Alice!" A man's voice echoed across the great expanse. She paused her intent to bolt and shifted sharply to see a young man striding across the marble floor. He was tall and good – looking with a rakish mustache. Jack Nickleby – Fizz's betrothed – arriving for the big engagement party weekend.

"What the – forgive the colorful vocab – bloody hell is going on?" he asked, dropping a soft leather portmanteau at the foot of the stairs. "Where's Crumpling? There's a police motor outside!"

"There's been a real hullabaloo," Alice said, accepting a kiss on the cheek. "One of the maids was killed, falling from the roof."

"Good God – how awful!" He looked dismayed. "Fizzy?"

"Corralled with the rest of the household while the police make inquiries. The second dining room but don't ask me for directions, I'm hopeless in this house."

"How did you manage to escape?" Jack brightened with good humor. "Hasn't old FitzPompey laid out salmon stuffed with sparrows or something?"

Alice laughed. "You sound like Simon. He's not wild about the menu either."

"That's a soldier." He shook his head and let out a theatrical sigh. "Well, I shall sally forth to the second dining room and check in with Fizz. Maybe Crumpling can conjure up a sandwich. Horrible wet trip from London."

"Glad you're here, Jack," she said, meaning it.

Jack Nickleby grinned at her. " Maybe we can all plough through this and escape to drink copiously elsewhere – say, Castle Fairlight."

"Be nice – this is Fizzy's big weekend." Alice laughed too.

"Oh, I'll be a good boy." Jack picked up his portmanteau and pushed off. "See you at breakfast, my friend!"

Alice watched him stroll off in search of a sandwich. She returned her attention to the staircase. *Now or never.* She slipped off her shoes and bent down to pick them up.

"Jack! Jack, *darling!*" came a loud call from the top of the stair. Before Alice could straighten with her shoes, she felt a wave of velvet rush over her right arm as a figure sailed past without so much as a vague, *I beg your pardon.*

Alice recovered quickly and turned on the step to see Dorothy Brier running down the last few steps, two at a time. The actress was still garbed in her scarlet velvet dinner dress and resembled an errant blood drop as she exited the stairs.

"Jack!" Dorothy cried in what seemed to be genuine joy and what Alice perceived as surprising intimacy. She was unaware that Dorothy and Jack knew each other. Admittedly, Jack Nickleby didn't appear as delighted. He stood, unsmiling, as Dorothy crossed the gilded floor as if she was late for the last train home. Another few clattering steps and she literally launched into his arms. She threw her arms around his neck and kissed him in a manner not usually reserved for casual acquaintance.

Alice realized she was staring with her mouth open. She closed it with a small cough and knew she ought to be politely retreating up the stairs.

"Oh, Jack! Thank God you've come! Dorothy kissed the side of Jack's handsome face. "I've been so, so bored. It's been the most awful few days and now I have to talk to the police …"

Jack's gaze was past Dorothy, extending up to Alice. "Steady on, Miss Brier," he said, still looking at Alice. He patted her back with all the romance of a doctor bidding farewell to the final patient of the day. "Perhaps you would like a cup of tea?"

"*Miss Brier?*" Dorothy sounded confused. "Jack — what are you …?" She pulled back a little and began to turn to see what held Nickleby's attention.

Alice had just a moment to avoid direct eye contact with the actress. She swung around and climbed the stairs with more alacrity than she thought possible in stocking feet.

"Oh," she heard Dorothy drawl, "the American. How dreary."

CHAPTER

18

Simon was surprised to note the arrival of *both* Dorothy Brier and Jack Nickleby to Palliser Park's second best dining room. The actress, still adorned in red – probably because she had keeled over, completely blotto, in her room – strode into the room as if she was leaving the artist's door at the Duke of York.

"Sorry, darlings," Dorothy drawled, "about missing dinner. I was shattered after that horrific scene. But just look who I found along the way!"

Jack Nickleby was on the threshold, grinning sheepishly. He looked well, Simon was pleased to see, and reasonably happy. Nickleby had weathered the war as a translator for the War Department, specializing in German and its various regional variants. Such a post, while stressful, didn't exact quite the same toll as active duty in the trenches. Simon didn't begrudge Jack his escape from The Continent.

"Jack!" cried Fizz, getting to her feet and darting across the floor to her handsome fiancé. "I'm so glad you're here. Have you heard what happened?"

"Miss Brier gave me the basic facts," he said glancing at the actress who was busy taking over Alice's former chair next to Lord FitzRobert. "Horrible. I'm sorry."

Simon watched Dorothy Brier as she made a performance out of condescending to sit at the table. She pointedly whispered something into FitzRobert's ear that made him smirk. The studied indifference to Jack's innate charisma and much admired charm set off a warning bell. He wasn't aware that Jack knew Dorothy Brier particularly well beyond Lord FitzRobert's orbit.

While Jack came to the table and settled next to his adoring Fizz, Lord FitzRobert's footmen rushed to provide the newcomers with some food and drink. The dining room had been thinning out. Perry and the Rothermores had been interviewed and then, much like Alice, had gratefully retreated to their quarters. Volkonsky, the repulsive Russian, was DI Saxby's current subject, leaving only himself, Fizz and Lord FitzRobert to discuss the weather.

"Simon – always good to see you," said Jack with genuine warmth. "I need a real friend at this thing."

"Well, I like that!" laughed Fizz, pretending to punch his arm. "It's supposed to be a high point in the trajectory of our lives."

Jack pretended that her tap had actually hurt and rubbed his upper arm. "You see before you, an abused man."

"Alice's parents threw a big wing – ding too," Simon said remembering their engagement party at The Savoy just before the war.

Alice's mother had exquisite taste and had secured the legendary Lancaster Ballroom to celebrate her daughter's upcoming nuptials. Glittering images flared up in his head like summer fireworks – crystals vases of orange – y pink roses, vibrant dance orchestra with gleaming brass instruments, a sea of beautiful women in sumptuous dresses, swirling with the twists in the music ... and joy. He remembered joy as something ineffably light and soaring ... *Alice was joy* – the most beautiful of all the beautiful girls. Joy. It had been easy to laugh ...

"Ours will be fabulous!" Fizz declared with gusto, crashing into his reverie and shattering his memories into shards. "Absolutely fabulous!"

Simon refocused on the occupants of the second best dining room. Dorothy Brier was knocking back a glass of wine, agitation visible in her clenched jaw. Jack Nickleby stared down at his hastily provided meal as if the secret to the lost colony of Roanoke was revealing itself in roasted potato.

"Your engagement party will be the high point of the summer," said Lord FitzRobert over his coffee cup. "As it should be at a great house such as Palliser Park. This house was built for entertaining the elite in its day and will again."

"But you survived all the fuss," said Jack, looking up at Simon with raised eyebrows, a hint of something more serious in his voice as if his trepidation wasn't entirely a put on.

Simon gave a small laugh. "I survived."

"Well, I hope *I* will. This parading of the condemned man is terrifying."

Fizz gave her fiancé another playful whack on the shoulder. "Idiot!"

Constable Brown appeared in the dining room. "Prince Volkonsky has been released by the DI. Who would ..."

Dorothy Brier sprang to her feet. "I'm next," she said in a flat tone.

"Where is His Imperial Highness?" asked Lord FitzRobert, watching his actress friend dispassionately. Simon had the momentary impression thatFitzRobert had a pretty good idea why the brittle thespian found him alluring.

"I believe the gentleman was intent upon going to his bed," said Constable Brown, watching Dorothy Brier as she swept past him. "Wasn't feeling well apparently."

"Come along, Constable," the actress' voice remained bored and flat. "This couldn't possibly be more tedious."

Lord FitzRobert pushed away from the table once Dorothy Brier's crimson figure had stalked out. He stood and stretched his shoulders. "I'm for bed as well," he announced. "What about you, Constance? Lots to do tomorrow with people beginning to arrive."

Fizz started to object but her fiancé patted her shoulder affectionately. "Go on," urged Jack. "Just going to wolf down this bit of dinner and do the same."

"I'll keep him company for a little while," Simon added, reaching for his coffee cup.

"That's good of you." Fizz beamed at him. "But won't Alice be wondering where her handsome husband has got to?"

Before Simon could fob off Fizz with some sort of banal reply, Lord FitzRobert coughed loudly and then waved at exhausted footmen who tried not to blanche at the notion of what His Lordship might require

"Off you go," he said with unusual thoughtfulness to his staff. "You are a credit to Crumpling. It's late and there is much to be done tomorrow. We can fend for ourselves."

The young men bowed, then darted from the second best dining room like hunted antelope. FitzRobert was known to be mercurial and a sudden fry – up for the entire household might be required before dawn. In the wake of the departing servants, FitzRobert excused himself as well. He wearily requested that *someone* – the identity of such a proxy for his magisterial person appeared unimportant – – inform DI Saxby that local police could show themselves out. Palliser Park was closed for the night. No pots of tea or sandwiches were to make their way to overworked policemen. He also made the point of bullying Fizz into retiring as well, issuing an edict that she was to be rested and flawless for the next day's important guests.

Fizz had sighed and acquiesced. She flashed both Jack and Simon an apologetic smile and resignedly trudged after her father, auburn curls glimmering in what remained of the dining room's candlelight.

"I can handle this. Why don't you go up as well?" Simon planned to check in with Saxby after initial interviews were complete.

Jack glanced at the door that had permitted Dorothy Brier to stalk over its threshold. "Don't have a wife waiting for me … yet."

"So," said Simon as he retrieved a cigarette from his case and tapped it against the metal lid, "how long have you been stepping out with Miss Dorothy Brier?"

Fizz's fiancé visibly started. His English skin flushed an angry red as if he'd been slapped. "I don't know what you're on about …"

"Oh, come on, Jack." Simon gave a short laugh. It had a harsh tone. "There are guileless youths collecting hymnals for their choirmasters who keep better secrets."

"Is it really that obvious?" Jack's handsome face contorted with shame. "Or did Alice tell you?"

"Alice?"

Jack looked miserable. "Alice saw … *something* when I arrived. Thought maybe she managed to tell you. But it's not serious, Simon! I met Dorothy at one of FitzRobert's dos and made the stupid mistake of agreeing to meet. I didn't think she'd be so … Simon, she's voracious! And she doesn't listen. I've told her it's over but she won't …"

"Steady on, Jack," said Simon. "I will say it seems rather awkward for poor old Fizz. Her big weekend and all that."

Jack nodded and sat back in his chair with a groan. "Dorothy will ruin everything. I thought, maybe, she'd understand – you know, being here for the engagement party. She'd understand that things would have to be different – that we have to move on with our lives. But Dorothy's digging her heels in."

""Would you like me to speak with her?"

Jack leaned forward, his eyes widening in both surprise and regret. "Dorothy is certifiable. Completely bonkers. Don't get entangled in all of this."

"I can be politely persuasive," Simon said, knocking some ash from his cigarette. "Leave Miss Brier to me."

CHAPTER

19

Alice hung up her dinner dress, grateful to be in a set of pale blue pajamas. Made of Sea Island cotton and incredibly easy to wear, the modern masculine design gave the pajamas a hint of daring. She wondered what it would be like to wear such comfortable clothes throughout the day.

"Medium dry sherry Number *Two*," Alice said out loud as she closed the wardrobe and retrieved her glass. "Far bigger than Number One, I think."

Accordingly, she poured herself a very large glass from a decanter that an anonymous Palliser Park servant had laid out with an assortment of other bottles of alcohol and oddly, tins of digestive biscuits.

"Oh, what the hell," Alice said, grabbing one of the gaily painted metal boxes. She might as well inhale a dozen cookies too.

A soft knock came at their bedroom door. "Lady Fairlight, are you in, beautiful girl?" said a Russian voice that slurred as a result of strong drink. "I long to speak to you."

Alice froze, panicked. The door was not locked. In another moment or two, she could be in the middle of a deeply unwanted interaction.

"Lady Fairlight – beautiful Alice," Prince Volkonsky continued to mewl through the door. "I know you feel the same about my good self. May I come in?"

Alice realized she had about thirty seconds to do something. Not enough time to cross the room and lock the door. Not enough time to hurl herself from the bedroom window because death would be preferable to an awkward conversation with the noxious Prince Volkonsky.

"Beautiful Alice?" He knocked again. "May I come in? I could be your darling Andrei just as you would like."

She could sense – like a springbok being tracked by an African leopard – that Prince Volkonsky would try the door handle next. He would discover that it was unlocked and enter unbidden. Boundaries meant nothing to Prince Volkonsky.

Next to the large four poster – everything in Palliser Park seemed to be oversized and designed for maximum impression – Alice dropped quietly to the floor. The rich Persian carpet worked in greens and unsurprisingly, gold was so thick that it absorbed any sound. She rolled under the bed, being careful to keep the cookie tin from rattling. From her new vantage point under the bed skirt, she could just see the floor extending all the way to one of two armoires and the drinks table.

As predicted, Andrei Volkonsky turned the ornate door knob. She could hear the well – oiled hardware sliding to the right and then the door opening with a soft swish. Alice immediately reduced her breathing to as little as she could get away with and winced as the prince's footsteps came round the foot of the bed.

"Alice, beautiful girl?" he called again. His voice now more tentative and interestingly, no longer slurred as if he'd sobered up crossing the threshold.

115

Alice heard him move towards the gleaming bathroom, looking to see if perhaps, she was in the bath and hadn't heard him at the door. Thwarted there, His Imperial Highness returned to the foot of the bed where he sat. She could sense him pondering his next move.

"Ah! A nice little drink has been poured," said Prince Volkonsky and the bed shifted slightly as he stood up. "Thank you."

She watched his peerless kid leather boots walk over to the drinks table where the glass of sherry had been left. There was a small clinking of crystal as, presumably, His Imperial Highness downed her medium dry sherry.

Then he wandered over to nearest armoire and threw open one of its doors. Alice could hear the hinges offer a modest squeak.

"So very nice," Volkonsky drawled over the sound of hangers scraping over the rod. "Gieves and Hawkes. He *is* exquisite, of course. So very elegant. So worth knowing."

Another knock came at the door and she heard His Imperial Highness activate the armoire hinges again as he abruptly shut down his prowl through Simon's clothes.

"Prince Volkonsky, may I ask just why you might be here?" Alice heard Mr. Spinner ask, unamused. She wanted to cry out in triumphant joy at his arrival, banishing the irritating and presumptuous Russian.

"You will refer to me as Your Imperial Highness in future," replied Volkonsky with imperious Russian drama. "I am awaiting Lady Fairlight. We became acquainted over dinner and I sensed that she wished to speak to me."

"I see," said Mr. Spinner, clearly unimpressed. "Her Ladyship is with her husband at present. Now be so kind as to hop it, Prince Volkonsky."

"In future ..." Volkonsky's voice was low, livid.

"In future, please refer any request for an imposition on Lady Fairlight's valuable time to Major Fairlight. I'm sure he'll know what to do about it."

Alice watched Prince Volkonsky's peerless kid leather boots march away. His Imperial Highness said nothing more but Alice could feel outrage billowing behind him like the wake from a great ocean liner.

She heard Mr. Spinner shut the main door. "Crikey – what a prat," he said with some vitriol.

Alice rolled back out from under the bed. "God bless you, Mr. Spinner!"

She popped up just in time to see her husband's former batman jump back in surprise at her sudden appearance.

"Your Ladyship?" His eyes widened at her modern pajamas and then he glanced away politely. "Are you quite all right?"

"Oh, yes – perfectly fine. I hid before he came in." Alice returned the cookie tin to the drinks table and saw that His Imperial Highness had, indeed, knocked back her glass of sherry. "He was pounding at the door, drunk, whining about how we had to talk or something."

"His Imperial Highness didn't appear drunk to me," said Mr. Spinner thoughtfully.

"I expect he's like so many professional weirdos – able to act almost normal when cornered." She retrieved a dressing gown from her own armoire and shrugged it on. "He was going through Simon's belongings when you interrupted him. Seemed more intrigued by him than me if truth be told."

"Allow me to ring for a pot of tea and a few sandwiches, Your Ladyship," said Mr. Spinner and he turned towards the door.

"Don't trouble your excellent self, Mr. Spinner, I can happily do that…"

"No trouble at all, Your Ladyship. Please lock this door after me."

As the valet seemed determined to go in search of food and tea, Alice followed him to the beveled door and dutifully locked it. Despite all the drama – both grievous and ridiculous – of the evening, she was really quite hungry.

CHAPTER

20

"Miss Dorothy Brier," said Simon. He had chosen a strategic location directly in the path the actress would have to navigate on her way to the ostentatious FitzRobert mechanical lift and settled onto a faux Louis XV armchair upholstered in a truly hideous needle – worked scene of Aphrodite dipping an alabaster vessel into a watering hole.

The actress, a little the worse for having inhaled Lord FitzRobert's expensive spirits, looked momentarily startled. To her credit, she recovered within seconds and flashed him a practiced smile.

"Major the Lord Fairlight," Dorothy murmured as he stood up. "How did you know I have been longing to ... umm," she cleared her throat and gave a short, coquettish giggle, "*see* you?"

"The local coppers satisfied with your performance?" he asked, taking note of her perfume – a rich blend of vanilla and amber.

Dorothy swayed towards him like a tigress on sleeping powders. She threw her arms around his neck, diamond bracelets clinking together with the effort. She rose up on the tips of her red satin shoes to kiss his unscarred cheek and then dropped a little to his neck.

"I could not help them," she said into his ear.

"Yes, but can you help me?" Simon asked.

"Try me," Dorothy breathed and reached up to shift his chin towards her. She rose again to press her lips against his. For a moment he almost felt drawn to the actress' confident allure but suddenly flashed on the memory of an unlucky soldier being struck by an adder as they performed a covert maneuver deep in a Belgian forest. The chap's shrill scream of surprise and pain had nearly sent them all to Perdition.

Simon grasped her shoulders and pushed her back gently. "I would like to talk, Dorothy."

"Talk?" She trailed a hand up his arm. "Can't you think of something better to do, my beautiful monster?"

He caught at her hand and plucked it from his coat sleeve. "Talk."

Dorothy tossed her head in frustration and then moved away, dropping down onto one of the Louis XV chairs with sigh. "I'm listening," she said in a flat, unaffected voice. He had the immediate impression that Miss Brier, illustrious star of the stage and, perhaps, other less savory ventures, was no stranger to serious conversations with authority figures.

"You and Jack ..."

The actress looked sour. "I see the little American ran, sniveling, to tell all she knew."

"She didn't have to – you know, you're fortunate that FitzRobert is either a perfect thicko or strangely amused by the serendipity of your," Simon returned to the homely Aphrodite and sat down, nonchalantly crossing his right leg, "desires."

"Go to hell. He likes what I am. He adores me." Dorothy threw him a look of disdain. "He laughs when I tell him what I do and what I think about you all. We laugh and laugh ..."

"You'll pull your claws out of Jack and you'll do it quick," Simon interrupted. As much as it was intriguing to learn something of FitzRobert's private sins – *if* Dorothy was actually telling the truth – he had no time to encourage her revelations.

"Now why would I do that?" Her smoky eyes widened with the challenge. "I like Jack. I like being in bed with Jack. I like stepping on that spoiled little minx he wants to marry."

Simon met her gaze. "Nonetheless, you'll drop him like a stone."

"I don't think I will. Dropping Jack for *you* holds nothing for *me*." Dorothy grasped the arms of the Louis XV and stood up. She was again momentarily startled when he mirrored her movement perfectly.

"Who said there wasn't anything in it for you?" He stood, looking down at her.

Dorothy smiled, triumph glittering in the rare violet eyes. There was a pellucid understanding that men would always offer her things of value. She expected it. She was entitled to it.

"Go on – tell me what's in it for me." She relaxed, awaiting the negotiation.

Dorothy Brier gasped as Simon reached out with steel trap speed, flipping her around into a locked hold. With the actress neutralized, he murmured into her ear exactly how he would remove her from the metaphorical chessboard and just what local sharks and assorted sea life would do to her famous face.

She was sagging in his arms, breath frantic when Reggie Spinner appeared, looking apologetic.

"Begging your pardon, Major," he said, ignoring Miss Brier's predicament.

Simon nodded. Then said to the actress who was still, "Off you go! We understand each other now, don't we?" He released her from the hold and gave her a gentle push. Dorothy Brier staggered forward. She looked to Reggie Spinner as if he might make sense of it all but the former batman pointedly avoided eye contact. With guttural sound – half growl, half sob – Dorothy broke into a run, hurling herself in the general direction of the mechanical lift.

"Interesting," said Mr. Spinner.

"Oh, she'll bounce back to her tedious self by tomorrow. That type always does." Simon let out a short breath and brushed his hands together, wiping off any invisible remnants of the actress. "Why are you not abed, noble Spinner?"

"Been a bit of an odd development, Major," replied the valet and he explained the unexpected presence of His Imperial Highness in the Fairlight quarters.

CHAPTER

21

Alice was poking at the fire with a very fancy andiron designed to resemble a Chinese dragon when the door knob rattled. She spun around; fire implement at the ready in case the repulsive Prince Volkonsky had returned.

"It's Simon," came a wonderfully familiar voice. "I've brought sandwiches."

"My God, there is a God!" Alice proclaimed, replacing the andiron and skittering across the bedroom to unlock the door. She found her husband standing in the massive hallway holding a silver tray loaded with food and had the winsome thought that Simon was the loveliest human being to ever walk the earth.

"Mr. Spinner told me you were peckish," Simon said as he followed her back into the room. "The kitchen staff likes you, apparently, because out came this heap of sandwiches."

"I couldn't eat much of dinner," Alice admitted.

"Unsurprising after what happened," he said, setting the tray on a chair seat near the fireplace."I'm quite interested in one of these roast beef …"

"Oh, there's hot coffee too!" Alice retrieved the silver pot from under a red cozy embossed with the FitzRobert crest. "You perfectly wonderful man."

Simon settled on the floor near the warmth of the fire. "I understand you had a visitation from our glorious Russian overlord."

Alice felt her stomach tip at the reminder. She handed Simon a cup of coffee and then sat down by the fireplace as well. Despite being June, the weather had been unusually cool and wet. Palliser Park might be ostentatious but the guest amenities were in keeping with Lord FitzRobert's view of his place in the world. Their unusually large fireplace was well tended by the upstairs servants – the rich flames ought to last another couple of hours.

"He is a most unpleasant individual," she admitted and went on to relate what had occurred after Prince Volkonsky knocked on the door.

Simon clenched his jaw as he listened. Alice could see that he was angry but also determined to not upset her by going into a tirade. She realized once again what a fortunate creature she was to have married such a kind and thoughtful man.

"I'm sorry I wasn't here," he said when she finished her tale. "I'd have taken great pleasure in breaking his imperial nose."

"We can't rough up Lord FitzRobert's golden boy." Alice bit into her sandwich. "But speaking of favored friends, have I got some hot news …"

"Jack and the Scarlet Spider?"

Alice almost choked on the roast beef. " You already *know?*" She coughed, disappointed. and scrambled to grab her coffee cup.

He clenched his jaw again. "I promised Jack I'd have a quiet word with Miss Dorothy Brier and get her to behave. He's desperate to break it off."

"I should think so! Poor Fizz!"

"Anyway, I had a word. Don't think I can get away with menacing *two* of Lord FitzRobert's guests – at least within twenty four hours." Simon sipped his coffee. "A pity. I really want to enliven breakfast by beating Prince Volkonsky to a pulp."

"So, she'll leave the field to Fizz?" Alice couldn't imagine the actress agreeing to stand down after what she saw in the Marble Salon. It seemed clear that Dorothy Brier considered Jack Nickleby to be her personal property.

"Oh, Dorothy will leave him alone – for now, at least." Simon reached for a sandwich. "Alice?"

"Hmm?" She was just thinking how lucky the world was to have sandwiches. So simple and satisfying – really a high point in the everyday lives of human beings.

"I am sorry I wasn't here." His quiet voice had turned serious. "Please forgive me."

Alice lowered her sandwich, a little surprised at the depth of her husband's feeling concerning her adventure with the obnoxious Russian. "I've rapped the knuckles of bigger palookas than His Imperial Highness. It's fine."

"It's not fine – you had to roll under a bed to hide for heaven's sake ..." Then Simon stopped and laughed. Alice thrilled to the sound of it – a genuine laugh. "That word – *palooka*," he said and laughed again.

She laughed too. It felt so lovely to laugh. "And I know so many of them – *Drop a dime!Beezer! Zotzed! Chicago overcoat!Harlem sunset!*"

Simon reached out and grasped her wrist, pulling her to him. He kissed her then – gently, tentatively, almost as if he was rediscovering how to express physical affection.Alice barely wanted to breathe in case she broke the spell – the magic that had given her melancholy husband a moment of genuine happiness. She felt him slide his arms about her waist as the kiss deepened and became more ardent. Throwing caution to Palliser Park's sea breezes, Alice threw her own arms around his neck and returned his passion.

22

Simon rose early as had become his custom. He liked dawn and the quiet that still lingered from the night. In the trenches and killing fields of Europe, dawn often offered respite from shelling or gunfire.

After kissing the sleeping Alice on the forehead, he made his way down to Lord FitzRobert's stable. Although much of the original stable yard had been converted into motor car and gardening facilities, a solid portion had been left to house farm and riding horses. Perry had acquired a former officer's horse from the Castle Fairlight project. A handsome bay with a blaze and four white socks named Colonel Lee. Perry was a reasonably competent rider but not brave. The burly, unflappable bay carried him safely where ever Perry might want to go – hunt field or across an Essex beach.

"Morning, Your Lordship!" said a cheery voice as Simon stepped over the threshold into the stable aisle. FitzRobert's stableman, appeared in an open stall door wielding a pitchfork filled with straw. "Forgive me, sir. Just getting a start on things. Be a busy day with all the guests arriving for the weekend. What can I do for you?"

"Mr. Brabinger, isn't it?" Simon replied, holding out a hand for the stableman to shake.

The horseman looked momentarily surprised at the egalitarian gesture but masked it and set aside his pitchfork so he could shake Simon's hand. "Right you are, sir."

"How's Colonel Lee been keeping?"

Brabinger's ruddy face lit up at the name. "He's a grand fellow – kind and sound as sterling. Young FitzRobert doesn't ride often so my daughter exercises the Colonel almost every day. She loves him, Your Lordship."

"I'm glad. You're right – he is a grand fellow," said Simon, feeling a flush of gratitude cross his senses. Grateful that a good horse had found the right home. Exactly what the Castle Fairlight scheme was about – finding safe sanctuaries for horses who had done their duty and deserved better than what the War Department saw fit to give them. "All right with you if I throw a saddle on him and hack out for a bit?"

Again, the stableman was clearly surprised by Simon's polite request requiring his approval. He covered up his fleeting reaction by nodding adamantly. "Of course, sir. I'd be happy to tack ..."

"No need – just point me in the direction of the horse."

"End stall on the right. You may remember he goes nicely in a kimberwicke." Brabinger reached out for his pitchfork. "Would you excuse me, sir, if I return to it? His Lordship will be wanting all hands on deck this weekend."

Simon spent the next thirty – odd minutes in a cherished occupation – puttering around horses which always acted as a soothing tonic. He put the muscular bay in the cross ties, grooming the gelding's burnished summer coat until it gleamed, cleaning hooves and combing out Colonel Lee's black mane and tail. The former officer's horse stood contentedly in the ties, enjoying both the attention and Simon's highly experienced grooming technique that not only cleaned but thoroughly massaged the muscles.

Once tacked up in Perry's Middlemore hunting saddle, Simon and Colonel Lee emerged from the stable area to a promising morning. The storm had cleared off, leaving a clear and bright sky. The North Sea, which formed Palliser Park's spectacular eastern border, churned silver, black and grey as if it hadn't fully released the night. He decided to wander down to Palliser's beach and allow the Colonel to soak his ankles in the cool surf. A thoroughly honest fellow, the bay was content to stride away from his stable and descend the long, tiered path that made a gentle incline down the cliffside to the beach below. It was beautifully graded and widened from what must have been the original 18th century path – something of an engineering feat in its way and must have cost FitzRobert the earth to achieve during the war years. He was particularly impressed by a low but stout fence line that protected beachgoers from the sea going edge. FitzRobert did think of everything in his obsession with Palliser Park.

Simon threw the reins out to the buckle, allowing the polite gelding his head. He awkwardly lit a cigarette in spite of the marine breeze and sat back in the saddle to take in the glittering views of the sea. It was rough out on the water – a remnant of the night's storm. Fierce white caps dotted the roiling water and out in the vast distance, he could spot fishing vessels heading out for cod and herring. An irony of the recent war was the notable rise in fish stocks. With commercial fishing almost at a standstill during the conflict, the sea had been able to restore her bounty to a level not seen since Palliser Park's Georgian foundation had been laid. Simon wondered how long it would take men to once again overfish English waters.

Once he and Colonel Lee made it down to the wide swath of sand, melancholy ruminations on the state of British commercialization had vanished – vanquished by a kind of unfettered joy brought by sharp briny breezes, roaring water and flashing sunlight. It was the best he had felt in days. Out on a horse in fresh air and for a little while, nothing was pressing him. A weight lifted off his shoulders as Colonel Lee stepped free of FitzRobert's impressive path and onto the sand. He was free – at least for the moment.

Simon pulled up the bay and took a long drag on his second cigarette since beginning the descent. He took in FitzRobert's improvements to God's natural plan, almost sighing at the affront. Four beach huts had been built up against the cliffside above the high tide mark to allow Palliser Park's owners and visitors to spend the day if desired by the sea. Expensively crafted to replicate the elaborate designs employed by Queen Victoria for her own personal beach huts, the wooden shelters provided not only breaks from changeable weather but a place for Palliser Park servants to lay out full meals for lounging guests. Meals that would have to be carried down from the house kitchen in heavy hot boxes along with chests of china, crystal, linens and silverware. No mean feat for the Palliser Park staff. He thought it likely that Fizz's gala weekend was the first real trial for the servants and the beach huts.

Colonel Lee knickered as a flight of seabirds looped past on the breeze. The gelding lifted his handsome head and snorted, inhaling some of the rich marine air. Simon patted the mountainous horse's neck.

"You want to fly, don't you?" He put the end of his cigarette in his pocket and picked up his reins. Colonel Lee jigged a little to the right, clearly anticipating stretching his legs. "Fair enough!"

Simon squeezed his leg, encouraging the bay to move forward into a gallop. Colonel Lee lit out cheerfully – thundering out towards the water and then arcing left to follow the beach.He laughed out loud, enjoying the horse's excitement at being out of his stall and larking about. The gelding even crowhopped as they streamed through surges of seawater that rolled over the sand before settling into a happy hand gallop.

Salty spray flumed up from the surf, drenching both Simon and Colonel Lee but neither cared. Each, in his own way, had been soaked in worse. The giddy sensation of flying down the coastline easily topped being damp. They galloped a good mile away from Palliser Park's fancy neo – Victorian beach huts and rounded an outcropping of the cliffside. On the far side was a pretty inlet featuring another gaily painted beach hut and a substantial dock that was large enough to welcome a good sized sailing yacht although at the moment, no such elegant visitor was moored to its solid pillars. To Simon's eye, it looked as if the dock had been there for a long while but had been considerably refurbished at typically great expense by Lord FitzRobert. There was another manicured pathway as well, emerging from the cliffs opposite the imposing dock. With two entrances to Palliser Park's spectacular beachfront, FitzRobert guests could either drop down to sunbathe from the house or arrive by sea going vessel. Despite his deep reservations about FitzRobert ostentation, Simon had to admit that it was an impressive layout.

"Colonel, old fellow," he said, pulling up the enormous horse. "We have a new route home."

The bay gelding let out a snort and then sighed. Clearly it was no news to the horse who had probably navigated the area a million times with Brabinger's daughter in the irons. Simon threw him the reins and Colonel Lee politely walked towards the entrance to the beach path.

Similar to the sister path to the south, it had been cleared and refined so that pedestrians, equestrians and carts could all easily negotiate the incline. To keep things from getting steep, the trajectory needed to long and winding – a side benefit is that it produced a pleasurable amble of a journey with striking views across the vast North Sea. The second path was even longer, snaking around a more complicated pattern of cliffside outcroppings. Again, FitzRobert had poured treasure into reinforcing potentially dangerous edges with a neatly made fence line. Simon appreciated that FitzRobert horses – and stable manager's daughters – were protected from falls. It was a level of ostentation that he could understand.

Colonel Lee was gifted with a huge, ground covering free walk. It was one of many traits that had made him an excellent officer's mount. Simon had the reins on the buckle, letting the horse pick his own way up the gentle slope of the beach path. They came around the final bend and up to the top, striding out onto the mainland. More than a mile in the distance was Palliser Park, its rear facade glittering with a pallid formality in the June sunlight. The extensive gardens, pool, croquet lawn and tennis courts rolled out from the house like God's carpet but finally gave way to natural Essex countryside.

Simon was interested to find that one of the property's original secondary buildings was still standing despite

FitzRobert's mania for orderly Georgian design. It was a stone cottage – early Tudor – in fine shape for its age especially given its superb position overlooking the sea and inlet below. It had weathered fierce marine storms since Henry VII busied himself sorting the Treaty of Redon. The cottage had probably been given to a succession of head gardeners or gamekeepers who must have been astonished daily by the sweeping views from the front windows. He bet it had a lovely central fireplace and a collection of quirky but cozy rooms. Simon decided he'd give a lot to spend his Palliser Park holiday in it – even sleeping rough with a bed roll and a chamber pot but doubted that Alice would feel as enthusiastic.

"Oh, let's have a little look, Colonel," Simon said, directing the gelding off the path and towards the 15th century cottage. "No sense rushing back if I'm not allowed to break Prince Andrei's nose at breakfast."

Once they'd reached the picturesque Tudor building, Simon swung down and led Colonel Lee towards one of two large lead glass windows by a heavy oak front door that still boasted original iron hinges blackened with age. It was also clear that the door had been fairly recently treated with linseed oil as the rich oak wood gleamed a little in the sun.

Simon avoided the pretty red, yellow and bottle green diamond – shaped panes, peering through a collection of distorted but reasonably clear ones. The cottage walls were unfinished fieldstone with a traditional open beam ceiling. A large hospitable fireplace was built into the north side. He could well imagine a main room – snug and warm against the sea winds – filled with horse brasses and comfortable, simple wooden furniture. Currently though, it seemed to have been pressed into service as a potting shed and general catch – all as if massive Palliser Park didn't have enough room to store all of the missing Templar treasure and then some.

There would be two or three rooms up some solid stone stairs he saw in the center of the cottage. Simon wondered if the upper floor was sound. If it was seriously on the point of collapse, that might explain why FitzRobert hadn't turned the Tudor cottage into a picturesque way station for guests with an interest in the dock.

Colonel Lee knickered behind him as if greeting a newcomer and pulled back slightly on his reins. Simon turned away from the stone cottage, spotting two riders exiting the same beach path. As they neared, he saw that it was Brabinger on a sturdy strawberry roan and a young girl of about thirteen on a grey cob – presumably his fabled daughter.

"What ho!" said Simon, leading Colonel Lee back to the path. "You've caught me out."

Colonel Lee knickered again as his stablemates drew up. The stocky horse took a step forward and extended his neck with another soft rumble. Simon patted the bay shoulder affectionately. Knowing that the honest, kind gelding had found peace and pasture friends made a sojourn to Palliser Park worthwhile.

"Your Lordship! Is everything all right?" asked Brabinger, pulling up and automatically glancing over Colonel Lee with a practiced, knowledgeable eye.

"Perfectly. I just wanted a gander at this wonderful old structure." Simon beamed at the pretty thirteen year old girl. He could tell by her soft hands on the reins and solid lower leg that she was a fine rider. That went a long way with him.

She beamed back at him. "Lovely, isn't it? Terribly haunted too!"

Brabinger snorted, sounding like one of his horses. "Haunted, my old Aunt May! Your Lordship, this is my daughter, Meg. She is of a fanciful nature."

"Oh, Dad," Meg laughed and then sobered as her father threw her a stern look. "Your Lordship," she said in a serious tone.

"I prefer *Major* actually," Simon replied before he put his left foot in the stirrup and swung back up on the big bay gelding. "Glad to make your acquaintance, Miss Brabinger. You clearly ride beautifully, I might add."

The girl blushed with appreciation. "Meg, please – Major."

"We thought we'd get the rest of the riding horses out for a stretch before all the fuss starts," said Brabinger, gathering his reins as the bored roan jigged sideways. "This is Jove – Lord FitzRobert's. Paid the earth for him. He's got a mouth of iron and no manners."

Like his owner, Simon was tempted to say but judiciously kept the *bon mot* to himself.

Meg laughed again. "We call him Jade in the family."

"Betty, the cob belongs to Lady Constance," Brabinger added as he tried to square up the pushy, fretting roan, "who rarely rides her."

Simon nodded and knew his honesty would be appreciated. "Unsurprised. She really can't ride down to the letterbox – just among the three of us, of course."

They both laughed, nodding in tacit agreement. Meg picked up her reins as Jove tracked sideways, nearly bumping Betty. The roan spun on his hindquarters and pirouetted away. Colonel Lee lifted his head and watched almost incredulously as if he couldn't believe his stablemate would be so rude.

"Will you ride back with us?" asked the stable manager before he gave Jove a warning tap of his spur. The roan snorted in annoyance but stayed in one place, chastised for the moment.

"Thank you. I will." Simon leaned forward and patted the Colonel's neck. "My wife will be looking for me by now."

"You wouldn't want to miss the breakfast, Major," said Meg as they pushed off together on Lord FitzRobert's perfectly kept property path. "They really lay it on for guests."

Simon smiled, hoping it came across as if he cared about elaborate breakfasts. "Tell me about this little house. Is it really haunted?"

The teenager lit up at the notion. "Oh, yes! I've seen things myself."

"Called Clara Mare Cottage," her father interjected as he jogged next to a placid Colonel Lee. "I'm told it was always a gamekeeper's domain in the Tudaburghs' time. His Lordship intends to renovate it as some sort of foul weather station for the dock or some such nonsense."

"Bright Sea Cottage," said Simon, thinking that some sort of a crew available to aid fishing boats or sailing yachts in trouble near the inlet wasn't a *terrible* idea and might upsticks the FitzRobert reputation with the locals. "Why is it supposed to be haunted?"

"The usual Wuthering Heights romantic rubbish. A gamekeeper – supposedly in the early 18th century – had a beautiful wife who used to spend many nights alone at Clara Mare while he tracked poachers or something. According to legend, one night during a big storm, she was menaced by a privateer or a highwayman or disgruntled poacher – it varies depending on who's telling the tale – and fell to her death trying to elude the villain on the cliffs. The gamekeeper – distraught at his wife's tragic end – dropped into a deep depression and hurled himself from the cliffside."

"That's why you can see ghost lights bobbing around the house or the cliffs at night," piped up Meg cheerfully. "Some say it's her. Some say it's him. Some say it's both and they're forever searching for each other."

"And you've seen this?" Simon had warmed to ghost stories. He'd seen strange things in the trenches of Europe. Things he couldn't fully explain. Chesterton's *The Everlasting Man* with its examination of the mysteries of faith and God's intelligence had come to mean a lot to him – had gotten him through some very tough days. *There are more things in heaven and earth, Horatio than are dreamt of in your philosophy* – and all that.

Brabinger shook his head. "Don't encourage her."

"Dad!" Meg pretended to be scandalized by his lack of seriousness. "You know both mum and I have seen the ghost lights."

Her father looked sour. "You see where she gets it. Not from me."

"Major, you just ask my mum," said Meg. "We see them all the time – well, at least, quite a few times. More often in the summer."

"Imagine that,' Brabinger laughed, "good weather brings out ghost lights. Almost as if footmen and maids were nipping out to meet each other for no good purpose."

To her credit, Meg accepted his theory with good grace. She shrugged with a giggle and admitted there might be some truth to clandestine servant activity. Simon thought about Polly Piety and wondered if she had ever met the mysterious fiancé by Clara Mare Cottage. Like the gamekeeper's wife, she had fallen to her death. Did Polly now haunt the roofline of Palliser

Park?Her essence reduced to a luminous orb that bobbed along on the night wind. Would God allow such a melancholy fate?

No, Simon decided with a clarity that surprised him, God would not. Whether servant or supernatural, Palliser Park's ghost lights were something entirely different.

CHAPTER

23

Alice was unsurprised to find Simon gone. He rode every morning at dawn in good weather and bad. Sometimes she went with him but also understood that time on his own was a restorative for her husband. He needed to be left alone in peace.

The weather outside their guest room windows looked surprisingly bright after the heavy storm of the prior night. It might be lovely to get out and take a walk around the extensive property, perhaps even get down to the beach. Fizz promised that the trek down to the sand was a perfect breeze now that her father had extensively groomed the trail. Alice admitted to herself that getting away from the main house would feel freeing. She now regretted her enthusiasm for a short summer holiday by the sea. Instead of a relaxing break, their Palliser Park sojourn was proving to be a cavalcade of automobile and human accident.

Still … Alice had to smile as she rinsed her toothbrush at the peerless modern sink in their peerless guest bathroom, they had spent the sort of night together that seemed to promise that the old Simon – the pre – war Simon – could return to her. Maybe Palliser Park would turn out to be an important marker on the road back for her husband. A final destination that offered laughter, joy and hope with lots of optimism tossed in.

She dressed carefully – a pretty cotton blouse with modish Oriental embroidering onthree quarter length sleeves and a high – waisted full skirt of celadon green. It was light and airy without being too casual for Lord FitzRobert's red – letter day of welcoming esteemed guests. Fizz and Perry's father was notoriously snotty on the topic of Americans. He'd be privately incredulous that the Marquess of Tash's son would marry a Yank because Castle Fairlight didn't require an infusion of American money. The Marquessate of Tash was one of most solidly fixed in Britain. Historically regarded as quiet, hardworking and wise, the Tash Marquesses had shepherded their considerable resources through prosperous and lean times, building both vast agrarian interests and canny investments. Hence the Marquess and his heir, Viscount Blayloch were decidedly *not* on the constant lookout for flush American debutantes whose pin money could be counted on to repair the roof. Indeed, Simon's older brother, Phineas, had married a country vicar's daughter who brought no money of her own to Castle Fairlight. They'd met at the South of England Hound Show and never looked back, sharing a passion for foxhounds and foxhound bloodlines.

Alice wondered how Phineas and Hazel were getting along with their two litters of hounds. With an outcropping of Welsh foxhound, the new puppies were growing into lighter, faster hounds than the traditional Peterborough type. Hazel had explained how the Welsh infusion could also produce exceptional brains and how excited she was to see the puppies move into the field one day. They'd be puppy walking, Alice decided. Getting the young ones ready for cubbing season.

Homesickness for her English family and comfortable, familiar environs washed over her. She'd rather be helping to walk Hazel's puppies and taking naughty Orson out for a run to the village. Why had she ever thought Fizz's party and Palliser Park would be a good idea? Even the concept of breakfast with its possibility of running into Prince Andrei upset her system and made her stomach ache with stress.

Feeling thoroughly unsettled, Alice emerged from their guest quarters. She could sensePalliser Park gearing up for Fizz and Jack's party. Maids were running around, getting rooms ready for very important guests who were arriving from further afield and expected to have a bed for the weekend. Somewhat lesser invitees – what Fizz called *the overflow* – would be put up at the village inn. It was a monumental undertaking.

She had married Simon in May 1914. War was looming so austerity and restraint were guiding principles for all social occasions. They had a small wedding at The Guards' Chapel attended by immediate family and Simon's fellow officers. A frothy white dress was not considered suitable for such sober times. Instead, she had worn an indigo blue walking suit made of a very fine silk faille and a flat crowned hat with a wide rakish brim. Simon had worn his long Royal Cavalry frock coat – a state of *undress* rather than formal dress – in keeping with the austere nature of the ceremony. The chapel with the walls and ceiling lined with standards and colours – many bearing damage and blood from historic battles going back centuries – informed them both what they were doing was important, sacred and genuinely, not to be entered into lightly.

No elaborate honeymoon either. They had spent their first night as man and wife in a staunchly Victorian suite aboard the Royal Scotsman train headed for Braemar and the Highland

Games. A colorful gathering of Scottish music, dance and sport had provided them both some careless joy before Simon needed to return to his regiment.And yet, Alice reflected as she wandered down Palliser Park's lesser guest vein to the main artery where truly important visitors such as His Imperial Highness and the Alastair Rothermores were billeted, despite all the vitality of the games, there was melancholy drifting over the event.The Scots were expecting war. There was a tacit understanding that some of the brilliant young men who so proudly showed off their best might never return to Scotland and, in turn, their proud families would know grief. What was profoundly sad – in hindsight – was that none of them: English, Scots or Welsh knew just how bad the *War to End All Wars* was going to be and the exorbitant price it would exact.

"What ho, Alice," said Perry as she came around the corner into the main hallway. The young FitzRobert was standing next to the portrait of the fascinating Lord Edwin Darnaway. He waved at her. "Going down to the feed trough?"

"Thought I might, yes," Alice replied, pushing memories of the Highland Games away. She took in Perry's somewhat odd location next to the Georgian painting and noted his passing interest in two maids who emerged from Prince Andrei's borrowed lair, carrying a load of bedding and empty wine bottles, "To be honest, you look up to something."

"Do I?" He grinned as she crossed over to join him. "Fizzy's still asleep. She won't be up for hours – too much champagne and constabulary. Dad's marching about, barking orders at the servants because everything has to be intimidatingly perfect."

"Isn't this Prince Volkonsky's turf?" she asked with a shudder. Her stomach turned a bit at the notion.

"It is." Perry glanced up and down the hallway. Various servants were moving through on their appointed quests.

"You waiting to escort him down to bacon and eggs?"

Perry laughed, his handsome face lighting up with the effort. "I wouldn't escort His Imperial Highness to his own funeral although I might privately hoist a cup of cheer."

"Why are you hanging about his lair?" Alice was surprised to find herself lowering her voice. If Prince Volkonsky was lolling about in his digs, she didn't want to alert him to their immediate presences. "He might come out any second."

"The prince isn't here. He left late last night – took Dad's Sunbeam 4 liter Tourer – heading for his doctor in London. His cold took a turn for the worse apparently."

"Oh, no!" breathed Alice, feeling as if a weight had lifted from her shoulders. "Do you think he might die?" She kind of regretted how hopeful she sounded.

"Dad's irritated. He wanted to show off his Russian toy prince tonight. His Imperial Highness did promise to be back for the actual party." Perry pushed his tortoiseshell spectacles up on his nose. "So do you want to have a look?"

"A look?"

Perry cocked his head towards the Russian prince's lair. "Been waiting for the servants to clear off. Don't you want to see if he's got a few Faberge eggs lying about?"

"You mean rummage through his belongings?" Alice flashed on the memory of Prince Volkonsky in Simon's wardrobe. "Perry, I'm surprised at you. Your father would be scandalized."

Perry looked delighted. "He would, wouldn't he? Listen, I just want to get a look at his piano score. He's been working on it for an age. Dying to find out if it's as rubbish as I think it must be."

"Perry, I don't think you should …"

"Oh, don't be a wet blanket." He grabbed her wrist and yanked. "Fortune favors the brave!"

Alice yelped as she stumbled after Lord FitzRobert's musically inclined son into the guest room of an exiled Russian aristocrat. Once Perry stopped pulling her along as if she wasOrson being escorted away from a plot of fresh grass, she had a moment to take in just what a top drawer Palliser Park visitor could expect. An echo of the great house itself – His Imperial Highness' hidey – hole was palatial, with sweeping views of the sea from a massive bank of windows. The furnishings were equally massive – high Rococo, Louis XV giltwood with lashings of ice blue satin, Calacatta marble and Greek statuary – presenting an almost overwhelming vista of luxurious comfort. The main room was so vast that a grand piano sitting in the furthermost corner didn't seem particularly large or out of place.

Palliser Park upstairs maids had done an excellent job. Alice could well imagine that Prince Volkonsky was a slovenly house guest who expected household staff to pick up his discarded clothes and meal trays. In his brief absence and despite other pressing assignments, they had managed to return his rooms to peerless condition. Everything looked polished, placed properly and thoroughly clean. She could smell lemon and beeswax. It was a combination of scents that always relaxed her. Something she remembered from her childhood – coming home from an afternoon walk with her nanny to take a nap in a pretty nursery that smelled fresh and clean.

Although the room was cleaned and readied, it was clear that the Russian prince was still in long – term residence. Beyond the piano, an ornate Louis XV desk was loaded with a mahogany Victor Victrola gramophone, stacks of wax recordings, papers and a cobalt blue Sevres vase with a small Russian Imperial flag planted in it.

"We really should be on our way," said Alice, feeling anxious about invading Volkonsky's room. She had the feeling he'd be unbearable if he ever came to learn of their encroachment. "I'm hungry."

"Hang on, Alice," Perry murmured as he made a direct line for the gleaming piano. "I've just got to view the great composition. This moving anthem of Russian pride and grief. I'm sure Chopin and his Polish dances should just step aside …"

He bent over the keyboard, sifting through the various scores on the music rest. "Satie, Scriabin … what – no Volkonsky? No tortured notes? No overused martial motifs?"

"Heap of papers over here," advised Alice. She crossed to the Rococo deskto admire the gleaming gramophone. It was a beautifully made thing – mahogany box, polished brass workings and an onyx bell hand painted with Art Nouveau vines and flowers. Fiendishly expensive especially for a penniless Russian aristocrat. Alice wondered if Lord FitzRobert or some starry – eyed, hopeless romantic moved by His Imperial Highness' tragic exile had acquired the gramophone. The thought made her feel mean – spirited. She didn't like Prince Volkonsky but losing everything from family members to property, position and means had to be devastating. Relying on the charity of individuals such as Lord FitzRobert would only add to brutality of his situation. Little wonder he lost himself in alcohol. Alice resolved to be more forgiving but even as she made the pledge, she found herself making a sour face. He was just so awful.

"More Scriabin," said Perry, flipping through the stack of sheet music. "Rimsky – Korsokov ... Borodin. The Mighty Five are all accounted for."

"The Mighty Five?"

Perry looked up from the desk and sighed slightly. It was clear that explaining the intricacies of serious music to the less enlightened was nothing new to him. "Five important 19th century Russian composers. Mily Balakirev, Cesar Cui, Modest Mussorgsky, Nikolai Rimsky – Korsakov and Alexander Borodin. In the 1860s they banded together to produce a kind of national style of Russian music."

Alice nodded. "Tchaikovsky didn't make the club?"

"Too influenced by Western music. You know what's not here?" He dropped the score he had been examining back on the pile and sighed again. "The Big *Six*. Where's the masterwork of Prince Andrei Volkonsky?"

She laughed out loud. "Obviously he took it with him. Too valuable to leave out in the open where the Philistine sons of wealthy men could scoop it up."

"You wound me," Perry said with a laugh of his own.

A dry cough came from behind them. "If I might be so bold, sir," came Crumpling's excruciatingly polite tones. "I would remind you that breakfast has been laid out in the second dining room."

They both slowly turned to face the loyal retainer who stood just inside the doorway. His craggy face was inscrutable, but Alice had the distinct impression that the butler was both dismayed and displeased by their foray into a guest's quarters. She couldn't fault him for that.

"Yes," said Perry, pretending to find his spectacles in need of a polish. "Thank you, Crumpling. We shall go down directly."

Alice cleared her throat. "I ... I just wanted to admire the prince's ... um, gramophone. It's lovely."

"There is a very handsome and highly similar phonograph in the music room, Your Ladyship," Crumpling replied, unfazed and unforgiving. "Recordings encompassing a wide variety of musical styles and tastes are to be found there as well."

"Of course," she said in a dry voice. "Thank you."

Like naughty children, she and Perry filed out under the watchful eye of Lord FitzRobert's perfect butler. Once free of the prince's rooms, Alice reached out and slugged Perry.

"Ouch!" he cried, rubbing his upper arm. "There is no need for your brutal American gangster style violence."

"Told you it was a bad idea." She laughed at his look of mock indignation.

"It's never easy when one searches out greatness." Perry shook his head. "I will not rest until I can feast upon the glories of ..."

"Maybe you can talk Prince Volkonsky into playing it at the party – a gift for the happy couple and all that."

"You interest me strangely." He raised his eyebrows, considering her notion. "How could he refuse?"

"How could he refuse indeed," Alice agreed. "Fizz and Jack will never forgive you though."

"That is a trifling matter if rare genius is unleashed upon an unsuspecting world."

Alice let out a laugh and broke into a run. "Race you to the second dining room!"

CHAPTER

24

After he had thoroughly rubbed down Colonel Lee and put the amiable gelding back in his stall, Simon nipped over to the main house. He headed for the second best dining room, noting as he went that Palliser Park was a veritable hive of activity. Servant drones buzzed hither and yon, attempting to fulfill Lord FitzRobert's persnickety vision of the perfect country house weekend. Although they had undoubtably been cleaning the massive house for the last week, they were still doing the final dusting, putting reams of fresh flowers into immaculate vases on an army of tables and organizing a king's ransom of food and expensive drinks worthy of Henry VIII's birthday. The next two days would be a real test of the staff's mettle. British households were really just beginning to return to elaborate social events and a new, younger servant class would have to learn how such things were accomplished.

Simon paused to allow one of the footmen to pass by with a basket of dishes unimpeded. Then he stepped across the dining room threshold, immediately assessing the various presences and more importantly – as a veteran of trench warfare – all available exits. The wonderful Alice sat next to Perry FitzRobert and they were grinning at each other about something. Lord FitzRobert stood at the sideboard, shoveling a heap of scrambled egg onto his plate. The Rothermores were across the table from Alice, sipping tea, looking vaguely ill at ease as if they'd grown tired of Palliser Park's grandeur and longed to be back home in less elevated surroundings. Simon thought they were on to something.

"Ah," said FitzRobert, glancing up from the collection of silver serving dishes. His gimlet gaze took in the boots and breeches with almost a shade of disapproval. "You've been to the stable."

"No better place to be in all the world," replied Simon. He smiled at Alice, who was beaming in his general direction.

Alastair Rothermore hoisted a goblet of orange juice in salute. "Well said, sir."

"Was it a good ride?" asked his wife, Edith. She also smiled at Alice as if to indicate she fully understood husbands with all consuming diversions such as riding or collecting brass rubbings.

"Splendid. Glorious views of the sea," said Simon. Suddenly very hungry, he moved across the dining room to make an assault on the breakfast dishes but made a point to pause by Alice first to pat her shoulder. "Morning, darling."

His wife looked up at him, her good mood evident in a bright, affectionate smile. "I was hoping to walk down to the beach – does the weather look as if it will hold?"

"I think so. At least for today…"

"I do hope you rode Jove," interrupted Lord FitzRobert as he selected a number of sausages. "He's top notch. Tattersalls, you know."

"I look forward to sitting on Jove," he lied, never having cared for hard – mouthed horses that would pull his arms from the sockets.

"Top notch," FitzRobert repeated and added a grilled tomato to his plate.

Simon left Alice's side to secure his own plate. Time to secure some basic information. "Bit thin on the ground," he said, affecting some surprise. "Would have expected everyone to be lining up for a hearty breakfast after the events of last night. I know I'm absolutely famished."

"Constance won't be up for hours." Perry made a horrified face. "Hardly a surprise, I realize."

"Jack's already up and out. We saw him heading out for a walk. Said he needed to clear his head before things got exciting," Alice offered. "He did look awfully distracted."

Lord Rothermere snorted. "Upcoming nuptials will do that to a man."

"His Imperial Highness has gone to see a doctor for his cold," volunteered Edith Rothermore, pleased to have useful information. "Apparently very poorly indeed."

Simon thought DI Saxby wouldn't be best pleased by the Russian toddling off before the investigation into poor Polly Piety's death was complete. If his instincts about Polly's schoolgirl coat of arms being Russian were correct, there was a strong possibility that His Imperial Highness could become the next reigning prime suspect.

Alastair Rothermore started to laugh but seemed to remember his host's fondness for the highly strung aristocrat. He pretended to cough instead.

"No Miss Brier either?" Simon added a short sigh to punctuate the observation, "And I was so looking forward to talking about her Lady MacBeth."

Lord FitzRobert turned away from the sideboard with his heaping plate. "Dorothy is also not at her best. She has decided to spend the day resting before dinner with our guests this evening."

"Very wise," said Simon.

He made his selections as the Rothermores engaged Perry with questions about the beach walk. Like Alice, they seemed determined to trek down to the sea. The arrival of the FitzRobert guests interested him more. If *DerGrabrauber* was focusing on Palliser Park, a weekend filled with milling guests and special events was an ideal opportunity to strike. On the continent, five were dead – three of the victims were members of their country's Reparations tribunal. In Britain, Sir John Redgrave and Colonel Sir Anselm Finch were part of Britain's Reparations Committee. It was hard not to argue that an attempt was being made to delay or halt proceedings that wouldculminate in Germany having to pay hugely for starting the War to End All Wars. Operatives in France – now also dead – had begun to relay information about a mysterious German or Germans they nicknamed *Grabrauber* who seemed, phantom – like, to slip in and out of intelligence zones, causing havoc and death but never leaving any metaphorical fingerprints. They called this phantom *The Gravedigger* because of the workmanlike simplicity of the murders – – written off as unfortunate accidents until the pattern of membership in reparations became clear. At Palliser Park, there were two Reparations Committee members in Lord FitzRobert and Alastair Rothermore, MP.

Was it possible that The Gravedigger was aware of his attachment to MI6 or was the Meredith and Sons lorry a bit of spy game serendipity – a genuine accident within an "accident"? Simon took his breakfast to the table and sat down next to his wife, who offered him a welcoming smile. He had a number of goals for the upcoming weekend, none involving frivolous fun by the seaside. Most important was Alice. He'd give up Lord FitzRobert to *Der Grabrauber* without a twinge of remorse to keep Alice safe. It was fortunate, Simon reflected as he sipped his own goblet of orange juice, that the murderous Teutonic Will O'the Wisp could not know that.

CHAPTER

25

Alice sipped her coffee. It was, she reflected, the last relative quiet before the wedding celebration. There would be another ornate dinner for Palliser Park visitors. A chance for those who came from far afield to greet those they knew and meet those they didn't. A general girding up for Saturday night as Fizz and Jack's engagement party – a ball really – would be, of course, be the weekend pinnacle. The Mount Everest of heavy hors d'oeuvres, French champagne andBritish spirits, dance orchestras, after dinner speeches and desserts drowning in heavy cream.

"You would like to hike down to the beach?" asked Simon, reaching out to pat her forearm lightly.

"Is it really a hike?" She had imagined it was a relatively simple gambol down to welcoming sand and brightly colored folding deck chairs.

Simon glanced over at Lord FitzRobert, who had settled next to Mrs. Rothermore and was telling her about his preference for some entity called The Carleton Club. "This is a substantial property," he said, pointedly lowering his voice to a murmur. "It's a fair walk. The full beach front itself is probably two miles long and has a dock large enough to welcome the biggest sailing yachts."

"Well, I'm going," Alice announced. The idea of being a substantial distance from all the bustle in the house was too tempting to be resisted. "I could use a good solid walk." She leaned in and whispered, "Just out of curiosity, what is the Carleton Club?"

Her husband looked amused at her question. "All Tory chums. Very political, very powerful."

"Oh," she said, envisioning politicos gathering to discuss arcane cricket rules and economic policy. Her own father had enclaves in Washington that he visited on occasion. "Hoisting excellent brandies and firming up the political platform."

"Exactly. Listen, darling – I'd love to amble along with you but I do need to have a word with DI Saxby first. Do you mind waiting a bit?"

Alice smiled and nodded. "I'm A – okay for later, Alligator."

She was delighted when he laughed out loud and dropped a kiss on her left temple. It was exhilarating to see Simon come to life – as if a silvery apparition suddenly took on the rich hues and dimensions of a real person. Maybe the trip to Palliser Park had been a positive decision after all.

Perry, who had been wolfing down an enormous portion of fried tomatoes, suddenly leaned their way. "I'm on chauffeur duty – ferrying guests from the village inn. Do either of you need anything from the tuck shop? They do carry a pretty decent range of tobacco."

Simon surprised her by asking if Perry might check and see if a telegraph from Mr. Spinner might be waiting for him at the post office.

"Telegraph? Surely Palliser Park has a telephone," she said and looked at Perry for confirmation.

Young FitzRobert shook his head. "Such modern conveniences have yet to fully reach the Essex coast – at least to private houses. Dad is demanding Brightsea step things up, of course and in fairness, he has offered a huge sum to assist. There are a couple of operating telephones in the village but those go out every time there's a storm so nobody is really too excited about the idea. You have service at the castle though – – *think* I remember that from my last visit."

"Castle Fairlight has, yes," replied Simon, reaching for his tea cup. "One below stairs and one in my father's study. He dislikes the notion of the party line intensely. All the different rings. Fortunately, as with Brightsea, no one in the area is much fussed much about the telephone so calls are blessedly few."

Perry glanced over at his father, who was currently discussing the next by – election and then pushed away from the table. "Anyway, I'm off shortly to the village. Dad wants everyone to arrive early so they can explore and fully appreciate the place."

"Any of them be arriving by sea?" asked Simon.

"You know, I think Sir George Jasper is bringing his yacht round. He's a keen sailor."

In her mind's eye Alice brought up memories of crossing paths with Sir George Jasper at various London social events. He was a handsome, charismatic individual – a natural politician who was keenly aware of the *best people* and keen to make propitious connections. Sir George didn't have a tremendous tug to make Simon – the second son of a politically unambitious marquess – one of his favored pals. However, the daughter of one of America's most prosperous industrialists was another matter altogether. Whenever Sir George spotted her, he was delighted to take up their acquaintance and tell her all he knew.

She suppressed a grin, seeing a sour expression skitter across her husband's face and disappear behind his grey eyes. Those eager to scale Disraeli's infamous greasy pole were not among his preferred company.

"Anyone else?" asked Simon, his tone light with the curiosity of small talk at table.

Perry stood up, snagging a piece of toast to eat on his way. "Not sure. We're not really boat – y people despite, you know, living here. We don't even have a boat." He threw a glance at his father, who was still in conversation with the Rothermores. "Yet."

He laughed and stepped away from the table. "See you both when the yoke of duty has been removed."

"Bye, Perry," said Alice. "Hope the weather holds."

"You and me both!" The young FitzRobert took a bite of his spare toast and headed for the door, saluting his father good – naturedly before he disappeared into the great beyond of Palliser Park.

Alice turned her attention back to Simon, who was spearing some scrambled egg. "Crumpling is miffed at me."

She saw his left eyebrow rise incredulously. "How could that noble steward possibly be miffed at you?" Simon asked before eating his egg.

"Perry talked me into riffling through Prince Volkonsky's room – by the way, it's very grand with blue satin, heaps of giltwood, piano and a fancy gramophone …"

Simon put down his fork and regarded her with displeasure. "You mustn't go anywhere near that drunken lout. He's lucky to be off seeing a wretched doctor or I'd have broken his nose by now."

"Crumpling caught us so no worries."

Her husband almost laughed. "Well played, Crumpling."

CHAPTER
26

Simon found DI Saxby on the wide steps leading to Palliser Park's impressive entrance. The young detective was directing his constable to find Crumpling and get the butler to sort out prospective servants of interest for an interview.

"Major Fairlight," said Saxby as Simon approached.

"Call me Simon. We're brothers in arms."

The DI offered him a tired smile. "Artemis Nyx Saxby. My parents were thoroughly convinced that I was going to be a girl – my father is a classics scholar at Cambridge – and failed to create a Plan B. My friends call me Nyx."

"Muster must have been hell." Simon winced.

Saxby let out a laugh. "Fortunately, most of the lads were *not* classics scholars. I went through the war as Artie."

"Fancy trappings did tend to fall to the wayside," Simon laughed as well and then his tone turned more sober. "I'd be curious to learn what you made of His Imperial Highness."

DI Saxby's handsome face looked sour. "High – handed prat. His grasp of English suddenly became more elusive. The Russian accent almost undecipherable. He managed to get across that he had been very ill and confined to his rooms. Seemed clear to me that he was mainly treating his illness with strong drink. His illness and lack of movement outside his guest room was confirmed by Lord FitzRobert and Crumpling. Why? You have other news on that front?"

"No," Simon admitted, realizing there was no actual value for a policeman in what he had to say. "Volkonsky just strikes me as the sybaritic type that might enjoy seducing extremely pretty servants."

"I would love nothing better than to arrest Prince Volkonsky for something, anything." Saxby stared out at the azure sea in the distance, mulling over Simon's idea. "He was in his room, playing the piano, when Polly fell. Crumpling brought me two upstairs maids who verified they'd heard him pounding away on the keys. Apparently, His Imperial Highness has been lolling about the place for an age now and driving the servants round the bend with his music."

"Pity. On second thought, Prince Volkonsky is too lazy to be bothered with the likes of servant girls." Simon held up a hand to indicate the lower steps. "Can I have a word? Away from the ears of this accursed house."

The Brightsea detective followed Simon down the steps. "Admit to being quite intrigued," he said once they'd moved a pace from the main house. "Is this going to be revelation from the Secret Intelligence Service?"

Simon almost started at the question. DI Artemis Saxby was even brighter than he had given him credit for – and he had assessed DI Saxby as a very clever, very competent investigator. "Why, Nyx," he said lightly, "I'm not sure where you would ..."

"You're *on the job* at Palliser Park," Saxby interrupted without any irritation. He just sounded amused. "Anything involving Lord FitzRobert, arms manufacturer, has to be in the sphere of national security."

Simon had to smile. He very much liked Saxby and had the keen idea that Kell might be wise to recruit the detective. They could use a network of the highly intelligent and battle hardened.

"There have been five killings – three on the continent and two here in England," Simon said, tacitly verifying DI Saxby's assumption about the SIS. "All men connected to the Allied Reparations Committee."

"Delaying the inevitable?"

Simon nodded, grateful for Saxby's acute perception. "There appears to be a German underground. Possibly remnants of their professional military class working together to disrupt post – war plans for the German state. One of them – it could also be a small team, mind – is a particularly adept assassin known as The Gravedigger."

"Lord FitzRobert is on the Reparations Committee, isn't he?" The detective coughed suddenly and then paused to take in a long breath of the rich sea – scented air. "Sorry – I took a little mustard gas over there … you might know how that is."

"I do," Simon murmured. He felt a real pang of sympathy for the young policeman. Castle Fairlight's family physician assured him that his lungs would recover eventually from the damage they had incurred from gassing but he wasn't so sure. "MP Alastair Rothermore is also a member of the committee."

Saxby coughed again and didn't reply until he'd had inhaled a few slow breaths. "This is a big weekend for Palliser Park," he said when he could.

"Yes, could be an opportunity for The Gravedigger. Lots of distractions and people. I suspect the removal lorry might have been one method of gaining access to the house or a mistaken attack on what they assumed was Lord FitzRobert's motorcar.

His Sunbeam 4 Liter Tourer and my Crossley are the same color," Simon said as they pushed off again and walked towards FitzRobert's seaward grounds. "Guessing The Gravedigger will try to put a checkmark next to Lord FitzRobert's name this weekend."

"What can Brightsea coppers do to help?" asked DI Saxby.

"We don't fancy one of our local toffs having his ticket punched by a German."

"I'd appreciate you making a right nuisance of yourselves and hanging about, with a weather eye. You know, it's quite possible that I'm wrong about this weekend, but my wife is here and I don't want her in the vicinity of German assassins."

"Understandable." The young detective inspector thought for a moment. "We can certainly drag our feet with the servant interviews. I actually have an invitation to Lady Constance's engagement party. Part of His Lordship deigning to acknowledge local officials. Brightsea's mayor and other minor mandarins will be attending as well."

Simon made a sour face. "FitzRobert must have some improvements he'd like Brightsea to feel pleased about."

"Yes – there is talk that he'd like to encourage sailing events, develop a yachting club or some such piffle. This is a stalwart fishing coast – Cod especially. Yachting seems pretty airy fairy to the locals."

"Wait until they get a look at Sir George Jasper," said Simon, recalling the politician who worked hard at appearing charismatic and approachable. He'd probably glide his sailing yacht next to FitzRobert's expensive new dock, leaping out, attired in the crispest striped blazer and sailing whites ever seen in Great Britain. Naturally, Sir George hadn't served with the Royal Navy. He was too valuable to waste on a destroyer guarding supply routes to the continent. Too valuable to provide support for exhausted allied soldiers. *He was needed at Whitehall.*

Simon held out a hand for the DI to shake. "Thank you being about the place today."

"Thank *you* for the first information drop," said Saxby, grasping Simon's hand firmly. "Not quite sure what to do about it all but we'll keep out an eye out."

"Will you close the book on poor Polly?"

Saxby's handsome face looked regretful. "Probably if nothing presents itself. These below stairs mishaps are notoriously difficult to unpick. The house closes ranks, creating a vacuum. Nobody wants to be the troublemaker or attract unfortunate attention from the employers. The grieving family is given a little offering, presented as a kindness but really a tacit understanding that no further questions need to be asked."

"I hope FitzRobert really coughs up for the Piety family."

"He won't. His ilk never does. He will spend more on cooking sherry this year." The DI took a step back and turned towards the chilly exterior of Palliser Park. "I should get inside to start this time honored tradition."

Simon thought again about how much he liked the young policeman. "Thanks, Nyx," he said, meaning it. "I have to take the wife out for some roadwork. She's absolutely determined to tread on Lord FitzRobert's beach."

CHAPTER

27

Alice was the last one in the dining room. Lord FitzRobert was gone, out to supervise the arrival of other guests. She guessed he really wanted to ensure that any new arrivals would be ushered through the gilded salon and up one of the impressive staircases or perhaps given a ride in the rare private elevator.

Excellent amateur watercolorists, the Rothermores escaped to the garden to do some sketching. Everyone else not employed by the FitzRobert family seemed to be still abed, resting up for the weekend of engagement events. She sipped her coffee and thought about her own day ahead. A long stroll, exploring the beach with a packed lunch — no need to be back at the main house for hours.

"Oh," came Dorothy Brier's voice, "it's you."

Alice looked from her coffee cup to see the actress sliding across the threshold, attired in a pleated cream colored skirt and matching blouse in a nautical design. She looked every inch the visiting queen of London's stages — expensive and sophisticated. An exquisite four — strand pearl choker graced her pale, swan — like neck. A little flashy for a morning costume, perhaps, but it did take away any cutesy quality that nautical fashion sometimes suffered from – Dorothy's looked grown – up and sleek.

"The dreary American – that's me," said Alice brightly – a cheer she did not feel welling up at the sight of the famous actress.

"I apologize for that misplaced remark," Dorothy replied as she headed for the sideboard to presumably cobble together remnants from the silver salvers for breakfast. "I was overwrought at seeing Jack. We are old friends."

"Clearly," Alice said and wondered if Lord FitzRobert had urged the actress to mend fences with those he thought might be useful. It wasn't that a minor Lady Fairlight had any genuine potential but her father, Jared Faraday – American industrialist and rumored future ambassador to the Court of St. James – most definitely had loads. She got up to leave, wishing to avoid further revelations if Dorothy Brier was feeling the yen to confide any.

"Your husband is a piece of work." The actress turned away from scraping scrambled egg onto her plate. "How ever do you put up with it."

Alice straightened her spine. "He's a good friend."

"And then some. Tell him I have bruises from last night." Dorothy Brier moved away from the sideboard, towards a chair. "Bastard."

Alice was very rarely struck for words but she just gaped at the actress whose famous face glimmered with condescension.

"Well, I … um, " Alice tried to formulate a reply but her brain wouldn't cooperate. Simon had left actual bruises on Dorothy Brier?

The actress set her plate down and reached up to her pearl collar as if to unlatch it. "Would you like to see? I'm hiding some of them under this."

Before Alice could cobble together a response to the incredible offer, a voice came from the doorway.

"I would," came Simon's voice. He sounded bright and interested. "Let's have a look, shall we?"

Alice watched Dorothy Brier freeze. She lowered her arms. "*You* don't need to see my neck," Dorothy said.

"Oh, but Alice does," Simon said, crossing from the threshold to the second dining room's gleaming walnut table. "You were so counting on my wife making an embarrassed break for it."

"It's all right," interjected Alice, horrified. " I really don't need to ..."

"My point is made." Simon smiled at the actress. "Do you need help with the catch?"

Dorothy squirmed, shrugging her shoulders as if she could hide from Simon. "Right then," she said finally, turning to look at Alice. "I may have overblown the notion of bruises. Wanted some revenge."

"Revenge?" asked Alice, mortified at being center in the actress' machinations. "Simon is a good friend to Jack and Fizz."

The actress glared at them both. "He's a bully! These military types are always bullies."

"Come along, Alice," said her husband, holding out his hand. "Let's find your beach. The weather is holding for a bit."

Alice fairly flew around the walnut table to join her husband. Rarely was she so eager to exit a room. Escaping the baleful presence of the scorned Dorothy Brier was something she wanted more than almost anything she had ever wanted in her relatively brief life span.

"For the rest of the weekend," said Simon as he offered an elbow to Alice, who took it with the fervor of Titanic passenger seizing a life preserver, "you can add Lady Fairlight to the off – limits list."

"Bullies!" spat Dorothy Brier. "You military sorts are all wretched bullies."

"One has the feeling," said Simon as squired Alice out into the vastness of a Palliser Park hallway, "that Miss Brier has had brush ups with the law in her past."

"A famous actress such as her prickly self?" asked Alice in genuine surprise. "Don't they have to keep a fairly above – board story so as not to offend the more delicate sensibilities of the ticket buyer? The vicar's wife or indeed, the vicar himself?"

Simon laughed. "A story is right. My guess is that Miss Dorothy Brier has, at least, three biographies. One for the public, one for associates in the theatre and one for her social environment – all overlap but don't always agree. I could bet the London Met have a more official one from a couple of decades ago."

Alice envisioned a tired paper folder in a battered file cabinet somewhere in the bowels of a police station. One that might contain arrest reports for all sorts of colorful things. "You mean," she asked, "Dorothy Brier might have been collared for ..."

"I doubt nothing when it comes to Miss Brier," said Simon, squeezing her hand at his elbow. "Did you manage to secure a packed lunch?"

She smiled up at him, thinking it was grand to hear him interested in food again. "And how! One worthy of Palliser Park – Crumpling promised it would be waiting for us down on the beach by a hut or something."

The walk was long but lovely. They followed the same path Simon had taken for his morning ride, strolling down the wide, beautifully manicured lane to the beach itself. Alice found the Essex coastline breathtaking. It was pure nature – wild and riven with sea winds – at odds with the carefully tended byways of Palliser Park. She wondered how soon the sea would take back the curated spaces imposed upon it by Lord FitzRobert.

The tide was out, allowing the beach great berth, dotted with glimmering tide pools.Beyond the sands, the sea was undulating deep blue, fading to a shimmer of silver in the distance. There was something liberating, deeply satisfying about walking by roiling water, hearing the murmur of the ocean and feeling the soft chill of the breeze pull relentlessly at one's hair. Alice was grateful to see Simon relax in the coastline's grasp. He held her hand as they made their way up Palliser Park's substantial private beach, even once, pausing briefly to kiss the top of her fingers. Seemingly, always wary – on alert – since his return from the war, she watched him breathe deeply in the sea air and his gait became less measured, less considered. He walked along carelessly, gazing out to the horizon's whitecaps.

They had just come round a bend in the craggy coast to see a small collection of brightly hued beach huts huddled by a massive new dock with all the sea – going accoutrements needed to welcome sailing craft or fishing boats of various sizes. It was impressive. A tribute to FitzRobert verve and ambition.

"Ahoy! Lunch ahead!" announced Alice, pointing to one of the beach huts – a bright blue one – by which a table had been established and covered with a white tablecloth that was flapping invitingly in the breeze.

"Just the thing – I'm famished." Simon broke into a run and pulled her after him. Laughing, the two half ran, half staggered over the rough, damp sand – surprisingly deep in places – until they reached the vibrant blue beach hut.

One of Palliser Park's young footmen appeared in the hut's open door. He was neatly dressed in trousers and a waistcoat but thankfully, not in full Georgian livery. Apparently even Lord FitzRobert had a standard for over – the – top displays – or Crumpling had quietly rescinded some edicts for the benefit of staff sanity.

Alice was still laughing from a wayward stumble around a clump of seaweed as she collapsed into one of the two chairs laid out for them. Iced water and champagne already placed upon the table by Crumpling's impeccably trained young footman – his name was Albert if her memory was correct. She watched as Simon fell into his own chair, swooped up a crystal goblet of water and settled back to drink it with a satisfied sigh.

"Much posher than a wicker hamper in a dog cart," said Simon, "with Orson in the draws."

Alice felt a pang of homesickness for her beloved ex – military mule. He had helped pull cannon across treacherous battlefields. He'd do anything for a peppermint and affectionate rubs on his over – sized ears.

"But I love him so," she said, picking up her champagne glass in salute. "To Orson!"

Simon lifted his water glass. "The Noble Orson."

The young footman brought out a variety of cold salads, chicken and ham along with some beautifully made French bread. "I apologize for not having a hot meal," he said, clearly anxious, "but Mr. Crumpling said Her Ladyship was adamant about a simple picnic."

"Good heavens, yes," replied Simon throwing Alice a look of approval. "We'd have been happy if you'd tossed us a paper bag with a couple of sandwiches."

Alice saw the footman let out a relieved breath as he refilled their water goblets from a peerless Georgian silver pitcher. "It looks wonderful, Albert. Just what I had hoped for."

Albert bobbed his head, still relieved that the meal had passed muster. He placed some butter on the table and prepared to make a polite retreat to the blue beach hut.

"Both His Lord ... *the Major* and I offer the deepest condolences on the loss of Polly. She helped me for a time and I just liked her so much."

"Thank you, Your Ladyship," the boy said with a catch in his soft voice. "We all loved her, Your Ladyship. She was a kind girl and so ... so ..."

"Pretty?" suggested Alice when the young man seemed at a loss.

Albert smiled. His blue eyes were momentarily distant as he remembered a fellow servant. "Yes – so pretty. Room seemed to brighten when she came into it and not just because Polly was a head – turner."

"I really pity her poor family and her beau if she had one," Alice continued, earning a raised eyebrow from her husband.

"I dunno about a beau," said Albert in his soft drawl. "She talked a bit about one though. A lad who was going to make her a proper wife. We nowt saw one. Mr. Crumpling says her family will be coming to Brightsea to collect her. Mr. Crumpling says His Lordship will do right by them. He's offered Polly a place in the cemetery."

"Very kind," murmured Alice, wondering again just who had been the mysterious man. The one who would have married and elevated Miss Polly Piety.

"Where is the servant cemetery?" Simon leaned back in his chair, gazing out to sea.

"It's behind the old gamekeeper's cottage," Albert said as he moved to refill their water goblets. "Nice place to end up really if you've got no one or your family's bit skint. Good of His Lordship."

After Albert had headed to the blue beach hut in search of cigarettes for Simon, Alice saw her husband pull his attention from the sea and level it in her direction.

"Doing a little detective work?" he asked, his voice less than pleased. "Don't trust the good DI Saxby to thoroughly interrogate the staff?"

She pulled a face at him. "I'm just dying to know who promised to marry that poor girl!"

"Be careful, darling, or you might get your wish."

Alice hadn't thought of that possibility. "You actually think someone might try and bump me off for asking about *him*?"

"Well, presumably Polly got bumped off." Simon winced. "Do Americans really say 'bumped off'?"

"Yep – we also say *bought the farm, cement overshoes, sleeping with the fishes*. We like to laugh at death in the States." Alice waved off his question with an impatient gesture. "So, you're saying DI Saxby thinks Polly was, in fact, murdered?"

Alice watched him sigh. She had the impression that he realized he had said more than he had intended to and was mentally berating himself – that allowing himself to relax had, in turn, made him careless. It was not the outcome she had hoped for with their long afternoon walk.

"I won't say a word to DI Saxby – I promise!" she said.

"You will not and you won't question any staff about Polly. If there is a HE lurking about and if this HE decided to rid himself of a clingy maid, you would be alerting him to both Saxby's investigation and your knowledge of it."

Alice leaned forward and laid a hand on his. "Do you think it's possible that the young besotted Curate Hayter was the one? The one who wanted to marry Polly? Maybe he realized she wouldn't aid his career in the Church."

"Hard to imagine an average Anglican curate slipping into the house, arranging a stealthy rendezvous with the victim on the roof, then successfully giving victim the shove andscampering away – all unseen by a FitzRobert or a FitzRobert servant."

She fell back on her beach chair, deflated. "Does seem improbable, doesn't it?"

"Saxby's really bright and competent. He'll figure it out. Let's stay out of his way and let him."

"If you insist," Alice said, sipping her champagne and still feeling a little flattened. Why shouldn't they try and discover who was Polly's murderer? Lord FitzRobert would want to bury the whole thing – she winced at the unintentional humor – and perhaps, SI Saxby would bow to his pressure.

"I do." Simon saluted her with his water glass, looking amused at her disappointment. "Why don't you tuck into some of Albert's lunch? He dragged it all the way from the main house."

"Good point and I could eat a platter fit for Henry VIII …
Good gravy!"

"*Good gravy?*" Simon's grey eyes glanced over the provided
lunch. "I spy no gravy."

"No!" Alice pointed out to sea.

Around the curve of the beach cliff, a sailing yacht
shimmered into view. A princely three – masted craft with a
glossy black hull and white superstructure. It was glorious –
cutting through the churning white caps like some kind of
obsidian dagger.

Simon turned to take in the vision of nautical beauty. "Ah,
Sir George Jasper has arrived."

CHAPTER

28

Simon leaned back in his beach chair and watched as Sir George Jasper's yacht maneuvered next to Lord FitzRobert's new dock. It was skillfully done, achieved by a crack crew of four. He suspected they were the same professional sailors that had helped Sir George win the Cowes Cup at the Royal Yacht Squadron Club. A bit of a scandal at the time as there was historic *understanding* that only amateurs should crew up for the Cowes Cup. As it had been a tacit understanding, Sir George's win – the club's first cup race after the war – was allowed to stand.

The yacht bore the name Sea Sprite in gold letters on her side. She was as lovely a sailing ship that had ever graced the English waters and Simon imagined the Sea Sprite slipped through the waves like silk. Not that he was a sailor. He was profoundly a landlubber. He'd take a good horse over the Sea Sprite every time, but even a committed horseman could yearn to step aboard a craft such as Sir George's.

As he ate some of Albert's provided cold chicken, a modest entourage of servants from the main house rattled down the beach path in a dog cart pulled by one of Palliser Park's farm horses. The sound of the tall chestnut's tack jingle and jangling had a sharp, bell – like quality in contrast to the deep rumble of the surf.

Lord FitzRobert, Alastair Rothermore, Sir George Jasper – a genuine trifecta if The Gravedigger, who seemed intent on disrupting, delaying or destroying the work of the Reparations Committee, was indeed on the game in Essex. Simon gazed out at the Sea Sprite, seeing Jasper's crew nimbly tie off the lovely ship as the man himself, Sir George Jasper stepped down onto the dock. The politician looked hale and well met. Even at the distance, Simon could tell he was a little flummoxed by the sparse welcoming party. Jasper had misread the warmth of the social contract if he had thought Lord FitzRobert would drop everything, leap aboard a jostling dog cart and make his way down to the dock to look at a magnificent object that he did not, as yet, have anything to rival. He watched as Sir George began to look about the cliffside beach, searching for rescue.

"Three, two, one ..." murmured Simon as Alice flashed him a puzzled look.

"Say!" called out Sir George from the dock. He waved energetically. "Can that be Lord and Lady Fairlight? How good to see you!"

Alice's cornflower blue eyes widened as she understood and belated turned to wave back at Sir George Jasper. "Hello!" she called out, her voice tinged with apology at taking so long to respond. "Care for a cold drink?"

The politician jogged down the massive new dock, floating down its crisp new steps to the beach and leaving the Palliser Park servants to load his weekend kit onto the dog cart.

"A cold drink sounds just the thing," Sir George declared, sailing up to their table as Simon stood up to offer his hand in welcome. "Lord Fairlight – a pleasure, sir!" After shaking

Simon's hand soundly, he turned to offer Alice a short bow. "Lady Fairlight, as lovely as ever."

"You are very kind," she said, holding a hand out to indicate an extra chair. "Please do sit, Sir George."

Simon saw Albert darting out from Lord FitzRobert's beach hut to assist. The young footman jogged across the sand, carrying a silver pitcher of something refreshing. He glanced up and noted the Palliser Park servants who had come with the dog cart, were now trying to hide sighs of frustration. It was a busy, fraught day for the household staff and there had to be enormous pressure to be back at the main house.Now, handcuffed to Sir George's whimsy, they settled in to wait for the illustrious visitor to decide what he wanted to do. Simon saw that the husky chestnut farm horse was bored and fractious at being made to stand on the warm sand.

"Sir George?" he asked as Albert finally reached them with his 18th century silver vessel.

The politician slid into Alice's proffered chair. "At your service, Your ..."

"Simon – please," Simon interrupted without apology. "Would you mind awfully if Albert told the dog cart it can take your belongings to the main house? You could walk back with us if you'd like."

Sir George glanced over his shoulder at the dog cart and its horse pawing irritably at the sand. "Oh, of course!" he replied, reaching for a freshly poured glass of lemonade. "Delighted to take a stroll with the Fairlights."

Simon nodded at Albert, who threw him a grateful look and headed off to alert his fellow servants that they could return to the main house with all of Sir George's baggage.

"Will your beautiful boat be staying all weekend?" asked Alice, earning Simon's admiration for deflecting the politician's attention from the footman's retreat and tacit understanding of what was being done for fellow Palliser Park servants.

"Oh, no – bit dull for the lads," replied Sir George in reference to the four professional sailors who kept the Sea Sprite in top shape. "I've given them leave to take her down south and have a bit of fun. They'll come pick me up on Sunday."

"That was good of you," Alice said, "Would you care for some chicken?"

"Thank you," Sir George watched as Alice skillfully dished up what was left of their picnic offerings. "Not a bad day for a cold lunch, is it? I take it FitzRobert couldn't be bothered with the old hot boxes, eh?"

Simon had a flash of servants lugging the huge wooden and metal hot boxes – so beloved of the Victorians for shooting parties and intervals at the opera – down to the seaside. He pretended to yawn, hiding his dislike of the notion.

"The staff is working very hard at the main house with all the additional people," Simon murmured as Alice deftly set a plate in front of the politician. Then he changed tacks entirely and asked in his brightest voice, "Are you sitting in with His Lordship on this reparations affair? Rummy business, that, eh?"

Sir George turned to look at him with newfound admiration. This was the kind of Westminster exchange that energized an innate pot – stirrer such as Sir George Jasper.

"Quite a thing, isn't it? Deciding how much to punish the wretched Germans." Sir George had another sip of his lemonade and then sat back in his beach chair with the satisfied aura of a man comfortable with his place in the scheme of things. "Do we strip them of everything or do we leave them some crumbs with which to rebuild their nation? You fought them on the frontlines, Simon. What say you?"

Simon saw Alice turn away from her admiration of the Essex sea and gaze at him in interest. He retrieved his cigarette case from a pocket, thinking about Sir George's question for a moment. "As a mere major in the Royal Cavalry, such decisions are beyond my remit, Sir George."

"But you must have an opinion, surely."

Simon closed his eyes for a moment, glimpses of German officers caring for their horses in all the mud, blood, boredom and terror flitting through his memories. "Good lads were out there on both sides," he said finally. "I don't wish to crucify them."

"Well said. I agree. We crucify the Germans now; we will live to regret it." Sir George helped himself to some bread from the communal basket. "Kick Germany while it's down and when it rises again, it will poison Europe with its bile."

Such common sense surprised Simon. He'd have bet money Sir George would have been a member of the Crush Germany brigade. He struck a match, lit his cigarette and inhaled. The tobacco smoke irritated his damaged lungs, but it hardly mattered any more.

"No Lady Stella?" asked Alice, changing the subject. George Jasper had married Stella Stanhope, daughter of the Duke of Danver. Considered the debutante of her year, she was exceptionally beautiful and exceedingly rich. The perfect bride for an ambitious young man.

"Lady Alice reminds us that this is a weekend for happy thoughts. No more talk of Germany," said Sir George, turning to address Alice. "My wife just gave birth to our second child and isn't up to travel, especially on the Sea Sprite. She's resting at home."

"My gosh! You must be over the moon," Alice cried in happy surprise. "Boy or girl?"

Her genuine excitement stabbed at Simon's heart. He knew she would love to have a child of her own and as a wonderfully healthy young American, Alice should have no trouble achieving such a joyous outcome. The fault resided with him. He wasn't a whole person anymore. He was hollow and broken. He had killed and killed and ...

"I'm pleased to say a lovely little girl," replied Sir George Jasper, patting Alice's hand. "We're naming her India. My wife's family lived in that fascinating country for some years and she has fond memories."

Simon stood up. He could see that his sudden movement had taken Alice and Sir George somewhat aback. In the distance, even Albert had spotted his abrupt change in position and was jogging back to see if he could be of assistance. There was no assistance for what ailed him.

"I think we should start back. There's a storm coming."

CHAPTER

29

Alice ran a couple of steps to catch up with her husband who was striding ahead on Lord FitzRobert's beautifully maintained beach path. She slipped her arm under his and Simon slowed to a stop.

"Sorry, Alice," he said.

"Nonsense. We should be getting back. The wind's picking up and Albert was glad to be done." She waved at the dog cart that lumbered some distance ahead of them on the path. The other servants had delayed their return so Sir George, Albert and Albert's lunch hamper could be added to the manifest. Sir George, perched in the back of the large square conveyance, lazily waved in reply.

Alice saw Simon glance away from her, his jaw tightening. He seemed remote – distracted, almost as if he was masking physical pain. She had seen it before and felt keen disappointment flood her thoughts. It was a step backwards. Something had triggered a mental retreat in Simon. He had faded into the wartime ghost.

"I've got my cap set on a long hot soak in that fabulous bathtub," she said in a bright tone. "The wind is really quite sharpish."

Simon turned slightly and gazed out to sea where Sir George Jasper's elegant sailing yacht was underway, heading southward towards a livelier marina. "A storm in coming in."

"Oh, I hope not." Alice followed his gaze. "Fizz is looking forward to dancing on the terrace. I don't see any clouds."

"It'll be a bad one," he replied with a certainly that Alice couldn't understand. As with other incidences of Simon's shell shock, she wasn't even really sure they were still discussing the weather.

They then walked the path that wound and meandered its way to the top of the cliffs. Alice always found Simon's fragile silences difficult, so she tended to chatter in hopes of soaking up awkward lapses. She provided cheery commentary on the seaward views which were, indeed, spectacular. Each time, as she did so, she scanned the horizon for any sign of Simon's impending storm. There were a few impossibly white clouds drifting with the sea wind but not the intimidating towers of grey and black she associated with serious weather. In fact, despite a goodly breeze, the sea looked ready for a painter's version of a perfect summer day. The sun was bright, setting off distant white caps like a scattering of diamonds. Sir George's yacht, the Sea Sprite had almost been swallowed up by distance – its crisp sails glinting occasionally as it arced southward.

Even the afternoon's sound – except for her incessant need to fill aural space – was peaceful from the tide's relentless drum to the tack jingling on the dog cart as it rolled ahead of them. It should be the perfect holiday by the seaside, but it wasn't.

They emerged from Palliser Park's cliffside path to a wide plain on which the majority of the FitzRobert property rested. The view across from the cliffside revealed Palliser Park's various rings in one dramatic line of sight. Formal Georgian great house in the distance surrounded by its acres of important outbuildings, elaborate gardens, a centuries old orchard, a substantial kitchen garden, modern tennis court and brand new pool. Farther out was the wild coastal acreage – open and wind riven as it had been since time began. The anomaly in the visual palate was an odd and ancient cottage that looked as if it had been thrown cliffside by some kind of a fairytale giant. A relic from Palliser Park's original and less ornate age, the place had a quaint, almost daffy charm – leaded glass windows, a wide arched doorway with black iron fittings and miniature turrets on four sides that gave it the look of a Mediaeval castle for garden gnomes.

Simon seemed fascinated with it. He had stopped to stare at the cottage's whimsical visage, studying the upper floor as it might answer some tangled question he had.

When she paused from one of her burbles – a commentary on her dislike of beets or as the British called it, beetroot – to take a breath, Simon pointed to the cottage and said, "Old gamekeeper's place. Clara Mare Cottage. I'm told it's haunted."

"As in an old gamekeeper's ghost? Did he die in a tragic shotgun cleaning accident or maybe bitten by a rabid fox?" Alice winced inwardly. She just wanted to kick herself. Why couldn't she stop babbling? "Who told you? Does he haunt inside or out?"

Simon walked towards the cottage. "Ghost lights," he said over his shoulder.

"Can we go inside?" Alice ran again to catch up. "I'd love to see the turret rooms."

"FitzRobert's got it locked up," her husband replied. His voice was soft, reedy and distant as if he was communicating from another dimension. As if he were really just interacting with his own thoughts. An aspect of Simon's version of shellshock – Castle Fairlight's physician, Dr. Derby, had told her that no case was alike. "Corbin and Eagle machined padlock. Good modern cylinder. Not impossible but tricky."

Alice had no idea what he was on about but then, when he had slipped into a state, she often couldn't follow his train of thought. She just continued to follow him as he made his way to Clara Mare Cottage. Simon walked up an old bricked path, passing by the Mediaeval front door and its new solid padlock. He seemed intent on heading off to Palliser Park parts unknown, disappearing around the rear of the old gamekeeper's cottage. Alice had a sudden vision of confronting one of Clara Mare's ghost lights alone.

"Hey, wait for me!" Alice darted after Simon, rounding the corner of the cottage and nearly ploughing into her husband who had stopped, hands on his hips, to gaze out at the land behind the gamekeeper's former digs.

Alice almost gasped. A couple of hundred feet beyond Clara Mare's outbuildings and what once had been the cottage's own kitchen garden was a scattering of weathered wooden crosses and small roughly hewn stone monuments. Gusting sea winds rattled the less substantial markers and wove haphazardly through untended clumps of wild grass. Alice thought it had to be the saddest, loneliest spot in all of Palliser Park.

"What is this place?" She shivered, sliding an arm under his.

"Servant cemetery," Simon said and pulled away from her, heading directly for the graves.

Alice watched him walk into the small cemetery, unsure of what to do. Something had set Simon back. He was spiraling again. Distant, lost in his phantom realm – a plane she'd never been able to enter.

Overhead, a seabird whistled sharply as if shrieking a warning. It startled Alice out of her own momentary reverie. She sucked in a short breath and for all practical purposes, leapt forward off the brick path and followed her husband into the servants' cemetery. It was just her imagination but she suddenly felt as if the ghost of one of the gamekeepers was just behind her, looking over her shoulder.

Alice shivered despite the June sun. Palliser Park was luxurious and beautiful but she wouldn't mind leaving as soon as they got back to the main house. An impossibility since Mr. Spinner had gone to London with the Crossley. Besides Fizz would be quite hurt and didn't deserve such cavalier treatment from a friend. Still, Polly Piety's death had, at least for her, cast a depressing shadow over Palliser Park.

By the time she caught up with Simon, he had dropped to one knee and was brushing dirt away from the letters on a small headstone.

"1887," he read out loud once she had stepped next to him at the gravesite. "Alan Cheavers – Butler."

Alice had a brief flash of some lofty Tudaburgh bellowing *Cheavers! For god's sake, where's my brandy?*

"My best guess is the Tudaburghs' awarded modest headstones to more celebrated members of staff such as butlers or housekeepers," said Simon as he ran his long fingers over the plain block letters. The headstone had once been a light grey but was now blackened with age.

Alice moved to a simple wooden cross that teetered next to Cheavers' more robust monument. Made of hardwood, the cross had started duty as a sturdy Christian marker but years of

sea storms, marine mist and wind had strained its best
intentions. Now the cross shifted slightly with every breezy
gust, the crossbar squeaking in quiet protest. It was, she
decided, an eerie sight.

She bent forward to read what inscription was left on the
tired crossbar. It looked as if there had been some attempt to
carve information into the wood and then paint the grooves a
hardy black.

" 'arriot Deal – Harriet, I suppose," said Alice. "Maid
1907."

"Deal – anglicized from the Germanic Diehl or from Deal
in Kent. Alternatively, a variant of Dale. Old English dæl –
place at the hollow or valley," Simon rattled off as if reading a
notation from some dry old tome.

Alice knew from experience that Simon, when coping with
his version of shell shock, often seemed to wander up and
down some kind of vast internal library. She looked over at
him. He had risen and moved on to another grave marker –
another of the exhausted wooden crosses.

"Barkus ... Grey," Simon read, reaching out to steady the
weaving cross. "Game ... it must be Gamekeeper. 1895."

"Then this was *his* cottage once." Alice turned away from
Harriet Deal's grave and gazed back at the Tudor dwelling. She
had the unsettling feeling that Barkus Grey could be standing at
one of the leaded windows, watching them. "Can we head to
house now?"

"When you think about it," said Simon pointing at Clara
Mare's various outbuildings, "the illustrious Tudaburgh family
chose a charming spot for their servants' final resting place."

Alice took note of what could only be Clara Mare's long
abandoned privy – the door of which faced the servant

cemetery. "Do you think Polly's parents will want her buried here?"

She saw him sigh slightly. "Without much means," Simon said, "they will see it as a kindness, which I suppose, it is."

"Can we head back?"

"Of course – sorry," Simon's reedy voice took on a thin edge. "Sorry. I am so sorry."

Alice put her hands on her hips and focused on her fragile husband, immediately relegating Barkus Grey and his haunted cottage to lowest priority. "You have nothing to be sorry about, Simon Fairlight. Not now. Not then. Not ever."

He tightened his jaw and turned to look back at the small, sad collection of grave markers. "Never imagine I don't know how fortunate I am to have you, Alice Faraday."

"As I, you," she said, meaning it. "How about we be happy together? Or, at least, let's go finish off the sherry in our room."

Simon was quiet, gazing at Palliser Park's shifting and shuddering crosses. "I could really use a sherry," he said finally.

"What are we waiting for?" Alice ran to his side and laced her arm around his. "An engraved lollygagger? That's gangster talk, you know."

30

He was hollow and broken. He had killed and killed and killed ...
Simon sucked in a quick breath and closed his eyes, willing the
repetitive chant in his head to cease. It was, as if, a gramophone
recording was playing in his head over and over. A noise that
could drown out anything and anyone within his orbit.
Fortunately, such flares of internal insulation happened less and
less as he adjusted to life away from the trenches. He fervently
wished he could identify exactly what brought on the bouts but
it was always different, always something seemingly insignificant
– a word, a smell or a glimpse.

When he opened his eyes, Alice was standing in front of
him, holding out a glass of sherry.

"Knock it back," she advised. "Then off to the bath. Soon,
we have to be bright and social."

"God," he said, accepting the small sherry glass. A bath did
seem appealing. Despite a summer day, the gusting sea wind
had gotten into his bones.

"You'll be interested to know that Lord FitzRobert does
not wish dinner suits to be worn this evening. Apparently, he
would like a rather more casual affair – a sort of effortless

summer holiday thing. Blazers and four – in – hand ties acceptable."

"Reggie Spinner will be shocked," replied Simon. "He does like proper mess dress."

"Speaking of Mr. Spinner, when does he return with the Crossley?"

Simon sipped his sherry. It was excellent. He expected nothing less from Lord FitzRobert. Even the toss away guest room stuff was of the best.

"Expect a wire from the superior Mr. Spinner today," he said, his voice tired. Occasionally the repetitive noise in his head came along with a wretched headache.

"A wire isn't a motor car with the ability to whisk us away," Alice said and sat down on the arm of his chair, "very early on Sunday morning."

Simon rubbed his temple in vague hope that the headache would relent a little. "Sunday?" Maybe by Sunday, he'd find proof that a German assassin was now operating within British borders.

"One of your bangers?" she asked, smoothing back some strands of his hair that had fallen forward into his face.

He nodded. What real proofs did he actually have that this assassin was in England, let alone targeting members of the British Reparations Committee at Palliser Park? He did have the two dead lorry drivers from Meredith and Sons. They had been dispatched by somebody who needed a large motor vehicle. It wasn't too difficult to surmise his Crossley had been hit because it looked very much like FitzRobert's Sunbeam. But if the blue lorry had been stolen by The Gravedigger, why hadn't the job been finished? Surely any assassin or assassins worth their salt would have screeched to a halt, returned to what was presumed to be Lord FitzRobert's Sunbeam and eliminated the target. Of course, he was profoundly grateful that it hadn't unfolded that way.

Suddenly Simon was aware that Alice was speaking. She tended to chatter when worried. He tried to concentrate on what she was saying, making an effort to push down the chant ... *Killed and killed and killed* ...

"I think I'll wear that vaguely nautical dress. A tribute to Sir George's arrival," burbled Alice. "There are about ten additional guests now with a fair amount extra stored away in Brightsea lodgings. Should almost be as big a shindig as Fizz and Jack's party tomorrow night but more blazers and four – in – hand – y."

"Darling, would you run that bath for me?" he asked. Alice looked surprised as he rarely asked for help.

"You bet!" She jumped off the chair arm and headed towards the peerless Palliser Park guest bathroom. "There's a lovely soap you'll like – honeysuckle. I'll set it out for you."

Simon watched his wife as she disappeared into the bath. Somehow fate had given him Alice Faraday. At his worst, he panicked that ever capricious destiny would take her away – one final punishment.

Headache powders and a very long bath had finally tamped down the loop in his head. Simon thought about *TheConservatory* with a mixture of wariness and genuine curiosity. The wariness was ongoing – a product of his post – war sensibility and his quest to identify the machinations of a German assassin. The curiosity centered around who might now be floating about Palliser Park enjoying Lord FitzRobert's expansive hospitality.

He was a little surprised that the glittering Marble Salon had not been put to use for drinks but decided that FitzRobert was saving it for the important event. According to Perry, the Conservatory had risen like the Phoenix out of what had once been a side garden. Glass, iron and stone had been lavishly applied to the construction of Palliser Park's own Crystal Palace as if the massive 18th century house needed any more living space.

"Why would anyone need to add another room?" wondered Alice, eerily seeming to hear his private thoughts.

They were walking from the lesser guest hallway to the main thoroughfare. It was reasonably quiet up in the guest barracks as most would already be downstairs, snagging alcoholic restoratives. Simon knew their presence was not pivotal to Lord FitzRobert's master plan so they could afford to be late – ish. The notion made him feel kind of fancy – free for a moment.

He thought Alice looked very attractive. She was kitted out in a nautical suit – navy blouse and pleated skirt with the traditional crisp white linen bib collar. A red satin ribbon tied into a jaunty bow gave the blouse a whimsical jolt of color. Perfectly chosen for a relaxed summer event. Alice flew the Fairlight family flag with elegance and beautiful manners. Americans were often dismissed as clueless in British society, but Alice proved more than up for the challenge. Indeed, it had occurred to him long before that Lady Constance "Fizz" FitzRobert possessed the kind of flamboyant coarseness frequently misattributed to Americans. He was proud of Alice.

Immediately, Simon felt the familiar flush of guilt cross his senses. *Why had he lived to return to Britain and Alice when so many good lads had not?* He shoved down the question as if it was an urge to vomit. Second guessing fate got him nowhere.

"We could try Lord FitzRobert's very fancy elevator," said Alice. "I think it's around here somewhere. I ..."

"Show me Prince Volkonsky's room," Simon interrupted. All of a sudden, it seemed like an intriguing proposition. Everyone was downstairs in the Conservatory. He'd be very curious to see if there was anything hanging about to link the louche Russian to Polly Piety. It would be highly gratifying to pin something on the spoiled aristocrat.

"Simon!" Alice breathed, her eyes widening in apprehension. "Crumpling was so upset with ..."

"Crumpling and the majority of servants will be at the beck and call of the FitzRoberts. Come along – let's have a look."

Alice threw him a withering glance over her shoulder as she obligingly left the accepted guest track. He followed her to a firmly shut door that was located near the bend into the secondary guest quarters. She stood back and pointed at the beveled door.

"*I* will stay out here," Alice announced, displeased. "A weather eye for the coppers."

"An excellent notion," he said, reaching out and grasping the doorknob. "Thank you, darling."

Simon pushed in Prince Volkonsky's door. There was still plenty of light streaming in from the spectacular bank of Georgian windows. A proper English summer evening wouldn't see genuine nightfall until ten o'clock or more.

His Imperial Highness' digs were lavish and expansive – exactly what a Russian aristocrat would expect as his due for breathing. An acre of heavy satin and giltwood. Even the grand piano, glimmering in the farthest corner, was full blown Rococo. It resembled some kind of mythical beast – broad and muscular with golden scales.

Simon crossed the rich Persian carpet to an overwrought Louis XV desk where personal items were stacked. Here was the diabolically expensive gramophone Alice had talked about. It was a beautifully designed thing. He ran his hand over the gleaming wood and brass fittings, then glanced at the stack of 78 RPM recordings. Unsurprisingly, perhaps, a selection of Russian piano and orchestral music but nothing that proclaimed Concerto or Sonata by Prince Andre Volkonsky.

The pile of musical scores revealed nothing with penciled notes from an exiled prince and tortured artist. Knowing Alice was anxiously pacing outside, convinced Crumpling was going to swoop down on them like an avenging angel, Simon made short work of the desk drawers. Nothing wildly unexpected – half empty cigarette packages, jars of ink, various pens, pencils, blank paper, blank score sheets and an English dictionary.He was surprised *not* to find half empty vials of cocaine thrown, forgotten, into dark corners.

He took a few minutes to run through the prince's wardrobe. Expensive suits, a couple of typically overblown Hussar uniforms, various colorful traditional Russian pieces including elaborate fur trimmed hats and embroidered velvet scarves. It seemed very costume – y, the contents of a theatre company's dressing room rack. All part of emphasizing close ties to old Imperial Russia.

The bathroom – even larger than their own – had been thoroughly scrubbed by attentive Palliser Park maids. Simon had no doubt Prince Andre was a domestic pig and left his extravagant quarters in a frightful state as easily as he accepted the courtesy of a breakfast tray. A pity really. The prince's muddle might have yielded something of interest. Expensive bottles of cologne – Creed, Guerlain, Floris – stood neatly in a row, awaiting their master. Not that Prince Volkonsky ever seemed to smell pleasantly of citrus or bergamot. His odor was more typically Eau de Sweat with sour high notes of the Distillery.

Simon was about to turn away from the bathroom shelves when something caught his eye. A forlorn tiny bottle tucked behind a tin of soap powder for hair. Not a glamorous vessel of masculine scent but a thin, inexpensive glass bottle that tried to look appealing with a small blue ribbon tied in a bow around its neck. He picked it up. The oval paper label read *Beaux Bouquet of Violets*. It was a cheap bottle of scented water that could be purchased in any village chemist's or tuck shop. A local Brightsea wife could pick up *Bouquet of Violets* for a few coins or it might be a gift that a flummoxed farmer or fisherman would choose, last minute, to give his beloved at Christmas. Even a skinflint Russian prince could secure his bottle of *Bouquet of Violets* while replenishing cigarettes in the village tuck shop. Perfect for dazzling an impressionable young maid from the Black Country.

Turning the small bottle around in his hand, it occurred to Simon that he'd seen another beribboned *Bouquet of Violets* recently. In Polly Piety's Princess Mary tin. Was it a connection between Polly and the louche Russian? The scented water was a cheap commodity easily available. Maybe His Imperial Highness bought a few at the chemist and then doled them out to the maids who cleaned his room in lieu of actual money. He had no evidence that Prince Volkonsky even knew that Polly Piety existed on the same plane as his exalted self. Just a gut feeling that the predatory Russian would have noticed the stunningly beautiful young maid and pounced. Polly had indicated to Alice that her engagement would be something of a step up for her.

And how – if it was, in fact, a Russian prince. Her Imperial Highness, Princess Polly.

Simon pocketed the bottle of scent. He'd give it to Nyx Saxby, who could use the information however he liked. It was too optimistic to think Nyx could build a substantial case against Prince Volkonsky. Pure conjecture was all they had – that and the unkind *hope* that Volkonsky was involved in Polly's sad death. But, not even the noxious Russian deserved to go to the gallows just because he was an appalling person.

If His Imperial Highness had shoved Polly off the roof – why? Even if the maid announced intentions to tell her family and friends about the engagement, the prince would just deny everything and paint the girl as delusional. No need for something messy such as murder. No one, especially Lord FitzRobert, was going to take her word above Russian aristocracy. Prince Volkonsky would have traded on that in one way or another all his life. It came to him as naturally as breathing. Maybe it wasn't Prince Volkonsky who had made a connection with Polly. Maybe it was someone else with more at stake. Someone a bit more dangerous.

Alice turned towards him as he exited Prince Volkonsky's guest quarters. She wore a relieved expression. No miffy confrontations with the august Crumpling.

"There are restorative beverages on offer downstairs," she said. "I want one."

CHAPTER

31

Alice was relieved to see Simon emerge from the prince's guest rooms. She was positive that Crumpling was going to swoop around a corner to make it abundantly clear how displeased he was with their poor manners.

"Satisfied?" she asked, making a sour face.

"You're right," Simon said as he offered her his elbow. "No sprawling scores for epic operas or concertos."

"Disappointingly dull," agreed Alice, slipping her arm under his. "I think he must take his work with him. Probably in a fiendishly expensive embossed leather case from Paris."

"Yes, and probably liberated from his last host's closet."

She laughed at the notion, imagining all the loot Prince Volkonsky had stuffed into his traveling trunk. All from confrontation avoiding Brits too embarrassed to actually ask for their possessions back. Perhaps even the lavish gramophone had been nicked from a well – meaning household.

The Conservatory – a metal and glass jewel box of a room – had been wonderfully prepared for Lord FitzRobert's guests. Alice thought of *Midsummer's Night Dream* as they entered the lavish hall. The FitzRobert's gardeners had created a fairy bower within the soaring glass walls. Immense potted trees and ceramic troughs of roses were grouped in idyllic copses throughout, providing both visual beauty and points of privacy within the expansive space. Cozy tables covered in crisp white linen and matching chairs were scattered hither and yon, encouraging relaxed, casual conversations. A quartet, placed in the very center of the conservatory, played popular melodies while FitzRobert footmen fanned out with sterling silver trays of drinks and hors d'oeuvres. The long English summer evening bathed the glass walls inbucolic warmth and golden light. It was gorgeous. Alice had to admit Lord FitzRobert knew how to enchant his guests.

As they were fashionably late, the majority of the guests had already assembled and were already one or two drinks in. Numbering roughly thirty or forty, it was a mixed group of various FitzRobert family members and friends who had traveled to Palliser Park from some distance. The following night's engagement party was set for vastly more invitees. That would be a real test of what Lord FitzRobert could pull off with his new house and new staff.

Alice looked around the conservatory, searching for faces she recognized. Lord FitzRobert was holding court under the branches of one of the massive potted trees to their right. He was sipping from a martini glass and making some kind of confident point about something to a small audience that included Sir George Jasper, Perry and several beautifully dressed women she couldn't immediately place from other parties. Dorothy Brier held her own court to their left. She was overdressed in a silver sheath of sequins and silk, ropes of amethyst looped around her long, swan – like neck. But, overdressed seemed to be her intent as she was surrounded by guests who seemed impressed to be in her orbit. She was a famous stage star. This was why Dorothy Brier was at Palliser Park – to dazzle Lord FitzRobert's more staid set.

The Rothermores were sitting by one of the glass walls, at a small table, talking to another couple of similar age. Clearly old friends from the warm, animated conversation – the happiest Alice had seen them since arriving at Palliser Park.

Alice spied a young man walking in their general direction. He wore a dog collar along with a rather rumpled grey suit and carried a glass of Champagne. She had an epiphany that it was the legendary Mr. Hayter, local curate and possible beloved of Polly Piety.

She moved forward to intercept the curate who stumbled broadly while passing a potted fern, giving an initial impression of the gawky academic. He teetered to a halt to ensure the majority of his Champagne had remained in his glass.

"Alice …" she heard her husband murmur.

Alice pretended not to hear Simon's warning. "It's Father Hayter, isn't it?" she said brightly. "Are you all right?"

He gazed over his Champagne flute at her, his blue eyes overlarge behind round gold spectacle frames. "Oh, yes," Heyter replied with nearly as much cheer. "Just didn't see that pot! Lovely gathering, isn't it? His Lordship is always so gracious to include a country curate such as myself."

"Forgive me for not introducing myself – Alice Fairlight," she held out her hand which Hayter shook vigorously, spilling more of his drink as he did so.

"Lady Fairlight, hello!" he cried. "His Lordship has told me what a lovely lady you are … and here you are … umm, proving him right again."

"You are very kind," Alice replied as he continued to shake her hand. "My husband …"

"Simon, Simon Fairlight." Alice heard her husband say and she felt him step next to her right shoulder. "A pleasure, Father Hayter."

"Major Fairlight!" Hayter finally released her hand and shifted his ferocious grip to Simon. "A pleasure indeed, sir!"

A footman approached, carrying a tray of Champagne flutes that matched the one in Hayter's free hand. Alice was grateful when Simon pulled his hand away from the curate's enthusiastic greeting and snagged a couple. He passed one to her and she took a grateful sip of the cold, fizzy wine. Just what she needed after the nerve – wracking visit to Prince Volkonsky's quarters. Instinctively she quickly scanned the room for any sight of the august Crumpling and thought she spotted him in the distance, having a word with one of the young footmen.

Alice returned her attention to the curate, who was telling Simon about his day sketching sea birds in flight.

"I'm a keen watercolorist," Hayter was saying. "Not that I'm ready for the Royal Academy or anything such as that, of course, but I do love it."

"Landscapes?" asked Alice, imagining that living on the sea coast would encourage such a niche for an amateur artist.

The curate shifted his beaming energy to Alice. "Oh, yes. Over the summer, landscapes and seascapes are just the thing. I actually prefer portraiture – in pencil and watercolor. You'd make a lovely subject, Lady Fairlight, if you don't mind me saying so."

Simon coughed slightly next to her. Alice glanced at him in some concern. His lungs had been damaged on the battlefield and she lived in constant trepidation that a chill could lead to a deadly bout of pneumonia or pleurisy.

"Do you have a particular subject in Brightsea that acts as your muse?" Simon asked with more interest than Alice would have believed of him. He had loved the arts as a student. The war seemed to have banished such interests to some lonely plane in his consciousness.

At this question, Hayter's delighted expression faltered a little. Genuine regret crossed his blandly handsome face and he suddenly sipped his wine as if it might steady him.

"A few hardy souls in my congregation are kind enough to sit for me," he said, sighed and then sipped his Champagne again. "But there *was* one face I longed to do justice to here. Classical beauty worthy of Aphrodite or Ceres. Her coloring was extraordinary – that bright, bright hair! Impossible now, of course. Poor, poor girl. Died in that tragic accident the other day. I was shocked."

"You mean the lovely Polly Piety?" Simon asked before Alice could frame the same question.

If the curate was surprised by Simon's familiarity with a house servant, he failed to show it. Instead, he nodded, sighing. "You took note of Polly's exceptional beauty? Also, a kind and jolly girl."

"I liked her very much," said Alice. "She was so looking forward to getting married. We talked about the wedding dress her mother was going to help create."

Hayter nodded. "She asked if I could marry them at All Saints in the autumn."

"Who was the fortunate lad?" Simon asked, his voice solemn. "We would like to extend our condolences."

"As would I," replied the curate with one more heavy sigh. "Polly never divulged that information. I had the impression that he was of a ... umm, higher station than her good self and that they both needed some time to settle the idea with their respective connections."

"A young farmer or fisherman, perhaps?" Alice offered, hoping that, perhaps, Polly had let a little more slip in her conversation with Father Hayter.

Hayter shrugged. "Possibly. I don't know. I did sense it was someone here at Palliser Park, though. Something about how Polly said they would leave *here* once married. Of course, she pronounced it *'ere* but it sounded personal, like her home. She liked art, you know. Showed me a couple of her drawings once after church. You know, a less artistic padre might have been annoyed that she had wiled away his sermon on *Brotherly Love* drawing sheep."

There was a brief pause as they all seemed to digest the thin snippet of information. Then Simon coughed again and begged their pardon for his momentary distress.

"Well! Shall we move to happier climes?" he said, saluting them with his Champagne glass.

"Yes, and if you two would be so good as to excuse me, I see my own intended has arrived!" Hayter had returned to radiating joy and good will. "I hope I can introduce you later?"

Alice pivoted slightly to see a local family arriving and by the way Lord FitzRobert was moving to greet them, she guessed an important local family. They were well turned out in handsome but not wholly new attire – so typical of the country gentry who didn't believe in being flashy or spending on new when old was of the best and perfectly serviceable. Parents, a son and daughter – the daughter, presumably Father Hayter's intended, was thin and pretty. Not a Polly Piety goddess but regular featured and blessed with a nice coil of shiny honey brown locks. Dressed in a white linen blouse and rose colored skirt, she looked unfussy and straightforward. Better yet, she looked happy and pleased to be present. Good signs, Alice felt, for a contented marriage. She was glad for the art loving curate of All Saints.

"We would be delighted," Alice heard Simon saying and she murmured her agreement as Father Hayter took off, tripping slightly over a rug edge, to greet his prospective new family.

"So *not* besotted with Polly Piety in the usual sense," said Simon softly into her ear.

Alice had to nod, watching as Hayter gave the smiling girl a peck on the cheek and turned to shake the hand of her father. "Just wanted to sketch a goddess with bright, bright hair."

"Thank God," said Simon. "My world makes sense again."

32

Simon spotted Nyx Saxby standing by the conservatory's glass outer doors. Doors that led to another of Lord FitzRobert's newfangled terraces. The long summer evening was still providing a warm light that bathed the Palliser Park grounds in a burnished gold. He longed for some fresh air and hoped Nyx would have some interesting intelligence after the staff interviews.

After reassuring himself that Alice was occupied happily in a conversation with Fizz, he made his way across to the Brightsea DI who was gazing down at his tank watch and yawning.

"Snagged you a Whisky," Simon said, holding out a glass of FitzRobert hospitality.

"Thanks be to Dionysis and any other gods of drunken revelry." Nyx accepted the crystal tumbler gratefully. "What a day."

"Stroll outside?"

The Brightsea DI nodded and reached for the handle of Lord FitzRobert's not period accurate French doors. He pulled it open. A passing footman looked momentarily anxious that he hadn't been fast enough to open the portal for a pair of guests.

Simon threw him a smile of reassurance and followed the detective out onto the tiled terrace. From inside the conservatory, the musical quartet broke into a cheery version of *Shine On, Harvest Moon* that sailed up, over the buzz of human chatter and laughter.

"I'm closing Polly Piety's case," said Saxby after downing a solid draught of the Whisky. "All the servant stories tally. No obvious candidates for her paramour. Nothing specific that indicates anything more than an unhappy mishap."

"You can put a line through Father Hayter's name," commiserated Simon and then told Nyx about the curate's artistic hobby.

The DI raised his eyebrows at the notion and drank another portion of his Whisky. "It did seem a bit of a reach. There has been a development however."

"Yes?" Simon pulled his cigarette case out of his breast pocket.

"Our Brightsea doctor took a look at Polly Piety early this morning – part of our standard case procedure. Brown just popped round with his findings. Miss Piety was with child. About four months along."

Surprised, Simon stopped removing a cigarette from its berth in the metal case. "And you're ending the investigation? Isn't this one of the most celebrated motives for murder – the inconvenient lady friend who finds herself pregnant?"

Nyx Saxby sipped his drink. "I agree. It leans in the direction of the inconvenient lady friend. If one Palliser Park servant had been able to give me something to follow up on. There's nothing. Not a shred. If I push, His Lordship will push back, protesting the affront to his household and my bloody – mindedness in portraying Palliser Park as a den of iniquity."

"Can well imagine the full force of FitzRobert disapproval." Simon pulled the bottle of cheap scent from his pocket and tossed it to the Brightsea detective. "Found this in the prince'sbelongings. It matches one I saw in Polly's quarters after her accident."

Saxby looked sour. "Volkonsky's on my short list. From what little I could glean from that noble Russian, he views servants as convenient objects to be utilized as needed. But I've got nothing on which to hang my worst suspicions. He was tucked away in his rooms, down with something like pneumonia, dabbling away at his music when Polly fell. Several servants confirmed this."

"I wonder," said Simon, watching as Nyx pocketed the bottle. Something pulled at the edges of his mind about Prince Volkonsky and his lavish guest quarters.

"And add to it, Lord FitzRobert's dismay at one of his treasured guests being troubled by the local plods. In a way, he'd be within reason. I've got nothing to hang any kind of a real murder investigation on." DI Saxby yawned again. "Sorry – it's been a very long day."

"And the two victims in the Meredith lorry?" Simon let the Polly Piety case go. He could see that the young Brightsea DI had shelved the case for the time being. No sense in using spurs on an exhausted horse.

"Unfortunate victims of toughs who wanted whatever they imagined was being moved by the lorry. We scoured the local area looking for anyone who saw anything, no matter how innocuous, concerning the blue lorry. You, Lady Alice and your man are the only ones with a story to tell," Nyx said, shrugging. "Do I *personally* think it was a mistaken attempt on Lord FitzRobert's well – being? Possibly given what you have told me, but I'd need a lot more before I could make such an accusation in my professional station."

Simon nodded, understanding the DI's predicament. "Fair enough."

They both sipped their respective whiskies, gazing out at Palliser Park's meticulously maintained lawn. It was a spectacular evening on Britain's east coast. As always, Simon was grateful to be out in the fresh air, away from things frivolous and ostentatious. As if the universe wanted to counter his feeling – inside the conservatory, the quartet switched to a lively rendition of *Ballin' the Jack.* He listened to the melody as it drifted past the French doors. The slightly muffled musical notes turned around and around in his head, beginning a metamorphosis into a very interesting idea.

"Nyx," he said, "did any of the maids mention Prince Volkonsky's piano playing? Anything specific?"

Saxby raised his eyebrows and thought for a moment. "Not much beyond his imperial edict that no one should disturb him and his genius while he's at the piano. Crumpling did mention that the prince seemed to have a preference for playing Borodin. Why?"

"One of the notable way stations of his guest room is an exceptionally fine gramophone and collection of Russian piano recordings."

Simon could see the idea flare up like a struck match in the Brightsea DI's eyes.

"Now that is something," Saxby murmured. "Volkonsky could wind up the gramophone and entice Polly Piety in for a bit of social engineering."

"Or nip up to the roof."

Nyx Saxby let out a short breath. "Or nip up to the roof."

CHAPTER
33

Alice thought that Jack – although superficially jubilant and extremely attentive to Fizz FitzRobert – looked tired. He had knocked back at least three dry martinis while listening to his betrothed's dizzy prattle with more interest than the prattle merited. She noted that on occasion, he did allow himself a moment or two away from Fizz's animated reverie. Every time his errant gaze trailed across the crowded conservatory, it ended up with Dorothy Brier in her silver sheath, dazzling a handful of Lord FitzRobert's guests. She smoked a cigarette from a thin black holder – thoroughly modern and thoroughly flashy.

Was it possible that Dorothy was more than a casual affair? Did Jack regret his official link to Fizz?

"So, I spoke with Clara," said Fizz, oblivious to anything but herself and her interests. "She's of the opinion that we should travel to America – New York, San Francisco – and avoid the Continent. What do you think, Alice? It might be livelier than France or Italy just now."

Alice watched as Jack pulled his gaze away from Dorothy Brier and refocused it on his vibrant fiancée. He offered Fizz a practiced smile, then waved at a passing footman to replenish the drinks.

"Alice," repeated Fizz with an exaggerated sigh. "America –
yay or nay?"

She jumped a little at Fizz FitzRobert's demand for her
opinion, mortified to have been caught staring fixedly at the
Jack – Dorothy connection. Fortunately, Fizz had enough of
the FitzRobert confidence that she rarely noted anything
beyond her current pursuits.

"Oh," said Alice. "Sorry. As an American, I insist that you
visit our fair shores."

"But aren't your brethren getting a bit silly about strong
drink – you know, with that wartime ban? That doesn't sound
lively or fun."

"Don't worry about it," Alice advised, glancing at Jack, who
was waving again at one of his future father – in – law's
footmen. "You'll always be able to find a drink in Manhattan."

Fizz let out a bright laugh. She reached over to pat Jack's
free hand. "Darling, it's America! I'll have Dad's secretary book
tickets on one of the ships crossing over."

Jack ignored her news bulletin, his face shifting from a kind
of superficial jubilance to annoyance. "Why can't I get a bloody
drink?" His voice was creased with sharp self – pity
unbecoming to a betrothed man who was supposed to be
deliriously happy with his path through life. "I just want a
bloody drink."

"You've had several already," Fizz FitzRobert pointed out.
"Leave a few for Dad's guests, will you?"

"Jack," Alice interjected quickly, hoping to avert an
awkward moment between the two, "tell your beloved Fizz
you'll go stateside. I promise to get my mother to throw you a
big party in New York if you do."

The handsome Englishman's mouth twisted in irritation – an unpleasant emotion that almost spilled over into words. Alice saw that he clearly thought the better of it, pausing to rearrange his features into his more usual affability.

"Sorry, darling," he said to Fizz, taking her hand and kissing the top of her fingers. "I have a bit of a headache. Of course, we will go to America."

"My poor, lovely Jack. I shall have Crumpling fetch you a powder." She gazed at him, her eyes soft with adoration.

Before he could respond, his future father – in – law – in keeping with the more casual nature of the evening – announced himself that dinner was being served. The conservatory erupted in a cacophony of happy, expectant conversation, glasses clinking and chairs being pushed back. The cheerful energy in the glass room suggested to Alice that the guests were aware of Lord FitzRobert's generosity as a host and anticipated a delicious dinner.

Alice got up from the cozy cocktail table and searched the room for any sign of her husband in the milling scrum of Palliser Park's guests. It was easy to imagine that he had escaped the hothouse excesses of the conservatory for a stroll outside. She just wished he had taken her along as well.

Perry emerged from the pack, unsteady and carrying a martini. He grinned at Alice before knocking back the contents of his glass.

"Shall I take you in?" he asked, handing the martini glass to a footman who was passing with a tray. His voice was giddy and bright with alcohol.

"Well, I was looking for Simon," she said, still scanning the conservatory.

"Oh, he's gone off with that plod, Saxby, from Brightsea. You know how these military types love to talk about the war and all that." Perry offered her his elbow. "Besides, wedded couples sitting together is so … so American. Shall I take you in, fair lady?"

"Yes," said Alice with a sour face. "We wouldn't want to be mistaken for Americans."

"You are the loveliest American I know!" he said, staggering a little as he slipped her arm under his.

"Perry, I am the only American you know."

"Untrue! I have met several while filing papers at the War Department." Perry made several florid gestures with his free arm that mimicked tossing paper at a wall. "Filing, filing papers for our brave stout fellows *over there*. Who knows? A few of those stout fellows might have lived because I followed strict alphabetical standards!"

"Off we go then," Alice said as several of the other guests took note of Perry's inebriated state. "You could do with some food."

Lord FitzRobert had elected to serve dinner in both the first and second dining rooms. With the emphasis on a casual warm – up to Fizz and Jack's grand event the following evening, the Palliser Park staff had assembled buffets in both rooms. These featured vats of beloved dishes – creamed vegetables, creamed potatoes, roasted potatoes, Potatoes Au Gratin, fried potatoes, fondant potatoes, salmon mousse pinwheels, mushroom tartlets, lobster and asparagus salad – all augmented by carving stations for roast beef and goose. Despite the attempt at a low – key summer holiday ambience, it was rather formal with Irish linen, heavy sterling silver serving dishes, towering candelabras and stacks of Royal Crown Derby.

The host himself settled in the first dining room — a vast space with walls of delicate celadon green that showcased two marble fireplaces in the Regency style. One fireplace had ornate carvings that represented Castor and the other, Pollux. Alice was happy to allow other guests the opportunity to sit at the grand main table with Lord FitzRobert. She escaped the first dining room and Perry, who had been asked by his father to look after George Jasper at the main table. She made her way to the other dining room, grateful for the opportunity to avoid Lord FitzRobert and Dorothy Brier, who would be holding court despite the informal façade.

"Alice," came her husband's voice as she nipped through the connecting door. She followed it to find Simon standing by the roast beef with two plates in his hands.

"About time you arrived," he said, cocking his head towards one of the small tables set up to help with guest overflow. "I've made you a plate — know you love a good, creamed spinach and about sixteen styles of potato."

"About time I arrived indeed." She had to laugh, following him to the small table. "You abandoned me to spend treasured time with DI Saxby."

"Don't envy him." Simon set their plates down and then moved to push in her chair. "He's going to try and persuade His Lordship to postpone Fizz's big do."

"Good luck with that. Why?" She smiled at one of FitzRobert's footman who had moved quickly to ensure they had wine.

Simon took the seat next to her. "He's gotten word from the Met Office that they are expecting a dangerous storm to come through tomorrow.Apparently, parts of Denmark and Norway really got smacked so they sent warnings off to us."

"I can't imagine Lord FitzRobert caring much about rain."

"According to Nyx, this area is prone to flooding. Every few years they get a real wallop – biblical smite of God stuff." Simon picked up his fork and pushed food around his plate.

Alice, about to sip some wine, paused. "Excuse me – did you say *Nyx*?"

"DI Saxby comes from a family of classical scholars. Artemis Nyx Saxby."

"Wouldn't classical scholars know it's a girl's name?" she asked in surprise.

Simon shrugged. "Something about expecting a daughter. I'm wondering if you ought to head to higher ground if Brightsea is going to be under water. I'll stay to help. If it gets as bad as I'm told, they'll need every able body."

"I'm not leaving without you and if you're going to stick around to help, I will too."

"What an obstinate young wife you are," he said and picked up his wine glass. "Aren't you supposed to walk three paces behind and attend to my every wish?"

"We Americans have very progressive ideas about marriage. Just ask my father," Alice took a forkful of creamed spinach and was unsurprised to discover it was perfectly cooked. She didn't envy Palliser Park's kitchen staff with all that they were expected to accomplish for the engagement party weekend. They had to be in a state of either cooking or preparing to cook ceaselessly – like Sisyphus pushing the boulder up a hill.

"Your mother is a formidable person," Simon conceded with a sigh.

"The proverbial iron hand in a velvet glove. Art dealers and opera impresarios wept to see her coming." She looked up to see DI Saxby approaching. The policeman wore a tired, vexed expression.

"A colossal waste of time," Saxby announced as he joined them.

"FitzRobert won't call off the party?" Simon asked.

Saxby slid onto a chair. "He deeply believes it's a tempest in a teapot. If there is, in fact, a dangerous storm, it will have weakened to barely an inconvenience by the time it rolls into England."

"Any truth to that?" Simon waved to the footman who was in charge of pouring the wine.

The detective rubbed his eyes wearily. "Possible it could unwind into some light drizzle, I suppose. The Met Office was pretty sharpish about, you know, moving with alacrity to avoid unnecessary deaths."

"That does sound pretty definitive," admitted Alice. "Let me get you some food. Do you prefer beef or goose?"

"Very kind of you. Goose, if it wouldn't be too much trouble," said Nyx Saxby.

The young footman finished pouring Saxby's wine. "I'd be happy to take care of that, sir. Goose and a bit of everything?"

"Thank you. Very, very kind." DI Saxby picked up the wine glass as the footman headed off to the carving station to secure some goose. "I have to get back to Brightsea and have the lads start readying for the storm. The last time the Norwegians warned us, the storm surge came in at twelve feet."

"How does Palliser Park fare in such weather?" asked Alice, wondering if its cliffside location protected it from flooding.

"It's situated better than most," Saxby admitted. "The Tudaburghs always opened the house to the village and locals if the flooding was bad. Not sure we can count on the FitzRoberts to do the same."

"I think Lord FitzRobert would do his duty to the locals," said Simon. "He yearns to be thought of as the benevolent aristocrat."

"How did he ever produce that glorious daughter?" sighed Nyx before he inhaled a long draught of red wine.

"You mean, Fizz?" Alice was surprised that the rather cerebral police detective was impressed by thoroughly modern Lady Constance FitzRobert. "Glorious?"

"Gloriously loud," said Simon flatly. "Gloriously lacking in couth."

Saxby shook his head. "All those coppery curls ... the way she laughs – she's so vibrant, so alive."

"Why, DI Saxby," Alice breathed, surprised again, "I believe you're really taken with Fizz."

The DI rubbed at his tired eyes again. "Ridiculous, isn't it? To be taken with a girl who's about to celebrate her engagement? What a perfect idiot."

Before either Alice or Simon could respond, the footman returned with a heaping plate of food and placed it before the detective, who gratefully tucked in.

"I'm famished!" he announced too brightly. "How about you two?"

CHAPTER

34

Simon sipped his coffee, relieved that the dinner was coming to an end. It was late. Many of the FitzRobert guests had either left for home or back to Brightsea inns. A few of the extended family and friends who were staying at Palliser Park lingered over hot drinks or a last glass of wine.

He still found English society events exhausting. Never his favorite way to pass time, before the war he would have navigated the choppy waters of elaborate dinners and parties without a thought.

Simon watched as Alice chatted amiably with the Big Two – Fizz and Jack, who had joined them for the dessert. Alice was just so beautiful. He loved the way her thick blonde hair glimmered gold in the candlelight. How her eyes brightened with humor and intelligence when she laughed – which was often. He was a fortunate man. He just wished he knew what he had done to deserve it. Why had he survived when so many were quietly decomposing in mass graves on the continent? What was the infernal algorithm?

He had a moment to think of his childhood nanny, Miss Pratt. She had taken a dim view of children feeling sorry for themselves. What would that excellent woman think of him now— moping about at a happy event. She'd shake her head and do what she always did, send him outside to do something useful. Thanks to Miss Pratt's notions of child rearing, he'd spent an unusual amount of time helping to muck out stalls in Castle Fairlight's stable. A vision flared up in his head of Cardinal, his father's temperamental chestnut mare. A big, rangy Irish bred mare, she hadn't cared for children and liked to snake her head out, nipping at him with angry, clacking teeth as he passed her stall. The day he had won her over with a carrot and an apple half had been a turning point in his eight – year – old life ...

An urgent shout brought him back to Palliser Park's second dining room. He refocused. One of FitzRobert's young footmen appearing at the doorway, shouting something about a mechanical malfunction.

"The elevator!" he heard Alice gasp. "Is someone in it?"

He was on his feet in the next instant and out of the dining room, heading for Lord FitzRobert's flashy new conveyance. It was what the military had taught him – to run towards conflict and crisis. It wasn't heroism or anything particularly special. Just what a soldier did. Human life wasn't cheap, wasn't cannon fodder even on the battlefield. Much of what a soldier did was an attempt to save lives, not take them.

Down the hallway and a twist to the right led Simon to the gilded cage lift. He came around the bend to see a knot of frantic Palliser Park servants milling around and up the staircase that bracketed Lord Rothermore's elaborate moveable birdcage. They peered up through the metal railings, gesturing helplessly. Clattering sounds on the tiled floor behind him meant that others from the dining room had followed.

"The bloody thing's seized!" cried another one of the FitzRobert footmen upon seeing Simon. "Mr. Rothermore, sir!"

"The lift has locked up?" Simon asked, moving in for a better look.

"Mr. Rothermore is in it, sir. It must have fallen and then ... I don't know, suddenly stopped. I think Mr. Rothermore slipped and hit his head."

Simon saw the bottom of the cage positioned about halfway between two upper floors. It hung slightly askew, swinging slightly on heavy metal cables. Something had gone badly wrong with the mechanism. A relatively simple pulley and cable system, it would be difficult to jam up the gears without some terrible form of misadventure.

He left the base of Lord FitzRobert's fancy machine and took to the steps, darting up two at a time. His chest wheezed with mustard gas scarring. Ignoring the pain, Simon pushed forward until he made his way to where the metal cage hung limply on its damaged cables. It resembled the jumbled inner workings of a broken grandfather clock.

Simon leaned over the banister of the original staircase. He could see the MP lying, breathing but unconscious, on the floor of the lift cage. Blood flowed from the politician's temple onto the monogrammed *F*. He glanced up at the heavy cable and pulley device that pulled the circular cage up and down the protective tunnel of gilded iron railings. The topmost pulley had been harpooned with a stout metal rod – ostensively some kind of catastrophic mechanical failure of the railing tube. It was clear that Rothermore would have to be freed – and quickly – before the cage went into freefall.

"I need rope and bloody quick!" he shouted, assessing that the cage would have to be pulled closer to the staircase and stabilized if any kind of transfer was going to be possible.

The next few minutes were spent in an urgent rush – securing the lift's cage and deciding how to best move from the steps to the cage's platform because it now hung between floor landings. Fortunately, the lift's designer had built a couple of rudimentary back doors in case of mechanical failure. These amounted to hinged panels in the tube rail that could be shifted out of the way.

Simon and two young footmen attended to one of the portable emergency doors first, sliding out several metal bolts and freeing the panel. They cleared it from the railing tube, tossing the railing panel to another set of footmen who got it down to the ground floor and out of the way.

"I'm going to nip over to the cage platform now," Simon said to his pair of anxious footmen. "If I can get Mr. Rothermore up – be ready to assist with the extra rope."

"Shouldn't one of us go with you?" asked Footman Ephraim. "Help with picking him up?"

"I'll go!" volunteered Footman Clarence. He was a sturdy lad who could probably pick up Rothermore without breaking stride. He was also considerably heavier than Simon.

Simon shook his head. "Cage could collapse with the extra weight. We'll just have to chance it with me. Ready?"

Clarence and Ephraim nodded, eyes widening with worry.

Simon gingerly made his way to the edge of staircase. He tied a section of another rope around his waist. Looking down, past the rope secured cage, to the ground floor, he could see the household gathered around the base of the stairs. Poor Mrs. Rothermore was in a state of near panic, leaning against one of her friends as if she might, at any moment, faint from stress. Lord FitzRobert was marching about, ordering the footmen with the railing panel to secure it in a nearby coat closet as if that was a huge help. As with everyone else, Alice was peering up, her face drawn and tense. He could tell she was not happy with his mission.Fizz, Perry and Jack instinctively flanked her, ready to support if the worst happened. Just beyond their orbit, Dorothy Brier stood. She gazed up at him, her eyes gleaming with a kind of atavistic interest that he found unsettling. Dorothy Brier hoped he would fail, hoped he would fall with Rothermore and the cage.

"Okay, lads," he said to Clarence and Ephriam, "pull it back so I can clear the stair edge."

The footmen quickly moved along the curving stair to pull the cage away so Simon could make his way down to the platform. Above them, the metal cable and pulley screamed with the pressure. From below, the Palliser Park household gave a collective gasp. He saw Alice give a start. She was ready to charge up the steps and take over the job from Clarence or Ephraim.

The cage was hauled back with a piercing shriek. There was just enough room. Simon swung down, jumping a short distance through the emergency door and onto the cage platform. He landed hard but managed not to hit his head or back on the stair edge. He even managed not to land on Rothermore's prone body which was something of a minor feat. Unfortunately, landing hard also meant that the lift cage rocked with more force. Above them, the harpooned cable slipped a little and the cage jerked violently. From the ground floor came dismayed cries. Lord FitzRobert shouted a demand that the whole mechanism stop twisting as if the lift cage were an irritating servant.

Simon almost fell with the sudden shift. He succeeded in not being thrown from the cage – mostly due to the efforts of the two young footmen who immediately worked to tighten the rope, stabilizing the rig. He moved to Rothermore, who was breathing hard and groaning faintly. An encouraging sign if his war experience was to be believed.

"Alastair," Simon said as he untied the rope from his waist, "you'll be out of here in a minute."

He gently rolled Rothermore onto his back. The rope was threaded around and under the MP's arms. Simon tied a solid knot and then bent in to pull the politician up. It was fortunate that Rothermore was not particularly large. He was able to brace the MP and maneuver him towards the cage's emergency door.

"Clarence – hold the cage if you can!" Simon ordered as he got Rothermore nearer the exit space. "Ephraim, have you got help?"

"Sir, I have!" shouted back the footman.

Rothermore let out a groan, beginning to regain his senses. He rallied enough to put some weight on his feet, allowing Simon to place him in the back door.

"W … what's," he murmured, "happened?"

"You're getting off this wretched thing," Simon said, checking the rig he'd devised around Rothermore's chest. "In a minute, you'll feel a big tug upwards. Not to worry."

Alastair Rothermore tried to respond but he seemed to drift away again, sagging against Simon.

"Ephraim – go, man!" Simon steadied the injured MP. Ephraim and the other footmen who had come up the stairs to assist, began to haul in the rope. Rothermore was pulled upwards through the emergency door. Simon supported the man's legs so he wouldn't twist or slip.

The onlookers on the ground floor cheered as Rothermore successfully ascended past the lift cage and up to where Ephraim could pull him to safety.

"Now, you!" called out Alice. "Simon, please hurry!"

Once Rothermore had been lowered to the stair landing, Ephraim untied the rope and threw it down to Simon. "Ready, sir?" he asked as Palliser Park staff members attended to Rothermore behind him.

The lift's pulley system screeched again – the pressure of shifting platform continuing to tear the rigging from its original moorings. Simon felt the floor jerk sideways and he fell back against the some of the remaining railings. The decorative cage metal bit into his back.

He looked up. The mechanism was actively grinding the stonework and plaster was falling like snow from the ceiling.

"Hold the gap!" Simon pushed off the railing and moved towards the emergency door, intending to spring up to the stair landing. The platform spun again, jerking the rope from Clarence's hands. Without the brace, the cage slammed into the staircase with a metallic bang that obliterated the cries of dismay from the ground floor. Simon fell to his knees and slid into the railings. He figured he had about a minute, maybe two before the whole system collapsed.

"I got it, sir!" shouted Clarence as he frantically reeled in the rope.

Simon sprinted for the gap. He hoped Ephraim would be ready.

The cage tried to twist again but Clarence managed to hang on. Simon slipped through the open space and sprang up towards the stair landing. The moment he did so, the cable and pulley mechanism exploded overhead in an avalanche of stone shards and plaster. Simon felt the rush of the cage and cable behind him as it hurtled to the ground floor, shaking Palliser Park's foundation as it crashed.

35

Alice stared at the pile of crushed and contorted metal that now filled the base of the staircase. Dust mushroomed up and radiated out over the ground floor. Her ears were ringing so loudly from the thunderous crash of the elevator that she could barely hear the astonished reactions of the other witnesses.

Nausea rolled over her like one of the waves coming into Palliser Park's private beach. She staggered a step to her right.

Someone took her arm. She thought it might be Perry but her hearing wouldn't allow her to be sure.

"Alice – can I be of service?" the muffled voice asked.

Alice was pretty sure she was going to be sick. "Simon ... is Simon?"

"He's pulling himself over. Look up and see. He's all right," the voice mumbled as if underwater or far away.

She made herself look to the stair landing and the underwater speaker proved to be correct – Simon was getting over the stair railing with the assistance of a couple of footmen. He looked in good shape although the plummeting elevator seemed to have slashed the sleeve of his jacket. She wondered – horrified – if the metal cable had bitten into

Simon's sleeve as it careened past him. Had it managed to wrap around his arm and hauled him away from the stair ...

Alice felt nausea flare like a Guy Fawkes Day firework – powerful enough to knock her off her feet. She began to weave, her eyesight blurring and ears roaring. Then Palliser Park's gilded hallway went black.

The emergency scene by the elevator was gone when her senses returned, replaced by one of Palliser Park's many ground floor reception rooms. Alice opened her eyes to see Simon gazing down at her, worry creasing his pale face.

"Alice!" he breathed, taking one of her hands in his. "Thank God you are all right."

"Stupid," she said, feeling like a perfect idiot. "How long ..."

"Only a few moments. Gave me a good scare though."

"*You're one to talk*," Alice pointed out with as much humor as she could drum up. She still felt unsteady. Maybe the elaborate meals at Palliser Park were just too much for her.

Another face peered over Simon's shoulder. One of the guests – a pleasant featured man in his fifties. He smiled at her in such an encouraging manner, she wondered if she was dying or being shipped off to a mental asylum. It was unsettling.

"Phineas Sherbrooke – FitzRobert cousin and doctor. I'd like to give you the once over if you don't mind. It's unusual for healthy young women to faint and your husband tells me you haven't been feeling tip top."

Alice felt irritated. "I did just see my husband nearly killed in a freak accident."

Phineas Sherbrooke continued to beam at her as if she were five years old and about to have a broken arm reset. "Indeed.

Probably nothing out of the ordinary. Good to make quite certain though."

Simon squeezed her hand. "Darling, Fizz can act as a de facto chaperone."

"I can!" sang out Fizz from the drawing room doorway. Apparently, she'd been loitering, waiting to be called into service.

Alice looked from Simon's worried face to the genial countenance of Phineas Sherbrooke, doctor and FitzRobert cousin. She felt rather than saw Fizz's anxious energy bleeding into the room. She was outnumbered and outflanked.

"Fine," she said, sighing.

36

While Alice was being looked over by Dr. Sherbrooke, Simon decided to return to Alastair Rothermore and see if the politician was ready to talk about what happened in the lift. Fortunately, there were other doctors to be found in the FitzRobert family tree and the more important one – a vaguely imperious Harley Street surgeon named Mortimer Threapwood – had been assigned to Rothermore. Alice had acquired the cheerful country doctor who maintained a surgery in Wiltshire. Simon liked him better.

Alastair Rothermore had been removed from the staircase and taken to the nearest room with a chaise lounge. He was sequestered with his devastated wife, Threapwood and a footman who stood by in case the doctor required anything. With the zeal of a Border Collie, Lord FitzRobert had herded his family and remaining guests back to the dining rooms for restoratives, leaving the patients in peace.

"Oh, Simon," said Esther Rothermore upon seeing him slip into the room. "Thank you for what you did. We are both really so grateful."

Simon shook his head. "Needed to be done. I just got there first. How is he doing?"

FitzRobert cousin Mortimer Threapwood glanced up from the bandage he was applying to the MP's head. "He'll be all right in a few days after some rest. Perhaps you would be so kind as to leave us ..."

"I echo my wife," Alastair interrupted in a weak voice. He waved a hand for Simon to come closer. "Thank you. She tells me you were incredibly daring."

Threapwood rolled his eyes as Simon ignored his request and took a chair next to the MP's chaise. The doctor finished tucking in the bandage, backing off to request hot tea from the footman. It was unclear who would be beneficiary of such a hot beverage and Simon hoped it was the Rothermores.

"What do you remember?"

Rothermore looked at him – exhausted but interested. "The bloody lift?"

"Yes – do you remember what happened?"

"I remember I was nipping up to fetch something of Esther's ..."

His wife sighed, shaking her head. "Never forgive myself. It was just a headache powder! Such a nothing little thing."

Alastair reached over to squeeze her trembling hand. "Got into the wretched thing," he paused to take a slow breath. "Got into the wretched thing and started to ascend ... then the gears started to scream ... the cage – y thing stopped, then dropped. I must have fallen. That's it."

"Anybody about? Anyone at all?"

The MP thought for a moment, wincing as some pain shot through his system. "Some young people had beaten me to the lift. They were a bit blotto ... I remember their laughter echoing up the staircase vestibule. Can't place who they were – maybe Lady Constance and her betrothed?"

"That," said Mortimer Threapwood as he returned to his patient, "should probably conclude this conversation."

"Fair enough," Simon said and stood up. "Thank you. I will make sure DI Saxby is informed. Perhaps you can avoid any more interviews."

He retreated, allowing the doctor to tend to his patient. Not much to indicate it was anything other than a faulty mechanism. Still, he'd give a lot to know the identity of the drunken guests who had been in the lift earlier. It wasn't Fizz or Jack. They had been in the dining room lingering over drinks with him and Alice.

Simon decided to return to the crash site before retrieving Alice. She would have some more time with the amiable Sherbrooke looking after her and that struck him as a very good situation. The idea of Alice seriously unwell really had the power to unnerve him. He felt faint reverberations of shell shock threading through his senses.

Alice was an excellent horsewoman with a knack for bringing out the best in highly strung or traumatized horses. He could always count on her to take care of their war scarred horses out in the hunt field. No mean feat, sometimes. He preferred to use a nice, soft – mouth eggbutt snaffle on such horses rather than the more typical and fashionable full bridle. The war horses had been pulled and jerked around Europe – usually in full bridles – and Simon had noted that the severe combination of curb and snaffle had an anxiety producing effect on some of them. He liked to reschool in an eggbutt or a low port kimberwicke. It often took a long time to restore faith that riders wouldn't hurt mouths with harsh hands and bits.Alice was a rider who reassured a worried horse. She had a lovely, quiet seat and soft hands. She could take an uncertain horse down to a stone wall in a noisy, frantic field and when she asked, it would find the confidence to fly the obstacle. That kind of riding took a steady nerve and true courage. She was not the type to faint dead away. He hoped Sherbrooke could provide some kind of opinion that would make sense of it. Until then, he would try to keep shell shock at bay – focus on Palliser Park's potent mysteries and The Gravedigger. A diversion. Something to puzzle out.

By the time Simon reached the destroyed lift, Lord FitzRobert, his family and friends hadretreated to the dining rooms for another assault upon the lavish provisions. Only a few members of the servant class remained to do what they could to tidy the appalling mess. They were stacking bits of twisted metal and trying to sweep heavy debris out of the way with inadequate brooms.

"Have you need of anything, sir?" asked Clarence, pausing to lean against his broom's handle. The young footman looked exhausted. They all did and the main event of the weekend had yet to start.

Simon shook his head. "Just having a look."

"Yes, sir. Quite something, isn't it?" Clarence said, returning to sweep a pile of dust and dirt towards a larger heap.

The hardworking servants were adding to several substantial heaps of debris that sat off to the sides of the staircase. Simon studied them, not at all sure what he was really hoping to find. He was not an engineer so the ruined pieces of metal cage and pulley chain told him no story of deliberate interference or mere accident. The sheer amount of dust was kind of intriguing. Palliser Park always appeared immaculate that it was hard to imagine so much detritus lurked in the crevasses of the building. Simon wondered if the explosion of the lift cage hitting the ground floor had literally shaken dirt from the foundation and floor tiles.

He left the crash site and headed up what had been a lovely Georgian stair before Lord FitzRobert's builders had stuck a stout metal edifice in front of it and spoiled the line. The steps were also covered in a fine dust thrown up by the accident. Lord FitzRobert's fancy lift had acted like a bomb when it slammed into the ground floor. Could it actually have damaged the house foundation? If so, FitzRobert faced yet another massive payout to restore his dream palace. It took Simon a few minutes to reach the top floor and by then, he was wheezing. The damage to his lungs from relatively mild exposure to mustard gas was an ongoing process – better than it had been but still debilitating. What it would have been like to suffer full exposure to it was almost unimaginable.

Simon paused, once he reached the highest landing, to catch his ragged breath. The dust particles that still lingered in the air were not helping matters and he leaned back against a wall to slowly exhale, trying to quiet his jangled nerves.

He coughed and felt his heart begin to race. Pinpoint lights danced in front of his eyes – something that happened when his lungs were overtaxed. The smell of the invasive dust was acrid, reminding him of the trenches. Disparate voices echoed in his head: *Hold the line! Hold the bloody line! Will this rain ever stop? Cuppa now, Major? I've been hit! Steady, lads, steady! Gas cloud to the west* …

It would be easy to stop the voices – just a few steps … and he, too, could fall … fall into silence …

Simon pressed his hands over his ears with a strangled cry. He pushed back against the wall, locking his knees so no forward movement was possible. Inhaling and exhaling slowly, in an ordered fashion, began to take the upper hand, banishing the voices and calming his banging heart.

Another few minutes of focused effort – he lowered his hands and let out a long, weary breath. It was time to try and be useful.

The chain and pulley system that had operated FitzRobert's opulent lift was effectively gone. A gaping hole in the ceiling plaster was virtually all that was left of a modern engineering feat. Looking up, Simon could see the oak floor beams it had been anchored into. These were splintered and would require serious reconstruction. The floor above held the servants' quarters. They would soon have a gaping hole to contend with as if their lives weren't inconvenient enough.

No obvious signs of The Gravedigger jamming up the lift. As with every aspect of the German Will O' the Wisp, there was only speculation. Never any direct or simple evidence.

Simon glanced at his tank watch and tried to imagine how long it would take a fairly fit person to nip up the staircase if that person was interested into reaching the main mechanism before a lift cage reached its destination. He had the notion to run an experiment in the morning with one of the younger footmen. Time a lad dashing up the stairs just to see what might be possible.

He descended the stair, wondering if Alice might be able to retreat to their guest quarters for some needed rest. Admittedly, he wouldn't mind tucking in for the night either. It would be a relief to get away from the FitzRobert dog and pony show. The decanter of sherry in their room called to him, promising warm, sleepy sensations. It was a pity, then, that he needed to take a walk before finally taking to his bed.

"Sir!" called out Clarence from below.

Simon glanced down to the ground floor where the footman now stood, waving a yellowed piece of paper. "Clarence?"

"Found this, sir, while I was sweeping up. Got your name on it."

Thoroughly intrigued, Simon came down the steps as quickly as he dared without reigniting the lung damage wheeze. He accepted what appeared to be an envelope from Clarence and murmured his thanks.

"It was in the rubbish," the footman offered, pointing to one of the piles of dust, broken metal and plaster shards. "You must have lost it in the fuss. Sorry, sir."

"Not to worry, Clarence. Thank you," Simon said, noting that the soiled envelope was from the Brightside telegraph office. He stepped away from the young footman and was about to open the message when Fizz FitzRobert suddenly burst into view.

She continued her agitated trajectory towards him, slipping an arm under his right elbow and wrenching him forward. "You must come right now. Right now!"

Simon shoved the telegraph into his pocket and without a care for his lungs, ran. Alice needed him.

CHAPTER

37

Alice sipped some tea that Dr, Sherbrooke had been kind enough to have fetched for her. She didn't know quite what to think. It had been quite a day. The sort of day that really demanded a hot bath and a good night's sleep. She longed for both.

"Alice!" came Simon's voice from the doorway. He sounded almost panicked.

"Hello, darling," she said before having another sip of the reviving tea. "How are the Rothermores?"

In addition to sounding panicked, he now looked baffled. "In some pain but expected to fully recover," Simon murmured as he crossed to join her. "I'm more concerned about ... well, how are *you*?"

Alice watched over Simon's shoulder as Fizz shepherded Sherbrooke out of the drawing room. She set her tea aside on a small table. Her husband sat on the edge of the couch to take her other hand. His own were shaking slightly.

"A little tired," Alice admitted. "Unsurprisingly."

"Unsurprisingly? You collapsed *and* you've been sick. Do you need hospital? Fizz said it was urgent."

She made a face. "Fizz! And you took that at her word? Fizz, really?"

"Do you need hospital?" he repeated before turning round on the couch to scan the room. "Where the bloody hell is Sherbrooke anyway?"

"I'm just fine, honestly." Alice felt a flush of euphoria cross her senses. She shivered with it. "Dr. Sherbrooke says we should know absolutely for certain in a few weeks …"

Simon stared at her, momentarily vexed. "A few weeks? You could be dead of the Bubonic Plague in a few weeks. What's his diagnosis for today, right now?"

"For someone who has a reputation for being awfully bright," Alice shivered again and laughed, "you are a perfect thicko.Dr. Sherbrooke thinks I've been a little off my game because I am going to have a baby."

Simon continued to stare at her. His frustration returning to flummoxed, shifting to sudden understanding fused with fleeting horror and then settled on wonder. He bent from the waist and kissed the back of her hands.

He straightened, radiating a kind of giddy awe. "A baby?"

"In about seven months, he thinks."

"A baby."

"Yes – a baby." Alice grinned, enjoying how far the simple notion had thrown her complicated husband.

"You and I … a baby?"

She laughed out loud. "You're sure the Royal Cavalry thought it was all right to let you operate machinery?"

Simon opened his mouth to say something but then clamped it shut. She could see that he was utterly speechless.

CHAPTER

38

Simon poured himself a drink from the side table. He looked over at Alice, who was sleeping deeply, her breathing regular and undisturbed by dreams. Tired from the events of the day, she had fallen into blissful oblivion not long after they had relocated to their guest room.

He wished he could settle in for long summer's night so easily. He wished he could settle in and thoroughly wonder at the thought of Alice becoming a mother. She'd be such a brilliant mother ... and he'd be a father. *What if a lovely, worthwhile child had to go to war* ... Simon took a swallow of his drink as his shell – shocked nerves crept up a notch. He forced himself to focus on the job at hand. There was one more task to accomplish before he could allow himself the luxury of thinking about Alice.

Wind rattled past the windows. Simon glanced out the nearest one, watching Palliser Park trees shudder in erratic breezes. A sea storm was somewhere out beyond the horizon. He wondered when it would sweep across the Essex coast – probably right in the middle of Lord FitzRobert's parade of bread and circuses. It certainly would give the ridiculous event lashings of an Edgar Allen Poe story.

Simon knocked back his whisky and headed for the door. Despite it being summer, he was dressed to stay warm. Coastal nights could be seriously chilly with a wind coming in off the ocean and he had a bit of a walk ahead. He slipped out, trying not to wake Alice, who clearly needed to rest – at least he assumed expectant women needed more rest than usual – and made his way down the quiet hallway. Palliser Park had shifted into slumber. There would probably be one or two servants lurking on the ground floor in case Lord FitzRobert or his guests needed something, but even noble Crumpling would have retired.

The great house was dark, save for some light under guest doorways and moonbeams slipping through windows. Lord FitzRobert had gone to enormous expense to refit massive Palliser Park with the most modern electrical wiring and plumbing systems to allow for very little reliance on the old – fashioned country house ways. Still, rural and coastal electrical cooperatives were pretty primitive and prone to failure especially after the exhaustion of war. Even the FitzRoberts couldn't force such entities to expand at a rate conducive to the comfortable London lives they had come to expect. As he did when in residence at Castle Fairlight where electricity was confined to certain areas, Simon carried his Ever – Ready *flashlight* as American born Alice would call it.

He hadn't turned it on as yet, preferring to nip along the darkened byways of Palliser Park without his torch alerting weary servants to the notion that a wandering guest might require something. Having turned into the main hallway that housed the most important individuals under Lord FitzRobert's roof, Simon heard the *click,creak* of a door opening. In the distance, light spilled out onto the hallway floor. Instinctively, he faded back against the edge of a large armoire that probably served, when fully opened, as a staging area for servants delivering tea or breakfast trays.

"We will never be free of him," murmured Jack, stepping into the shaft of light. "Never."

"I can take care of him," replied Dorothy Brier with a strange confidence for an aging actress who required a rich benefactor to bolster her prospects. "You'll see – it'll be all right. You secure the purse. We have to have money."

Simon watched from the shadows as the lithe actress wrapped her arms around Jack. Their kiss was passionate and familiar. They clearly had been together a long time and were as comfortable as an old married couple. So much for Jack's protestations to the contrary. He wondered how Fizz would feel about being reduced to *The Purse*. Deeply unamused would be the least of it, surely.

"I know you're the best at what you do," said Jack quietly, once they'd pulled apart, "but he's far too clever. Not too proud to admit that he scares the hell out of me."

"Forget him. Things have changed. You have to convince that wretched girl to elope – we can't wait anymore."

Simon saw Jack shrug his shoulders, apparently uneasy with his assignment. "You can't tell Fizz anything," he said defensively. "She has to have a traditional wedding."

"Once the ink's dry," Dorothy Brier paused to kiss Jack's cheek, pressing her body against him seductively, "I'll take over."

"He'll never allow it. Never."

"Leave him to me," she reiterated. "It's the least of our worries."

Dorothy pulled Jack into another deep kiss. Simon leaned back against the wall and squashed the frustrated groan that rose in his throat. Apparently, Jack was actually an unappealing idiot being led around by a terrible woman and whoever HE, the puppet master, was in their circle.

"I should go," said Jack once she allowed him to draw back. Dorothy gave him a little push. "I need some sleep anyway."

Simon surreptitiously lowered himself so that a large reproduction William and Mary armchair would provide more cover in the dark hallway. He didn't fancy having a conversation with Jack especially as there was a strong possibility that Jack would end up with a broken nose.

He held his breath as Jack took a lit candle from Dorothy, then headed up the hallway. The small white candle emitted an erratic umbrella of light that billowed around Fizz's duplicitous fiancé. Simon hoped the fluttering golden glow wouldn't capriciously reveal his hiding spot. He couldn't imagine a more awkward scenario – even worse if he gave Jack that well deserved punch in the mouth.

Fortunately, Jack appeared absolutely wrapped up in himself and his perceived troubles. He passed by the William and Mary reproduction chair without hesitation, never glancing to his right and discovering a crouching and highly irritatedcavalry officer. Simon stayed where he was until Jack disappeared around a corner and he heard Dorothy's guest room door click shut.

The central hallway returned to uninhabited with nary a servant creeping along with tea and digestive powder for a visitor who had eaten too much of Lord FitzRobert's sumptuous buffet. Simon emerged from behind the William and Mary chair. He let out a breath and wondered what he ought to do about protecting Fizz from the dread duo. From Alice, who managed such affairs, he knew the wedding itself being planned for the following spring. There was time to address Jack's deplorable behavior before legal instruments were involved and, of course, always the chance that he would reveal himself as a rake before the Fairlights needed to act. Dealing now with Jack gave him less time to find the Gravedigger and stop the bumping off of notable persons. He had to prioritize the job at hand.

Simon made his way silently past Dorothy's door and down to the ground floor without encountering any other living souls housed within Palliser Park. He slipped outside through the conservatory's costly new and patently faux French doors.

Outside was windy, wild and cool even for a summer night. Simon felt a rush of elation. It was so much better than being trapped inside Lord FitzRobert's vast gilded cage. For a second, he was thankful to the Gravedigger for setting him free of the house. There was even a moon that provided just enough visibility to allow him to avoid switching on his clever American flashlight. Simon remembered what the troopers used to say at such moments: when tea actually got boiled in the trench or an extra annoying rat got picked off without much fuss – *Life is grand, ain't it?*

He moved from the conservatory terrace to one of the formal garden paths that connected eventually to the cliffside and could just make out the outline of the former gamekeeper's cottage in the distance. Moonbeams glinted off its leaded glass windows. Simon could see how such flashes could be mistaken for ghost lights although if he was right, there was an even more vivid reason lights could haunt Clara Mare.

A brisk sea breeze pulled at his hair and jacket as Simon jogged along the cliff path. His scarred lungs ached with the effort but he ignored the pain and kept up the pace. Worth it to test his theory that the structure was just a little bit more than a gardener's storage closet.

By the time he reached the flagstone entranceway, the wind off the sea had turned the night very cold. Simon shivered as he stepped onto the stonework. The sea below the cliff was roaring as the waves churned against the beach and pier. Nature's way of announcing that a major storm was en route. Jack's reprehensible behavior wasn't the only force that would be buffeting the fancy engagement party.

Simon paused to breathe. If done slowly and with some focus, it helped banish the effects of the damage to his lungs. While he did so, he scanned the old gamekeeper's cottage – Clara Mare – in the silvery light of a summer moon. It's cheerfully Olde England outlines and leaded glass windows made him wish again that he could see what the original Tudaburgh family house had looked like – probably a lot more enjoyable than the formal Georgian pile that currently had pride of place.

He had noticed earlier when out with Alice that the dust and detritus that one might expect to find clogging an essentially abandoned structure had been recently disturbed. The lock on the door had new scratch marks by the keyhole that also suggested recent use. It was, of course, perfectly possible a Palliser Park servant would have suitable reasons to nip in for a gardening tool. For example, Poor Polly Piety had yet to be returned from Brightsea for burial in the servant cemetery so no one needed to rifle through the cottage for a sturdy shovel. If not a member of staff, who else might be using the old relic and why?

The cottage was relatively remote. Inhabitants of the house wouldn't find it a convenient place for quick visits. It was close, however, to Lord FitzRobert's brand new dock. He was not a sailor but assumed it was possible for a sea craft to sidle up to it in the dark of night and easily be undetected if the boat handlers weren't too noisy about it. Could an outsider or outsiders be trespassing on Palliser Park grounds and if so, for what purpose?

Simon stepped up to the arched door and examined more closely the modern padlock that had been added to keep the cottage secure. Secure from what was unclear. Perhaps Lord FitzRobert was worried some wandering local would purloin an old bucket. Under the beam of his American flashlight, he could see fresh scrape marks in the mechanism.

Fighting a trench war taught men many unusual skills. Passing many long, dreary hours in a trench also occasionally led to gaining unusual skills beyond the immediate needs of the battlefield. One of his was lock picking – learned from a trooper named Alfie Poole from the Birmingham slums. There wasn't a lock that Alfie Poole couldn't crack given enough time. The trooper had proven invaluable behind the lines in reconnaissance missions when supplies were short and during some of the long down times between maneuvers, Alfie Poole had battled boredom by teaching Simon basic lockpicking.

Simon pulled out a set of lock picks from his trouser pocket. A peacetime present from Alfie after Simon had secured him an officer's commission with Sir Vernon.

He selected the one that Alfie would recommend for a modest job and slipped it into the keyhole, making short work of the padlock. After the correct tinkering, the lock clicked open just as Alfie Poole promised it would. Simon pulled the hasp across and pushed in the former gamekeeper's front door. The heavy wooden door gave a sigh as it swung free of the threshold and its ancient iron fittings rattled a little.

Simon stepped over the wide threshold typical of the era in which it was built. He was proud of Alfie Poole. Just as invaluable to the service as he was in the trenches, Alfie — despite the kind of working class background that ought to render him of little interest to persons such as Sir Vernon — had earned unfettered respect from the intelligence fraternity and a promotion to lieutenant. He almost smiled at a memory of Sir Vernon revealing that the background investigation of *the colorfulPoole* had produced a report that teachers in Alfie's grim slum school had dismissed him as little better than retarded. In reality, Alfie Poole had been the brilliant head of his own crime syndicate — specializing in second — story work. Barely a teenager, he directed seasoned professional thieves in a complex network that had spread across the Midlands.

Simon dismissed recollections of Alfie Poole as he scanned the former gamekeeper's cottage. It must have been a charming place once, with a muddle of rooms, whitewashed plaster, open beams and large central fireplace made of the same stone that had been used for tombstones in the servant cemetery.Simon could see how a blazing fire in the fireplace would warm the entire cottage, making it quite a comfortable sanctuary against a cold seaside night or after long day tending to Palliser Park duties.

But, if he were right, Palliser Park's haunted cottage just might be something else as well. The mysterious lights floating along the cliffside and around Clara Mare's modest cemetery might be the lonely shades of long dead Tudaburghs or their servants. He had seen inexplicable events on the battlefield and would never discount a good ghost story.

That said, a convenient building within walking distance of a natural harbor might be an ideal stash for some profitable smuggling. A wily gamekeeper could put away a nice pension, assisting the passage of illicit goods into England. Maybe past Tudaburghs spearheaded the whole scheme. He could imagine the temptation of acquiring French wines during Napoleon's tantrums. After the last war, Simon wondered if Clara Mare might be a useful place for The Gravedigger. He had to be within striking range of the main house to do vandalism such as stripping the rig of a lift cage or whatever else was planned to disrupt the work of the British Reparations Committee.

"Or I could just be a perfect thicko out on a fool's errand," Simon murmured, testing the wide wooden planks in the central space with his foot. He tapped the wood in several likely spots, hoping for a hollow sound that might indicate a void under the floor.

When sounding out the ground floor revealed nothing of particular interest, Simon checked the walls for any possible hollow spots. Then he moved to the other smaller rooms including what was once the kitchen still outfitted with an iron stove, long empty shelves and sturdy wooden pegs.

The entire cottage had been cleared of traditional furniture and household goods – no whimsical Restoration Lowboys or fireside benches. There was a sizable collection of gardening tools and a few packing crates that contained nothing more exciting than paper packages of seed.

Simon shifted his interest to the first floor. He quickly ascended a narrow stone set of stairs that twisted up to where the former sleeping quarters were located. Even more barren than the rooms on the ground floor, the largest space had been pressed into service as storage closet for a few shabby old trunks and wooden boxes. The air was heavy and stagnant as well – the odor of damp stone, mold and old wood rolled over him like the tide coming in. Dead flies littered the floor boards. With luck, he could make short work of the upper rooms and retreat.

Outside, the wind rustled around the upper level of the cottage, warning that the sea storm was coming. Simon handled his American flashlight carefully. He kept the beam as doused as much as possible. It wouldn't help to add to the Clara Mare ghost lights legend.

"Perhaps I am, indeed, the perfect thicko," Simon said out loud to the old building as he stepped into the last of the abandoned bedrooms. Floors and walls had been solid in the others – no mysterious airing closets with hidden compartments for illicit French wines.

The final bedroom – from what he could tell with his pale light source – was probably the prettiest in its day. Two large latticed windows overlooked the cliffside and in the moonlight, Simon could see out to the churning water beyond the craggy rocks. He decided it must have been pleasant with an overstuffed bed and a cheery fire going in its own fireplace. Rather a lovely fireplace too – even if the actual firebox was small and shallow. It had a handsome wooden chimneypiece that once must have displayed some of the gamekeeper's prized possessions.

Disappointed, Simon let out a short breath. He ought to get back to the main house and try to get into bed without waking Alice. Maybe he had been wrong about the Gravedigger targeting Lord FitzRobert and Palliser Park. Maybe the lorry had just been an unusually violent robbery. Maybe the lift had actually been some kind of odd accident. Maybe he was just wrong.

"And now, the perfect thicko goes home," he said, turning to find his way back to Clara Mare's stone steps.

Then Simon paused and returned his gaze to the fireplace with the rather nice wooden mantel. A fireplace built on an inside wall. A fireplace – inexplicably for a country cottage – that did not share a chimney with any of the lower rooms.

He stepped in for a closer look at the relatively fancy woodwork surrounding the firebox. The mantel was solid with side pieces embossed with some desultory, non – specific flowers. Kneeling, he aimed the flashlight at the base and discovered that it didn't quite drop flush to the floor.

Simon stretched his fingers under the gap and gave the side panel a solid tug. He was gratified when the heavy mantel began, grudgingly, to pull forward.

"Brilliant – false wall hide!" he breathed as the faux fireplace gave a cracking groan and swung open on hidden interior hinges. Palliser Park's former gamekeepers did indeed top up their Tudaburgh pittances with some good, old – fashioned smuggling. "Well done to you, ye olde game …"

The smell hit him first. If the stagnant air from before had seemed unpleasant, the fetid, rotten odor from the hidden space was overpowering – and it was a smell Simon knew all too well. He reeled, almost dropping to his knees. The wretched sweet sour smell of death. The smell of rotting flesh. Hundreds of blowflies billowed out, riding the wave of foul decay liberated from the gamekeeper's secret hide.

Simon staggered to lock his knees and combat the nausea that had risen up in his system. He waved away a horde of flies and aimed the American flashlight into the dark space that was hidden behind the false wall. Not a huge cache for a ship's hold of fabled pirate treasure chests but perfectly adequate to secret away bottles of wine and valuables. The amber light from the flashlight bounced around exposed wood and beams, revealing an ingenious plaster and wallpaper construction that effectively sealed the hide and helped it keep its secrets.

The secret that Simon's light found was not an outlawed bottle of brandy or someone's silver tea set. It was a human body– seemingly dumped in the rear of the hidden closet – sitting against the back wall with the limp posture of a man who had fallen asleep on the train. Despite devastating effects from the blowflies that continued to swarm over the corpse's visible flesh, Simon recognized the ruined face. His Imperial Highness, Prince Andrei Volkonsky of Russia.

CHAPTER

39

Alice sat on the edge of the bed and wondered just where her husband had gone. It was very late. She imagined the entire house with the exception of the Fairlights and a few exhausted servants was deeply asleep.

Feeling annoyed, she got up to pour herself a glass of water and pondered drawing a hot bath. It was an uncivilized hour to soak in a tub but immersion in warm, steaming water would soothe away her rumpled feelings. After all, she was accustomed to Simon's late night excursions. He often disappeared late at night to read or if in residence at Castle Fairlight, take a stroll to the stables. There was always something to do in a stable even if it was making sure none of the horses had divested themselves of a blanket or fly mask.

Alice sipped water and noted that Simon's paddock boots were missing. That meant he had decided to make a break for the outside for a walk in the June moonlight. A very appealing idea and she was further irritated that he hadn't invited her along. They were on a holiday together and ought to be doing their adventuring together. She hoped the whole *with child* business wasn't going to get all molly – coddling. Simon had another idea coming if he assumed she was going to sit in some

246

kind of confinement, sewing linens or some other tedious
pastime. The current American thinking for expectant mothers
was plenty of sunshine and exercise. Fortunately, her Harley
Street physician was young and was much of the same opinion.

In fact, she was going to get dressed and head out to find
Simon. He had either gone to the Palliser Park stable to see
what the horses were up to or had decided to walk along the
cliff path. Because Simon probably wouldn't want to step
unannounced into a stable that wasn't his, Alice guessed he'd
opt for the cliff path.

Despite the early summer, Alice knew it would be cold out
by the water and in the wind that was bringing the powerful
storm from the north. She threw on her jodhpurs, a sweater
and tweed jacket. Her lovely new lightweight jodhpurs already
felt just a bit tight about the waist. Would she be a veritable
walrus by Christmas? It was daunting.

Alice made her way out of the guest room and into the
darkened labyrinth of Palliser Park's hallways. She walked
carefully and quietly towards a secondary staircase that would
take her down to the ground floor. Fortunately, there was
enough moonlight streaming in from the house's Georgian
windows to guide her past all of Lord FitzRobert's hallway
furnishings without any serious incident. Simon, she noted, had
taken his beloved EverReady. A birthday gift from her father to
his son – in – law, the flashlight had been the hit of Simon's big
day. It had completely dwarfed the green marble horse head
bookends she had been so positive would entrance him. Men –
who could ever really understand them?

One of Palliser Park's secondary stairs took her down to
the main floor. Alice had lost count of how many staircases the
sprawling Georgian house actually possessed. They seemed to

pop up everywhere as the original architect clearly had twigged to the notion that the aristocratic Tudaburghs would demand prompt servant responses despite vast distances in the house. She was glad to avoid the elevator area with all of the rubble and congratulated herself on navigating without much fuss to an outside door.

It was a windy and wonderful night, Alice decided as she dropped down some terrace steps to one of the lawns. The night sky had been brushed momentarily clear of clouds by the gusting breeze that billowed through garden trees and hedges. Although a cloud bank would be drifting in as the storm drew closer, the remarkable clarity of the sky allowed moon and stars to flash brilliantly in the cold upper air. It felt exhilarating to breathe the night in and head out in search of her husband.

Alice felt strongly that Simon – not wishing to step into another man's stable unannounced – would have lit out for the cliffs where the silvery views across the sea would be fascinating and beautiful. She let the moonlight lead her through Palliser Park's garden rings to Lord FitzRobert's perfectly tended path that wound along the cliffside. The sea was pounding the beach below, roaring as it struck sand and rocks. Jets of salt water sprayed up with every crash against the rock, glittering briefly in starlight before falling back into the black tide.

Pausing to gaze out to sea, Alice was enchanted by ship lights bobbing in the dark distance as various large vessels battled rough water. She imagined the ship captains were anxious to tuck into nearby harbors to ride out the coming storm. These were commercial shipping vessels too large to find safety at Lord FitzRobert's new dock. They required the spacious ports of Southhampton or Dover. She wished them well.

She turned away from the sea drama and strolled along, breathing in the sharp, briny air. Overhead, marine birds wheeled and whistled in the erratic wind. It was a lonely sound but also crystalline and beautiful like a pure notes of coloratura soprano.

"Now, that's interesting," murmured Alice as her attention left soaring sea birds and refocused on Clara Mare on the distance.The old gamekeeper's cottage was a whimsical outline – a perfect setting for the ghost stories that swirled around it. She stopped and stared. Two fluttering orbs of light were floating towards the cottage.

"Ghost lights!" she breathed, breaking into a run. If a morose shade of a jealous gamekeeper's wife was wandering the cliffs above Lord FitzRobert's dock, she wanted a good look at it. If Simon was on the path somewhere, he'd be investigating errant ghost lights too. With a bit of luck, she'd see a real ghost *and* catch up with her mercurial husband.

40

Simon doused what little light was still emitting from the EverReady. Men were approaching Clara Mare. Through the latticed windows, he had caught sight of them coming up from Lord FitzRobert's new dock. They carried lanterns and were clearly headed towards the cottage.

"Care to bet they are here for you?" he said to Prince Andrei's slumped corpse.

He pondered his options. It was crucial *not* to meet up with the cottage intruders. They had probably murdered His Imperial Highness or, at the very least, were in the employ of whoever had shot the Russian prince in the head. Such individuals would be quick to rid themselves of a witness and he didn't fancy dying so soon after surviving the war.

Simon pushed the false fireplace back into place and hoped that in the night shrouded cottage, it wouldn't be immediately noticeable that the old smuggler's hide had been recently disturbed. He heard heavy footsteps scraping over the stonework outside the building. They'd be in the cottage in another minute or two. That meant an escape down the stairs and out through the kitchen was not a viable plan.

"And now, the Perfect Thicko is trapped," he murmured, scanning the abandoned bedroom for ideas.

There was only one way out and that was through the leaded windows. Not his favorite escape route as heights always made him anxious but infinitely preferable to confronting the prince's murder ring. Adding to his difficulties was the need to allow the interlopers to enter the cottage before using the window exit lest one of them spot him out on the roof.

Downstairs, Clara Mare's main door rattled. Simon unlatched one of the large latticed windows and shoved it open. He hoped the noisy entrance through the front door had masked the squeak of the iron window hinge and waited.

"I don't like it," said a voice loudly – Estuary accent. A Londoner. "I don't like it at all. That lock's not supposed to be hangin' open. Who's been in 'ere?"

"Gardeners," replied another London voice – dismissive, even bored.

Simon heard the same heavy boots scraping over floorboards. They were closing in on the narrow staircase, seeming to suggest that the dead Russian was, indeed, the point of interest. He threw a leg over the window ledge and gingerly slipped off the bedroom floor, trying to keep errant sound to a minimum. The roof was old slate – damp and skiddish. A gusting sea wind pushed at him as he emerged onto the roof. It rattled the window sash, making it very difficult to pull shut while exiting. Fortunately, the roof line under the bedroom windows was not steep, allowing him to find a spot to wedge himself against the ancient rain gutter and exterior wall. On the negative side, the old latticed window had failed to close completely.

He prayed the heavy old hinges and hardware would keep it from catching in the sea wind and pulling open, alerting the trespassing toughs to his escape strategy . Simon clutched his flashlight to his chest and braced against the wall as the latticed window glowed gold with the arrival of the men with their lanterns. From his vantage point, jammed to the extreme right of the window, he could just make out a corner of the bedroom and into that corner lumbered a bullet headed Englishman in a sailor's thick sweater.

"Cor – the stink," said Bullet Head, disappearing from the sliver of the room visible to Simon.

He could hear the false fireplace being pulled open amid repulsed commentary from the cottage trespassers. As thought, the two were in Clara Mare to take charge of the prince's body, presumably to dispose of it. Given the sailor sweater and the direction from which they emerged, Simon assumed they had arrived by boat. If a murderer needed a body to disappear forever, a murderer could do worse than dumping that body far out at sea.

And who had actually shot Prince Andrei in the head? The *hired muscle* as American Alice might say or had The Gravedigger struck at the prince – perhaps mistaking the Sunbeam's driver for Lord FitzRobert? If it wasn't an error of opportunity, why had the Russian been murdered? Had he seen The Gravedigger or seen something else he shouldn't have?

"What a bleedin' fool's game," said Bullet Head's partner – in – crime, suddenly appearing at the latticed window.

Simon almost slipped, pushing back against the cottage to stay out of the window's sight line. His heart raced at the dangerous surprise. Fortunately, the stiff breeze that rattled around Clara Mare's odd roofline disguised the scrape of his boot heel against the ancient slate.

"That's a big sea," observed Partner – in – Crime, pushing open the latticed window for a better look. Simon pulled back to avoid being struck by the glass. He barely took in a breath, prayed that the cottage interloper wouldn't decide to take a hard right and catch a glimpse of his hiding place.

"We'll be lucky to be done before it gets rough." Bullet Head's companion continued, his voice glum. "Don't fancy being out there in a real blow. Out and back. Out and back if we're lucky."

"Give us a hand!" snapped Bullet Head from somewhere in the room. "Not hauling this leaky bag on me own."

The Partner – in – Crime grumbled unintelligibly and abruptly pulled the latticed window in. With a sinking sensation, Simon heard the cottage trespasser rattle the old hardware as he latched it shut. No way back into Clara Mare. He was effectively caught out on the roof.

Simon shifted slightly, studying the cottage roof. The slate tiles glimmered a slick grey in the damp night air. Not only did he need to find a way down, he had to find it quickly if the two sailors were to be followed. It would be very useful to see the boat they'd managed to slip next to Lord FitzRobert's new dock.

Hoping that Bullet Head and the Partner – in – Crime would mistake any slips on the slate roof for general buffeting of the sharp sea wind, Simon gingerly moved from the relative safety of his hiding spot. He scrambled up to the crest of the roof where bright moonlight allowed a commanding view of the cliffs and the sea below. There by the FitzRobert dock, rocking in the high surf, was a lovely sailing yacht. One he had seen before. The *Sea Sprite* – Sir George Jasper's personal ship.

41

Alice paused to catch her breath, leaning with one hand against the abandoned privy. She had run almost the full length of the cliff path but had swerved off, heading for the servant cemetery. On the fly, her strategy had whittled down to the idea that ghost lights would probably float towards the sad little collection of weathered crosses and grave markers.

She took deep breaths, grateful that the moonlight had kept her from stumbling over a rock, and scanned the cemetery. No ghost lights. No translucent, glowing gamekeeper's wife gliding towards her final resting place. No Simon either. It was going to be a long trek back to bed ...

Something clattered on top of the privy roof and then thudded to the ground behind her. Alice started in panic, about to let out a shrill cry. A hand covered her mouth, brutally cutting off any further sound and an arm wrapped around her waist. She struggled sharply against her attacker.

"Be still, you silly creature," Simon whispered severely into her right ear. "We're in a bit of a jam."

Alice almost collapsed with relief but quickly straightened her spine as the notion that they were in some sort of tight spot became the dominant issue. She allowed him to pull her down

into a crouching position behind the old outbuilding. The privy
– a classic "one – seater" – was basically just a four by four
wooden box with a door that faced a path from Clara Mare's
kitchen.

Simon pulled his hand from her mouth but made a very
soft shushing sound. She nodded her understanding. Her heart
was thudding in excitement and panic.

"I tells you something's movin' about," came a thick
London accent from Clara Mare's garden path.

Alice saw a golden light cross over into the space between
the cottage and ramshackle privy – someone was holding out a
lantern. She pulled her legs up to her chest to make her frame
as small as humanly possible and hoped the speaker wouldn't
think to investigate behind the old outbuilding. She felt Simon
squeeze her shoulder in an attempt to be reassuring.

"Wind," replied another London voice. "A branch. A bird.
A cat. Come on – we'll be lucky if we don't end up in the drink
like this bloke."

"Nuffin' to chance," the first man insisted, his voice almost
petulant. "The gov says nuffin' to chance. I 'eard something on
the bloody roof! We should check and see if someone's about."

"About?" His companion snorted. "The only someone
about is this dead git and he ain't tellin'."

"I 'eard …"

"Not chasing after the 'ousekeeper's cat. *Come on*," the other
man repeated. He was clearly getting very annoyed. "Sea's
getting big. Don't fancy drowning out there."

Alice watched the gold light undulate as the suspicious
Londoner moved lantern back and forth scanning for any hint
of … *them*. She froze, barely breathing. Simon had moved very

quietly into the kind of crouch that would allow him to spring at any approaching attacker.

"Right then," the first voice relented. "This place gives me the bleedin' willies."

"Just grab your end," his friend snapped, "and stop fussin' about like a girl."

The original speaker replied with a profane description of his companion but seemed to move to assist as instructed. Alice watched the lantern light withdraw from the area about the old privy. Despite the pounding surf from below the cliffs, she could just make out a few scraping sounds as their boots crossed Clara Mare's stone kitchen path.

"Stay down for a bit longer," Simon whispered into her left ear. "I want to be sure they've moved on before we venture out."

Alice nodded. She felt absolutely knackered and cold in the rising sea wind. "Who are they?" she asked as quietly as she could.

"I will explain all once we're tucked into our little room," he said, rising up and peering round the edge of the privy. "Right – think you could run again if I need you to?"

She nodded again. Anything to avoid a meet up with the rough Londoners who seemed to be toting around a *dead git*.

Alice watched as Simon scanned beyond the old outbuilding. He was wheezing slightly so his lungs scarred by mustard gas had been taxed by whatever he'd been up to before rescuing her from a nasty run – in.

"Stay close." Simon reached down to grasp her hand. "Don't hesitate if I tell you to do something."

He pulled her after him. They left the back of the privy and crossed to the rear of Clara Mare. Hugging the cottage wall allowed them to move towards the cliff path without alerting any dangerous persons to their presence. Alice tried not to trip over any errant rocks or clumps of coastal grass in the gloomy shadows of the cottage. It wouldn't do to roll an ankle and have to limp or be carried all the way back to the main house.

Simon paused ahead of her once they'd reached the far end. Again, he scanned the views beyond the old gamekeeper's cottage. This time she moved next to him and looked as well. On a normal evening, she'd be dazzled by the vista in front of her. In the sharp, blue moonlight, the cliff edge provided a dramatic frame for a wild and vibrant sea. The storm had not yet arrived but huge, angry waves were announcing its approach and if such omens were to be believed, it was going to be one heck of a blow – out.

It was Lord FitzRobert's dock, though, that provided the greatest revelation. Tied off, rolling up and down in the high surf was a beautiful sailing yacht. It's sleek, knife – edge design set off, even in moonlight, by a glossy onyx body and crisp white trim. Alice could see a few lit lanterns swinging wildly on deck and in the wheelhouse. She could just make out the dark figures of the ship's crew – one onboard and two on the dock. They were focused on moving an object onto the craft.

"Now's the time," said Simon. "We're going to dart to the path and head back. I don't think they'll spot us."

"Is that the *dead girl?*" she asked, watching as the two figures wrestled with something human sized and awkward.

"Yes," Simon said and took her hand again.

The sea wind buffeted them as they left the relative sanctuary of the cottage, running across the scrub grass to Palliser Park's cliffside path. Alice looked back for a moment – the two crew members continued to mill around the yacht but appeared to take no notice of people up on the cliffs. Relief coursed through her. There wasn't going to be an ugly clash – at least not immediately.

They ran, using moonlight as their guide, until reaching Palliser Park's outer rim of gardens and tennis courts. Simon pulled up by an apple tree and braced a hand against it, wheezing.

Alice tried to catch her breath. She felt as if she might be ill. Her stomach lurched with the effort of having gone flat out from Clara Mare.

"Was that," she paused to take in a shaky breath, "the *Sea Sprite?*"

Alice saw Simon nod, still wheezing. "Sir George Jasper is transporting dead bodies?" she asked, finding it difficult to reconcile the affable politician with death and misadventure. At the very least, she couldn't imagine the proud yacht owner happy to put decaying human corpses on his immaculate ship.

Simon finally pushed off the apple tree. He inhaled deeply and exhaled without the mustard gas wheeze. When he spoke, his voice was low and serious. "We're going to move through the garden very very quietly. I don't want anyone seeing us outside the house."

"In case, Sir George – or someone – is out and about checking on the status of dead bodies?"

"Clever Alice," Simon said, actually smiling although it was rueful and a bit bitter. "No one must know what we have seen tonight. You understand?"

"I understand that you are going to have a hell of a story to tell me," said Alice. She stood up straighter as the nausea and unsteadiness seemed to be drifting away on her second wind. "Have you got the EverReady?"

Even in the shadow of the apple tree, Alice could see his face looked pained. "I dropped it on Clara Mare's roof," he admitted. "Up there somewhere, probably in five pieces."

"One hell of a story," she repeated.

They moved quietly and with purpose through Palliser Park's formal garden rings, keeping mostly to the shadows along the perfectly manicured pathways. Alice noticed that Simon looked up frequently, scanning the main house's sea facing windows. She guessed he was searching for any sign of someone watching – perhaps, with a spy glass – for sight of the *Sea Sprite* heading out. She saw nothing unusual in Palliser Park's bank of Georgian glass. No glimmer of light or movement.

Finally, they reached the same door she had used earlier and Simon ushered her inside. He indicated that they should maintain silence while they returned to their guest quarters and sanctuary.

Palliser Park felt like some vast mausoleum to Alice. She wondered if Alexander the Great's lost tomb would have the same sealed up, dry and heavy sensation when it was eventually found. By contrast, the far older and more storied Castle Fairlight had a quirky, almost cozy charm even when one was creeping downstairs to find the sandwich tray the staff always left out on a sideboard for hungry souls. Alice decided she couldn't wait to return to the castle for the rest of the summer and again, berated herself privately for dragging Simon to Fizz's wretched engagement week. Trucks knocking cars into ditches, pretty girls falling to a horrible death, elevators crashing, Jack stepping out with his future father – in – law's girl and Sir George Jasper's boat crew moving a dead body. What an unmitigated disaster.

They slipped up a secondary staircase and emerged to the first floor's main hallway. Alice breathed in relief. All that was left was a trip up the central thoroughfare and a hard left into the smaller, less ornate second tier guest wing. Piece of cake.

Just as that pleasant notion crossed her mind, someone with a lit candle came into view. Someone headed down towards them. *Piece of cake*, Alice sighed. Didn't Marie Antoinette say something about cake?

Simon suddenly swept her into a kiss. He wrapped his arms around her and pressed his mouth against hers with urgency. She responded in kind until the approaching member of the household coughed loudly and the candle illuminated the area around them like a police search light.

"Crikey, you two," drawled Perry. "You've got a room, you know. Don't make lonely bachelors feel even worse."

Simon backed away and Alice turned to see Lord FitzRobert's son in his rumpled dressing gown, grinning at them. He held out a silver candelabra with four burning candles of various heights.

"I woke up absolutely starved," Perry admitted. "There must be a mountain of food left. Keep me company?"

Alice shook her head. "Sorry, Perry. We crept down for a raid already. I've got to get Simon tucked in – he's had a lot of wine."

She felt Simon swing an effusive arm about her shoulders. "That's right," he announced with a slight slur. "At least five glasses. Isn't Alice beautiful? She's the most beautiful girl in the world!"

Perry laughed, jostling the candelabra. "Well, never thought I'd actually see Sober Sides Simon blotto. Nicely done and much deserved, sir – and yes, I think Alice is the most beautiful girl in the world."

Alice almost blushed and moved quickly to slide an arm about Simon's slender waist. "Such piffle! Come along, Simon – let's get you to bed."

"Here, have a candle," said Perry, pulling one out and handing it to her. "It's easy to get hurt in the dark."

"Thanks, Perry," she said and meant it.

"I'm a lucky man," Simon added, slurring again.

Perry laughed, moving off towards the secondary staircase. "That you are, my friend. On the other hand, I'm just hoping to find some cooked goose and maybe some of that blueberry trifle."

CHAPTER

42

Simon poured out a couple of sherries while Alice changed back to a nightgown. Despite it being summer, coastal nights could be quite bracing and he was cold. The guest fireplace in their room was kitted out with everything needed for a fire – a luxurious state of affairs for anyone who had spent years in the trenches – so he'd gotten one going as soon as they'd spilled into their room. As much as he had hated years lost to the war, he had to admit it forced him to become far more competent at a variety of skills that, previously, his social class would have precluded.

"That *was* a hell of a story," said Alice as she left the palatial guest bathroom. Simon almost caught his breath at her casual beauty. His wife was any chap's daydream. Tall and elegant. Bright, bright gold hair haloing a face of such classical symmetry, it could have been immortalized in a Sandro Botticelli painting – a Venus. How had the second son of a rustic marquessate managed to capture the heart of such a creature?

"Why would Sir George's crew hide a body in Clara Mare?"

He hadn't told her that the body belonged to His Imperial Highness, instead spinning a fluid story about stumbling across sailors with a body and hiding on the cottage roof to avoid detection. He left out the faux fireplace and any real details. He'd have vastly preferred it if she hadn't spotted the *Sea Sprite*. The less Alice knew about the underlying dangers at Palliser Park the safer she was.

Events were shifting about faster and in far darker ways than he had ever imagined possible. His original plan had been to hunt for clues about a German assassin named The Gravedigger in the orbit of a man who would be a likely target. Hopefully learn if such a Will 'O the Wisp actually existed and wasn't just a phantasm of nervous operatives in the UK and on the Continent. He wasn't particularly sure if the existence of The Gravedigger had been revealed, but something deadly was on the prowl at Palliser Park. It was on his mind to get Alice away from the house the next day if possible. With a bit of luck Reggie Spinner would be back in the Crossley by morning and could whisk Alice back to London.

Reggie Spinner. Simon paused, holding out a glass of sherry to his wife. Something tugged at his memory. *Mr. Spinner's telegram.* The one that had been found up on the stairs in all the rubble. It sat, unread, in his jacket pocket.

Alice collected the sherry. "Simon?"

"Oh," he shook his head, "sorry. I was thinking."

She yawned and wandered towards the bed. "Why would Sir George have a dead body on the Sea Sprite? He doesn't strike me as a man who would care for messy corpses."

"Agree, actually. My best guess? Sir George is the unwitting master of some seaworthy thugs."

"Smugglers — that sort of thing?" Alice's face shadowed as she thought about possible crimes such a ship's crew could be plotting. "Are you going to let Sir George know?"

"This is something for DI Saxby. I will have a word," Simon said. "Beyond that, we saw nothing. We know nothing. We are here for an engagement party. Promise me, Alice?"

She made a face. "How boring."

"Alice?"

"Oh, yes – I promise," Alice had a sip of sherry as she got into bed. "Just few hours before all the hoopla starts. Do you think it would be horribly rude if we gave breakfast a miss and slept in?"

"No one in this house would even notice," said Simon over his shoulder. He opened the armoire door and started hunting for his summer blazer.

"Perry would," Alice said behind him. She sounded a little pensive. "Poor Perry. He gets steamrollered by both his father and Fizz. FitzRobert never lets him forget he filed papers for the Ministry of Defense all through the war – wasn't strong enough for the fight. Maybe we should have joined him for some of that goose."

Simon shoved some of his belongings aside in his hunt for the wayward blazer. "Perry was lucky to file papers. Didn't end up dead in a ditch." He was immediately sorry for his brittle tone. But if the disappointed fathers of frail young men only knew what the war had been like ... scores of young and not so young dead soldiers flared up in Simon's memory. In trenches, in ditches, on fields, hanging on barbed wire ... shot, machine – gunned, bayonetted, knifed, gassed and blown apart ... fresh blood, sticky old blood, viscera, vomit, tears ...

"Simon!" breathed Alice.

Her voice brought him back to the guest room. He realized he had fallen against the wardrobe; a tear was running down his face. Alice had left the bed to run to his side. She had a hand on his shoulder and was murmuring comforting words.

Embarrassed, Simon righted himself. He wiped at his eye. "Forgive me." His voice was hoarse. "It's been a ... long night."

"Let's go to bed," she said. The careful, neutral tone Alice chose stabbed him like a German bayonet. He must have been very difficult to cope with since his return from the front. So much of his reintroduction to polite society was lost in a fog.

"Go ahead, darling," he murmured. "I'm all right – give me a moment, will you?"

Alice rose up and kissed him on the cheek – the scarred side. She returned to the bed without another word. Simon let out a short breath. He was tired so vigilance was needed. Shell shock was insidious and took him hostage under the veil of exhaustion. He needed to focus on the job at hand. The job that would protect members of the Reparations Committee if, indeed, the Gravedigger haunted Palliser Park. The job that would protect Alice.

He returned to the line of clothes and pushed a few shirts out of the way, finding the blazer from Lord FitzRobert's overblown *casual* buffet dinner. Inside the breast pocket was the battered telegram from Reggie Spinner.

Examining the exterior of the small envelope, Simon was convinced – despite the damage sustained in the crash site – that it had been opened. Hard to imagine that any of the Palliser Park staff would have taken a peek at a guest's communiques. They were either old enough and well trained enough to ignore the temptations of below stairs gossip or so young that they were still anxious only to be noticed by someone of Lord FitzRobert's powerful personality for excellent service.

He took a seat on one of the wingback chairs by the fire and pulled Reggie's telegram from the filthy envelope.

Coat of arms not Russian. German Bavarian. Counts of Arco auf Valley. Anton Graf von Arco auf Valley, Nationalist, currently in prison for assassination of Prime Minister Kurt Eisner. Only other extant member of immediate family, Brother Albertine employed as Ministry of Defense translator in post – war Europe. Currently listed as MIA after car bombing in Germany. Presumed dead. Will return in Crossley Saturday.

Simon rested his head back against the chair. A Bavarian coat of arms? He had to admit he hadn't seen that as a possibility. Where the hell had Polly seen the coat of arms for a tiny Bavarian fiefdom belonging to the Counts of Arco? Was the surprising man that was going to marry her of German Bavarian extraction? He had seen most of the Palliser Park staff and they seemed a solidly English bunch. In fact, it was hard to imagine Lord FitzRobert employing any Germans in his household given post – war feelings about Germany – wouldn't serve to suitably impress his guests.

He read the telegram again. Albertine Graf von Arco auf Valley had been a translator for the Ministry of Defense. Jack held that job currently in the post – war mop up in London. Jack was fluent in German and a number of German dialect variants. He wondered if Jack had ever come across Albertine Graf von Arco through Ministry workings in Europe. It was a pity Jack had proven to be unreliable or he might have a word. As Jack was now clearly connected with Dorothy Brier, who was a direct conduit to FitzRobert, he'd keep his questions to himself at present.

Polly's coat of arms was German. A Bavarian family with such fervent nationalistic leanings that one of them had murdered Kurt Eisner. The Gravedigger was German with such fervent nationalistic leanings that he was removing key members of Britain's Reparations Committee to thwart or slow its work. A very thin thread to pull through a broad tapestry of national security issues but it was *something* ... at last.

CHAPTER

43

Alice overslept and when she finally opened her eyes, she wasn't a bit sorry about it either. The day of Fizz and Jack's engagement would be one filled with complex preparations – almost as weirdly complex as hiding dead bodies for later transport to watery graves. Every benighted servant would be in a fluster, toiling away to make sure the daughter of the house had a special evening. Wise guests would stay well out of the way. She intended to make excellent use of the idea.

She sat up and stretched, stiff from their adventures by Clara Mare. Simon was gone. Still out on his morning ride. A glance at the windows revealed imperfect weather for a June fete. It was windy and cool. Raindrops dappled the window glass – heralds of the massive storm the Met Office had warned DI Saxby's police force and entire eastern coast about. The storm that Lord FitzRobert thought wouldn't deign to disrupt Palliser Park's social debut.

A knock came at their door and Alice jumped at the sharp rapping sound. She pushed off the bed and grabbed a dressing gown from the footboard.

"Forgive me, Your Ladyship," said a Palliser Park maid once Alice had opened the door. The girl – maybe twenty years old –

looked a bit flustered and her thick brown hair was escaping its hairpins in spots. Crumpling would be horrified. "I'm running behind but I have a breakfast tray for you, if you'd like."

Alice realized that she was, in fact, pretty hungry. "Thank you! How lovely."

The maid stepped backwards in the hallway to a wheeled cart on which were stacked a series of neatly put – together wooden trays of breakfast items. She picked one off the top and brought it into the guest room.

"All the same – sorry," the girl apologized, looking even more flustered. Alice guessed that some of the guests had been dismayed, preferring the more traditional sideboard buffet. "Where would you like it, Your Ladyship?"

"Oh, on the end of the bed would be fine," Alice indicated the direction and the maid dutifully lugged in one of the heavy trays and laid it down.

"Mr. Crumpling asked me to let you know that lunch will be a buffet and to apologize for any lack of service before the big party."

"Are you all on the run?" Alice asked with a kind smile for the anxious girl.

The maid smiled in return as she tucked some of the loose hair behind her ear. "Yes, ma'am. His Lordship is having a right strop too." She lowered her voice to nearly a whisper. "He's not been through one of our storms before and don't know what we know. Locals been sending their regrets all morning."

"Is it really going to be a bad one?" Alice glanced at the windows. Trees were tossing left and right in the stiffening wind. She wasn't really sure if she was inquiring about the incoming storm or what she had witnessed last night. Sir

George's sailing yacht must be far out to sea by now, with a dead body in its cargo hold.

"Think so, ma'am. Flooding for sure. Locals looking to their own today." The maid bobbed a curtsey and headed for the door. "Good morning, ma'am."

Alice waited until the door was pulled shut before attacking the breakfast tray. Famished after dashing along the cliffs the night before, she lifted the lid on the nearest plate and discovered a hearty pile of scrambled eggs and sausage. None of it was even remotely hot but she was hungry enough that it didn't matter. If Simon was lucky, there might be some cold eggs and sausage left but she wasn't making any rash promises.

Another knock came at the door just as Alice tucked into a piece of toast. "Alice?" came Fizz's voice from the hallway. "You there?"

"Come in," Alice called out after quickly swallowing her bite of bread.

The door swung open again and Fizz sailed across the threshold, effortlessly vibrant in a pale yellow linen dress, her rich coppery hair pulled up in a simple knot. Alice thought her friend looked every inch the daughter of the manor – enviably confident and self – assured. The sort of carefree rich girl who didn't know her family's property was being used to shift dead bodies around.

"What a disaster!" Fizz announced, hurling herself into one of the wingback chairs by the fireplace. She wrinkled her nose at the breakfast tray. "Horrible breakie – sorry."

Alice helped herself to a forkful of scrambled egg. "It's fine," she said. "You were saying?"

"The party's an utter cock – up." Fizz threw both her legs over the arm of the chair and shrugged. "I don't think anybody's coming. Regrets coming in left and right."

"Apparently this part of the Essex coast does flood in a big storm," Alice said. She watched Fizz sigh deeply. "You can't really blame people for needing to protect their land and houses."

Her friend groaned. "*I* understand that. Dad doesn't. He's furious that weather is getting the better of him and his plans. So! Anyway – it's going to be a smaller, more intimate event. Perry and our driver have already been sent to Brightsea to start collecting everyone at the inns. We're lucky that we put up the musicians so they're already here."

"It'll be a lovely evening." Alice hoped she came across as suitably reassuring. In truth, it was going to be a scaled down summer soirée in the middle of a tempest. They could probably all fit into the main dining room and play board games while the rain hammered down. Hardly the grand social event of the summer that Lord FitzRobert had envisioned.

"You know, I don't even care,' said Fizz, waving her arms in a dismissive gesture. "Jack's being an utter ass."

Alice worked hard at keeping her face neutral. "Oh? Is he frustrated in the same vein as your father?"

Her friend threw up her hands again. "God knows! Probably. He's just acting very put upon. Had the nerve to say Dad wants him to perform all weekend like a trained monkey."

"Gosh," said Alice, thinking that being in the middle of Fizz and her father's mistress ... er ... *special friend* was producing high level stress for Jack. Not that she felt sorry for him. "How did you respond to that?"

Fizz made a sour face. "Well, I wasn't very politic. I said *Dance, Monkey, Dance*. I may have even called him Chim Chim. He didn't think any of it was a bit funny. Stormed off to pout. Anyway, once you've gotten dressed, we're all gathering to play cards in the library. Apparently, Sir George is a genuine card sharp and can perform actual sleight of hand."

Sir George Jasper. Alice thought of his crew arriving to whisk away a dead body. It might be interesting to sit next to him at cards and see if it might be possible to discern if he was more than just a gormless employer. Simon would hate the idea but he was off on horseback somewhere and unavailable to voice any objections to a same detective work.

"I'll be right down!" she said and picked up another piece of toast. "What fun!"

44

Simon asked Jade – Lord FitzRobert's difficult roan gelding – to slow from bright posting trot to a walk. As a favor to the stable manager, Brabinger, he had taken the horse out for his morning ride rather than the more placid Colonel Lee, who was older and didn't require as much attention.

He found he rather liked the rangy horse. Jade was young and opinionated but also quick, highly athletic and brave. If he didn't already have a castle stable yard filled with horses needing to be reschooled, he might have made FitzRobert an offer. Jade could be a genuine showjumper with some slow and solid rebuilding. He had developed an interest in showjumping, having seen competitions before the war and had been on the hunt for the right horse when military service interrupted such frivolous notions.

"I saw the Ghost Lights last night!" shouted Meg Brabinger over the wind and surf. She had come along on Betty. The cob had a propensity to get fat so daily exercise was important.

They drew up to halt on the cliffside path. The views over Palliser Park were spectacular even on a grey and drizzled morning. From where they stood, letting the horses relax, the horizon stretched from grey roiling sea, Lord FitzRobert's new dock – with no sinister sailing yachts attached – to Clara Mare and Essex countryside beyond.

"Really? At Clara Mare?" he asked, patting Jade's thick neck.

The pretty teenager nodded and brushed a streaming lock of hair out of her eyes. "I was up very late – our dog, Esme, had her puppies early … in my room. Anyway, I looked out my window and saw them floating about the cliffs!"

"How eerie," said Simon without a hint of humor or sarcasm. Not only did he believe there were, indeed, strange doings that occasionally crossed the paths of living persons, he thought covertly moving a Russian prince's murdered corpse was legitimately eerie.

"My mother has a camera," Meg sighed. "I would love to get a picture someday."

Simon stood up in his stirrups, gazing out over the cliffside to Lord FitzRobert's empty dock. Sir George's beautiful yacht was long gone. *Out and back*, the sailor had said. *Out and back if we're lucky.* He turned the phrase around in his head. *Out and back if we're lucky.*

"Meg," he asked, "how would you ride to Brightsea if you wanted a ginger beer at the tuck shop?"

She picked up her reins as Betty shifted sideways in the sharp wind. "We do that all the time! Mum craves chocolate. Just down the entrance and onto the main road."

"What if you wanted to avoid the entrance and the main road?"

Meg laughed. "You mean if, say, I wanted to sneak into Brightsea to buy vampire novels and an ice cream without necessarily letting my parents know?"

"Yes – exactly," Simon forced himself to laugh a bit. He thought both Meg and her illicit trips to the village to snag gory penny dreadfuls were delightful but actions at Palliser Park were shifting in a dangerous direction. He wanted back doors and options.

The teenager pointed in the opposite direction of Clara Mare, back towards the main house. "Palliser Park has several fields for His Lordship's dairy cows and horse turnouts. I would go through the first one and then take the old drover's path into the village. It takes a lot longer but, to be honest, it's a pretty hack and no worries about motor cars."

"Show me," he said, expertly gathering up his reins.

Meg accepted the challenge with a grin, urging the cob forward into a trot. Betty looked slightly miffed at the request and crow – hopped in annoyance. Simon followed on a very alert Jade, who had been bored by the rest stop and was ready for a change.

They cantered down the cliff path. The roan gelding snorting with excitement in the cold wind, leaned into his bit with all the gusto of a horse ridden with heavy hands. Simon's shoulders ached from holding the gelding in – it was like restraining a freight train. Still, Jade possessed an effortless, balanced gallop. The horse was a natural athlete, sure and cat – like.

Meg took them past the main house, stables and outbuildings towards an expanse of open country. Unlike the wilder land that encompassed Clara Mare, the fields were old line cultivated pasture – as green and verdant as Palliser Park's formal lawns. Simon marveled at the Essex coast's variety of terrain. The pasture land was surrounded by ancient stone walls probably constructed by early Tudaburgh serfs and maintained through the centuries by their descendants.

"I like to hop over just over there," said Meg, pointed to a section of the wall next to a heavy gate. "The footing is solid on both sides."

Simon squeezed his legs against Jade's sides and asked the sturdy gelding to make an approach to the wall. The horse went without hesitation, floating over the four – foot wall as if it was nothing and landed softly on the other side.

"Fine fellow!" breathed Simon, patting Jade's neck as he pulled him up to a standstill. Maybe he would have to make FitzRobert a fair offer.

Meg came over next. The reliable cob had to make more of an effort at the wall but landed easily as well. She pointed again across the pasture at another stone wall in the distance.

"We can get to the drover's path over there. I'll show you!" She took off on Betty, galloping boldly towards the obstacle.

Jade jigged sideways in the violently blowing pasture grass. The gelding was anxious not to be left behind by his stablemate. Simon waited until the cob was safely away and then allowed Jade his head. Lord FitzRobert's horse bold forward, rolling across the pasture with the energy of a hawk diving at its prey. They sailed over the stone wall and joined Meg, who was cantering next to a line of old – growth apple trees.

"Here," she called over wind creaking in the apple trees and the heavy beats of the horse hooves on the field. Drawing down to a walk, Meg turned into the trees where a well – worn path wove through the orchard and continued long into the distance. "This is the old way before the main road. *It* doesn't flood like the new road to Brightsea."

"How new?" asked Simon as they stopped to admire the medieval route. He didn't object when Jade took a bite of an apple from the nearest tree.

"About 1800. Something about moving military artillery when Napoleon was expected to invade." Meg smiled ruefully. "Brightsea gets most of its fresh water from River Dobbins. A big storm floods it and the new road."

"But not the old road?"

"Takes longer," she said, throwing her leg over the knee roll of her saddle and quickly checking her string girth. "I think it arcs around and approaches Brightsea on a slight elevation so water runs off. I'm not saying it doesn't flood a bit in a whopper storm but not like the main road. Those medievals weren't stupid."

Simon gazed at the *old way* – a sturdy path through the creaking apple orchard – and thought about the sailors hauling Prince Andrei's dead body to the *Sea Sprite*.

Out and back if we're lucky.

Out and back.

Back.

CHAPTER

45

Alice managed to retrace a path back to the library. Not her favorite place after Polly Piety's terrible fall and she was grateful that the weather meant that its terrace would not be pressed into use.

The remaining houseguests had, indeed, collected in Lord FitzRobert's impressive library where beleaguered staff had made a map table into an impromptu drinks bar – tea, coffee, hot chocolate and juices were all laid out with exquisite care. Later, Alice imagined, lunch would be wheeled in and another buffet would be laid out with all sorts of delicious dishes created from the previous night's offerings.

Looking about the book – lined room, she saw that both Doctors Threapwood and Sherbrooke were present but not the Rothermores. Alastair Rothermore was probably not up for social events and she doubted that his attentive wife would leave his side. There was a gathering of various FitzRobert uncles, aunts and cousins who had been given the coveted invitation to stay at Palliser Park rather than one of the inns in Brightsea. Sir George Jasper was at the map table, pouring a cup of tea. Fizz and Jack were deep in what appeared to be serious conversation by the new French doors – and in a touch of irony, they were bookended by Lord FitzRobertand Dorothy Brier on the other side of the room. Perry was missing, of course. He was dutifully making the guest retrieval runs to the village.

Alice decided a hot chocolate would be the best way to start her well – behaved guest behavior and have a chat with Sir George at the same time. She made her way to heavily laden map table and arrived just as the politician was picking up his teacup.

"Lady Fairlight!" he said, seeming genuinely glad to see her.

"Alice, please," she replied. "I'm dying for a hot chocolate."

Sir George beamed at her. "Allow me." He set down his tea and reached for the silver chocolate pot, pouring her out a cup.

"Thank you so much." Alice gave him a grateful smile. "What a chilly day for June!"

"Indeed, it is," he said, handing her the cup – in the Aynsley Old Indian Tree pattern.

She was immediately covetous, having always yearned to have a set of the rich, sophisticated pattern for her own. It was difficult to justify the purchase of new china when the Fairlights had so many sets floating about the family. They had been given formal Royal Crown Derby from 1815 – foxhunting scenes, Minton from 1830 for luncheon – Roman god, Mercury, griffons and fruit urns around the rim and Royal Worcester from 1860 for breakfast – English game birds. All venerable and deeply appreciated but, perhaps, not quite the pattern for a young couple on the cusp of 1920.Alice felt a stab of guilt. The world had been at war and she was pining after fancy china.

"And where is your gallant husband?" Sir George asked, interrupting her china reverie. "Surely he must want a hot drink in this weather."

"Out riding. Every morning whether clear, wet or snowing."
Alice sipped her hot chocolate. It was just what she needed
after the long night darting about the sea cliffs. She wondered if
the jovial man in front of her was aware that the *Sea Sprite* was
transporting dead bodies or if he was, as Simon suspected, a
clueless yacht owner with a devious crew.

"Now that's a red blooded Englishman! Well done to him."
Sir George held a hand out to indicate two nearby leather club
chairs. "Would you care to sit down?"

"Tell me about your beautiful ship," she said, once they had
settled down. "Where did you find her and how did you ever
become interested in sailing?"

"Well, we are a sea – faring nation," Sir George pointed out
as he set his teacup on the little table between the club chairs. "I
rowed at school and my dear father had a passion for the sea.
He took me sailing on holidays. When I was older, I crewed for
him in various cup races. His boat was called *The Pride of
Glanford*. She wasn't big so the two of us could manage her
pretty well."

"*Sea Sprite* looks awfully big to me."

Sir George looked pleased at the admiration in her voice.
"*Sea Sprite* is a big yacht. I knew once the war ended, it would
mean the freedom to sail the seven seas again and I wanted to
take my wife and show her the Mediterranean – Rome, Greece.
That kind of voyage requires a big boat."

"And a bigger crew, I suspect," she said, sipping the hot
chocolate. "How did you manage to find sailors? Weren't they
all pretty much taken up by the Royal Navy?"

"I lent *Sea Sprite* to the War Office. She's quick and nimble.
They used her for covert and non – covert reconnaissance

missions to Europe – the last being mop up in Germany, hauling War Office staff back and forth. When I got her back, I inherited her crew of four. They were being mustered out and asked me if they could stay with *Sea Sprite*. Seemed a good fit at the time."

Alice noted a slight stress in his voice and decided to pursue the small chink in Sir George Jasper's jovial armor. "Sounds as if you might have changed your mind about a big crew."

He threw a glance out the nearest library window as if something distracting might blow up to talk about instead. "They're crafty sailors," Sir George admitted, his face turning melancholy, "and I deeply appreciate their service during the war but … they're kind of rough cobs and I want my wife to feel comfortable aboard *Sea Sprite* this summer – especially with the baby. After this sail, I think I'm going to engage some of the amateur youths at our yacht club. They'd enjoy a summer in the Mediterranean before heading back to university."

Alice knew that Simon had been right. Sir George was clueless about his crew. Indeed, they were rougher cobs that he might ever imagine. She couldn't wait to update Simon with what she had managed to ferret out and felt some pride at demonstrating genuine detective abilities.

"What an absolutely marvelous holiday!" she said with enthusiasm. "Speaking as a wife, I agree with you about university sailors. Much better atmosphere."

Sir George seemed to relax as he smiled at her. He was about to add something when Fizz swept into their midst. She was clutching at Jack's arm as if he was under arrest for trying to flee.

"Did I hear the words *marvelous holiday*? Do tell!" Fizz's voice was artificially bright. Alice wondered if she and Jack were still fighting.

Sir George sprang up to offer the daughter of the manor his chair. "I was just telling Alice about my plans to head to Italy and Greece for the summer. You know, both your brother and your handsome fiancéhave sailed the *Sea Sprite*."

Alice looked up at Jack who had tight face as though he was battling annoyance or anger. She saw him visibly unclench his jaw and force a smile.

"Yes, indeed," Jack said as Fizz retracted her claws and slid into Sir George's vacated chair.

"I didn't know that!" Fizz cried as if it was the most interesting news bulletin she had ever received. "Darling, one of those tedious trips over to Germany when you had to translate all those files for the War Office?"

Jack nodded. Alice noted that he looked quickly in the direction of Lord FitzRobert and Dorothy Brier. She also took the briefest of glimpses and saw that Dorothy – resplendent in soft green walking suit and a gloriously long strand of shimmering pearls – was clinging onto His Lordship with the same kind of fixated determination as his daughter, Fizz.

"She's handsome, is she not?" Sir George pushed a little for verification, pride evident in his swelling chest.

"I was very fortunate to be aboard." Jack nodded again. "Comfortable and beautiful."

Before Alice could ask him what he thought of the crew, Lord FitzRobert cleared his throat and commanded the attention of the room.

"Lunch will be brought in," he said, patting Dorothy's hand which lay over his forearm, "so you will be very well fed. I insist, however, that we now find partners for a little Bridge tournament to wile away what's left of the morning. Dorothy is a brilliant player so I am claiming her."

Alice caught Jack returning to a clenched jaw. It was clear to her that Jack, despite protestations to the contrary, was still wrapped around Dorothy Brier's long, elegant fingers. What it meant for Fizz and the evening ahead, she could not guess.

46

"Going to be a bad one," said Brabinger as Simon returned the roan gelding to his box stall. The stable manager was topping up water buckets as his lads had been conscripted to the main house for party duty.

"The storm?" Simon unlatched Jade's halter, watching as Jade pivoted in the stall and went to the hay in his manger.

"Been awhile since we've had a humdinger. Pity it's clashed with Lady Constance's big night."

Simon stepped out of the stall and pulled shut its door. "Will the horses be all right?"

The head stableman gave a nod. "Tudaburghs were a crafty lot. Palliser Park never sees much damage during a flood. We'll be fine here even if the party is a non – starter."

"Meg told me you served with the Imperial Yeomanry?"

Brabinger nodded again. "South Africa. Mounted regiment."

"Got the wind – up," Simon said, using military slang for acute battle anxiety. He took a moment to consider what he was about to say. "I'm thinking you and the family might want to do a pretty immediate skive."

He saw Brabinger consider the covert message from one trooper to another. The horseman looked uneasy and leaned against the stall door, clearly thinking hard about why a major with the Royal Cavalry would need to intervene in Lord FitzRobert's affairs.

"FitzRobert wouldn't take well to someone swinging the lead," Brabinger replied in a way that let Simon know he had understood the high seriousness. "It would have to be an *Imperial FU*."

"I believe things are going to get a little sticky tonight. Jerry doesn't want a vote on reparations."

The stableman let out a short sigh in appreciation of Simon's pointed understatement. "You might need an old Tommy."

"I'm trained for this kind of nonsense." Simon hung Jade's halter and shank on the hook next to the stall door. "With luck, the party will only be ruined by bad weather. I'll see that the horses are looked after."

"We'll skive," said Brabinger, pushing off the door. "Within the hour."

"You could do me a favor if you had a mind," said Simon, retrieving a small notebook he always carried in a pocket and scribbled down a line. "Would you send this telegram at the next best opportunity? Can you read it out loud so I know you've deciphered my handwriting?"

Brabinger accepted the scrap of paper and peered down at it. He recited Sir Vernon's contact information and then the actual message – *Fairlight needs assistance with black horse*.

Black horse was code for a sticky wicket – serious trouble. Sir Vernon would understand he was requesting tactical support. He wasn't absolutely positive he needed it but the *Sea Sprite*'s sailor had uttered the word, BACK. *Sea Sprite* needed to navigate rough seas and then return before the storm fully engulfed the Essex coast. It didn't require a genius to sort out that the Gravedigger or a creature of the Gravedigger's ilk was circling Palliser Park like a hawk stalking a field mouse and Fizz's engagement party was where the hawk was planning on diving to secure its prey. Besides FitzRobert, Rothermore and Jasper, there was another member of the Reparations Committee who had managed to snag an invitation to stay at Palliser Park – Sir Henry Frost, celebrated economist and old school chum of the other three. If the goal was to break or indefinitely delay reparation decisions, removing the four would achieve it in a single blow.

How the single blow would be administered was not clear as yet and it was possible, of course, that the unexpected storm had already disrupted carefully laid plans. Plans that he, now, – – with genuine sadness – had to accept included Jack Nickleby and Dorothy Brier. How and why Jack Nickleby was involved wasn't clear as yet. *He scares thehell out of me.* Simon would bet a sizable amount that it wasn't Lord FitzRobert Jack was worried about – it was the hawk.

CHAPTER

47

"No trump," said Lord FitzRobert as if the fate of the world depended upon the outcome of the trick. "East wins with the King of Hearts."

The East was Sir Henry Frost, who accepted the scattered applause with a good natured grin. He turned to Alice, who was West and held a Jack of Hearts. "That's the tournament done. Good thing too. I never want to see a playing card again ... for at least a week."

Alice smiled back at him. Frost was handsome man with craggy features and thick beautifully manicured salt and pepper hair. He was just the sort of Englishman she liked – immaculate manners and didn't take himself seriously.

"I'm not much for cards," she admitted.

"Really? You play a good game," Frost said.

Alice was about to launch into a tale of her mother's legendary Bridge parties when the library doors opened. Two of the young footmen wheeled in a large cart loaded with covered dishes, followed by other servants carrying trays.

"Lunch!" proclaimed Lord FitzRobert, standing up. "All very casual, don't you know."

Dorothy Brier, who was South, also stood and looked down on Alice with a bitter sort of gleam in her handsome eyes. "Congratulations. You Americans always seem to elbow your way to the front."

"I must protest," said Sir Henry, patting Alice's shoulder. "After all, *I* played the King of Hearts and I'm as English as ... well, as something English ... toffee?"

Alice sensed that the actress knew better than to take on Sir Henry Frost, old school friend and contemporary of her paramour. Indeed, Dorothy forced a laugh, then averted her eyes, murmuring something about needing a drink.

"Come along," said Lord FitzRobert in a tight voice. He didn't look particularly pleased with Dorothy. "You can help organize lunch for everyone."

Sir Henry Frost sat back in his chair and shivered in a theatrical manner as Dorothy stalked off with a toss of her perfectly coiffed head. "That had to sting. Reduced to organizing the lunch like a housekeeper."

"You don't like Dorothy?" Alice asked, deciding to elude the bonds of social propriety which might suggest remaining politely mum on the topic of mistresses. A massive storm was coming that might wash the Essex coast away – why not shoot for the moon?

"Of course, not my place to like or dislike her under Fitz – y's roof but," he lowered his voice to almost tacit, "clearly a pot stirrer. I don't think she helps him especially with the children. You see, their mother, Lydia, was a lovely lady. Fitz – y's always been a bit of a blowhard even back in dear old school days. Lydia tempered him. Far too good for him, of course. Her death was hard on the children especially Perry – poor blighter."

Alice watched as Dorothy made desultory efforts to direct the servants. The Palliser Park staff well trained by Crumpling – a butler's butler – were having at it, politely ignoring her and getting the job done. Other guests were beginning to rise from chairs and gather in chatty clumps to discuss the deteriorating weather.

"I'm grateful that Perry didn't have to go," she said, not quite sure why she had brought it up. Part of her felt just a little resentful that Simon had endured the trenches while Perry had spent the war in comfort and safety. "He was bored at the War Office shuffling papers but, at least, he was spared combat."

Sir Henry's face turned both thoughtful and a little melancholy at her words. "Speaking as his godfather, Perry has always been a fragile boy. Something of a disappointment to a hale and hearty chappy such as Fitz – y. It might have been better if Perry had gone over and seen a bit of action."

"His Lordship might respect him more?" Alice considered how Perry often acted as an adjunct staff member, running Lord FitzRobert's errands.

"Respect himself more too, I suspect." Sir Henry sighed and gripped the arms of his chair in preparation for standing. "Shall we join the ravenous wolves?"

Alice wondered if there were more story behind the sigh. She hadn't noticed that Perry felt marginalized by not performing more active service for Britain during the war. He seemed reasonably content to do his bit at the War Office. She had always sensed that his responsibilities were a little more extensive than just putting stamps on files and that he had enjoyed the brushes with genuine power. *And* apparently, Perry had even been sent over to Germany after Armistice on the *Sea*

Sprite. No mere file clerk would be shipped over to support British interests in the post – war mop up.

Even with Dorothy getting in the way, the servants managed to assemble the buffet lunch in record time. At His Lordship's urging, the bored housebound guests drifted into a line – the gentlemen politely standing back to allow the ladies to go first.

As Alice reached for one of her coveted Indian Tree plates, thunder cracked overhead with an unnerving cracking sound – like a shotgun going off in the house. It rattled the window cases and empty crystal goblets laid out on the table. She froze in surprise – as did everyone else in the library. Then there was some nervous laughter as both guests and servants turned to look out the room's bank of windows and fancy new French doors.

Beyond the library glass, trees whipped and shivered in a fierce, cold wind. Overhead, the sky was a slate grey broken by occasional flashes of lightning. But out at sea, there was a black cloud wall roiling towards the Essex coast. Alice had watched some severe storms come and go but she thought what was roaring across the water from the North looked some kind of Viking monster. She'd never seen a cloud bank as black – the wall of onyx undulated like a massive panther stalking the coast.

Another clap of thunder rattled the room. Alice jumped slightly and felt immediately foolish. She lived in Great Britain. A good soaking storm was nothing new or a cause for particular worry. Knowing that the gentlemen were patiently waiting for the chance to attack the buffet, she shook off her momentary fright and focused on selecting some of the dishes that the beleaguered kitchen staff had conjured up out of the previous night's dinner.

"Lemonade, Your Ladyship?" asked one of the young footmen as she reached the far end of the map table.

"I would kill for a cup of tea," she admitted.

He set down his pitcher of lemonade. "I will bring one to you straight away, Your Ladyship."

Thunder continued to roll overhead as Alice carried her plate a distance away from the main activity. She wouldn't mind having a short break from social chat and being able to sip some hot tea in peace.

Earlier, she had spotted a couple of comfortable reading chairs and side table off by a freestanding bookcase. The perfect place to hide out and hope that her husband would make an appearance.

Alice had just settled into her chair when the footman tracked her down and handed off the cup of tea. She thanked him profusely, dropping back into the highbacked chair to sip the smokey Chinese Oolong tea and listen to the thunder. She closed her eyes for a moment and concentrated on breathing. There was no doubt that along with the exciting news of an expected baby came fatigue. She just didn't have her usual stamina throughout the day. What was it going to be like when she was much further along? Even with a pile of new mystery novels, sitting around all day would be so tedious.

Another rifle shot crack of thunder made Alice open her eyes. She gasped in surprise. Perry had taken the chair next to her. He gazed at her over the rim of lemonade goblet and then waved with daffy good cheer at her startled jump.

"Released from indentured servitude as a lowly taxi driver," Perry said, saluting her with his lemonade. "Wasn't much to do in the end. Most of them had already toddled off back to London to escape the weather. The once mighty guest list has been reduced to a mere handful. Poor old Fizz."

Alice almost sighed. She had been looking forward to a few moments alone. "Do you think your father will plough ahead with everything as planned?"

"The servants are removing most of the tables in the Marble Salon." Perry rolled his eyes theatrically. "He's pushing on – as ever. *Fizz will be celebrated*, come hell or high water!"

Thunder rolled overhead. "Probably high water," said Alice.

"Oh, I wouldn't completely rule out hell," he laughed. "Night hasn't fallen yet."

"Perry," she said, setting aside her tea, "Sir George mentioned you sailed *Sea Sprite* to Germany for the War Office."

Perry's laugh died away. For the briefest of moments, he looked almost shocked. Then he had a drink of his lemonade and recovered. "I did, yes," he allowed in genuine dismay. "Sorry – even though I am a very, very unimportant file clerk, that trip was supposed to be covert."

"No worries – I really just wanted to ask you about *Sea Sprite's* crew."

He stared at her, utterly baffled. "The crew?"

"What did you make of them? Sir George thinks they're a bit rough for his summer voyage to Italy."

"I don't know … to be honest, I was sick as a dog both ways. Spent most of my time being sick over the railing. They seemed good at whatever it is they do. Made good time and all that." Perry made a dismissive gesture with his hands. "Who cares?"

He leaned forward and tapped her knee with his hand. "You want to break out of here? We could go grab a bottle of champagne and find a place to watch the storm come in."

"As lovely as that sounds, I am a bit tired."

Perry pretended to wipe tears away from his eyes. "Oh, come on, Alice! Imagine all thelightning bolts. Come on – it'll be such fun and not boring like ... here."

"Well," Alice said, wondering if a few minutes of storm watching would help wake her up for the evening's event, "lightning might be kind of exciting ..."

"Sorry, Perry," came her husband's voice. Simon sounded amused. "I insist on having my wife all to myself."

Alice looked up and saw her husband drawing up. Still in his riding clothes, Simon waved Perry out as he approached. "Off you go," he said to Perry, who laughed and dutifully vacated the wingchair.

"Fine," said Perry. "I need to fill a plate full of goose sandwiches anyway."

Lord FitzRobert's son and heir sauntered off to the buffet table while Simon took over the spare chair. "Shouldn't you," he asked, "be eating your own goose sandwich?"

"Not that hungry. Have some if you like," Alice thought he looked more tired than she felt. "You missed the big breakfast tray – I ate yours too. Good ride?"

Simon reached over and snagged one of her sandwiches. "Very informative," he said but didn't illuminate how. "This is going to be a devastating storm. Nyx will be in Brightsea manning the proverbial watchtower which is a shame because we could use him here."

"You'll be unamused but I did have a chat with Sir George about the *Sea Sprite* ..."

"Alice." Simon did indeed look unhappy. "You have to stop playing detective. There are dangerous forces at work in this house."

"Yes, yes – I understand and I'll hang up my deerstalker hat, but listen first." Alice told him how Sir George planned to dismiss his yacht crew and that both Perry and Jack had sailed *Sea Sprite* to Germany on covert post – war assignments for the War Office. She was gratified that he looked thoughtful and serious while digesting her news.

"Does seem likely Sir George is clueless about his crew carting around corpses. I'm glad," he said finally. "And now, we're going to wash our hands of this. We're going to keep our heads down and get the bloody hell out of here once Mr. Spinner returns with the Crossley."

"Will he be back today?" Alice asked. She missed the quietly competent Mr. Spinner.

Simon nodded as he selected another sandwich from her plate. "Unless the storm causes delays on the road. He should be back before Fizz and Jack's party begins."

"No joy there either. Fizz is fed up with Jack being moody." Alice went back to sipping her tea. She found that the Oolong both settled mild nausea and helped to relax her nerves. "It's going to be a bang – up evening. His Lordship is livid that the guest list has dwindled to a meager group but is going to frog march us all through the whole thing anyway."

"Promise me that you will not go off alone. You stick with me or Mr. Spinner once he returns."

Alice remembered the *Sea Sprite's* sailors hauling away the body of some unfortunate soul, presumably to dump it out at sea. "Oh, I promise all right."

Before Simon could reply, a massive lightning bolt split the sky outside the library windows – a jagged streak of white hot energy. Thunder followed immediately, breaking overhead with a violent cracking sound.The fragile rural electrical system collapsed, plunging the library into dreary greys of a stormy afternoon. Heavy raindrops struck the glass with the ferocity of an American gangster's tommy gun. The monster from the north had finally arrived.

CHAPTER

48

Simon rolled Alice's intel about *Sea Sprite's* covert trips to Germany around in his mind. Jack Nickleby was a translator for the War Office. Not only was Jack fluent in German, he was fluent in German culture and hence, a highly effective interpreter of German intentions whether verbally or on paper. Had he been got to, somehow, on one of his trips to post – war Germany?

From his chair next to Alice, he had a pretty good view of Lord FitzRobert's guests. Despite weather taking out the majority of invitees, the *Big Four* remained. FitzRobert, Sir George Jasper, Sir Henry Frost and Alastair Rothermore were all present under Palliser Park's Georgian roof. The perfect opportunity to torpedo the Reparations Committee's work. These men would be central in deciding just how much Britain would punish Germany for its part in starting the war to end all wars.

He shifted his focus to Dorothy. The actress was standing close to Lord FitzRobert in what seemed to him was an attempt to centralize her power in the room. All she had in society was her connection to the FitzRobert family. No one who mattered cared about Dorothy Brier's matinee idol status. Indeed, the aunts, uncles and cousins would be unenthusiastic about her as Lord FitzRobert's late wife had been very much admired. FitzRobert's friends might find Dorothy possessed a kind of lurid fascination but, for the most part, she was just a cipher in English society.

Dripping in pearls and cashmere, she had taken pride of place next to Lord FitzRobert. They were ostensively engaged in conversation with the illustrious Sir Henry Frost and Dr. Threapwood – well, at least FitzRobert was. His Lordship was animated and gesturing, although, even at a distance, Simon thought the bonhomie looked a bit forced. He was putting on a big show and needed everyone to know all was well. Dorothy, on the other hand, was quiet and wore a fixed expression of polite interest in what her paramour was on about. Her eyes, though, were directed over His Lordship's perfectly tailored shoulder at another couple. She gazed with the focus of a predatory cobra on Fizz and Jack.

Simon switched his attention to Jack Nickleby. Gloriously blond, the zenith of English handsomeness, Jack may never have had real money in his pocket, but he possessed luck and if he played that hand properly. He was about to marry one of the wealthiest heiresses in the world. For a man who was grabbing the proverbial brass ring with both hands and performing loop the loops with it, Jack looked miffed – irritated with the universe. He glanced several times away from his betrothed, checking on Dorothy before returning his attention to Fizz who, like her father, was overly enthusiastic and eager to promote the joys of the day.

Jack and Dorothy – illicit lovers. Simon rested his back against the wingchair and remembered what he had overheard the night before. They were both under the thumb of someone who had been pulling their strings. Someone who intimidated Jack. Someone who wouldn't let them go.

He wondered if Jack would tell him who the puppet master was – with some judiciously applied pressure. A brutal shortcut would be worth the unpleasantness. There wasn't a lot of time to discover who he was really up against. The *Sea Sprite* would be returning to the FitzRobert dock soon if it wasn't already there.

A light wave of clapping interrupted his thoughts. Simon refocused and saw Alastair Rothermore limping in, attended by his loyal wife. The MP looked a little pale and winded but otherwise in reasonable shape. He accepted the applause with good humor and settled in a chair while a footman rushed to bring him a plate of sandwiches.

"Oh, I'm glad he's all right," said Alice. "Really banged up his ankle though."

Lord FitzRobert held up his hands, seeking the room's attention. "You may have noticed Palliser Park has lost power in the storm. This is common out here. The local electrical authority is fairly primitive."

There came an appreciative swell of rueful laughter.

"Staff has been making sure every room has both candlesticks as well as oil lamps. Let me assure you that the Marble Salon looks its best in candlelight and we will have a marvelous evening! We will be a much smaller group but no less enthused to celebrate the engagement of my daughter, Constance, to Mr. Jack Nickleby. After our dear Rothermores have a bit of lunch, I am going to suggest that we break to ready for the evening ahead."

Sir Henry Frost stood up. He held out his goblet of lemonade. "A toast to the FitzRoberts! Thank you for a splendid weekend despite the weather."

A spate of *Here Here!* rose from the gathering of friends and family, followed by more applause. Rain hammered down on the terrace outside. The sky was growing darker except when lit up by streaks of lightning. Nyx had said that the Met Office worried that it might be the storm of the century.

Simon saw Jack beg off from Fizz. She didn't look best pleased but put on a good face about it after he kissed her cheek. Jack shook a few hands as he left including Lord FitzRobert who, like his daughter, didn't look absolutely delighted. Jack strode from the library, failing to acknowledge either Fairlight as he passed.

There was another crack of thunder and when it died away, Simon heard Esther Rothermore telling Fizz that many men suffered from engagement anxiety – that her own Alastair had taken up knitting to cope and had made himself so many string vests, he was still wearing them after twenty – odd years. Simon guessed Jack was not riddled with anxiety about making a legal contract with vast wealth. Jack was panicked that something might blow up to prevent it.

"Darling," he murmured to Alice, "let's nip upstairs while the going is soft."

Alice nodded, appreciating the reference to safe ground for horses to move across and pushed up from her chair. "Wouldn't mind putting my feet up," she said. "Boy howdy – I'm already getting so lazy. Who could know being expectant was so exhausting?"

"At least you're stuffed with goose sandwiches and curried veg," Simon replied, offering her his elbow.

She made a face at him. "Thank you. That helps so much."

They were not the only guests escaping to their own devices. Others were abandoning the library at a pace, leaving beleaguered servants to clear up yet another buffet. Simon maneuvered Alice ahead of the main exodus in an effort to avoid being delayed by either Perry or Fizz. Both FitzRobert children looked ready to do some venting, and Simon had neither the time nor the interest in coddling their social angst. There were enough extended family members about to listen to their curated tales of woe.

Simon locked the door to their guest quarters and turned back to Alice. His lovely American wife was divesting herself of her shoes with a relieved sigh. Outside their borrowed windows, hard rain and wind gusted against Palliser Park's pale stone. It was only the opening salvo, the outer ring. Conditions would get much worse.

"Could you start a fire?" she asked, indicating the cold fireplace that overburdened servants had failed to tend. "I'm going to sit in that chair and drift off. Fizz said I could borrow her maid, Elyse, to help with my hair. She should turn up in an hour or so. Drinks at six, dinner, etcetera to follow."

Simon crossed to the fireplace and retrieved a box of matches on the chimneypiece. "I'm off to have a little look around," he said, bending down by the firebox to assess what was needed to rebuild the coal fire. "You will lock the door and no one – not Fizz, not Perry, not Elyse the maid – will enter until I return. Are we clear?"

"Yes, Major Fairlight, sir!" She gave him a crisp salute.

"At ease, Trooper," Simon said as he stacked coal over kindling. "You might make yourself useful, though, and light a few lamps."

The servants had left a handful of Victorian oil lamps in the room along with an additional canister of paraffin and lots of old fashioned candles. Simon had to admit Lord FitzRobert ran a tight ship. Palliser Park ran like a military operation. Since the FitzRobert money came from a century of arms dealing, it made sense.

Between the two of them, the guest room brightened with light and heat. He hated to leave cozy, warm environment and Alice. She looked tired, Simon thought, as she dropped into the overstuffed armchair by the fire. It was going to be an exhausting night. He desperately hoped Alice could cope.

"No one is to enter this room while I'm gone," Simon repeated. He handed her a small glass of medium – dry sherry. "Lock the door behind me."

"Understood," said Alice.

He reached out and laid a hand on her tawny gold hair, running his fingers down the side of her face. "I love you, Alice." His voice was very quiet, very somber.

"That has a rather funereal quality," she said, catching his hand in hers and pressing it against her cheek.

"I may ask some very difficult things of you before this all comes to an end. You must do them without question – like a soldier on the battlefield. Can you do that, Alice?"

"I'm an American," His wife replied. "We're doers, not talkers. You ask your difficult things. I won't disappoint."

Simon bent over and kissed her forehead. "Back soon. For now, your entire job involves resting."

Armed with leather bag over his shoulder, Simon stepped out of their guest room and then paused, waiting to hear Alice lock the door behind him. He took a moment to exhale. Tendrils of shell shock were trying to wrap around his rib cage and crush his heart. It was painful. He sometimes felt as if he were made of broken glass – every way he turned cut and slashed.

The lock behind him clicked. Alice was safely in – for the moment. He breathed again. No time to splinter in self – pity. No time to run for cover in the trench. He had to go over the top and do his job.

Simon inhaled and then exhaled slowly. He forced himself to push forward, heading for Palliser Park's roof. He needed to do a general recce of the area – if the weather would allow it. Following the same route to the roof he had taken the night Polly Piety had fallen to her death, Simon slipped through the staff rooms and up the twist of stairs to the attics. With the FitzRobert party so close to starting, every servant was employed doing something for the celebratory night, which meant that their floor was essentially deserted. He appreciated the ability to move quickly without needing to explain himself to Crumpling or any other servant who might have spotted him on their turf.

Once he made it to the attics, luck found him again. A pocket of calm – a bubble of milder weather – was drifting over the area as if the monster storm was taking a brief moment to collect itself before continuing the attack. Rain had abated to a light drizzle and the wind was constant but not damaging. Visibility had increased too.

Simon moved outside from the attics. He headed for the windward side, being careful not to slip in significant pools of water that had formed on the roof's surface and found a solid spot next to one of Palliser Park's decorative Roman statues – a very miffed looking Hera. Pullinga pair of binoculars from the leather bag, he first trained them out towards to sea. The surf was huge and angry. It rolled onto the beach in towering gun metal grey waves. Simon doubted Lord FitzRobert's brightly colored beach houses would survive the storm. The incoming tide looked as though it had risen halfway up Palliser Park's craggy cliffs. Across vast miles of jagged white caps, the horizon was black with another wall of the monster storm. The worst of it was yet to come.

Shifting the glasses to take in the expensive new dock, Simon saw the riggings of a boat twisting in the wind. The *Sea Sprite* had returned – along with Sir George's duplicitous crew. He studied what he could see of the yacht. She was lashed to the heaving dock, riding up and down on the massive tide and probably taking on a lot of salt water as waves violently crashed over her decks. No sign of the crew. No lights gleaming in the windows of Clara Mare. They had to be there, hunkering down and waiting to complete their instructions – and Simon could guess the battle plan centered on the four members of the Reparations Committee.

Simon turned his binoculars further inland. Palliser Park had been built on a rise in medieval times to avoid flooding. He trained the eyeglasses towards the village of Brightsea. It was too far away to get much beyond the ancient Anglican church steeple but he also guessed that there was already considerable flooding. If the tide was rising on Palliser Park's sturdy, protective cliffs, the lowlands would be seeing a juggernaut of seawater rolling over the local inlet. It could be catastrophic once the main body of the storm arrived.

He doubted Mr. Spinner would be making it back any time soon. A pity. He could have used his ever useful and quick witted former bat man. It also meant that there was no quick out for Alice in the Crossley and his more dangerous Plan B would have to suffice.

CHAPTER

49

Alice looked at two gowns in the guest wardrobe. Both had been made by House of Worth before the war. Like many women in Britain, she wore out of date fashion after Armistice Day. On the continent, Europe was digging itself out and French fashion houses had yet to fully recover. In the British Isles – among the upper classes – it was considered quietly correct to wear pre – war finery to important social gatherings and events. New frocks were ostentatious in a country where so many had lost everything: fathers, uncles, sons and grandsons.

One of her pre – war Worth dresses was a deep rose satin with silver embroidery and the other, a frothy confection of lemon yellow silk georgette and hand – sewn flowers. Alice leaned towards wearing the lemon. It just felt more younger and more summer – y – reminding her of the fancy birthday cakes her mother always presented on such important occasions. The satin dress was a little heavier and more formal – but, perhaps, more appropriate for a party in the middle of a gale.

She felt silly, foolishly vain for even looking at them. It had been a terrible week with two violent incidents – one of which had left poor Polly Piety dead. Then there was the corpse that been tucked away at Clara Mare by Sir George's strange crew.

Now a storm was bearing down on the Essex coast that could bring devastating damage, even death, to Palliser Park's neighbors and the charming village of Brightsea. Who cared what she would wear to Fizz's ridiculous engagement party?

Alice let the dresses fall back into the line of clothes hanging in the wardrobe. She'd decide in a bit – probably the rose satin. There was time to indulge in the guest room's greatest luxury, the completely modern bathroom with its deep tub. Maybe even read a few chapters of the newest Scarlet Pimpernel novel as she soaked, inhale some calming lavender scent from generous jar of bath salts provided by the house and try to ready herself for whatever was worrying Simon so much.

She could tell he felt the engagement party was going to be the center of danger. Something that went well beyond Fizz deciding to hand Jack his proverbial hat. Alice wondered for a moment if such a notion could have emerged out of Simon's shellshocked nerves. It was just possible that Polly's death and the elevator crash had pushed him into seeing a phantom danger … *what was she going on about?* Sir George's yacht crew had been carting around a corpse in order to dispose of it at sea – presumably to avoid calling attention to a murder. Alice shook her head, annoyed at her quibbling. He was right. Something was up. She trusted her husband's instincts and always had.

"League of the Scarlet Pimpernel – where the heck did you go?" Alice murmured, glancing about the room. She spotted the book on a small table by one of the Georgian rectangle windows and nipped across from the wardrobe to secure it.

The weather outside the window had let up somewhat. It was still raining but was no longer a grey sheet dropping down hard on every surface. Thunder still rumbled but from a distance, warning of a renewed wave that would be rolling in. Alice watched the trees in Palliser Park twist and turn with less erratic violence. Picking up the novel and about to turn away, her eye caught movement on one of the garden paths. A burly looking man was jogging towards the house. He looked wet and cold with hands jammed into the pockets of a heavy navy pea coat.

Navy pea coat. Alice stared down at the man in dismay. He was every inch a sailor from the nautical cap on his head to the wide cuffs of his rough trousers. The *Sea Sprite*, one of Sir George's ships, must be back after dumping the body. She jumped back from the glass when the sailor glanced up. Her heart was racing, pounding against her ribcage.

Where had Simon gone? Should she go against his wishes and leave the sanctuary of the room to warn him? Alice moved back to the window and cautiously looked out of the rain splattered glass. The sailor was no longer in sight. She wondered if he had actually gone into the house. That meant he could be anywhere.

The door handle to the room gave a squeak as it moved up and down. Alice caught her breath in surprise and backed up against the front of her wardrobe. Someone was testing the door – a servant would knock politely. She heard murmuring outside and caught the words *locked, why?*and *asleep.* Two voices – one high pitched enough to be a woman. Then the other side of the door went silent.

Alice allowed herself to relax. She let out a long, quavering breath. Simon was right. There was something very wrong about Palliser Park.

Then the silence was obliterated by a series of sharp knocks at the door. To Alice's jangled nerves, the banging sound was ear – splitting. She instinctively shifted along the heavy furniture piece and pressed herself into the narrow space between it and Simon's wardrobe as if it could shield her from the unknown persons outside her door. She waited. In her bones, she knew answering the door would be a deeply regrettable mistake.

There were more hushed voices. The higher pitched woman's tone sounded agitated. Alice strained to pick up any words or phrases. She thought she could pick out *help, hell* and *what now?*

The door handle was tried one more time – not covertly this time either. The would – be intruder rattled the hardware as if frustrated or desperate. Alice pressed against the side of her wardrobe, willing the mysterious visitors to leave. Tension ratcheted up through her body – a confluence of fear and anger at the unwanted intrusion into her life. She actually thought she might burst into tears over the sheer unpleasantness of these people and whatever it was they intended to do if they had been able to breach the door.

Silence returned to the hallway beyond the guest room. Alice wiped at her eyes and crept out from the slender space between the wardrobes. There might be time to catch sight of them if she were brave and careful. Identifying them could be crucial.

Alice darted across the room and pressed her ear to the door. She couldn't make out any telltale sounds of lurking bad hats.

"One to get ready, one to really think about it …" Alice whispered as she picked up the key from the drinks table. "One to go."

She shoved the key into the lock, turned it and pulled the door open a few inches. Peering out, Alice saw that the smaller hallway that held the second tier guest rooms was deserted. Not even a maid was scurrying about, checking on the coal tins. Certainly, no clandestine types waiting to pounce on an anxious American.

Alice considered emerging to find Simon. She was genuinely rattled and longed for the reassurance of his presence. Surely, she would be safe out in the open with the FitzRobert household coming and going. Servants would be everywhere, assisting with the party preparations. And maybe Simon would need her help. Maybe the people who had been at the door would be looking for him as well.

Simon had told her to stay buttoned up in their room. He had specifically said not to open the door to anyone. The tacit admission was that no one was off his prospective villain list.

Alice retreated back into the room and shut the door. She locked it and replaced the key on the drinks table. Simon had led men on bloody battlefields. He had stared into barrages of cannon and gatling guns. He had hunkered down in clouds of mustard gas. His lovely face came into her thoughts – with its brutal bayonet scar.

She would wait for Simon. He knew how to deal with Palliser Park.

CHAPTER

50

Simon ducked back into the attics, grateful to be under a roof. The storm was regaining strength. Rain had begun to hammer down again. From where he stood, immediately under the roofline, it sounded like a bank of German Maschinengewehr 08s at full fire.

The German machine gun – known as MG08 to those unfortunate enough to be opposite it – was the most efficient and deadly of the large water – cooled guns. It shot 400 to 500 rounds per minute and had successfully mowed down legions of British soldiers. He had seen what MG08s could do to a man ... or a horse.

Simon's damaged nerves flared and his vision began to blur in the stress. He swayed a little on his feet and reached out a hand to balance against one of the window frames. There was an alien voice deep in his head that rose in his fragile moments – *It would be so good to go.*

He blew out a short, intense breath. No time to wallow in self – pity. Alice needed protecting as did the four members of Reparations Committee and any of the other guests who were in the way of whatever was planned. Simon stood up straighter and opened his eyes.

As he looked at the problem, there was one major objective: find out who was behind the events at Palliser Park and prevent any harm coming to innocent parties. In order to accomplish it, Alice had to be safe so he could do what needed to be done.

But first, a recce to assess both what his movement options were and where *Sea Sprite's* sailors were if they had managed to infiltrate the house.

Simon pushed away from the attic window when the sound of a door slamming made him freeze in mid – step.

"Crikey," came a voice in one of the other rooms that made up the rabbit warren of attics. Simon recognized it as emanating from one of Sir George's sinister crew at Clara Mare. "Don't like this. Don't like it at all. Bad enough we 'ad to 'andle that ..."

"Jerry," interrupted the voice's companion, clearly bored. "Who the bloody 'ell cares?"

At least, he now knew the *Sea Sprite* gang had indeed made it into the main house and that two of them would be based in the attic. Simon also knew he wasn't ready to take them on just yet. He needed to make some kind of decision before Sir George's sailors discovered that they had an eavesdropper.

Simon chose the window. The pounding rain was a nuisance but it would mask any creaking in the casing. He was out in the proverbial flash and had the window back down just as shadows in the room appeared in his peripheral vision. Pressing hard against the wall – squeezed into the narrow space between two attic windows – he was grateful to the storm for covering his escape. With luck, the two wouldn't spot the rainwater on the attic floor until he'd made a complete exit from the roof.

Exit from the roof. The sharp marine wind sent shards of rain into Simon's face as he thought about the best way to get off the roof without alerting anyone – blameless or sinister – to his efforts. Surprise was his only real advantage. He had to get off the roof, assess where the chess pieces were and make a workable plan to disrupt any attacks on the Big Four.

Returning through the attics was out. If he tried that and was confronted by the sailors, he'd have to neutralize them – a conflict that might be loud enough to attract attention. He didn't want to lose the element of surprise until he knew what his personal Will O' the Wisp, the Gravedigger, intended to do and how many people were needed to accomplish it.

With the attic route closed and without any convenient scaffolding left over from Lord FitzRobert's massive renovations, he was left with only one possible avenue for escape. The Victorian feature that FitzRobert would have strengthened and improved – Palliser Park's plumbing with its extensive cast iron pipes. A long, slippery pathway down to the ground.

Thunder rolled overhead, reminding him that lightning could be another danger as he anticipated moving across the roof's surface. High winds, pummeling rain and potential lightning for a descent that would be tricky in the most bucolic of weather.

Still, there nothing else left to do and he was fighting an unknown clock. Simon looked at the window to the other side of him. He carefully reached into his rucksack and retrieved a small cosmetic mirror he'd stolen from Alice. Shifting it to an extreme angle, the room he'd just left was partially in view. It looked as though the sailors had left it to explore other parts of the attic – probably to find an old chesterfield to sit on as they waited.

Simon moved swiftly past the second window and again, pressed himself against the wall. He employed Alice's mirror again to scan what he could of the attic room. No sailors. Safely over the first hurdle.

Returning the mirror to his bag, Simon peered through the curtain of silver rain at the acres of extensive roof that rolled out from the attic level. He was lucky that Palliser Park was a traditional mid – century Georgian with a complex but reasonably flat roofline. Much easier to transit than Clara Mare with its sloping slate tiles. He'd have to move fast though to avoid the possibility of the sailors spotting him and sending up an alarm. It was unlikely in the storm that they'd hear him clattering along or catch a glimpse of him in the downpour but it was worth avoiding.

Simon studied the roofline and identified a likely spot for cast iron pipes. Lord FitzRobert and the Victorian Tudaburghs before him would prefer the majority of such pipes to be tucked away in corners and notches in the building's basic structural footprint. He spotted just such a corner to the left of him – a large early Victorian enlargement of the kitchens had required a major multi – story addition to the rear of the house. Such was the pain and expense of retaining Palliser Park's formal Georgian lines.

"Throughout the decades," Simon murmured, lighting out for the corner with its hoped – for bank of pipes, "boys have been escaping their tutors and irritating mothers by shimmying down the pipes. How difficult can it be?"

He darted through the rain, splashing through massive puddles on the roof. By the end of the weekend, Palliser Park could be suffering from all sorts of disastrous leaks. The corner proved to have exactly what Simon had guessed it would – an elaborate system of thick iron pipes that ran from the servant's floor all the way to the ground. These pipes not only ran up and down but forked sideways as well, providing the intrepid house climber handy footholds. It was literally a cast – iron ladder of sorts. Simon bet lots of Tudaburgh boys had nipped down to freedom over the years.

But he was forced to admit, they had one thing he didn't have – easy access. The roof and attics didn't require plumbing. The nearest arm of the pipes was attached to the servants' floor below him. To reach it, he would have to get over the stonework that closed in the roofline and drop down to the next floor.

Simon stared down at the lattice of pipes. Rain soaked his clothes and plastered his hair against his skull. It would be a dodgy maneuver in excellent summer weather. In both sharp wind and water, potentially fatal. But with the attic route closed to him, a drop over the side was the only option.

"You chaps will help, won't you?" Simon said to one of Palliser Park's Roman gods that dotted the roofline. He reached into his wet rucksack and retrieved a pair of suede riding gloves. After pulling them on, he took out the length of thin rope that he always kept tucked away in his old campaign bag.

Simon worked quickly. Selecting the nearest god – a Mercury with a maniacal grin – he tied a solid knot around its base and then another one around his waist.

"The best laid plans of mice and men," he said, testing the security of the knot. It would hold.

His time in the trenches had taught him hesitation was dangerous. Once committed, one had to just get on with it. Simon swung his legs over the wet stonework barrier that ran along the edge of the roof. He slipped an arm around one of the decorative stone balusters and eased off the barrier, immediately feeling a painful stress in his elbow as it now helped support his hanging body weight. Dealing with height would never be his first choice but the rope's support gave him some confidence, allowing him to withdraw his arm from the baluster and start a cautious swing towards the top pipe in the plumbing lattice. After going over the edge, the life – saving pipes were only a couple of feet away, but it seemed like a nautical mile as he built up the trajectory of his rope swing.

It took four or five rotations but finally, the rope swung him close enough to grasp at the top pipe. The cast – iron pipe was dripping with rain water so his first grasp slipped and he sailed backwards precariously. Another two swings to rebuild the reach and Simon hooked his right hand around a metal bracket. He found a lower pipe to lock his feet onto and gingerly used his left hand to untie the rope.

"Not too slow because the clock is ticking," Simon murmured to himself to steady his nerve, "but not too fast because unmoored and wet."

Simon began the descent. He moved with steady purpose, shifting down from one cast iron pipe to the next. Only managing to incur one major slip – the soaked leather sole on his boot skidded off a lower foothold and he made an abrupt, terrifying drop. Fortunately, his rough suede riding gloves allowed for a desperate grab at one of the pipe brackets and arrested the fall. The full stop resulted in his knees cracking painfully against the exterior wall but, otherwise, he was all right for the moment. Simon took a brief pause to collect himself and express salent gratitude for sturdy stable gear. He had grown up in the English countryside and had survived four years, three months and two weeks of war – much of it in open trenches – and yet, he doubted he had ever been quite so drenched with rain water.

As a man who didn't care much for heights, he had promised himself he wouldn't look down – that taking a good look at the long way down could actually cause a stupid mistake. Nonetheless, Simon peered through the hammering weather at the ground. He had already tripped up so he figured a glance downwards couldn't make anything worse. The view revealed good news. His sudden plummet had been unnerving but it *had* provided something of a shortcut. Just one more floor to go and his feet would touch blessed earth. The happy notion gave him renewed energy and he focused on the descent, stepping down from one pipe outcropping to the next.

There were no more surprise slips and Simon jumped to the ground. He rubbed his aching elbows, mulling over his next move. It would be best not to be observed by staff or guests through Palliser Park's Georgian windows. He would to need to move with covert speed to try and assess the extent and location of the enemy forces. With a bit of luck, the puppet master who might or might not be the infamous Gravedigger had decided the *Sea Sprite* crew would be sufficient for carrying out whatever disruptions were planned.

With two of Sir George's sailors waiting in the attics, that left – from the rough head count he had made the night before on Clara Mare's rooftop – two more to be found and *neutralized* as Sir Vernon liked to say.

Then Simon was on the game again. With most of the guests upstairs, the ground floor would be dominated by Crumpling and his staff readying the Marble Salon for Fizz's engagement fiasco. He kept close to the house to avoid being inadvertently spotted from upper windows and moved as quickly as he could to the stable where it might be possible *Sea Sprite's* corpse handling crew had decided to hole up. Above the stable was the Brabinger family's living quarters – another potential hide – y hole.

He retrieved the Webley Met Police revolver from his rucksack on the chance that Sir George's sailors wouldn't be pleased to see him. Slipping through the tack room – Webley at his side – Simon peered into the main aisle of Lord FitzRobert's beautifully restored stable. All appeared quiet. The horses were calm – unexcited by either invaders or the relentless storm. Colonel Lee left his hay and nickered at him in hopes that a carrot or apple might be forthcoming.

"Sorry, old man," Simon said, crossing the barn aisle to rub the big bay's head. Always a horseman first, he automatically eyed Colonel Lee's water trough and saw that it was full.

After checking every stall, the feed room and grooming stations, Simon found an interior staircase that led up to the Brabinger flat. He quietly ascended the steps and tried the oak door at the top. It was firmly locked with no signs of forced entry.

That left mechanical horsepower. The garage where Lord FitzRobert kept his sleek Rolls Royce and other vehicles such as the missing Sunbeam Prince Volkonsky had supposedly driven to his doctor. The other conveniently located spot to stage a coup at Palliser Park. If the last two members of Sea Sprite's crew weren't there, Simon guessed they were either still aboard *SeaSprite* or in Clara Mare biding their time, waiting for some pre – ordained signal. Given the way the yacht had been yawing in the huge tide, he assumed they would choose the old gamekeeper's cottage.

The garage was new but had been meticulously designed to resemble the long established Tudaburgh stable. It would be difficult to find a more elaborately appointed private garage anywhere in Britain or Europe. Any mechanical problems could be directly dealt with at Palliser Park so His Lordship never had to be bothered to seek out a lowly repair shop. His chauffeur – a former color sergeant named Hopkirk – ran the garage like a military operation.

Simon approached the FitzRobert garage, pondering how best to proceed. He wasn't anxious to use his Webley in a direct confrontation yet and decided to walk the perimeter of the outbuilding, scanning for any indication that the *Sea Sprite* crewmembers were inside.

As with the stable, the building seemed quiet and what he could see through the rain splattered windows was unexceptional – no lurking bad hats. Simon brushed water away from a window glass and took a closer look. The FitzRobert Rolls Royce sat in its bay. Gleaming and elegant, it was the reigning monarch of the collection. He narrowed his eyes and moved closer to the window pane. One of the Rolls Royce's rear doors was hanging open. Not the manner in which the disciplined Hopkirk would allow such a magnificent motor car to be treated.

Simon reached down and grasped the handle of the bay door. He hoisted the wooden panel up to take a closer look at the interior of the garage. Rain pounded down on the door, providing an umbrella for Simon as he stepped into the Rolls Royce's space. He was grateful to be out of the weather for a moment despite needing to check every corner for a hulking figure intent on doing him harm.

There was no one. Not even the dutiful Hopkirk. The garage was tomblike – motor cars sat silently in their slips like metal Egyptian sarcophagi.

"Hopkirk?" he called out before approaching the Rolls. "Hopkirk? It's Major Fairlight." There was no response and he wondered if the chauffeur had been recruited to help in the Marble Salon.

Simon took a look in the back seat of the car. Nothing of genuine interest. He was reminded again of an Egyptian tomb – one that been opened and robbed.

A muffled thump caught his attention. Then there came several more as if someone or something wanted his attention. Simon tracked the rhythmic thumps. He held up the Webley. It might be a feint by one of the *Sea Sprite* set to lure him in.

The insistent sounds led him to a large fitted cabinet in the rear of the garage. He could see the latched door shifting out and back as something shoved against it.

Simon unhooked the latch and then jumped back as the door flew open. Hopkirk had been kicking it with his feet. The chauffeur had been brutally bound and gagged. His forehead was bruised from a blow to the head.

"Thank God, Major," he gasped once Simon had pocketed his revolver and liberated him. "I thought you might be one of 'em. Gave me a right crack on the skull."

"It's a corker," Simon agreed, handing him a handkerchief from his hacking jacket pocket. "Sorry – it's wet."

"Feels good," said Hopkirk with a raspy breath. He pressed the soaked linen against the bruised swelling. "Got the jump on me. Out like a light once they conked me, but I think they wanted to disable the cars. What the blazes is it all about?"

Simon helped the older man to stand and get to a stool. "I'm not entirely sure. Something to do with His Lordship's post – war work for our government."

"His Lordship is an important man."

"Do you still have your service revolver?" Simon asked.

Hopkirk nodded, still holding the handkerchief to his temple. "Up in my flat."

"Let's get you upstairs and go from there." He offered Hopkirk his arm and the chauffeur rose unsteadily from the metal stool to accept it. "Can you describe these louts?"

Hopkirk proved to be observant as the best color sergeants tended to be and gave Simon a clear view of two sturdy, working class sailors that matched the pair he'd seen in Clara Mare. He guessed they were also the set who had invaded the attics. That left another unaccounted for and if he was right, he was probably tucked into the old cottage more than a mile away, armed with a spy glass and awaiting signal by lamp. Given distance and time issues especially with the storm, he would have to wait for him to come in.

"How can I help?" rasped Hopkirk as Simon settled the former soldier onto a chair by the kitchen table. "Want to do my bit."

"I think you've done your bit," said Simon, moving to fetch him a glass of water from the modern sink FitzRobert had installed in the staff flat. Then Simon spotted a bottle of aspirin on the counter and brought it along as well.

"Wouldn't mind having a go at the blighters," said Hopkirk almost wistfully. "There's a box of bandages in that cupboard if you don't mind."

"Could use a set of eyes up here – I think there may be four moving about," Simon said. He set the tin bandage box down on the kitchen table and flipped it open. Behind him the bubbling tea kettle whistled. "Let me take a look at your conk."

Hopkirk lowered the now red handkerchief and tilted his head up to the light. It was a simple scalp laceration – superficial but bloody. Pretty typical of scalp wounds that he had observed on the battlefield. As with most soldiers who had toiled in the trenches, Simon had become an excellent emergency nurse and had helped stitch up much trickier injuries.

He cleaned stoic Hopkirk's wound with some hot water from the kettle. With the blood cleared away, the laceration proved too shallow to require a stitch or two. He could hold it together with a pressure bandage.

"No needle and thread then?" asked Hopkirk as Simon packed the abrasion with clean bandaging.

"You are in fortune's breast pocket, my friend."

"Thank you, Major." Hopkirk remained still as Simon wound cloth tightly around his forehead and secured it with a pin. "You're a good lad." His voice was weary. "What's your brilliant plan?"

Simon appreciated the informal language of soldiers. "Not sure if it qualifies as a plan," he admitted. "Once I know where the black chess pieces are, I'm going to take them off the board."

The former soldier reached out to grasp the handle of the tea mug Simon had brought him. "You trained in behind – the – lines guff?"

Simon knew Hopkirk was referring to inglorious and brutal guerilla tactics. "I did my share over there," he allowed. Some people might not want to share company with a man who had done the things he had.

There was a thoughtful pause while the older man sipped his tea. "You're a good lad," he repeated, once the mug was returned to the table top. "You need me – I'm here."

51

Alice heard another knock at the door – quiet though, not sharp and angry as before. Still, she froze, remembering how frightening the mysterious visitors had been. It felt clear to her that had she opened the door, she would not have escaped, unscathed.

"It's me," came Simon's voice through the wood panels.

"Oh, thank God," she said, running to unlock the door.

He stood in the hallway in soaked riding clothes. "I'm freezing," Simon admitted, almost sheepish. "Have you got the fire going?"

Alice flung her arms around him. "Where have you been?"

"Now you're wet as well," he pointed out.

"I care not," she said, pulling away from the fierce hug. "Yes, the fire is going. Come on in and listen to what happened. Through the window, I saw one of those sailors from the *Sea Sprite* in the garden, heading for the house."

To her surprise, Simon nodded and then moved with alacrity to their fireplace. He stood in front of the coal fire and divested himself of his hacking jacket, tossing it on a nearby chair.

"There are *two* and both of them are currently hiding in the attics. Somewhere there are two more ..." Simon winced, "too."

"Just what the hell is going on?" Alice joined him by the fire. "Someone ... well, more than one actually, tried the door. They banged on it – I think they thought I was asleep and they would wake me so I'd answer."

"It wasn't Fizz, or maybe Perry, looking for a shoulder to weep on?" Simon asked. He was unbuttoning his wet canary vest and tattersall shirt. "Fizz has a pretty heavy hand. Perry's a bit of a fool."

"No." Alice felt cold despite the coal fire in June. "It was strange. I just knew that if I had opened that door, I might never be seen again."

For a moment, she watched genuine grief shudder across her husband's highly planed face. He reached out and pulled her into his arms, pressing her tightly against his chest.

"There are four men at Palliser Park who wield a great deal of power over Germany's future," she heard him say into her right ear. "I believe there is a plot to disrupt that power and Fizz's engagement party is the focus."

"Lord FitzRobert, Sir George Jasper, Alastair Rothermore and Sir Henry Frost," Alice guessed, thinking about the most notable members of the guest list.

"Clever Alice," he murmured, still holding her close.

"What are we going to do?" She decided not to inquire as to how her husband had come to the notion of secret plots to unravel post – war political machinations. It felt as if Simon had pieces to a puzzle – a puzzle she knew nothing about.

Simon pulled away and kissed her forehead. "Drinks will be dished out in about an hour. Can you get ready? We need to make an appearance."

"Just an appearance?"

"A little sleight of hand," Simon said with an enigmatic flair that came off as unintentional. He just looked tired and distracted. "I'll explain it all later."

It took roughly an hour to make the transition into suitably polished guests for Lord FitzRobert's celebration for his favorite child. The ladies maid Fizz had promised would turn up was delayed assisting other guests so Alice did her own hair, twisting it into a simple chignon. Because they would be making what Simon termed *an appearance*, she figured anything more was gilding the lily.

She decided to wear the rose satin. The whole visit to Palliser Park had been riven with the melancholy and sinister culminating in an evening in which a German plot would be unveiled. A frothy lemon yellow frock seemed utterly wrong – a mean joke.

"Simon," Alice said as her husband crossed to one of the windows to have a gander at the late afternoon storm. The long English summer's day meant there would be light until almost ten o'clock. Glorious for an engagement party in fine weather. Poor Fizz.

"Rain's letting up a little," he announced. "Maybe we'll get a brief lull."

"Simon," she repeated, as he turned away from the window and started adjusting an insecure cufflink, "why would four British ex – navy sailors turn into agents for Germany? That just doesn't make sense. You know *helpin' ruddy Jerry* after this awful war."

Alice saw her husband stop suddenly at her words. She watched as an expression of realization flicker across his face and disappear, replaced by one of genuine sadness. Both vanished as he turned to focus on her and her question.

"Oldest motive in the world, I expect – money." Simon made a half – hearted adjustment to the sleeve of his traditional tail coat. "I miss Mr. Spinner's brilliance at final inspection."

She was a little surprised that he wasn't in the Blues and Royals frock coat uniform that he preferred for more formal social events – even their own wedding – and said so.

"Not for this circus," he said and seemed to force a smile. "You look lovely. A little plain, perhaps, but lovely. No jewelry?"

"No decorations?" Alice countered. *Not for this circus.*

Simon tilted his handsome head in recognition of her riposte. "Touche. We understand each other."

He offered her his elbow and she took it with a little breath for courage. "Can you, at least, tell me how this all begins?" Alice asked.

"You and I are going to wander through the drinks, making sure that we are clearly seen and at some point, you're going to feel very faint."

"Actual acting? Not sure it will pass Miss Dorothy Brier's muster but I'll try."

Drinks were being handed out in Palliser Park's gallery on the ground floor. It was narrow and long, running a length next to the Marble Salon. In the Tudaburgh's day, the gallery would have heavily featured family portraits from various eras and some reasonably good landscapes. Given the later rise of the family in society, the FitzRobert era offered far fewer family portraits of any note although many excellent landscapes and nautical pictures had been acquired to fill empty Tudaburgh spots.

Whoever was left from the once mighty guest list had already arrived by the time the Fairlights managed to reach the gallery. It had taken a little longer than expected as all the routes to the double staircases in the Marble Galley had been sealed off by interior doors. Apparently, Lord FitzRobert wanted a spectacular ceremonial opening of the Marble Salon for dinner and dancing. Even the hired musicians and servants had been cleared out of the salon as they were needed in the gallery or in the kitchens.

Alice had requested an orange juice as she didn't want her nerves dulled by champagne or gin. She scanned the gallery – intended to have been a suitable venue for a large number of summer visitors to Palliser Park, it now swallowed up the hardy clutch of roughly thirty who had survived the storm purge – and saw that everyone had done their best to honor Fizz and Jack. The guests were beautifully attired and attempting to fill the half – empty gallery with vivacious conversation of the kind one expected at jolly social events. The Palliser Park staff was crisply uniformed and performing a variety of tasks with the kind of flawless attention to detail that would be making Crumpling a satisfied butler. The visiting musicians were stationed near the massive double doors of the Marble Salon, dutifully churning out cheerful versions of Baroque and Victorian favorites.

Lord FitzRobert was holding the center, talking too loudly with Sir Henry Frost and gesturing grandly with his glass of scotch as if he could, single – handedly, make up for all the missing guests. Fizz, who by all rights, was the actual focus of the evening, was laughing with Sir George Jasper and the Rothermores. She was legitimately stunning in a bright white evening dress that imitated Roman style – her gleaming russet hair caught up underneath a new tiara of diamonds and citrine. Family members and other guests, intimidated by the yawning size of the gallery milled around the central drinks table and musician stand. There was still no electrical power so a collection of bulbous oil lamps had been pressed into service as heavy cloud cover had stolen the late summer daylight. The Victorian lamps with their sentimental hand – painted glass domes clashed with high Georgian formality, but no one seemed to mind. Alice guessed every candle in the house would end up being used in the Marble Salon.

"Doesn't it feel like we're standing outside some kind of ancient tomb?" Alice murmured before taking a sip of her orange juice.

Simon saluted her with a small glass of sherry. "Let's have a word with Fizz and then you can make your stage debut."

Alice took her husband's elbow and they started to cross the inlaid floor to where Fizz FitzRobert was laughing – like her father, far too loudly – and knocking back a large gin martini.

"Oh, no, you don't," came Perry's voice from behind them. He took Alice's other arm. "Not without me. I took a nap and overslept. Dad will be livid. I was supposed to help organize the aunts."

"Perry – using us as a shield?" Alice shook her head. "Will you never learn?"

"He never will," said Simon.

Fizz spotted them approaching and made her apologies to Sir George and the Rothermores, darting over to meet them.

"I'm already absolutely tanked," she announced with another loud, almost harsh laugh. "Had at least three champagnes!"

"Where's Jack?" Alice asked, looking around for Fizz's handsome intended. "Shouldn't he be here squiring you about?"

Fizz tossed her head – the diamond and citrine tiara flashing in the glow from the oil lamps. "Dad has him ready to read a poem or something up on one of the staircases – you know, as the doors open. Oops – I've ruined the surprise ... *surprise!*" She giggled and looked about, "I need a footman ..."

"Perhaps, slow down on the grog?" Perry said, his tone hopeful.

"No homespun wisdom from you," Fizz snapped and turned sharply in his direction, her eyes flashing as brightly as her jewels. "Dad's ready to have you drawn and quartered. Aunt Honoria was lost for most of the afternoon!"

"I fell asleep!" he bleated, instinctively ducking behind Alice's shoulder.

"You're useless. You had one little thing to do and you couldn't even ..."

A scream interrupted Fizz's scathing review of Perry's failures as a brother. A full throated, terrified scream – one that would have been louder if the doors to the Marble Salon weren't sealed. It was followed by another muffled scream.

Guests and staff members in the gallery began to twist and turn in panic. Hired musicians in the middle of an excerpt from Vivaldi's *Spring* screeched to a dead stop. Lord FitzRobert froze in mid – gesture, his face alternating between indecision and disbelief. Alice recalled the incident with the elevator. Was this the start of what Simon had been fearing?

Her husband slipped his arm from under hers and took off at a run for the doors to the Marble Salon. She followed – not because she was brave and thought she could actually help but because she wanted to stay with Simon. Whatever was happening or would happen, they had to stay together.

Simon was the first one to the door, Sir Henry Frost and Sir George on his heels. She saw Simon twisting the key and then flinging the double doors open with such force that they banged into walls.

The screaming was louder with the doors open. Shrill, unhinged. Alice nipped into the Marble Salon just behind Sir George Jasper.

A maid was standing at the bottom of the west stair in a state of utter hysteria. She held a lantern and long tapers in shaking hands. It seemed clear that the girl had entered the Marble Salon to light candles and something had frightened her beyond the capacity to cope. The quaking girl was looking up, pointing, screaming.

Alice looked up. In the dull glow of the lantern and a bank of candles that the maid had managed to light, she saw Jack Nickleby hanging from one of the balcony balusters, a cruelly thin rope wrapped around his neck. He slowly turned from one side to the other – a terrible creaking sound every time Jack's body spiraled to the left or right. She couldn't stop herself from focusing on Jack's terrible face – grey, eyes wide open in horror. Something wet and dark dropped on his forehead. Then another struck his cheek. Black rain drops.

She looked further up. Up to the balcony rail where Jack had tied the rope. Dorothy Brier was lying over the rail, lifeless arms reaching down as if to try and pull Jack to safety. Blood was dripping down from some, as yet, undiscovered mortal wound. It coursed down her arms and fell from her fingers.

More people pushed their way into the Marble Salon, jostling Alice. Like His Lordship, she felt frozen in place, unable to make a decision about how or where to move. She could hear shouts and new voices screaming all round her, echoing in the enormous space. Lord FitzRobert's household was shifting into full out pandemonium.

"Jack!" shrieked Fizz from somewhere behind her. "Jack!"

Suddenly Alice felt a strong arm encircle her waist and pull her from her rooted spot. It was Simon. He moved her with surprising speed to the gallery beyond the horrifying tableau in the Marble Salon.

"Keep going," he murmured in her ear as they slipped past milling people and servants who were arriving to see what had gone wrong.

Ignoring the panic, Simon led her away from the Marble Salon and towards the nearest exit. Alice looked anxiously behind her as they headed to the foyer. No one gave them a second glance. The focus was entirely on Jack and Dorothy. They ran through the main doors and clattered down the narrow, wide steps of Palliser Park's formal entrance, instantly pummeled by rain and wind.

"Where are we headed?" Alice asked breathlessly, pausing to kick off her satin pumps. "Simon, why would ... why would Jack kill himself?"

"He didn't kill himself," said Simon in a flat voice.

Alice's head reeled at the thought. Someone had hung Jack Nickleby. Someone had murdered Jack and presumably, Dorothy Brier as well.

"I need your help," said Simon, pulling her along again through the rain.

She peered, bleary – eyed in the downpour, at where their destination might lie.

"The stable?" she asked. Thunder rolled overhead.

"If you don't think you can do it," he said, "you can hide in the Brabingers' flat until I fetch you."

"Oh, I'm going to help all right," Alice replied, wiping a heavy strand of wet hair out of her face. "You just tell me what to do."

"Good – you're the only person here that could get it done." Simon yanked open the sliding barn door and they ducked inside, out of the weather. He shut the door again, plunging the stable aisle into semi – darkness. There was just enough grey light to move around without tripping over buckets or tack trunks.

He took her up a set of stairs to a landing and a fine old oak door. A brass plaque that read *Brabinger* was mounted on the wall next to the door. Alice watched, shivering in her soaked dress as Simon rooted around the ledge above the door, looking for a key. When he actually found one, he unlocked the door and they stepped into a neat, attractive family flat.

"This way," said Simon as they walked deeper into the Brabinger home. He was picking up items as they went along – a flashlight from the kitchen table, an anorak off a coat rack by the door.

He stopped at a bedroom. A small room with pale green and cream wallpaper, a shelf of silver cups festooned with county fair ribbons and window curtains with large romantic flounces. A girl's room.

"Meg will have warm riding clothes – dig up what you can and put them on. See if her jodhpur boots will fit you."

"I like the idea of warm dry clothes. Are we riding out of here?" Alice crossed to Meg's cupboard and pulled open the door. The clothing rod held many bits and pieces suitable for a riding habit.

"*You're* riding out of here," Simon said in the kind of voice that defied any contradiction or argument. "I need you to get to Brightsea and Nyx. If there's flooding, he'll be using the church as headquarters. It's on higher ground. Tell him I could use any help he can spare. If Mr. Spinner made it to Brightsea, send him along too."

Alice swallowed hard. "You're not going to do anything brave but ultimately futile and stupid, are you?"

"I'm just going to try to keep people from getting hurt."

"FitzRobert, Jasper, Rothermore and Frost," she recited and yanked a pair of heavy weight jodhpurs off a wooden hanger. "You know, I thought for a bit that it might be Jack. He's never had any real money. Fizz can be oblivious yet expensive… but now, of course, it isn't him."

"He was part of it," said Simon without emotion, "but no longer needed and had gotten unreliable."

"My God," Alice resisted the urge to gasp like a character out of ladies' novel, "you *know* who's behind all of it."

"I think I do, yes." He turned away from her. "Hurry, Alice. I'll saddle a horse for you in the meantime."

When she returned to the stable aisle, Alice was reasonably dry and kitted out in Meg's winter – weight riding clothes. The girl's boots were a little snug but would work just fine in the current emergency. She also wore a large waxed anorak that probably belonged to Meg's father and a wide – brimmed felt hat that might be Mrs. Brabinger's.

Simon had a huge strawberry roan horse fully saddled and out on the cross ties. The horse pawed the stable floor irritably with his left fore. Alice had the impression that the gelding was coiled up with energy, ready to explode.

"This is Jade," said Simon, patting the roan's neck. "I won't lie – he's young, opinionated and pulls like a freight train."

"Great." Alice made a sour face. "How about that nice little Cob over there?"

"He's also incredibly athletic and brave. If any horse can get you to Brightsea in this gale, it's this one." Simon unhooked Jade from the ties. "Let's get you up under roof."

Alice took in a deep breath and stepped to where Simon could give her a leg up into the saddle. As soon as she settled in the saddle, the roan gelding jigged to the side, anxious to be off and away. She collected her reins expertly.

"Ready," she said as Jade pawed the ground.

"You're going to your right – I'll let you through the gate." Simon handed her a flashlight. "Hop the wall on the other side of the pasture and go right again – there's an old drover's path that resists flooding unlike the main road. It'll take you to Brightsea."

"Ready,' Alice repeated and hoped she was right.

Simon pulled open the stable doors and Alice urged Jade out in the rain. The strong horse surged forward, glad to beout of his stall. She was heartened to see that the weather had slowed for a moment and was now just a steady drizzle. The summer evening light was holding so she could even see reasonably well.

She directed Jade through the opening Simon made with the wooden cattle gate. The horse snorted in the drizzle and then nickered at a group of cows that were bunched together in the storm.

"See you later, alligator," she said to Simon.

"Mind how you go, Alice." He reached up and took her hand for a moment.

Alice nodded and squeezed her legs against the barrel of the large roan gelding. The horse was delighted to be asked to move forward and shifted immediately into a gallop. She had to admit Simon knew his horses. Jade's gallop was balanced and powerful – agile like a cat. He covered the pasture easily and flew over the wall at the point Simon had recommended.

After a successful landing on the other side, Jade crowhopped in excitement. Alice reached down to pat his neck and then pulled him up for a moment – just to look back. One last look at her husband.

She gazed across the pasture in the silvery summer light. Simon was already gone.

CHAPTER

52

Simon made good time back to the main house. Getting Alice off to Brightsea on the roan gelding had taken a toll on his internal clock. The upstairs duo had undoubtably lit a lantern in one of the attic windows to reel in the remaining *Sea Sprite* crew. He would be surprised if they weren't already in place for the centerpiece of the drama.

If he was right about the Gravedigger's identity, there were two possible ways it could unfold: FitzRobert, Frost, Jasper and Rothermore would be taken as hostages aboard *Sea Sprite* and transported to Germany where they would be highly useful in a variety of ways to an underground resistance movement. The other option was a flamboyant on – site execution designed to terrify the British people and delay the Reparations Committee's work indefinitely.

The power was still out on the Essex coast so Palliser Park looked gloomy and abandoned in what light remained in the summer storm. Simon approached the side door most conveniently located to one of the secondary staircases. The quickest route he had discovered earlier when he sought to avoid the central stairs in the Marble Salon and nip up to their guest room covertly. He paused before trying the door and

337

instead, leaned against it, retrieving his revolver from a trouser pocket.

As always, shell shock's tendrils of panic threatened to weave their way up through his nerves, choking off his ability to think and react. He felt sick as if his nerves emitted some kind of poison.

Steady, lads, steady – he remembered the calm basso voice of Captain Alfred Deller as they readied for an assault on a German watchtower – *Nothing here we haven't done before.*

Simon let out a short breath and pushed in the door. *Over the top and on we go …*

The vestibule was shrouded in dappled light and empty of human occupation– no servants moving around anywhere. He could hear muffled shouts, cries of distress, breaking glass and the echo of a rifle shot from the distant Marble Salon. He guessed all of Palliser Park's household was now centralized in the Marble Salon – the kitchen staff would have been rounded up by the later crewmembers. It's what he would have done if such an assignment had fallen to him.

It was well past time for an assessment of just what he was up against. Simon took the secondary staircase carefully but with as much speed as he could manage without causing loud creaks or footfalls. He made it to the next floor without issue and headed in the direction of the Marble Salon.

Essentially, Palliser Park's first floor was built around the towering Marble Salon. All roads, as it were, led to the crowning achievement of Lord FitzRobert's restored Palliser Park. The two massive staircases opposite each other served as the main thoroughfare to what was both a great hall and ballroom – the heart of Palliser Park. A long stretch of open hallway connected the stairs and served as a viewing gallery with its gold gilded balcony. Of course, currently, the view included two brutally murdered bodies.

Simon came up the main hallway of the guest wing as he been trained to do – fast, silent but pausing at every possible juncture to scan for enemy presence and moving on. He saw that the interior doors that could close off the Marble Salon to preserve heat or conceal servant activity before parties, were standing open. There were two streams of voices rising up – getting clearer with every step that he took – those in peril and those in charge.

Again, *if* he was right about the Gravedigger's identity, it would still be hidden and would remain hidden to protect future operations. The Gravedigger was far too important, too useful to squander.

"No one will be hurt," a German voice rang out over the terrified sounds of Lord FitzRobert's partygoers. Simon pictured poor Jack still hanging from the baluster below the German's feet – a victim of his own desires. "All will be well."

Simon was grateful that the storm had knocked out power. The Marble Salon was in half light from its rain whipped windows, providing deep shadows in pockets. He backed up into one of them – an extreme corner by one of the interior doors and scanned the visible wedge of the balcony.

A tall, powerful figure prowled the Marble Salon's balcony. Mid – thirties, blond, dressed in a coarse black sweater, wool trousers and heavy boots, the German carried a Bergmann MP 18. The MP 18 was a submachine gun favored by the *Sturmtruppen* – small assault groups who specialized in surprise and the most brutal trench combat.

Simon shifted for a slightly wider view. He failed to spy any of the English sailors but counted two more Germans on the stairs opposite. Tough looking men in black armed with Karabiner 98Ks – shorter, trench tested versions of the Gewehr 98. The Gravedigger wasn't using Sir George's four crewmembers. These were *Sturmtruppen*. Disciplined, well trained and deadly.

Simon wondered if the *Sea Sprite's* crew was still alive or if they had even realized what the plot actually was. It occurred to him that they may have thought they were doing Britain a service by getting rid of what he now knew was a *Jerry* corpse – Albertine Graf von Arco auf Valley, German translator turned faux Russian prince. Of course, they hadn't just dumped Albertine into the drink, they had also picked up Gravedigger's strike team somewhere and brought them to English soil. Was it possible that the *Sea Sprite* sailors had bought the whole plan as a covert British operation – maybe believing Sir George tacitly approved of what they were doing? He'd check the attic when there was a moment and see if there was anything he could glean.

"All will be well," repeated the one with the MP 18. He appeared to be the erstwhile leader of this faction of *Sturmtruppen*.

The Germans might be in control of Palliser Park, but they had a major problem. Simon suspected that the plan had been to swoop down on Fizz's engagement party, secure the members of the Reparations Committee and get them out as hostages to Germany. They hadn't counted on the most powerful storm in recent memory to strike the Essex coast. If they lit out now for international waters, *Sea Sprite* wouldn't survive the hundred – foot waves out in the North Sea. They had to wait for the weather to break.

He still had a small window in which to operate. The cock –
up in their plans would make the Germans nervous – as
Sturmtruppen, their instincts would be to eradicate dead weight
and clear out if things got tight. *Sturmtruppen* were not soldiers
who waited. They were apex predators who sighted prey and
charged without mercy.

53

Alice began to understand Simon's faith in the red roan. He was strong but naturally balanced, keeping his feet underneath him even in wet conditions of the cow pasture. She had trotted away from the stone wall, following what appeared to be well − used shortcut into an extensive orchard of apple trees.

A steady rain pattered down on the leaves with a dull rhythm − at odds with erratic thunder and flashes of lightning. She tried to see in the fading light where an old drover's road might cut into rows of trees roiling in a stiff wind. It all looked the same in the rain. The land was rising slightly as Jade jogged along the worn trail. The gelding shook his head in annoyance as a thin tree branch was blown by the wind past his ears but he didn't shy. Simon was right. Jade was a stable fellow.

"But you do pull like a freight train," she said, stretching her shoulders and then stroked his mane. "His Lordship must have hands of iron."

They trotted on, searching for the fabled road to Brightsea. Speed was important but asking Jade to gallop when the path was unknown risked an injury to the horse and it was essential to make it to the village.

The rain shifted from steady to pelting and with visibility dropping, she didn't see it. Jade did – he slid to a stop and pivoted on his hind legs, leaping to the side in one massive bound. Although genuinely taken by surprise, Alice stayed with him. Simultaneously, an ancient apple tree split under several centuries of storm and crashed across the shortcut with a hideous cracking.

Grateful, Alice cried out her thanks and threw both arms around Jade's neck as he pranced with excitement. If Jade hadn't moved like quicksilver, the deadfall would have gotten them both. She sat back up and added several solid pats to his rain soaked shoulder.

"You are an excellent boy," she said, her voice shaking and heart pounding. Like Jade, she wanted to prance with nervous energy. *Mother Nature, Destiny, Zeus, the Universe or whatever – a girl and a horse just eluded your grasp …*

Lightning streaked to the north. The whole area was lit for one dazzling instant and in the flash, Alice spotted the old drover's road. It was just beyond the fallen apple tree, up an embankment.

Alice gathered her reins. The stout gelding snorted and shook his head, happy to get back to work. She squeezed her legs around his barrel and he moved off without trepidation.

"Jade, my friend, let's see if we can get around this thing," she said, wiping rain from her face.

The apple tree had completely wedged itself between several other trees. There was no way immediately around it. Over the tree was the only real option. Alice estimated that the tree's trunk as it was positioned on the path was roughly three – six, four foot and well within the capabilities of the roan gelding. At least in fair weather and with decent light. As it was, in foul weather and twilight, they'd be lucky not to come to serious grief. Riders had been killed attempting less treacherous obstacles.

Alice took Jade back down the soggy path, deciding that a short, four – stride approach would be their best chance. Her father – a fine horseman and long – time whipper – in for the Hudson Valley Hunt Club – always told her that long approaches to fences invited disaster. *Along approach*, he would counsel, *gave a young or inexperienced horse too long to think about things.* She did not want to give Jade too long to think about all the reasons he might not want to jump a recently fallen tree in the middle of a storm.

"Okay doke," Alice said, shortening her reins in case Jade decided to go off to the races on the landing side – *if* they landed on the other side. "Let's go, boy."

She trotted Jade around in a small circle, picking up the gallop as they returned to the path. Jade clattered through the mud, locked onto the oncoming obstacle despite the curtain of rain. *One stride, two, stride,* Alice counted in her head and upon reaching the third stride, she squeezed his sides, asking for the effort.

Jade sailed over the apple tree in a huge effort, easily clearing the trunk and landing safely on the other side. A young horse, he was impressed with himself and threw in a couple of minor bucks – a horse's version of an athlete punching the air with excitement after scoring a victory.

Alice ignored his silliness and urged him on. The horse flew forward and bounced up the embankment to the old drover's road. With some finessing, she managed to pull him up one last time before lighting out for Brightsea and quickly checked his girth. Once the saddle was secure, Alice collected her reins for the final push to the village.

Thunder rolled dully overhead and the rain thinned a bit – a brief lull. She gave Jade the nudge, he immediately broke into a canter and then into a full hand gallop. A few seconds later, they were streaking towards Brightsea and help for Simon and Palliser Park.

CHAPTER

54

Five *Sturmtruppen* including the one swinging around a MP 18 submachine gun. Simon shifted slightly in his hidden spot, trying to catch a glimpse of the ground floor and the subjugated household. A world of difference from four hearty sailors without much in the way of special training. He'd been an idiot to have underestimated the Gravedigger.

"You can help us," called out the Number One from his elevated position on the balcony. "And by helping us, help yourselves, yes? Speak up if you know someone is missing from this party."

Time to move. Simon retracted himself from his overlook. It would only be a matter of moments before someone was forced to admit the Fairlights were absent. He was losing some element of surprise. The *Sturmtruppen* would soon be looking for him.

At least Alice was away from Palliser Park. He sent up a fervent plea to the universe that she had found the old road to Brightsea and was able to manage the difficult roan gelding. Knowing Alice was, at the very least, on the precipice of being safe gave him a kind of internal permission to do what he had been trained to do in war.

Simon headed back to their guest room. It couldn't be a hidi
– hole for long – they'd come after him, Bristol fashion, in
short order. He ran as lightly to avoid creaking footfalls but
realized that the raging storm outside the house would probably
obliterate such ordinary noises. A few moments in the room
would allow him to regroup. The single up – side of being
hunted by *Sturmtruppen* was that such an effort would require
them to split up to make an effective search. They would be
overconfident, imagining that the Fairlights would be easy
marks.

"The dear old room," Simon murmured as he nipped into
the secondary guest hallway and their quarters.

It all looked so ordinary. Their room was just as they'd left
it – a bit untidy in the rush to get ready for Fizz's party.
Glancing at a bottle of Alice's favorite perfume made him
momentarily nostalgic and grateful – profoundly grateful that
she was on a good horse and away from Palliser Park.

Simon pushed aside frivolous thoughts and concentrated on
the practical. He threw open the wardrobe and pulled out a
metal case that always accompanied him on trips. Inside were
useful things – extra ammunition, lock picking tools and various
weapons for close – quarters combat including his trench knife.
After selecting a few pieces, Simon stripped off his damp
tailcoat and white shirt, planning to change into some sturdy
country clothes.

He was throwing his shirt on a chair when the muffled
sounds of people moving outside in the hallways made him
freeze in place. The Germans were moving ever faster than
anticipated.

Simon reached for his trench knife – a nasty blade based on
a Bowie but with the addition of brass knuckles on the handle,

running from butt to bolster – and moved into the glamorous white tiled bathroom. He slipped behind its door and waited, barely breathing.

It didn't take long. Simon had to admit German efficiency was commendable. Number One with the MP 18 had issued orders and his *Sturmtruppen* were mercilessly following them. There were five of them in an enormous house of complex design. Number One would need at least one in the Marble Salon to keep order. That left three on the hunt. They would underestimate him, believing him to be a husband protecting his wife – that the Fairlights had been fortunate enough to elude the initial round – up and were cowering somewhere in the house. Basic locate and control duty.

The handle to their guest room jostled and then Simon heard the door creak softly as it swung in. He grasped the trench knife's handle tighter, holding the weapon flat against his bare chest. One of the bathroom cupboards featured a mirror on its door. He had positioned it so he could see most of the main room in the mirror's reflection.

A single member of the rogue *Sturmtruppen* cautiously stepped into the room. He, too, was in a well – worn black military sweater and wool trousers. A Balaclava was rucked up on his blond hair, available to conceal his face if needed. The German had a Karabiner 98K in his gloved hands. It was a short version of the Gewehr bolt action rifle and much more useful in close – quarters work. There was a semi – automatic Mauser C96 hand gun on his belt. The former soldier was a lean, killing machine.

Simon watched in the mirror as the German turned slowly in a circle, assessing the room for any pertinent information. The soldier spotted the abandoned tailcoat on the chair and went to examine it. Simon swore silently – it would be clear to the German that the coat had been out in the rain. *Why hadn't he tossed it in the wardrobe?* These were the mistakes that got men killed.

The German pivoted and approached the bathroom. One last thing to check off the search list before exiting to relay information back that the missing guest was in the house somewhere. Simon tensed behind the bathroom door as the *Sturmtruppen* soldier came closer. He heard the man mutter something. His German had been learned in the trenches so it was school boyish at best but he thought the soldier said, *There is no honor in this.*

It almost made Simon regret what he had to do next.

The *Sturmtruppen* officer stepped across the bathroom threshold. It wouldn't be a thorough recce if the German didn't make absolutely sure no one was hiding in the bathtub. Simon had made sure the shower curtain was pulled shut to pique interest. The officer took two strides towards the bath and reached for the white curtain.

Simon sprung, wrapping his right arm around the surprised German's throat, jerking him backwards and off his center of balance. His left hand went up to grab a sturdy handful of blond hair. Before the flailing soldier could regain his footing, Simon propelled him forward and slammed his forehead down on the edge of the pedestal sink. The German groaned as bones in his face shattered against the porcelain, blood from a broken nose splattering the white basin. Just for good measure, Simon did it again and then, once more to be thorough. The straining *Sturmtruppen* officer's body relaxed, slipping to the floor, dead.

He could have used his trench knife. Faster, quieter. But he wanted the German's clothes. A knife left holes and lots more blood.

55

Visibility was deteriorating as Alice and the sturdy roan gelding galloped the drover's road. The long summer light was surrendering to the storm. She could see how the old road with its higher rise resisted flooding. But both local rivers and sea inlets seemed overwhelmed by storm surge. Sections of the drover's road had fast – moving water ripping across it. Jade had bravely leapt over several smaller runs and they had continued through the rain.

She brought up the horse. His sides were heaving with exertion – a side benefit being that with exhaustion, Jade had stopped pulling and was trusting in Alice's sensitive, soft hands. Once Jade had shifted down to a standstill, Alice listened, trying to place a sound she thought she had heard over the thunder and rain.

It came again through the gale – bells. Brightsea's church tower was ringing their bells, calling out sanctuary to all those who needed shelter. Alice was sure that if the power hadn't been knocked out, she'd be able to see the village lights.

"Hear that? Brightsea, boy!" she cried out in the rain. "We're almost there."

Jade tossed his head, content to stay put for the moment. Alice closed her leg and asked him to move on. For the first time, the horse hesitated. He was tired. He wanted to find a spot out of the rain and wind. She asked again. He snorted irritably but picked up the trot and then the canter. They were off again into the storm.

Until they weren't – about two hundred yards farther and Alice was forced to draw up a frustrated Jade. A section of the drover's road had collapsed, leaving a yawning gap filled with rushing water. She could just see, in the last of the summer light, the broken edge of the path. It was, she reckoned, a good eight – foot stretch from one side to the other. The current was too strong to cross on foot. If they attempted a jump and didn't make it, they'd be washed along with the fierce flood water.

Alice was pondering the two unappealing possibilities when a new sound caught her attention. A barking dog. She looked around in the rain – a lightning flash momentarily illuminating the immediate area. A black and white sheepdog was racing towards them, barking furiously and wagging its tail in excitement. The dog careened in next to Jade, trembling and looking up at Alice, as if asking for rescue. Jade pawed his right fore against the wet ground impatiently, clearly unimpressed.

Alice sighed. She bet a lot of farm animals were struggling in the massive storm, separated from their usual places and people.

"Sorry, Jade," Alice said, reaching down and grasping the farm dog's collar. She hauled the shaking animal up to the saddle. Jade was astonished and said so by jigging in a circle anxiously.

The sheepdog licked her face as she settled him over the saddle pommel. It would be something if all three of them could get over the gap.

"All right then," Alice said as she squared up her reins and got Jade's attention. "It's up to you, my friend. We can either end the night enjoying some hay in Brightsea or take a long drop to the next world."

She swung Jade around and had him perform his small circle at the trot. Then he broke into his canter and headed for the terrifying gap. The sheepdog seemed to understand it had to make itself small and still. It pressed against Alice, allowing her to manage her reins without interference.

Three more strides would decide their fate. Alice held Jade together, supporting him with her leg and keeping her hands quiet. He rolled towards the yawning gap and in one last enormous effort, lifted himself into the wet air. It was a jump of a lifetime – deserving of every silver cup ever given in any horse show she had ever competed in, America or Great Britain. He arced over the roaring water in a flawless bascule. Alice could feel the cold flood water striking her boots and legs as if it wanted to knock them down into the current. The next instant Jade landed solidly on the other side. He shuddered upon hitting the ground and snorted, exhausted.

"Very good boy!" Alice cried and stroked his tired neck. "Very, very, very good boy."

The sheepdog agreed, barking happily.

"You're a good boy, too," she said to the dog who licked her wet face again.

Brightsea was not far from the collapse. She could make out the church tower in the flashes of lightning. Alice hoped Simon wouldn't mind if she allowed the exhausted Jade to walk in and knew that he'd do exactly the same thing if he were in the irons.

Another ten minutes and they clattered onto the high street, heading for the official emergency headquarters in the village church. She was grateful to see that the village itself appeared to be in reasonably good shape. No obvious flooding. Sandbags had been carefully deployed everywhere indicating that Brightsea had seen a few severe storms and knew what to do.

The closer they got to the church, the busier the village became with people arriving in farm drays, motor cars and pony traps. All Saints itself was lit up with storm lanterns and looked almost cheery in the rain. On its front steps, she could see the Reverend Father Hayter welcoming his parishioners and giving directions. His black habit was flapping in the wind, reminding her of a raven. Just a few more steps and all three of them – horse, girl and dog could stop.

"Lady Fairlight!" came DI Saxby's voice. Alice looked around to find the detective jogging across the street to intercept her. He sounded worried and surprised to see her.

Another *Lady Fairlight!* rang out from the opposing direction. It was Mr. Spinner on the run from the church steps. She had never seen him sprint with such speed.

Alice pulled up Jade as they reached her and looked down at them – one on each side of Jade's dripping neck. She handed Mr. Spinner the black and white sheepdog. "Simon sent me," she said. "He needs all the help you can give him."

56

Sturmtruppen – Zero. Simon Fairlight – One.

Simon had left the dead German in the bathtub. There were two more to take off the chessboard before he dealt with the central issue in the Marble Salon. He hoped that if he were spotted moving through the shadowy house, the borrowed clothes and wool balaclava pressed down over his dark hair would identify him as one of the *Sturmtruppen*. Might buy him an out if the other Germans took it at face value.

The Karabiner 98K was slung over his shoulder, mainly for show. He wasn't ready to use a bolt action rifle or a revolver. Too much noise. Too flashy.

Simon worked his way down the main hallway, taking advantage of the deepening gloom in the house and ducking for cover when lightning lit up windows. The house was sporadically alive with sound. He could hear the echo of *Sturmtruppen* Number One dealing with Lord FitzRobert's bluster as His Lordship made demands. The fact that such irritants were being tolerated tended to indicate that the *Sturmtruppen* were waiting for the weather to break so they could exit with political hostages. Not that they wouldn't just mow every breathing soul down if a quick retreat was needed. That was how the *Sturmtruppen* operated – shock and death.

There were other noises beyond the rolling thunder – doors banging open, heavy boots stepping from carpet to Palliser Park's gleaming wood floors. The two German soldiers had divided the hallway and were systematically clearing the rooms. Occasionally, they would regroup and update. Simon had been tracking the two for several rounds of room clearing, waiting for his best chance. It had become a dodgy maneuver. As the natural light diminished, the house intruders had pulled out flashlights and weren't shy about casting the beams about as they searched.

He dropped down behind one of the hallway's reproduction William and Mary armchairs as one of them exited a nearby room. The German came to the center of the main first floor thoroughfare and called out something about *zigaretten*. Simon instinctively ducked lower as the second rogue *Sturmtruppen* soldier emerged from his search and scanned the immediate area with his flashlight. Fortunately, the second German performed a perfunctory pass, keeping the beam at chest height and didn't go low where he might have spotted Simon under the chair legs.

They lit up cheap Heer and Flotte military ration cigarettes. Simon strained to hear and put his trench education German to use. There was some general moaning about how few cigs ended up in the ration packs by the end of the war followed by one of them commenting that he had been pretty disappointed with a recent Tom Mix western called *Fighting for Gold*.

Simon pieced together information that one of them was named Karl and that they both wondered where Dieter had gotten himself off to in the recce. He made a mental note in his head: *Sturmtruppen – zero Fairlights, Simon Fairlight – Dieter.*

He picked up another sentence that roughly translated into *Gunter doesn't pay us enough for this shite* – and wondered if Number One with the swagger – y MP 18 submachine gun was Gunter.

The unnamed one decided once the *zigaretten* break was over, he'd find Dieter and bring him in so they could search the ground floor. Simon watched Karl nodding as he dragged heavily on his cheap Heer and Flotte. Then he reached out and knocked three times sharply on an end table. Simon tucked the practice into his mental file on the *Sturmtruppen* as it was one of their communication devices – a way of announcing one's presence ahead of time so someone wouldn't fire in low visibility.

"Ich gehe jetzt aufs dach und mache den Englischen clowns den rest. Spater gibt es weniger zu tun," said Karl, tossing his spent cigarette onto Lord FitzRobert's excellent Aubusson carpet and crushing it with his boot. Simon watched, chilled by the casual cruelty of the threat and the waste of a fine rug.

I'll go upstairs to the roof and finish off the English clowns. Less to do later.

Simon tightened his grip on the Karabiner. His rough translation was enough to verify that the hapless English crew of the *Sea Sprite* had been led up the proverbial garden path. They thought they'd been working in aid of the British government – extremely well paid, of course. That in itself would have been a major red flag to a thinking man. The British government rarely paid well for anything. But Jack – the very picture of British virtue – would have made it all seem so believable.

He sighed. Did he really want to let Karl put a bullet in the head of the duped?

CHAPTER

57

Alice gratefully accepted a cup of tea from Father Hayter. She had collapsed on one of the All Saints pews, tired but anxious about Simon and all the others left behind at Palliser Park.

"Thank you for collecting Sandy," said the curate, referring to the black and white sheepdog, who had been padding after him and now sat, offering Alice his paw. "I am so very fond of him."

"Well, he *insisted*," she replied, shaking Sandy's paw. "Poor fellow. Awfully far from the church."

Hayter nodded. "My own fault. I lent him to Ted Hiller for the day. His dog, Kip, has an injured paw and Ted needed to move sheep before the storm set in. Sandy loves to work sheep … anyway, he must have decided to light out for home once the thunder started."

"Glad Sandy found us." Alice sipped her tea. It wasn't exactly piping hot but the town ladies and farmers' wives were doing their best to keep kettles on and sandwiches flowing.

"Us?" Father Hayter blinked.

"Oh, sorry," she almost laughed at his misunderstanding, "my horse, Jade."

"Ah! Of course." He straightened as a farmer came up, asking a question about extra sandbags. "If you'll excuse me, Lady Fairlight. I've got to organize this."

Alice watched Father Hayter head off with Sandy trotting at his heels. She wasn't just grateful for the lukewarm tea. She was thankful to all of the kind people of Brightsea who had warmly included her as a fellow storm refugee. When she had slipped down from the exhausted Jade's back, several farmers had taken charge of him. There was a stable to the rear of All Saints where members of the parish who traveled to church by horse or in pony traps could put up their animals. Although the stable was crowded with equine evacuees, Jade was rubbed down dry, fed and given a clean, comfortable slip stall.

Mr. Spinner materialized through the clutches of tired people, carrying a blanket from the Crossley. He found her on the pew and laid the blanket across her lap.

"DI Saxby is out in his car trying to determine road conditions, Your Ladyship," he said, his face drawn with worry. "Apparently one of the sea walls has been breached. The village has been cut off with collapses on all the usual arteries. Even the old road – the drovers' way – has seen some flooding. Do you think I could make it afoot?"

Alice thought of the yawning collapse in the ancient pathway as an overwhelmed local stream revised its course and swept over the land. She shook her head. "We barely made it. Probably worse now. Please sit down, Mr. Spinner. No need to be formal just now."

"With Your Ladyship's permission, I had thought to take a turn at a bell rope. The ringers are awfully tired and…"

"Absolutely. Go," she said. "Anything we can do to help. I'll be boiling some pots of tea myself in a minute."

Her husband's former batman turned to go, hesitated and then refocused on her. "Your Ladyship, your husband ..." Mr. Spinner thought for a moment before continuing. "Your husband is a very capable man. It's difficult to explain but he has a certain ... skill set."

Alice leaned forward. "Things he learned in the war?" She was always anxious to learn more about Simon's experiences under fire.

"Yes, Your Ladyship." Mr. Spinner looked relieved at her understanding. "If anyone in England can protect your friends, it's the Major."

She felt tears springing to her eyes. Of course, Simon would possess such abilities. Of course, he would be an actual knight.

58

Simon came up the attic stairs after the one called Karl. It was impossible to keep the steps from creaking, hiding his approach from the German intruder so he darted to the top and knocked three times on the door.

"Ja. Kommen," came Karl's response. He sounded relaxed but distracted like a workman concentrating on a project.

Yanking the balaclava down over his face, Simon pushed in the door and stepped over the threshold. The *Sea Sprite* sailors were on their knees, arms bound behind their backs. They were both crying. He'd seen it many times on the battlefield – even the biggest working class toughs could hit their breaking point under fire.

"Siehst du? Britische babys. Auf nimmerwiedersehen!" said Karl, his back to Simon, his service revolver pointed at the head of one of the weeping sailors.

You, see? British babies. Good riddance!

"Good riddance, Karl," said Simon in his schoolboy German.

Karl turned around with a puzzled expression. "Ernst?"

Simon squeezed the trigger of the Webley. Karl staggered backwards. His craggy Germanic face radiating surprise and dismay. Then he fell and was still.

The Englishmen on the floor had stopped crying and were sniffling, trying to figure out why they weren't dead like Karl. Simon pulled the balaclava off and moved to unbind the sailors who both sagged in relief once their arms were free. One of them looked up at Simon, bleary – eyed while the other rubbed tears away with his dirty sleeve.

"You do know you're complete idiots, right?" said Simon.

"Right you are, sir," replied the one who was gazing at him as if he were St. George after slaying the dragon. "We are idiots."

"Thank God, you're a Brit," said the other in a thin voice that threatened to dissolve again into tears. "We thought ... we ..."

"You *thought*." Simon made a sour face. "Where's your other crew member?"

"Alan's 'oled up in the cottage to look after *Sea Sprite*," replied the one who was still staring him with awe. "They need 'im to sail 'er out again."

"I counted five Germans. Any more I don't know about?"

The sailor shook his shaggy head. "*Sea Sprite* can only 'andle so many and we were supposed to take Sir George and 'is mates to Germany for the meeting."

"The meeting?" Simon raised an eyebrow.

"Big secret meeting with the Yanks. To make Britain stronger."

"Oh, *that* meeting – was King Arthur coming along too and Henry the Eighth?" He went over to retrieve Karl's weapons. "Your names?"

"I be Bert and that's Toby."

"Do you think you two could hold this attic and not accidently shoot each other?" Simon held out the Karabiner and the Mauser revolver. The sailors took them a little gingerly but nodded.

"And no matter what you hear – do not come out to help me."

Simon left them arguing over what to do with Karl. Bert wanted to chuck him in the next room. Toby was in favor of a sheet and few gratuitous kicks to the ribs. He pulled the balaclava down over his face in case Ernst popped up unexpectedly. If Ernst thought he was Karl or even Dieter for a second, he'd hesitate before shooting, stabbing or bludgeoning.

He moved down the stairs to the servant's floor. No sign yet of Ernst flying up to report Dieter's demise. It was hard to believe the *Sturmtruppen* officer hadn't discovered his comrade in the bathtub but Palliser Park had a lot of ground to cover.

The floor was deserted. All the servants were corralled in the Marble Salon with Gunter and his hostage minder. As Simon descended to the next level, he worried that the Number One – Gunter – was getting bored watching frightened people huddled together. Gunter might be mulling over the possibility of using his MP 18, ridding himself of everyone including the four millstones he was charged with bringing back to Germany. The original plan must have been for a fair weather drop, grab and run operation. On a beautiful June evening, five Sturmtruppen would have swept in on a shockwave, identified the members of the Reparations Committee and gotten out. All probably accomplished under two hours. That was the trademark of the *Sturmtruppen* – deadly speed. The storm had turned their standard attack style into a dreary waiting game.

Gunter had to be thinking that with the much smaller guest list, it would be far simpler to just eliminate everyone in Palliser Park. They had been counting on rampaging chaos in a huge milling party to swoop in and out – no one able to provide reliable descriptions. But what Gunter had now was a long, tedious wait in which Lord FitzRobert's guests could do nothing but accumulate accurate information. Gunter had plenty of ammunition for roughly thirty guests and a handful of servants.

Of course, Simon considered as he reached the first floor, they'd made a mistake trusting Bert and Toby to take out Hopkirk and disable the motorcars. That must have been a last – minute addition once Gunter realized the storm would delay an exit and he wasn't yet ready to move the full team out of the staging area at Clara Mare.

He was grateful the Brabingers had evacuated and *Alice* … Simon paused and let out a long breath. He sent up his deep hopes that she had made it to Brightsea in one piece. Alice was a brilliant horsewoman. Surely, she struck a truce with the difficult roan gelding and the old road resisted flooding. He should have put her up on Colonel Lee – the bay was slower, less agile but steady and …

Simon closed his eyes, forcing thoughts of Alice into the background. She had the power to disrupt his rhythm, something he couldn't afford. The electric weaving of shellshock began to rise – nausea, unsteadiness. He leaned back against a wall, pulling the Karabiner against his heaving chest. *It would be so good to stop …*

A sound of a rifle rattling on its shoulder strap cut through the thought. He opened his eyes. *Sturmtruppen* Ernst emerged from the secondary guest hallway. The soldier looked grim, ready to boil over with anger. Apparently, Dieter had been found. He glanced at Simon and then at his trench watch. Simon noted that it was of English military design and knew that Ernst had stolen it off a dead Brit.

"Dieter ist tot und sie verschwenden zeit. Erdgeschoss! Beweg dich!" snapped Ernst, making the fatal mistake of not taking another look at Karl.

Dieter is dead and you're wasting time. Ground floor! Move! Simon watched the German start up the main hallway at a jog. He shifted the Karabiner behind his back and secured his trench knife, moving after Ernst. It would be any second now. Seconds away from Ernst realizing his slip.

59

Alice had just handed a plate of sandwiches to one of the farmers who had come in from sandbagging when DI Saxby found her. He still wore his raincoat and fedora – both dripping with water. The young policeman looked tired. Of course, they all looked tired, she reflected.

"Sandwich, Detective Inspector?" she said, putting one on a plate. "You're here ... no good news, I'm guessing."

"Call me Nyx, please." DI Saxby swept off his sagging fedora and ran a hand through his damp hair. "I'm sorry, Lady Fairlight, I ..."

"Alice, please."

"Alice, I have taken the motor in every direction. There's no reaching Palliser Park until the water drops. Probably sometime tomorrow." He shrugged off his raincoat as well. "I'm told the worst of it is over."

"Well, that's good news anyway." Alice silently sent up anxious prayers to God that He would look after her husband and all the people trapped in the great house. She knew that Simon's faith had been shaken by his experiences in the war. He still politely attended services but she could tell he had stopped listening to God's voice. Surely the God she believed in would not abandon Simon.

"I beg your pardon," she said, realizing that Nyx Saxby had spoken to her without getting a response.

Saxby tilted his handsome head, his eyes exhausted but sympathetic. "No worries if you aren't able but would you go over what you saw, one more time?"

Alice sighed and handed him a sandwich plate. "Let me fetch you a mug of tea. I could use a break anyway."

It wasn't easy in the crowded church to find a quiet spot. Even Father Hayter's office had been converted into a nursery for sleepy children. They settled on the Sacristy with Alice sitting on a stool between the vestments and a cupboard while Nyx leaned against the heavy wooden table where Communion elements were gathered.

"You heard screaming?" He took a bite of the fish sandwich and looked grateful for it.

Alice nodded. "Terrible. Simon took off to see what he could do and opened the doors to the Marble Salon. It was ... It was awful."

"Jack Nickleby – hanging by his neck? Dorothy Brier dead from unknown causes?" Nyx asked, clearly taken aback at such brutal crimes in his generally bucolic Brightsea district. "Murder, suicide."

"No. Simon was sure Jack didn't kill himself. He didn't tell me how he knew. Then it was all just a big rush to get me on a horse."

Nyx's voice was kind. "He wanted you out of there."

"Simon had to have guessed that the storm would cut off Palliser Park." Alice felt tears rising again to her eyes and she fought to keep them from escaping. She let out a breath and sat up straighter. Of course, he hadn't really expected she could send back help. He had just wanted her out of there.

The DI opened a cabinet next to the table and withdrew a bottle of wine. "God will provide," he said, also snagging a couple of water glasses usually set aside for deacons and priests with scratchy throats.

"Oh, no," said Alice, blanching. "That's Communion wine."

"I think God would insist." He poured out two small glasses and handed one to Alice. "It'll steady us."

Alice sipped the rich and sweet wine. Nyx was right. It did feel reassuring.

"And," Nyx's voice softened a little, "how did Lady Constance fare? She was all right when you left – physically, I mean."

"Fizz was frightened," Alice replied, remembering how her friend had recoiled in horror at the sight of Jack hanging in the Marble Salon. "She wasn't hurt though."

Nyx Saxby nodded and looked away, pretending to be interested in an altar cloth.

"You kind of …" Alice searched for the right word, "*approve* of Lady Constance, don't you?"

The Brightsea detective almost jumped at her words. In trying to recover, he succeeded in knocking over an altar candle. He also blushed – a tough thing to get a battle hardened war veteran to do.

"I hope to …" Nyx fumbled to straighten the candle, "to see her again … someday."

"Maybe tomorrow," said Alice.

He turned to look at her. Genuine hope in his blue eyes. "Maybe tomorrow."

CHAPTER

60

By the time it occurred to Ernst that he had been sloppy, it was already too late. He executed a dead stop and pivoted, slipping his revolver from the holster. But Simon had moved faster, taking advantage of Ernst's angry distraction and getting in close. He brought down his arm sharply and cracked the rogue *Sturmtruppen* soldier's wrist with the brass knuckles of his trench knife.

"You, English," growled Ernst, his face twisting with pain at the sudden blow. He dropped the Mauser C96 and staggered to the right, holding the broken wrist against his ribcage.

Simon kicked the Mauser farther away and continued on. It was one of the lessons an effective close combat operative learned – keep pushing forward, never give the opponent valuable seconds to think and regroup.

Although Ernst's dominant hand had been damaged, he pulled at the Karabiner that had been slung over his shoulder. He was quick despite pain and had the rifle in place. Only operating the bolt action with his broken arm slowed him down.

Simon had been one step ahead of Ernst from the start and he kept his advantage. Ignoring Ernst's frantic fumbles with the

Karabiner's bolt, he moved in close – almost chest to chest as if they were waltzing – and made highly accurate use of his razor sharp trench knife. Four vital strikes, any one of which would be fatal. *Never stop. Never give the opponent an escape route.*

Sturmtruppen Ernst looked surprised as Simon stepped back. He dropped to his knees and tipped to the side, falling lifeless onto the floor.

Sturmtruppen – zero Fairlights. Simon Fairlight – Dieter, Karl, Ernst

Simon knelt, removing the British trench watch from Ernst's left wrist. He pocketed it and turned his focus to the Marble Salon. It was finally time to address the central problem.

He returned to his former position by the open double doors. Pressing into the shadows, he needed to get a sense of how things were developing in the Marble Salon. More lamps and candles had been lit so that the gilded room was brighter and glittered gold. Dorothy's body had been removed from the balcony railing and laid on a decorative bench. Probably the same one Jack had been forced to stand on before he was pushed over the edge.

Simon saw he was right about Gunter. The *Sturmtruppen* leader was pacing the balcony walk. He looked tense, ready to clean up and clear out. Unnamed Number Two was at the base of the opposite staircase, leaning against the newel post to mind the Palliser Park household.

Both guests and servants seemed as listless as their bored keepers. From what he could make out, they were clumped together, sitting at various round tables. Undoubtably suffering from differing levels of shock, they were mute and exhausted. There was no more indignant – and useless – outrage, no sobbing, no frightened shrieks, no bargaining. They were just waiting for it all to end.

Gunter paused. He shifted the heavy submachine gun on his shoulder and gestured at the other German. "Sie sollten inzwischen zuruckgekehrt sein. Das gefallt mir nicht."

They should have returned by now. I don't like it.

Number Two straightened up. "Wahrscheinlich rauche ich. Ich gehe."

Probably smoking. I'll go.

Simon tensed. He pulled the balaclava mask down over his face. It was time to flush out the true puppet master who had pulled all the strings from the beginning.

He stepped through the doorway, onto the balcony above Palliser Park's great hall. His presence had a jolting effect on the room. The captured household members noticed the change after a long, tedious wait. They sat up in frightened anticipation – their voices returning to nervous murmuring. Gunter turned to him – at first, annoyed at an underling's delay and then rigid with the realization that he wasn't Ernst, Dieter or even Karl. The *Sturmtruppen* leader's hands automatically went to the MP 18 …

Simon shot Gunter with his Webley at close range and without breaking his rhythm, switched to the bolt action rifle and shot unnamed Number Two. The sharp cracking sounds electrified the Marble Salon. Terrified shouts and cries went up as the household threw themselves to the floor, ducking behind and under tables. There was a deluge of jangled noise as crystal glasses and pieces of silverware crashed to the marble floor in the mindless panic.

"What the blazes is going on?" demanded Lord FitzRobert, rising from a crouch to his full height. The master of Palliser

Park looked as if he had just about enough of the intruders and understood a coup might give him some bargaining power. "If you could just tell us what you want, we could end this."

Simon had to admire His Lordship's moxie. He glanced behind FitzRobert – Fizz was hunkered down with Perry. Both of them were grey with exhaustion. Fizz looked utterly drained, defeated. He'd never seen her less than silly and lively.

He pulled the black balaclava off and tossed it aside. As the mask hit the ground, an incredulous silence followed – almost a collective intake of breath. They stared up at him, astonished. Then a couple of young footmen stood up and starting cheering. Guests and servants followed suit, rising from their hiding spots behind the tables to join the lads.

Simon hated it. He felt as if he'd just taken a bow for a performance in a stage play. Ignoring the tribute, he left the balcony and came down the steps. *Sturmtruppen – zero Fairlights. Simon Fairlight – Dieter, Karl, Ernst, Gunter and No Name*

Guests and servants were dealing with their escape in different ways. Some dissolved into fresh tears, others with nervous titters and anxious questions. Many just found a place to sit and hung their heads, breathing. Crumpling – the ultimate butler – immediately returned to service, checking the state of his staff and organizing the young footmen for various essential tasks. The FitzRobert cousins, Doctors Threpwood and Sherbrooke, were already assessing some of the more traumatized for shock.

When Simon stepped off the stair – the Karabiner still over his shoulder, trench knife at his waist – he was surrounded by grateful people anxious to shake his hand and give thanks.

"Expect you must know how we all … feel," said Lord FitzRobert, his normally overbearing style replaced by trembling emotion. "You saved my family, my friends, my staff." He made an expansive gesture that encompassed the room. "How can I ever ..."

"Given the chance, any Brit would have done the same," Simon interrupted. He caught a glimpse of Fizz and her haunted face behind His Lordship's wide arm movement. She had returned to a chair and was quietly crying into a rumpled handkerchief. Perry stood behind her, awkwardly patting her shoulder.

"You might cut poor old Jack down," he added. "It upsets Fizz."

Lord FitzRobert almost cringed at his thoughtlessness towards the dead man and his daughter. He nodded, calling for Crumpling to see about Jack and then moved away to actually assist in the retrieval. For the moment, it seemed possible His Lordship had undergone something of a personal epiphany. Simon wondered if it would stick and then realized he actually didn't care. He just wanted to find Alice and go home.

"What I want to know is *why?*" Sir Henry Frost broke into his thoughts. "What's the whole bloody awful business about? Seems such a lot of anguish for common robbery."

Sir George agreed. "What did the hell did they want? Couldn't make heads or tails out of it."

"Four members of the Reparations Committee were to be taken as hostages," said Simon as he walked to one of the nearest tables and picked up an abandoned water glass. His hand was covered in drying blood. "The weather held them up or you'd all be on the *Sea Sprite* now headed for a German port."

Sir George Jasper looked incredulous. "*My* ship? That *Sea Sprite?* But my ship is down south with the crew. Not due back until the end of the weekend."

"*Sea Sprite's* currently riding out the storm tied up to His Lordship's new dock," Simon said before knocking back the entire glass of water in one go. He was tired, sore and thirsty.

Sir George – the ultimate politician – was actually speechless. He sat down on the bottom step of the staircase and rested his head in his hands morosely.

The last of the Big Four – the MP, Alastair Rothermore – came up and patted Simon on the shoulder. "Thank you, Major Fairlight. That makes twice that you've saved me from disaster. You've also made it possible for me to take Mrs. Rothermore and put Palliser Park in the rear mirror forever. Well, when the roads clear, that is."

"You say that so easily." Sir Henry sighed. "Clearly, Germany is desperate to derail the reparations process. They could well try again."

Simon put the glass back down on the table. A bloody imprint now marred the crystal and its etching of the FitzRobert coat of arms. He dumped the Karabiner 98K and his trench knife on the table as well. People in the Marble Salon who were unused to such things, stared with wide eyes at the brutal weapons of war.

"Good question," he said. "Let's ask the one who pulled all the strings."

Simon pivoted slightly on his heels. "How about it, Perry? You planning any other attacks?"

It was as if the Marble Salon had lost internal power and everything slowed to a crawl. The focus shifted to Perry FitzRobert, who was still standing behind a weeping Fizz, his comforting hands on her shaking shoulders. He had stiffened his pale face momentarily drawn in anger. It quickly reformulated into shocked and hurt.

"I don't … I don't know what you're talking about, Simon," Perry breathed, his eyes glittering with tears behind his spectacles. "I would never hurt … anyone. You all know I c … couldn't organize a church tea. That's Fizz's and Dad's … area. *Dad!*"

"Simon," Fizz lifted her tear – streaked face to gaze at him, "what are you saying? Perry rescues foxes. He doesn't hunt them."

"I am mortified and stunned," announced Lord FitzRobert. "To accuse Perry of treason – Simon, do you need to sit down, settle your thoughts? You'll see you're mistaken."

"I'm not," said Simon. He felt the room turning against him – aunts, uncles, cousins and friends saw pale, frail Perry with his tortoiseshell spectacles quaking behind his more vibrant sister. How could a music academic and file clerk be the leader of such desperate men – desperate *German* men?

Perry pointed a nervous hand. "Simon suffers from shell shock. Fizz told me!"

Simon watched as sympathetic faces turned in his direction. They now understood he wasn't well. Hadn't they just witnessed him kill two people without a pause?

"How did it all start, Perry?" he asked, ignoring the rest of the Marble Salon. "There you were – something of a strange genius – filing away the War Office's classified papers, learning things, tucking away information for future use. Information, perhaps, on an actress named Dorothy Brier who, before the war, was the longtime mistress of Bernhard von Bulow."

Simon shifted his gaze to Lord FitzRobert, who was turning red with rage, embarrassment or both. "You may recall that Prince Bulow was Germany's Imperial Chancellor and ardent supporter of German world domination."

He returned his attention to Perry, who was breathing hard and gazing back with narrowed eyes. "Imagine, knowing this creature now had her hooks into your father. When did the idea occur to you that a file clerk with your level of trust – *the son of Lord FitzRobert* – could fiddle the system? It wasn't hard for someone of your intelligence and skills – someone who was filing away all sorts of War Office papers – to find and redirect money. Substantial sums of money."

"You are absolutely bonkers, Simon." Perry shook his head sadly. "Please stop."

Simon glanced around the Marble Salon. People were listening, intently. Even Lord FitzRobert has ceased making derisive noises and was staring at his son.

"At first, you probably just wanted the money to produce one of your operas, but that idea had palled. So dull, so insignificant in the world of men. Money allowed you to capture Dorothy's interest. You reeled in her sympathies and avarice. She worked for you now – gathering information and even better, actually finessing situations and people."

"Dad," Perry's voice took on a pleading note, "he's a nutter. Please make him stop."

Fizz rose from her chair and stepped back from her brother. "You used to borrow pocket money from me all the time," she murmured, her eyes widening with pain. "The new flat in Mayfair ... I thought they'd just given you a proper salary."

"Then you got to sail the *Sea Sprite* to Germany on an errand for the War Office," Simon continued. Attention in the room had become rapt. Sir George left his seat on the stairs at the mention of his yacht and came to stand next to the Rothermores. "You connected with your sister's beau over there – a translator. Jack was skint. He was always skint and desperately needed money to keep up with Fizz's crowd. You recruited him. He introduced you to another translator – one that worked for Germans this time and had all sorts of interesting, useful connections. Albertine Graf von Arco. Recruited him, too. You started playing both sides against the middle – stealing money from the British and being funneled money by what was left of the German *Weltpolitik* to carry out assignments on English soil."

"Jack was part of this? *My* Jack?" Fizz's voice rose so high, it cracked with strain. "What have you done, Perry?"

Perry turned from his sister to his father who continued to stare at his son, alternating between sadness and mortification. "Dad," he begged, holding out a trembling hand, "you know me. You know I could never have done these things. You know how useless I am. Isn't that what you always call me – Clueless Perry? *Why can't he be more like his sister?*"

"Perry." Like Fizz, his father's voice broke under the pressure. "You're a traitor and a murderer."

In the space of a heartbeat, Perry was transformed. He shed the poor rich idiot skin and straightened his spine, advancing on his father "I murdered no one!" he snarled. "No one!"

Simon curled his fingers around the Webley in his trouser pocket. He had no wish to use it. Sir Vernon would want Perry alive so he would give up his connections on both sides of the

378

sea. Besides, Simon knew Perry would have a revolver on him somewhere. If Simon were not careful, Perry would use it and graduate to murder.

"Who's the Gravedigger?" Simon asked in a sharp tone. One that demanded answers – as if he were disciplining a child.

Perry threw him a patronizing smile. "That stupid name. Typical War Office blather." He gestured up to the balcony. "Dorothy was already an assassin when I met her. She specialized in seducing," Perry carried the gesture over to his father, "*old men* and popping their cogs. Before the war, Bulow acted as brothel master and rented her out to men he wanted to remove."

"Sir John Redgrave?"

"Of course. He was on the Reparations Committee. Dorothy was an expert in the tragic accident." Perry again wheeled on his father, "By the way, Dad – your time was almost up. She loathed you."

A tear dropped from Lord FitzRobert's eye. He said nothing and looked away from Perry, his jaw trembling. He had ruined his son. There weren't enough lavish houses, important friends and gleaming objects in the world to hide such failure.

"The accident with my motorcar," Simon pushed him again. *Never stop. Never give an opponent an escape route.*

"Jack. He thought it was Dad in the red Sunbeam." Perry was starting to enjoy unspooling his secret life – revealing to his family that he was a good deal cleverer and more ambitious than they ever imagined. "Jack wasn't nearly as good a killer as dear Dorothy. Dorothy was an artist."

Simon stepped closer, hoping to find a moment to subdue the young Englishman without incident. "But Jack killed the two lorry drivers?"

"She helped. Loved the kill."

"The lift collapse?" Simon moved forward with the question.

Perry backed away from Simon. The audience of guests and staff began to scatter across the great hall, anxious to get out of any potential line of fire. Something bad, something final and terrible was about to happen. No one wanted to get dragged under when it blew up.

"Of course, Jack failed to rig it properly. Dorothy was bored stiff. Just wanted a little fun so it didn't matter who got caught in it."

"And how could that possibly serve your interests?" Simon asked, taking another step closer to Perry. The younger man was flushed with anxiety and excitement. Beads of sweat rolling down his agitated features. He was utterly panicked but also thrilled to finally dispel his genial idiot image. If Perry could be kept talking, a moment would present itself to overtake him without any more violence.

"Them!" Perry cried, throwing an arm out to indicate members of his family and then specifically, his father who stood watching his son with horror etched on his face. "*Him!* His precious plans for his favorite. The grand party – the social event of the summer. That stupid, extravagant lift that was going to impress everyone. Who cared about any of it? I let Dorothy run."

"And Albertine Graf von Arco?"

"Prince Volkonsky," Perry laughed harshly, pacing Simon across the great hall. "We needed Albertine to go everywhere, know everybody, collect information. Who would be intrigued by a penniless German prat? But a glamorous Russian aristocrat? For example, *my Dad*," he swung around to focus on his devastated father, "fell for the whole melancholy Russian exile story hook, line and sinker."

Simon continued to push Perry back by pressing him physically and peppering him with questions. "Why'd you kill him?"

"Because he was stupid!" the young Englishman spat, still retreating from Simon. "Albertine fell for that nothing girl. Thought he was fooling me with his illnesses and his phonograph records – pretending to play that wretched piano Dad bought him."

"So, Polly had a *tragic accident* and Albertine objected. Did he threaten you?"

"Albertine wasn't that stupid but he was drinking heavily. Wanted to marry *the maid*, can you believe it? He'd have compromised us all eventually." Perry backed into one of the tables and almost fell. When he recovered, he held a small snub – nosed revolver in his hand. "You know, I discovered Dorothy and Jack had their own little plan. Once Jack married the moron that is my sister, Dorothy would get rid of Dad. Then Fizz. They'd have all of her money."

Simon didn't want to kill Perry. Young FitzRobert was not a professional soldier like the *Sturmtruppen* five, but he was completely mad and dangerous. Bodies littered his wake even if he hadn't actually put them down himself.

Before he could make a final decision on how to relieve Perry of the revolver and get him to the ground alive, a strange sound tore through the Marble Salon's air. A long, eerie cry of pain and rage – a human soul wounded beyond all endurance. Almost supernatural in its raw power.

Fizz, with the ferocity of an Irish banshee, snatched up a silver candelabra and brought it crashing down on Perry's head and shoulders. She shrieked with rage and heartbreak. The young man looked genuinely surprised, dropped the snub – nose and then toppled to the floor. Fizz flung the candelabra away as if it had burned her hand and burst into tears. She sobbed with wild, unbearable grief.

Her father came and put his arms around her.

"I'm sorry," he said. "I'm so very sorry."

CHAPTER

61

It was two days before the waters fully receded from the Essex coast. The storm itself had passed over England, en route to bedevil Ireland and the north Atlantic. Under a warm summer sun, Brightsea began to dig itself out of sandbags and mud as it had many times over the centuries. Rural roads remained treacherous for motorcars but were drying out enough for horses to pick their way through the mud and debris. Farmers and their families sheltering at All Saints began to make their way home on foot and horseback. The sea remained rough with only larger ships challenging choppy waters.Brightsea's inlet with its fishing boats and docks had seen considerable damage. Fishing families were landlocked until they made repairs to tangled boats, lines and docks. The locals were philosophical about it all – they'd been through it before and would again. It was simply life on the Essex coast.

On the third day, Alice and Nyx Saxby were finally able to saddle up and ride to Palliser Park. The New Road – developed at the Duke of Wellington's direction when Napoleon was expected to invade the British Isles – was finally passable to those fortunate to be astride a horse. Despite the warm June sun, it was an anxiety – filled ride. They had no idea what they would find at the great house.

"Here we are," said Nyx, once they'd reached Palliser Park's impressive gates. He looked over at Alice. "If it's particularly ... difficult, you'll return to Brightsea and alert my constables."

"Understood," Alice replied, her stomach twisting with fear.

They passed through the pillars and urged their horses into a gallop. Nyx's borrowed cob was placid and unflappable. Jade, after a couple of days of rest, was bursting with energy. Even the muddy ground couldn't repress his high spirits. He snorted in the summer breeze, pretending to shy at a butterfly and tossing out a couple of light – hearted bucks. Normally, Alice would have found it funny, even kind of exhilarating. As it was, she held him together, grimly, and worried about what lay ahead at the FitzRobert estate.

They splashed through puddles pooling on the gravel path as Palliser Park's formal Georgian lines came sharply into focus. She saw Nyx throw her a puzzled look. It could have been a scene out of the great house's past – at the main entrance, uniformed soldiers were clattering down the wide stone steps while two footmen carried out a long rolled – up carpet on their shoulders.

One of the soldiers spotted their imminent arrival and broke away from the group to wait for them.

"You must be Lady Fairlight," said the young officer, offering her a small bow of his head. "The Major said you'd probably turn up bright and early."

"The Major!" Alice breathed, feeling the leaden knot in her stomach lighten a little. "He's all right?"

The officer gave her a cheerful nod. "He's in one of the dining rooms. Can I take your horse to the stable?"

"I'm Detective Inspector Saxby, Brightsea Constabulary," said Nyx, swinging down from the borrowed cob. "Just what is the situation here? What of Lady Constance?"

"Yes, sir. The Major said to expect you as well. If you'll accompany me to the stable, I can give you the details."

Alice jumped down from Jade and handed the reins to the officer. She ran to Palliser's entrance, leaping over a puddle on the way and took the stone steps two at a time. Careening into the house, she nearly collided with Crumpling who was directing the removal of another carpet. He looked unsurprised at her frantic intrusion and simply pointed in the general direction of the dining rooms.

She ran on – past maids pushing carts loaded with breakfast trays and around two of Lord FitzRobert's elderly aunts who were strolling, deep in conversation. Alice caught fragments of *Never live it down* and *Dear Constance* as she clattered past.

The second dining room was empty but murmuring voices informed her that the main was, indeed, occupied. Alice ran across to the connecting door and threw it open with a bang.

"It'll be some time before we can properly interrogate the wretch," a tall, hawkish looking man was saying as she burst over the threshold. "Oh, dear," he added, turning his head to look at her.

Simon who had been leaning against a sideboard with his arms crossed, turned as well. Relief and joy replaced the serious expression he had been wearing.

"Alice! You made it to Brightsea!"

Alice darted from the doorway. "Sorry!" she called out to the older man, hoping he'd forgive her brash American manners and then threw herself into Simon's arms. He hugged her fiercely and for a long time – well past any British notions of what was suitable in mixed company.

He kissed the side of her face several times, repeating *Well done, darling. Well done.*

It was only after the hawkish man in tweed coughed twice that Simon reluctantly drew back. Alice saw that her husband had tears rolling down his scarred cheek. He wiped at his eye and cleared his throat.

"Lady Fairlight," the man greeted her andbowed slightly.

"Darling, this is Sir Vernon Waldegrave Kell – my superior," said Simon, keeping an arm around her waist as if he couldn't bear to completely let her go.

Alice held out a hand for Sir Vernon to grasp. She suddenly noticed the main dining room looked as if it had been commandeered as a kind of military headquarters. Files and papers were stacked on the table along with a typewriter and all sorts of other equipment.

"Sir Vernon," she replied. "Forgive me but I'm astonished that you're here. The roads …"

Sir Vernon bowed again over her hand. "I arrived by Navy frigate two days ago. *HMS Greyhound.* It's moored out there in deep water."

Alice was rarely without words. All she could do was stare at Sir Vernon as he retreated to his makeshift desk. "I'm sure the Major will explain it to you," he said and then murmured enigmatically, "all within reasonable parameters, of course."

Epilogue

Castle Fairlight – December 31, 1919

Castle Fairlight traditionally laid out a New Year's dinner for family and local friends. With many of the usual attendees away fighting in the war, the event had been put into abeyance for four long years. So it was with special exuberance that they gathered to see in a new decade – one they all hoped would bring the end to such terrible conflicts.

Simon did feel a kind of peace as he surveyed the comfortable old castle room filled with people he loved and admired. Over the past few months, it had settled deep in his bones. He actually slept at night. Laughter came more easily. The tormenting voice had stilled … for the most part.

It was the alchemy of Alice. His clever and kind American wife who found genuine joy in life. Life with all its flaws, disappointments and grief did not discourage Alice. She did not bow down to pain. She welcomed the novel and the new. Honored the ancient and the wise.Alice was not afraid of the world. She held up a torch, lighting a way through the darkness and he was beginning to stumble along the path.

He carried a tray of drinks across the drawing room. After dinner, the inhabitants of Castle Fairlight and their various guests had broken up into smaller groups for quiet conversation and some wry observations about a year in which the world's battlefields were finally silent.

Alice, heavily pregnant and due at any moment, had settled onto a chair by the fire and was chatting to their own conclave. He thought she looked a tired – living in an ancient pile such as Castle Fairlight might appear romantic to an outsider, but it was impossible to heat and even the simplest errands involved tromping up or down stairs – but also happy. By tradition, Fairlight children were born at the castle and Alice was determined not to let the side down by enjoying the modern comforts of a London hospital. Stubborn American grit.

Simon stepped into the circle of friends and set down the tray. "Let the trumpets sound, I have returned with the requested refreshments. Hot tea for …"

"Let me help, sir," said Reggie Spinner, rising from the couch.

"Stand down, Mr. Spinner," replied Simon as he handed the teacup to Alice. "I can manage to pass around a few drinks. It took all my brains to remember the order. Speaking of which, Scotch and water for you."

Reggie Spinner took the glass and saluted the group with it. "Thank you, sir."

"Champagne." He handed a flute to Lady Constance FitzRobert, who accepted it with a grateful smile. She looked radiantly happy too – life had moved on for her as well.

"And," Simon sighed theatrically, "a glass of beer."

"Potion of the gods," said Nyx Saxby from his place next to Fizz. "Do not think to mock the gods, my friend."

"But on New Year's Eve? Bacchus is weeping." Simon secured his own champagne and took the chair next to Alice. "How is Brightsea these days, Detective Inspector?"

Simon saw Nyx glance warily at Fizz. She sipped her champagne, seemingly unaffected by the question which might stir up nightmarish memories of the past summer. In the months after Perry had been whisked away by Sir Vernon to god – knows – where, much change had come to Palliser Park. Sir Vernon had a tale fed to Fleet Street about an armed robbery gone terribly wrong – something that briefly electrified the British public before getting lost in the deluge of flood stories – so no one was at all surprised when Lord FitzRobert no longer wished to spend his valuable weekends and holidays in the house. His Lordship auctioned off most of Palliser's contents, then turned the enormous estate into a long – term nursing hospital for injured and retired members of the armed forces. Something, he promised, the FitzRoberts would underwrite indefinitely.

"Brightsea is freezing at the moment," Nyx said. "Unusual amounts of snow. We've gone back to horses for a lot of things."

Alice brightened. "How is Colonel Lee?"

Saxby had bought both Colonel Lee and Fizz's cob from Lord FitzRobert when the house was undergoing the change into a hospital. Jade had come to Castle Fairlight to join the ranks as had the Brabinger family. Simon really needed extra help with his project reschooling former cavalry horses and Brabinger was the perfect choice to run the burgeoning riding school.

"He's lovely – ever the perfect gentleman." Simon watched as Nyx reached out to take Fizz's hand. He looked somewhat nervous as she squeezed his fingers tightly and nodded. "So, we've got a bit of news ..." he began in a soft voice.

"I know it must seem awfully, awfully soon and all that," burst in Fizz with her customary vivacity, "but ... well ... Nyx and I have gotten married. Special license, I – do's at the local register office. Dad was there. It was absolutely killing us not spilling the news at dinner!"

After a second of stunned silence, applause and glass clinking broke out among the friends and rippled over the drawing room as the good news spread. Soon they were surrounded by the rest of the Fairlight family and friends eager to congratulate a young couple who had been through so much the previous summer.

Mr. Spinner held up his whisky glass. "To Detective Inspector Saxby and Lady Constance – may you always know fair weather."

"God, I hope so," Nyx called out over the cheers.

Alice laughed, taking Simon's arm to get to her feet. "Fizz – a detective's wife! No one will ever believe it!"

Constance beamed at her new husband. "I shall make a very good DI's wife, thank you very much. At least I will spend my whole life trying."

"She already has big plans for my office," Nyx said to much laughter.

"Well, it's so dreary – all those file cabinets," replied Fizz to even more cheers and laughter.

Simon lifted his own glass in a private salute to Alice, his family, friends and those he had known and lost on far away battlefields. Life found a way.

In the crush of congratulations for the Saxbys, with all attention on the new couple, he stole a moment to pull Alice into his arms. She seemed grateful for the extra support, resting her head on his chest with a small sigh. Someone cranked up the phonograph, then *Auld Lang Syne* spun out into the atmosphere. Like Guy Fawkes fireworks, fresh rounds of cheers and toasts went up around the drawing room. A new decade had arrived – one that promised peace and renewal.

"Happy New Year, Alice," he murmured, kissing her forehead.

"Happy New Year." She smiled up at him. Then winced and gave a little start. "Oh," she added, frowning, "how interesting."

Concerned, Simon stepped back to look at her. Alice looked a bit flushed but otherwise, all right. But then she winced again. "Alice?" he asked, his voice urgent.

"Well, I, for one, am glad Doctor Adams is a guest," Alice said before pausing to gasp. "The baby … is coming."

Reggie Spinner was already at his side. "I'll fetch the Medic, sir."

Simon helped Alice return to her chair as the thrilling news traveled across the drawing room. He dropped down by the chair arm and took her hand. "I don't know where we're going, my darling," he said, shaking his head at the nonsense of life, "but we're going there together."

She tried to laugh but sucked in a sharp breath instead. "Just try going anywhere without me."

Simon was profoundly struck by the kindness of people as everyone rushed to help in some way. Mr. Spinner was organizing the room with quiet efficiency. Ladies had already decamped to the kitchen to boil water and collect the needed items. Fizz was kneeling next to Alice, holding her other hand and offering all the right, comforting words. Nyx was making the dash to secure the doctor's medical bag from a car. His brother and other men were moving furniture at Doctor Adams' request. His father was elated, so rattled by joy that he kept making the error of announcing that Alice was *foaling*.

New life found a way.

www.ingramcontent.com/pod-product-compliance
Lightning Source LLC
Chambersburg PA
CBHW020015120726
47903CB00004B/1303